HYPER

VOLUME I

WHITE KNIGHT

MARA ROTUNDO

ISBN 978-1-0686182-0-8 (eBook)
ISBN 978-1-0686182-1-5 (paperback)

Published by Goldmund.

www.hyperaeon.co

Contents

This book is for those who survived both love and the pandemic. To my best friend, Iulia Popa, my friend Frank Steel, and my other half Steven—your immense support has been a lifeline.

PART ONE

ILLO TEMPORE

CHAPTER I

In the sky over the town of Belmont, there lay a flurry of clouds, like layers in a cake: fiery sunset colours up top, then silky pastels morphing into grey down below.

The uppermost slowly shifting like lazy lovers' arms, creating ephemeral creatures of wonder in a golden glaze. Pink arms, hopeful, lustful. Wind played with their shapes at a steady pace. One looked like a horse in battle for a split second until replaced by a warrior queen, floating togas wrapped round her form. If you looked again it was just golden lace. And these shapeshifting sculptures hung quietly in the sky. But as you lowered your gaze, the clouds turned to leaden menace.

It was a small ordered town with precisely drawn streets and quiet houses that seemed dormant and expectant. Something brewing, strange calm over town.

As you zoomed into central roads, an old Victorian house stood out. Façade of blue, violet detail. The whole thing popped out among the rest like turkey on a Christmas dinner table. Obviously the neighbouring buildings tried to emulate the style, but lacked the courage of such colours and their paint faded grey. Less joyous, resigned to be extras in the play.

Inside the large wooden frame of the main window on the third floor was a perfectly coiffured pot arrangement of rose geraniums. In the breeze, curtains fluttering. The floor squeaked with steps of people walking, winter lights casting warm reflections over a classical interior.

The monotonous murmur of television news offset by voices talking, chilled, to each other.

—You brought the other cup, darling? You know I like my china. I don't like my tea in your silly mug.

Eris Clemens, the lady of the house, put the mug back on the coffee table. It read "Best Wife" in handwriting font. She was sat in front of the large TV, and as evening set in, was almost bathed in its light.

—Right away. Said her husband, absent-mindedly. He was stuck at a desk the other end of the large living room, hunch back over his two computers. Their light bathed him in blue, and emphasized the chummy double chin. He looked anywhere between 30 and 60, but he was mid forties and rather chubby.

—Actually, deario... why don't you go. I am working here. Your.. and he gestured vaguely in her direction... mug, can wait.

Eris, elegant woman of much younger age, was left a bit tense by the response. She took a deep breath and decided to once more brush over this slight lack of courtesy. These benign acts of marital indifference had long become normal and a price you learn to live with.

Lithe, delicately defined bone structure, carefully dressed in a tailored pant suit and red tie—Eris Clemens was a woman like a boxing fist in a velvet glove. Her black eyes like laser following objectives in space, pinning them with feline precision. Features deceptive in their feminine sweetness, sharp cheekbones and rather severe pout just a hint of the character within. In her wavy hair, her hand gestures you could just about glint a suppressed sensuality.

Very comfortable in her skin, but restless, she was trying to enjoy evening tea with her husband before leaving to town for a double event: her book launch, and his evening sermon. He wasn't fond of decadent rituals like tea, as he called them. He preferred decadent things like Coca Cola and cheeseburgers, preference otherwise apparent in his convex mid section and heavy breath every time he stood from his desk—which wasn't very often.

She stood up to go to the kitchen and fetch her pretty porcelain tea-ware, when the loud bell of the corridor landline rang. It almost never did. Everyone had her mobile number. So in thin heels she strutted to the phone. She picked up. She listened.

—Hello, Ms Clemens? Is this Ms Clemens? Eros? ...

—Yes, it's her. Her voice thundered: It's "Eris", not "Eros". And she picked the TV remote to quiet the news as she struggled to hear the grating person on the other end of the landline.

But something caught her eye as she strutted back and forth in front of the TV. The local news said something of the dam uphill, some 16 miles North, which displayed a newly discovered structural problem. The technical words uttered with faux authority by the news-presenter were a tad lost on Eris as she was also trying to make sense of the other lady, on the phone. At the same time Stan stood up and walked the opposite way shouting "blast!", angry at his computers.

—Sorry, what happened? Eris tried to make herself heard. Who is this again?

The news-presenter used all the gravitas of her tall hairdo to shake fear into the home public:

—"And in the absence of urgent intervention, say the 10 striking engineers and workers, this security weakness threatens the fine balance between the 30 blocks that constitute the dam and could submerge the whole town of Belmont under its colossal wave. The management of the dam company are in talks with the disgruntled workers, now on their third day of strike".

—Wait, what? Eris lifts left eyebrow like a question mark. Menacing eyebrow it was—often resulted in casualties.

—My aunt is dead?? Which aunt? She shouted, in a swift, fencing move—TV remote in hand to switch the damn thing off; in a deft twist casting her eyes at the high ceiling, where she was supposedly projecting the image of this interlocutor with bad, bad news.

—Sorry to give you this news, Madam. Your aunt was found dead yesterday; you were given as next of kin and her attorney, my employer, needs a word with you. Also, since there are no other relatives, you are responsible with her affairs.

—I... oh, God. I understand. Sure. When? Yes, I'll be there. Very soon, thanks. Of course, thanks a lot. Good night.

Silence fell in the flat. The squeaking, the TV, the voices stopped.

Eris slammed the phone on the table and collapsed on the sofa. Sinking in. Room now heavy and grey.

Stan, where was Stan? They needed to go. It was all too much, at once. Dear God. Should she cry? Could she? Did Aunt Ely mean much to her? When did she last call her? She couldn't think. Emptiness opened and absorbed the whole room with her.

***

Meet Daniel Graf. A face bit like a golden retriever, and shoulder-length hair fluttering in the breeze. Determination digging a crest in his unibrow, green eyes hungry with desire to prove himself. Squinting hard—too much sunshine for his taste falling over the edges of the stadium, masking the crowds. End of timeout. It was kick-off. Daniel, in his white and blue colours, puts his helmet on and semi-crouches defensively, ready to jump. In a matter of seconds, quarterback throws him the ball, he receives, runs. Runs harder. His 6'2" give him an advantage across the gridiron. Defenders slam into him mercilessly, he takes it with a bit of gusto, like enduring pain from bigger team mates his moment to shine. Like a professional punch bag. He runs, holding the ball like a precious baby, gets tackled, pushed down, throws himself into a defensive curl, then outwits everyone and jumps up on his feet showing the ball to the referee, triumphantly. All over in a matter of seconds. The crowd is elated. Touchdown. Not too much of a crowd, but Daniel isn't a wide receiver with the NFL. Just a semi professional non league player in his downtime from a scintillating career as a scientist. You know, for athletic brownie points, to dispel any notion that he's merely a geek; geek, yes, but also jock—he was proud of being this unique, insecurity-dispelling package. Daniel was very ambitious. Broad spectrum ambition.

Locker room after the game. Daniel calls out his mate, Andrew.

—Hey, Andrew, look: I've got girly pants on.

Andrew explodes in laughter, they elbow each other and wink. Hey, Ian, look at this silly ass.

—Ha! They say. Pose for us, dude.

—Nah, I am shy. And Daniel sort of pretends to hide his mid section behind golden, smooth muscular arms. One of the be-towelled linebackers, a mountain of a man, slaps Daniel playfully on the ass while passing by, so Daniel pulls down his towel as comeback.

Everyone is laughing, putting their most masculine laugh on.

You could see them leaving the building one by one or in groups towards their cars, enjoying the last bits of joyous male camaraderie, ready to go back hat in hand to the Missus once home from the game. Their allotted time for warrior cosplay over—now, the evening encircled them like a tranquillizer fog with the sweet smell of home cooking and screeches of kids' play. And that was the real reality.

He hobbled into the entry way with his big bags full of equipment and the helmet hanging off his rucksack strap. She was there, opening the door to him. A purple haired short girl with stout thighs and big bosom. A five foot advertisement for fertility. Wifely smile welcoming the hero just back from his battles, ready to feed him.

Bowl of camp stew steaming on the table behind her. Round face with ultra large cheeks and lips like a letter box hole.

He was everything to her, hero, saviour, centre of the known universe. She woke up in the morning to fix his breakfast, she was there on his way to work to fix his bag of snacks for the day; sometimes, she spent the day in his cafeteria at university, keep an eye on him. He was her life's investment, her precious treasure. When she had a moment, which she often did—she had no job but housework, she would avidly watch Disney stories of little fairy tale princesses (her) carried in the strong arms of a prince (him) at sunset. She'd been lost in a kink hole, he found her online and rescued her from the hills of Alabama. Years and years back, and now they just rode the routine. They loved their own image in each other, and there was this perfect synergy of damsel in perpetual distress saved by the white knight. This dynamic validated Daniel to his core. Gave him that puffed chest feeling, dilated pupils kind of thing. She needed a daily saviour from the hardships of kitchen life, and grocery shopping, and random people who looked at her a bit weird. He was always available to save her from the emotional turmoil of all these daily struggles.

She was his cheerleader. Their joint efforts focused on his academic accomplishments. No small deal, being an MIT scientist. You could almost see Liddel—his pet name for her—on the metaphorical pitch: short skirt, crop top uncovering rubenesque folds, in a slow motion pom-pom dance. "Give me a D, and A, N, I, E, L" in a timid high pitch voice. This metaphorical routine played out every morning as he set off to be an important man of science. He exited the home with his laptop bag and restless hair, grinning, satisfied to his core because this petite woman drowned him in so much adoration. And him back? Yes, of course he adored that she adored him. Because she was good for him. Because she regarded him as a God. Her devoted presence in his life meant they were a team of two working on the "Daniel Graf" project.

Any day now, he would get tenure. He needed a new line of clothes for that event. And they were discussing options together.

—Shall I wear a tweed suit like my European colleagues? He asks while playing with his hair. Like, waistcoat, handkerchief, the works. To look the part, you know? I'm not a starving scientist anymore, he *modestly* giggles, underneath his golden brown curls.

She said she liked the idea, but secretly wondered how she'd look next to this new him: presently, she had the outward appearance of a goth retired into Harajuku girl: mini skirts, pigtails. Tired eyes encircled in black, Hello Kitty underwear. She wanted to be cute and loved, but she hadn't quite cashed in on her high-achieving boyfriend's *White Knight* check in order to improve herself into the next stage of life, adulthood; she had rather used it as a pretext to hover indefinitely in that cute state where submissive smiles and learned helplessness trigger male protection and safety.

Of course, sometimes he saw her secret tears. He offered a hug to console her. But no deeper input. Most of all, avoided like the plague any idea of telling her what the truth of the situation was, because that could trigger her, and make her cry, and he just liked his domestic bliss. He just liked his peace and quiet as he came down from work, not to spend his important evenings on hard talks with the missus about her lack of direction,... he was often tired from his important work and all he wanted home was to eat, relax, watch Marvel movies and make silly jokes with the missus. Oh, how she was happy when he laughed at her monkeying around! Sometimes she thought about ways to make him laugh throughout the day. She would do something silly in the kitchen and tell herself with a smirk: "oh, wait until my boo hears this; oh, he'll like this". She was correct. Whether funny or not, was irrelevant. What mattered was the frivolous intent and the generation of laughter and eluding problems. War in Syria? Let's not talk about that, too dark. Political turmoil? Ah, who cares, we have apple pie tonight, darling.

Bills gone up? Ah, it's OK, you work a good job, honey boo. You have your consultancy checks too. And the happy days went on and his successes were marked by lovely trips and homely dinners and laugh and fun and Julianah grew more and more in her role as the woman behind the man, so much so that it became printed in her facial features, the body posture—always ready to serve, life's complexity trimmed at the side to make room for just him, and being good for him, and being a good wife. Hovering next to him in helicopter position ready to be snapped into service at any time.

While he blossomed with such exquisite service, she was drained of life, of energy, personality. There were two sides to her character: the cheerful side he saw, which was a fiction she delivered to make him happy, and the lifeless, depressed side she hid from him. And as she had no others, friends or family, this was a cross she carried entirely alone.

He kept getting better. Collected diplomas and trophies on his living room shelves. Travelled worldwide in high demand, shook hands with important people, drank sake with Japanese scientists and played golf with Californian start up execs. While they remained strongly connected at the relaxing Netflix-and-pie level, the rest of the base of their lives floated apart day after day, like moving tectonic plates. The abyss between forming out of everyone's sight. Well, out of their own sight. It would have been obvious to everyone else had they shared their lives with anyone, but they didn't.

And this was a tectonic shift the girl could sense with her gut instinct. An instinct like an amorphous ball of sensations, resisting being unfurled into words and cognitive form.

And the more she felt it, the more she talked about strengthening bonds.

—We can go shopping for a nice wool jacket for yourself tomorrow if you like. And she smiled edging her head sideways. At the mall where we looked for my dress that day.

—Oh, right, any success with your wedding dress? He asked with a piece of bread in his mouth.

—I found one, actually ... she got shy. Cutesy shy, rocking her hips.

—Right, let's buy it, no? Drive to the mall next weekend.

She went quieter and brought him more bread. Yes, but..

—It's in this shop in London. It's on Instagram, but it's in London.

His eyes widened. Can't you buy it online? She remained feet from the table and sort of hid her wide frame behind tiny clasped hands. No, she whispered softly...

—Was thinking of flying there, she started... has to be custom made, you know these dresses nowadays are made for anorexic bitches. I'm womanly! She giggles, slapping her belly. It would be so romantic... I love it when we travel together.

—Of course, sweetheart. We could take a nice trip on my spring break. He said after a while. You will look so pretty in it. Of course. He smiled absent-mindedly and fondled her head. His attention had already shifted back into himself. Thinking of important science stuff. "Young Scientist of Great Promise"—his recurrent "Nature" headline fantasy, springing in his consciousness day in, day out. Map always drawn out in his mind's eye of his career horizons, other people more of a distraction.

She was happy like a poodle. She saved the listing on his tablet and started making starry eyed plans. She imagined herself in the London wedding dress, projecting the fantasy onto the wall before their sofa, above the TV and next to the bookcase that displayed his books and trophies. She saw herself as once more a manga fairy in a princess tulle dress, twirling around until his strong arms collected and placed her safely in... the kitchen. Where she put an apron straight atop the wedding dress.

———⟨⟩———

—Why, Miss Edgenstein, you have your anxiety attacks again? Switch back to decaf, it may help. Often times these...

—No, no, Mr Roughshod. I tell you, I am not crazy—it's the stuff, the plague...

—Yeah, yeah. You said. Says Stan looking over her shoulder to the next person, signalling them to come in. Gently ushers her out with a compassionate face also full of slight boredom. There is no plague, we've long left that in the past now, Miss Edgenstein. You need a husband, you do! And if not, a pet! Actually even better!!

He laughs, but with a light stress undercurrent. Sometimes he feels like he carries the world on his shoulders, and soft tolerance for people's inane witterings combines with fatherly concern for their woes. That's Stan.

His practice always full. These days monster cues in front of his office, where he also conducts his other work as an actuary in his rare downtime. Many laptops dotted around the place here too. It's the Stan way.

This stream of congregants keeps him fresh and chock full of empathy. Then he retreats in geeky endeavours to empty a bit of that burden. Calls himself a mathematician and a high intellect, but one thing has so far escaped his observation: there is a worrying number of congregants worried about this Chinese virus and he tends to dismiss them all as just "nerves", "too much caffeine". His news intake has gone down since his workload doubled. Slight tendency in Stan to downplay the matter since his empirical data shows most of the women focused on the insidious virus tend to be his most sensitive "patients", who have for years come to him with a number of pro blems... some more real than others.

His applied maths not the best. As he's hunched over his laptop fiddling with numbers, the phone screen is abuzz with WhatsApp group messages of concerned citizens—his neighbour group, the Jewish school mates, the activist group... all mentioning the occurrence of this threat. Perhaps a virus escaped from a lab, man made, or maybe just nature having had enough of people running amok destroying things and time is nigh for a new natural selection round. Theories abound. Notifications ping blissfully ignored in the background. Stan looks out into the abstract landscape in his head. He remembers Eris, fondly. Cannot help but think of the sweetness of their evenings together, starts wanting to wrap up. Looks at the phone briefly, a pang runs through him, ignored. He is a man who has taught himself to ignore too many warning signs. Sign of genius, or perhaps a fool. We'll see which.

Miss Edgenstein in front of the practice, on the grey streets. Gesticulating to the other ladies, agitated. She knows what she heard. People don't always take her seriously, bit of a Cassandra complex. Women every-where smelling danger, calling attention to the news but dismissed as "hysterical"; old story. People showing preconceptions against showing emotion, even when the emotion is life-saving fear of a coming train. But she tells them, she saw those Twitter posts straight from China, late night... it was scary. Hazmat besuited folk, collapsing in broad daylight... awful.

Other mothers interrupt all at once, either asking for detail, or tutting in indignation looking at each other with meaning... "Edgina at it again". They all wear similar grey clothes and have the same height and emit the same aviary sounds during debate. It's like a pack of geese has gathered to debate international relations. Emotion seeps deep into each vowel, facts can't just be facts, and statements can't just be data, they need to be pregnant with emphasis. These women have hearts. And wombs. And screeching kids attached to their hands or hips. But they feel. And truth is, they're correct. The virus is approaching. Not here yet. Not yet out of China. But it's reproducing. And it could be bad. Nothing is known. But people don't always take people like Edgina seriously. People sort themselves in two camps: gullible believers, and cynical deniers. More a matter of predisposition and personality, than true assessment of facts. Even though they all carry smart devices brimming with data. But such is life.

Tall, portly, Stan overlooked the street with protective eyes. He wasn't a friend of regular haircuts so his hair flew in big blue eyes. That's why he carried a little yellow plastic comb to discipline it with, on his person at all times. Sometimes, talking, he'd use the comb to gesticulate and mark his points, like a conductor's baton. But not now.

Eris drove her black Tesla into the alley. Everywhere she went, glamour and sparkle came with her. The car approached the pavement like a graceful large cat. Quiet engine, sexy curves, and Eris' curly head popping through the window, framed by the glow of large mabe pearls.

—Hello, Chubby Sticks! The street lit under her 10,000 Megawatt-smile. A smile she wore everywhere, which captured so many souls she kept in a tiny bottle around her neck. Maybe they didn't get her substance, but they couldn't resists the primal pull of so much charisma and lust for life.

Stan, kind, a bit tired, loved her for who she was within. His face lit up, his eyes smiled deeply.

—You finished for today? And she checks her lipstick in the mirror.

—Yes, I am finished, bunny. I wish I'd go home. So tired.

—But you promised me, I've got this thing. I need moral support. She gesticulated with bejewelled hands on the wheel and making her whole bosom wiggle in outrage.

—No, don't worry, I am not saying no, just be warned I'll be low energy. Probably nap in a corner.

—Ah, well, no change then. She arched her left eyebrow right out of the window while starting the engine.

On arrival to the venue, she walked confidently through fans. Clutching Stan's elbow, using her own to gently nudge people out of the way with a sweet smirk, but a fundamentally jaded air.

—Doesn't get fucking easy, does it!

—What you complaining about, baby?

—I don't know. It's a bit boring. This bit, you know? She cuddles into him to confess.

—It's all boring if you ask me, he shrugs.

—Yeah, yeah, I know, Stan. It's all boring, life is over, let's shoot ourselves here on this pavement.

It's not boring overall. I get it. The need to do this, to keep doing that. She says, marking a little circle into the floor with the tip of her shoe.

—What is "that"?

—You know.

—No.

She rolls her eyes. Pushes her face into him, through gritted teeth.

—Writing, ideas, the high stuff!!

—Oooh. Yeah, that's good. He combs his hair. Your little *arts & crafts*, yeah? Good to express yourself, get it out of your system, ready to work on higher stuff.

Inside, swarms of people, not all here for her event. Old gothic building with faded walls of a different world order, different time, clashing with the artefacts, posters and chatter of a new generation that fills its tall halls and staircases with laughter. There's a bit of a sinister echo in the ancient woods and stones if anyone cared to listen. But everyone busy with their little bubble.

Flicking through history books there was a tall silhouette with long curly hair, lost in lecture. There was elegant focus in his gestures and demeanour. His careless clothes gave off an air of sexy cool only the young have, who'd look good in a bin bag, because the screaming health of the young body overshadows style and frills. Even lost in thought, resting pose, the body ready to lunge into action—all the *elan vital* flowing through the veins, that restless tension in the muscles. This kind of allure emanated strongly from Daniel's presence in a dark corner of the book store, unbeknownst to anyone, not even himself.

Then Eris started speaking. She was bathed in light, and her movie star appearance went well with her careful mannerisms and vivacious hand gestures. She was composed, funny, good at what she did. It didn't hurt she had her own style: classical, always dressed to the nines; always a tie, or bow, the flash of an antique watch; velvets and silks draped to both hide and emphasize the body. Feline feminine wiles luring you in to then stun with a gregarious, masculine confidence; a laugh devised to defuse and expose the tension created by her physical persona like fireworks in a room.

She gazed at her notes.

—See, she starts. My contribution to feminism is... so it goes a little like this. The story goes many established male authors traditionally stole from their wives who couldn't put their names on anything, because... well. Patriarchy, etc. You know the phrase, "the woman behind the man". I want to redress this historic injustice. I also steal ideas from my husband and put my name on it. That's the real feminist victory! Any talented woman can write something great herself and slap her name on it nowadays. But to really have equality of the sexes, you need to even out the thieving!! That's where we have to catch up, ladies. I am doing the tough work for all of you.

Chuckles sprinkle across the room. Some applause. She continues.

—So, say hello to the real "woman behind the man", my husband Stan Roughshod! She laughs and points to her left, where Stan stands and nods kindly, amused.

Autograph time. People circled her drawn to the charm, the happiness, the style and some, the curves so emphasized by tailoring and hundreds of yoga hours.

Bit of a break, whispering to her agent and Stan. She makes her way back to the table, grinning widely to an impatient crowd.

Then Daniel saw her. He walked closer to the front. Now he was carrying her novel, "My Olarion", under his arm. He ran his hands through his hair and squinted harder to take in every detail. She struck him as familiar. Not that he'd seen her before. But he sort of recognised her from his dreams.

Stale dreams he pushed back ages ago thinking they don't exist and he doesn't deserve them. He knew he wouldn't get noticed, so he didn't even try. Like hypnotized, he meekly went to ask for an autograph, and she barely looked up, despite putting on her default Hollywood smile and chattering sweetly to him and others at the same time.

The boy felt something deep and unknown. The boy was not a boy, he was 29. But she made him feel like a boy, he was one, in front of her. And she didn't even acknowledge him. Flustered, possessed, he walked away. He walked into the night and it started raining. He didn't notice. He had to lean against a wall, and breathe deeply. Tectonic plates started shifting and he had motion sickness.

———⸎———

"January 6"—the date flashes across her screensaver, selfie of her and Stan at the beach.

—I can't finish this sake. And she slams a tiny violet cup on the table, in the dim lit restaurant.

—So leave it! Stan answers, not even lifting an eye from his phone.

—What!! It would be a crime against humanity. Tiny Japanese kids slave away in a labour camp for this very sake, and you expect me to throw it away?! She says, but she had finished about five already. A sort of happy tunnel vision took hold of her.

—Let's think of the children, huh?!

She laughs at his joke, he laughs at her laughing. A chummy complicity between them.

—By the way, have some work to do again at the office. I am not be able to drive you tonight.

It's the workload, I'm far behind and can't postpone, spent enough time on you this week already. You always slow me down with your events.

—Of course. My aunt's death is why you can't have nice things. Eris gasps sarcastically, kicking off one of her shoes under the table. The dainty thing rolls down in its velvety splendour, red sole sticking up. Unwittingly, Stan steps right on it, nearly squashing 1K worth of shoe. Eris waves the waiter.

—Excuse me, which desert do you recommend? I am after something fruity. And she punctuates the sentence with a slow blink, like she's talking to a cat. When she does, microscopic glitter falls off her lashes in front of her pearlescent skin. Waiter, big handsome boy who's not seen much of life yet, picks up on it subconsciously and eagerly recommends a few things:

—Madam, the apricot frangipani tart is very popular; and.. leaning, whispering towards her.. my personal favourite if I may, Madam, is the strawberry truffle, with coconut rum. To die for! He says, jumping joyously on his toes.

—Hm.. and she thinks with her lips.. that's tough! I think I'd like to have both but this time only, I'll settle for the apricot, thanks—and she nearly winks to the boy. Personable, she was. Affable, people said. Unbearable, said enemies. She was about as unbearable as apricot frangipani tart, if you were strongly against that sort of thing. She slams the menu on the table and looks Stan in the eye, her huge, black eyes swallowing the space between them.

So many years between them, so many frontiers passed. So many memories.

—Look, I'll drive myself to my aunt's house in the morning. No problem. But just so you know, bit unfair I can't count on you at such a time.

—It wasn't a good idea to go so late anyway. It's a difficult journey through the mountains, neither you nor I like to drive there in the dark.

—Well... that is true.. she looks at him edgeways. Maybe it's all for the better, she says.

Then she pokes her finger in the air:

—You are Mr. Let Down. That's who you are, mister.

—I am not your mister, buddy!

She looks at him, through him. Nodding gently to herself.

—Turgescence!

—What??

—Not familiar?

—Made up word, right?

She chuckles. No! It's the property of plants, and perhaps all living creatures, of being plump, juicy, alive because so full of water and nutrients. You dig?!

Despite tired eyes trying to carefully follow her explicative gesticulations, he seems more and more befuddled. Reverts to default, which is his phone.

—Look. And she leans forward over the table. Grabbing him by the collar, closer. I mean youth. How youth looks, and feels. Like that waiter. Did you see his skin, bursting with life? That's youth. His bright eyes?

That doesn't seem to enlighten Stan, who smiles helplessly.

—Well... she continues... getting closer. In fact, I like them young.

—You do?? Who's them?

—Boys, stupid!

—I am a boy, bunny... Your boy. Stan says, looking boyish and old at the same time. A rare skill Stan seems to have perfected in so many years of thinking young but moving old.

But she tuned out. She's watching the crowd, busy, colourful. "Turgescent".

CHAPTER II

It was one of those grey humid evenings that make everyone restless and depressed. The streets had a distinct acoustic to them, as if you could sense both rain and thunder, and destabilizing winter heat. No one knew what season it was any-more. Few cars around, and grey silhouettes crossed the streets whispering into phones.

The Emporium was an events centre in the old town of Johnnyville. No one knew how it sprung there looking like the architectural exercise of a 5-year old, dwarfing elegant historic buildings that must have once looked imposing dominating the skyline. The kind of place that suited the X-Factor type events that took place in its viscera. Culture was being made there: just not high.

The panellists knew each other for donkeys years, being chummy to each other over swimming-pool-sized takeaway lattes.

—Do you think it will go on, I mean what have you heard?

—Yes, we might have to cancel. We should prepare as usual but be ready to cancel or postpone if and when we're told no, said the artistic director with calm emphasis.

—What? Who says that?

—It's orders from the top.

—Which top?

—Government.

—What? The old dance teacher lady preferred to be slightly disconnected from all this kerfuffle.

—GO-VERNMENT!

—I STILL CAN'T HEAR, Go Ornament?? What in hell's name? She exclaimed to everyone's cheerful surprise.

—Dude, you're being stupid. It's the fucking coronavirus. Things are getting shut down. *"Venues with large groups of people were advised to not operate"*, one of them reads off a paper, slamming his finger on the text.

—So? It's advice! Merely.. advice. Go forth, my man! Be brave! And she rearranged her things on the table.

—Look, I can't just. There are lives involved, OK? It's potentially a very bad thing. I've seen some things... let me tell you...

And then it all fizzled out and the auditions started.

There was a swarm of applicants, but not like in other years. They all wanted to showcase their special skills and make it big. In a corner, shy, anxious, was Julianah. Around her, a dear friend, and her boyfriend. Pepping her up: "you're good, you can make it through, you've got real talent."

Thin pigtails with pink ribbons, white ruffled mini-dress. Outgrown roots in her purple streaks. A dishevelled adult baby, but with heavy make-up and sharpie-drawn eyebrows. She was stooped over as if to hide her very ample bosom, her body had grown into this shape. Waterfalls of beads and chains on her chest, clinking and popping with her scarce moves. While very developed in the lateral plane, with the silhouette of the Michelin man, her demeanor, in the way she held modest hands, her little girl clothes spoke of wanting to be small. Smaller. Her act? A foot sized poppet that looked like an anime version of her. A baby that talked in her hands. Julianah was an amateur ventriloquist.

The judges went quiet when her time came. Between stupor and "genius" their collective minds navigated a whole spectrum of possible reactions. But they were sober grey haired professionals, so they kept a poker face and looked ahead while Julianah took to the stage, timidly. Steps heavy, anxiety crippling. The doll—her double—started to sing a Korean pop song. A collection of shrieks and whispers and guttural sounds. It was like the ghost of a murdered child haunted the hall poking everyone's eye. The girl kept a stubborn face while the doll leapt into a surreal life of bizarre horror. Her face spelled stale held back tears. Her whole energy in a fierce clench of the jaw to mask an internal scream. The doll's song a hymn to a childhood the ventriloquist was clinging onto with despair. Marking stages of dissonance and dissociation in broken tones and onomatopoeic sounds.

And the judges wouldn't have it. It was not what they were looking for. Not the performance they sought for their TV show.

—Do something else, .. Liddel! The elder man adjusted his black rimmed glasses and gestured her to stop. She hesitated. Her sad eyes lit.

—I can dance... um...

—No! I mean find another occupation, darling. This isn't working out for you.

It was a blow of death. Once more she put her soul out there only for cruel judges to cast her out. The earth was pulled from underneath her feet. Worse than this feedback, the solemn silence of the others. Give me harshness, she thought, I can bare the sound of it, but the embarrassed silence of the panel was cutting her fragile heart into thin slices, then frying them. They were embarrassed for her. She was an act they were anxious to skip and forget. Her work, her soul. Her heart and soul. Well, a doll. Daniel was once more worried. He gestured to call her off stage but she wasn't moving. Panellists started coughing and looking into their papers.

Then it irrupted.

—No, it's not fair!! No! Give me another chance!! I can do this, I can, I can!!! Sonic boom of her feet stamping down on stage waking everyone's focus towards this central act. As she uttered the words a rain of tears and mascara came down her face. The black tears mixed with snot as she descended into an aggressive melt-down. She reached her tiny hands towards the judges as she screamed an infernal shriek.

Daniel froze, the panel frozen and time with them. It was no longer January 2020, but a time loop Julianah had been spinning on for decades. The same shit, over and over, and over and over again. Her little girl heart couldn't cope.

—I am the best, I am the real deal, not like the others!

—Escort her out please. Is there anybody here with her? Please take her out. This is unacceptable.

Their faces spoke of basic sympathy, but the clock was ticking.

A black ballerina took the stage with modesty and calm. Her poise brought confidence and cleared the air. For the show, the panel and the contestants a crisis was over with a sigh of relief. But for Daniel and the small group, a crisis just began.

—Can't you tell her it's only hurting herself?

Her friend whispers to Daniel. He's old and wise.

—I did, don't you think I did?? Daniel blurts with sudden exasperation.

—There are other things she could do, find a hobby, this is just.. and he looked away. It's just... Well, nuts.

Daniel looked as though brusquely awaken from a dream. Livid.

—Nuts??

—How do you mean!

The other was confused: Well you know...

—No, actually, John—I don't.

Their eyes met but their minds didn't.

—Look it's all a setup, OK? Daniel seemed to want to believe it. Gesticulated a lot in an attempt to persuade himself. He looked towards the restroom where she was lagging.

—I know all about it, OK? It's a setup, the casting director is screwing the ballerina, he knows it's all a show.

Julianah is very good for them, she's just that wacky artist they need, but they don't understand her, she's too honest, that's always her problem... Daniel spoke in one breath looking between the toilet door where she was and the wall behind his pal's back. John couldn't believe his ears.

—Dan, man... I know and respect you both, you make a very cute couple.. but don't you think you're exaggerating a bit? She's talented, no doubt, but I'm sure the reason they prefer the ballerina is that the ballerina is just more professional... you know?

—Look. Daniel stared coldly at his friend. I don't tolerate this negativity. This wouldn't be the first time I broke off a friendship over criticism of Julianah. OK?? She was spectacular! She's a bona fide artist, a misunderstood genius. And he emphasizes with his hands stretched wide. Julianah walks over. John takes one step back. Daniel runs his hands through his hair: "No more of this, please". He's tense.

Julianah approaches in a cloud of stale depression. She'd been so darkly depressed since the dawn of time that it's now written in her countenance, her body. Shoulders sunken, neck absent. The walk, slow and menacing.

John shakes his head. Daniel shakes his. John makes his excuses and leaves, with a last sympathetic look towards the girl. "Good luck, Julianah. Next time, hey?"

—Look, the judges just don't know how to recognize talent, he says affectionately. Hugs her. Whispers in her ear, you're beautiful, you're intelligent. You're too good for them. She doesn't quite believe it, but it doesn't matter whether it's true objectively, because he is saying it. Her prince believes she's a princess. Their reality is what they tell each other and the rest of the world can beat it.

Later that evening, when she's showering, he's onto a little research. Leapt on the sofa, laptop in his lap. "Eris Clemens" in the search bar. His OSINT methods patient, thorough. He can work out the best of hidden information, like for instance, the fact she was looking for a tenant for her house in Dahut. No advanced stuff: he just tracked down her personal Facebook and did some deductions from chats with friends. She wasn't the most private of small celebrities. Then he scanned all the ads in Dahut and found a few that could be hers: not many, small town, not much going on at the minute. Not quite sure what to do with this information yet, but he'll find something. He performed some mental maths: his work took him to Boston, Massachusetts, three times a week. Johnnyville, Boston, an easy drive. But Dahut Boston was even easier. Half hour commute. Could base himself there half week and justify it to Julianah, say the commute too much. Work always solves so many problems.

So when Julianah walked in slowly, he just swiftly changed the screen to a blank Word document and sat there looking loving. It was a small rented living room covered in chintz. Dolls, candles and flowers everywhere. For the first time in what seemed like eons, Daniel was gazing outside this universe. He liked his woman, but his head heavy with dreams. Dreams that now had a map. And the map lead from their little abode in the outskirts of Johnnyville, to the nearby Dahut. To her door. In his active imagination, she opened the door to new universes. Fresh air, he took into his plump chest.

⬦―――≪≫―――⬦

In the morning sunshine of early January 2020, Eris got in her car and set off to Dahut, her late aunt's town. It was a two hour drive through the mountains, past the dam in Sirius and the artificial lake. In the guts of the mountains the roads were tough and insecure, and at the other end she knew nothing of what she'd find.

She was driving alone so she used the opportunity to play Billy Idol's "Rebel Yell" album with an open roof. Felt good to leave behind the fearful uncertainty in Belmont, where cases of the virus arising, people worrying, yammering; felt good to cut a line through the forest to a task that will take her mind off stuff.

She loved the fresh perspective of lonely trips. She travelled much for work, and felt free when she was away. At first she thought it was just because she liked to travel. Then she slowly realized she also liked being alone, smelling youth, adventure again. Stan was getting on her nerves a bit. Lectured her on many things every day.

"And do you say that with the weight of your 20 stones?"—she'd quip sarcastically.

She was sort of the bread winner, her financial success outstripped his. She made things happen. He kind of tagged along, pissing on her parade occasionally when she got too happy about frivolous things; lecturing her on morals and higher goals. She loved him, they were good for each other. He made her laugh so hard her abs hurt. But surely there was more to life than this?

At first she left Belmont via back roads, then she joined the valley. Driving up to the reservoir, and through peaceful cottages in the sun. When "Eyes Without a Face" played on the audio, she felt transported. By the time "Flesh for Fantasy" came on, she was... hard to say. In a state of longing? Something she yearned but not quite sure what. It was time for something. She drove on.

Then she got to the lake. She drove right past the dam, and remembered what that news item said about mechanisms controlling the blocks in its structure. Hmm. Should she worry? Maybe not yet. Ten minutes later she was stood by the lake taking pictures and breathing the mountain air. The lake surface looked metallic and cold. Bit too perfect. She couldn't resist googling for information on the dam. What if it collapsed on the way back? Belmont would be submerged. Disappear like Atlantis. The place that never was.

Turns out the structure was solid because of this labyrinthine structure inside, with dozens of corridors and galleries. The dam was built of 30 blocks affixed together and controlled by the many control panels in the guts of the dam; one wrong command and a domino effect could be triggered. That's why it was secured with guards walking past, so no one could trespass. People used to cross the fence and get in to photograph the cold dark corridors, but some got lost and never found their way out. Kids with their Instagram. Or Tik Tok. Risk their lives for a picture.

And then she drove on. It was quiet and beautiful. With the exception of this bit where she had to pass over a very high viaduct, suspended on a rocky mountainside. Narrow and with the car rolling down the road, rocks fell into the abyss below. She slowed down, turned up the music. Music made it feel more like a scene in a movie and less like scary real life with consequences. And then it was nice again. She probably listened to that album three times in total by the time she got to Dahut.

And she parked, not quite recognising the place she'd visited years back. Her good old aunt... bit estranged, bit mad. Second degree anyway. Well, she was in for some work. She didn't even know why Ely died. Oh, dear. She said to herself.

This little man emerged from the cottage next door, with a big object covered in a blanket. He was James, she remembered him. But it was James with a wig that barely covered his white hair.

He walked over and put the box in her hands.

—Hi, milady. He even curtsied. This... is yours!! I have suffered enough, he chuckled.

Eris couldn't quite make heads or tails of what just happened.

—Well, oh, hi Jam..!

—It's not James!—he shrieked before she could finish. It's Graciella, thank you.

Oh, okay. Anyway... she looked at the box now in her hands. Well, what is this? James pulled the blanket off to reveal a cage with a cute little hamster inside. It was huge and it smelled.

Oh dear, again. She said.

—So...? her face asked for explanations.

—Well, obviously dear: your aunt whom you haven't had the grace to come visit in a very long time.. had a pet, this little fella. Since she died, and by the way I found her, I took in the pet. Now it's yours. Happy to be free, I don't like pets.

—Oooooh, came the long exhale from Eris' red lips. I see I've set off on the right foot. Well, either way, thanks, Jam.. Graciella. How are you? All good?

—Yes, yes, I am good. I am not so good after what happened.

—Why, what happened?

—Well, it was all very weird. One night I was drinking tea with Ely on the porch, next night I was calling her an ambulance that never came, then she's dead from a cough.

Right away, Eris put one plus one together and said: Coronavirus!

But Jam/Graciella was adamant it wasn't.

—How do you know?

—Well, I know, dear! And he twirled and set off.

—No, wait, Eris' voice softened. Come by, please, I'll make you tea.

Tell me all about it, and what you've been up to—haven't seen you in ages!

—Ha! I am not going back into that festering plague infested hole!

Lightning on Eris' face.

—Plague?!

I thought you said it's not corona.

—I don't know what it is, girlie. I am not going there. I ran out of heart medication.

—Oh, okay.

Eris just wanted to appease the situation and get in: "I am deeply grateful for all you've done". They did have to talk. She had to handle the affairs from this point onwards and Jam... Graciella had been fabulous help, a good Samaritan.

So she walked in, set down the little creature with an air kiss. She looked around. Ah, what a place.

Eyes the surfaces for a work area. Sees this art deco gem, a bureau bookcase, in a corner. Dyed Venice pink on the inside, with antiques and books and memorabilia dotted through the dusty shelves—the museum of her aunt's lifetime. On one of the shelves, a bust of Adonis. Or Narcissus. She wasn't sure.

She sits down and puts her laptop on the open bureau, which is a bit shoddy. Takes a deep breath, looks around.

Work beckons. Stuff to solve. But she's used to that. A deep sigh.

Wide tall rooms... curtains fluttering in the wind. Reading nook with large wooden bench in an enormous bay window... covered in furs and an assortment of velvet cushions that told a whole medieval fairy tale, like a serialized tapestry. Overlooking a fairy tale garden, a river running through it. And it was a West facing window, so every evening sunset would provide entertainment for the solitary figure wrapped in a blanket on the bench.

She feels sad. Some forgotten memories from her childhood, Ely around, giving her plums and doughnuts. Always doughnuts, she made. Once even with acacia, a splendour. Everyone liked them. A horrible final sadness overtook her. She missed seeing this woman. She will never see her again. And look how she lived. A vibrant woman. When was the last time she spoke to her? Oh My God. A year and a half. They talked about... doughnuts. And bland pleasantries. Ely congratulated Eris on her successes, which she followed with curiosity on her

Facebook, where she always gave a heart, and a short message "love this, love you". What horror. Eris had to grab her head to hide the thoughts, for fear they might open an abyss. She had no time for this. Pain and horror suppression, her specialism.

—Albion Cottage is such an amazing house! So beautiful, so quaint. She was just a third degree relative, but it would seem wrong to sell and ruin this ample abode she curated so carefully. I don't know what to do... She runs her fingers through her hair on call to Stan, who suggests:

—Find a tenant, darling.

Yes! Divine inspiration like an earthquake on her face.

—How did I not think of it?! Of course.

—See, you don't keep me around for nothing.

—Yeah, true. You're the idea man. Thanks, Chubby Sticks.

So like that she decided to keep the house. It was so sweet here. Huge windows opened, meadows opened, linden trees and song birds. It was like a different little world. Between morgue visits and lawyers talks and other draining administrative business, she enjoyed every minute. One day she put her best pearls on, tights and another black dress. She always looked a bit like a 50s movie star. When relaxed, a 70s film star. With thin hands she flattened her velvet creases while looking in the mirror.

Wandering towards the alcove window with a nice cup of green tea, she noticed a squirrel digging a hole to hide a big monkey nut in the yard, "aw, how cute". Nature... she smirks. Serenity.

Then her eyes wander towards a nearby magpie that stood observing but like it wasn't. Five feet away or so. "This looks exciting". Eris sat down and looked closer. The magpie was onto the peanut. Poor squirrel wandered off in a frenzy, the magpie shamelessly approached. The squirrel came back, magpie backs off. It was becoming a soap opera. Then of course squirrel went off into the world and eventually the magpie, with a determined face, rushed, undug the peanut, balanced it into its peak and flew off.

—Ah, sighed Eris. How sad for the poor squirrel. Then she remembered other things she had to do. She walked to town, and on the way back, sunglasses and Billy Idol still blaring in her ears, merrily strutting down the road in kitten heels. Something shakes her off the secret sort of party inside her mind: eight cute round baby faces playing on the pavement all go quiet and stare right at her. Girls, boys, between 2 and 5. Angelic blonde faces. Eris smiled, amused. The silence continued after she surpassed them, so she turned back to see the eight baby faces still round and staring but this time their faces had turned 180 degrees to follow her around. Like sunflowers chasing the sun. She exploded in laughter and the kids too. She turned again, they went quiet again. She suddenly adored this town.

On approaching the house she heard a loud, not bird song, but bird screech. The magpie. The magpie and the squirrel were having a fight in a cherry tree. It wasn't clear how remorseful the magpie was, but a cat also approached. Started to look like a turf war. This time, the magpie flew to the highest point on the street—a lamppost, and started to screech a loud defence against the charges. She sounded hysterical, frankly. The squirrel realised she lost. She did, but as she walked off, she wrapped herself in a gorgeous bushy tail, as a consolation prize. Magpie had nothing of the sort. Cat, having scared both off, walked off, aloof. "Well, what a day"—said Eris. And then she threw herself right in the faded pink of the baroque sofa, when she heard a ping. Email.

"*Dear Eris,*

I saw that you advertised a room more than a week ago. Is it by chance still available in the near future? I am a lecturer at the MIT, looking for a room. I need the room for weekdays mostly, it makes my commute easier

(going back to my partner in Johnnyville at week-ends). Happy to do chores.
  Best wishes,
  Daniel"

Then she went to the morgue. And it was dark and cold, but she had to do it, because no one else in the family was there. She was taken down the corridors by the coroner and noticed how grey she looked. Gray and deeply... sad? Must be a tough job to do, spend all this time among the dead..

—Ah, no it's a job like any other, said the doctor, while looking dead.

That light in the eyes, that's supposed to sparkle? Nope. None of that here. Eyes that saw too much death to make the difference between life and death. Lights off.

—It's no different than living people, and she smiled. But a smile like a tense mechanism of ropes and pulleys activated to lift her leaden cheeks.

Anyhow. Here we are. And she pointed to a door. Eris could swear her hand sounded rusty as she did.

Wait. What did she die of? Eris had a flash of intuition. She wasn't always the most intuitive, but, lately, there was a sense that stuff was happening in the world and she better pay attention, and it suddenly felt relevant. Like, what if what killed Ely was the virus? This virus everyone talked about, no one knew what it was.

The coroner was from another planet. She was adamant it wasn't.

—How are you so certain?

—Ah, I see so much of this. Elder single ladies don't have such a lengthy lifespan, you know...

—I suppose, added Eris, confused. But ...and she didn't want to offend the Dr... but there still is technically a cause of death, no?

—Loneliness?

—The virus?

The two ladies words' crossed each other and so did their confused eyes, but it didn't lead to fruition. The coroner was a bit in her own world, probably eager to get this over with and go home and have a tall drink. Long Island Ice Tea, or so. Maybe two. Or ten.

And there she was. Ely, like she'd never seen her before. Eris crumbled a bit. But on the outside, firm. It was mostly guilt. She just lived in her little world, champagne in hand while her own blood relation wilted away.

—So you think there's no risk then?

—How do you mean?

—With giving her a normal funeral, if she by any chance had the virus...

—Look, I wouldn't worry about this, said the doctor with confidence. It's not all as gloomy as they make it out.

—Oh, OK I'll make the arrangements then.

And as she rushed home in the dark, heels clacking on those poorly lit small town streets, she thought of the email and how fortuitous it was. She might solve the problem sooner rather than later and go back to her gorgeous life. Ah, what cosy idea.

"Dear Daniel,

You can come and visit anytime. I'm looking forward to showing you around.

Eris"

Then she slammed her laptop shut, yawned and dragged her silken robes down the corridors to a warm bed.

The streets were restless and wet. Rumors escalating. Yes, it was coming over. Yes, it was bad. Easily transmitted. Dangerous. People died in mysterious ways. No one knew what it was and how far it went. The TV news reported more and more each day but the government wasn't catching on.

The upper echelons still seemed to believe you can shrug it off and leave it down to natural selection. They even said so proudly on TV. "TAKE IT ON THE CHIN"; "YOU'LL HAVE TO ACCEPT YOUR LOVED ONES MIGHT DIE". It didn't sound very reassuring, unless you felt you had some magical immunity. But what would the criteria be? How would you know you have it? What if the virus liked healthy young people, and fancied killing them? All those power smoothies and gym hours for nothing. You couldn't know... No one did. The news and the fear approached town like a bad mist. And it wasn't even just the town. Or towns. It was all over. You never felt how small and round the world was like now. Bad news circled the planet in no time straight from people's phones. Into other people's phones. Who read bad stuff happening across the world in their bed late night, with only the blue light of their screens. Suddenly the whole world was one scared tribe, leaving aside wars and colors and stupid concerns and going down a few notches in that almost cosy level of animal fear, which makes you seek another warm body to cuddle to, instead of this obsessive focus on competing everyone, everything, to death. The shared problem of Covid for the world over brought them all together. Unified in fear.

Thank God for the internet. No guidance anywhere from the government; except for China, but they were bad-mouthed as the quintessential iron fist that came down to isolate and separate the infected lepers from the healthy in overly brutal manner. In Belmont, in Dahut, an oasis of late stage internet freedom whereby people met and discussed in cafes what can they do. Then went back online to gossip. Online, offline. And again.

How can they protect their families. Their old. Suddenly the facts of cruel life became more stringent: everyone knows the old get old, and ill; but here came a virus that apparently wipes off the old and ill so as to punish them, like an evil hand of natural selection on steroids. Why do it the old fashioned way, when you can speed it up and leave the young and sexy roam the world free? Why indeed. The hipsters, the bon-vivants, the people who always took it easy, one salted caramel éclair at a time, felt some kind of itch in their behind to do things better. It became clear it was in their hands. No, the old and the lazy won't do anything. The voice from the TV either. The people started to take matters into their hands and read the web, find advice, advance. Leave parcels on doors of the needy. Set up group chats. Sometimes protest.

And so it was in this atmosphere that Daniel embarked on a journey to meet his new interest: Eris Clemens, the glamorous writer. Defying his usual over-cautious spirit, he travelled to Dahut and knocked on the door. But unlike everyone else, he already wore a mask. It was not even mid January. The gates of hell were yet to open.

All it took was a few hair brush strokes and a shave. His semi pro athlete physique carried him well. A spring in his step, like a teenager. Typical college canvas tote hanging on his broad shoulders, hair fluttering in the wind. General lie to the dutiful fiancée. Absent minded kiss on her thin lips. Out the door, into the winter. And off he went.

When he knocked on Eris' door, she was already there, by accident. Tea in hand, dressed in a few layers of cashmere and black leggings that showed her svelte figure. But of course, not missing, her massive pearl earrings, her antique rings, her wavy hairdo and discrete makeup. When she slammed the door open with her signature Hollywood smile, Daniel froze a little. There she was again. The Goddess. He was naturally nervous, but this was bolder than anything he'd done. His eyes betrayed him. So he just thought he'd mask it with more timid charm, and extra politeness.

When her intrepid black eyes sunk their blade into his pudding face, a champagne cork popped somewhere. The earth's rotation took a hit, the magnetic poles confused each other. She felt him melt, and he let her feel it.

But Eris was a worldly, polite professional. What happens at THAT level—subconscious, lust, whatever—doesn't disturb the matters at hand, she can control several plot-lines. So she greets him calmly, gestures him in. Sits him down on a sofa.

In a split second, she had to make a decision: sit on the peach and gold antique sofa opposite to him, or closer to him on the white settee he was busy getting cosy in?

Like a vulture, she twirled her long cardigan and landed next to him. Arms dominantly to the sides. He felt small, though so much taller.

—So... Lovely email, there, Daniel. Promising.

She internally had a question mark over the word "chores", but she didn't mention it. Too much going on.

—So you'd like to live here.

Looking calm, glowing, he rolled his curls off his face to answer. His voice came out soft. Like a whisper. Like he was tired and yearned to be washed ashore.

—I do. I have a position at the university... and he waited for her to be impressed. But she wasn't, easily.

—Which one, sorry? And she takes a sip, and he watches surreptitiously. He watches her closely, everything. He's captured and focused hard to hide it, to appear normal. Her arched eyebrows, cheekbones and rose lips become the Bermuda triangle of his composure, his very soul.

This sense of secret mission for something that wasn't clear to him raised his pulse a little. And he generally had the heart rate of an Olympic swimmer.

—MIT.

—Ah. She positions the cup so that the handle aligns with the edge of the coffee table, squinting for a second like she's seen something.

He sees that. But he has to continue.

—So, I really live in Johnnyville with my fiancée. We don't want to move fully as she has a life there, and friends. But I'm a bit tired of the commute. This is so much closer, and quieter. I'd, of course, only need this for half the week. Weekends I'm home.

—Hmm, yeah. She nods. She seems to be elsewhere again. He wants to know where. He's scared. Doesn't she like him? But she has to!

He continues.

—The place looks great, you said it's central, and it is. He takes in the interior. Large living room, ceiling so high, your echo gets lost and back to you the next day. The earth tones of the antique furniture, the art on the walls, the large bay windows opening to a magic garden. Looks like a fairy tale, really. But mostly, she looks like a fairy tale. She's from his teenage dreams.

Back to the room. Eris looks at him sideways and says, "Yes my late aunt had exquisite taste. Runs in the family, actually!" Her crystal laugh fills the room, populates it. He smiles along, but bit confused. He's not used to feminine confidence; thrown off balance by it.

—Yes, it does. Late? What happened to her?

—She passed recently. No one knows why.

—Oh. My condolences.

—It's OK. Eris looks away for a second. I... Won't be here much myself. Maybe a little, to work sometimes. I love the place. But I live in Belmont.

On hearing this, his hopes sink like the Lusitania.
"Make her stay, make her stay".
—Oh really? He sounded almost natural.
—Yes. I'm also married.
—I'm engaged, he corrects her.
—Oh, I see. Well I have a husband back home. Not
that he's too possessive. I pretty much have my life.
—Is he also a writer?
Eris stops and stares in his face. How... who told
you I'm a writer?
—Well... Blushing, looking down, to hide that he's
been caught. You're a bit famous...
—No, I'm not. She says, almost harshly, with re-
sentment. I'm not THAT famous. And she downs a
whole cup of green tea.
—I read your stuff, he said, with a very controlled
smirk. She knew what the controlled smirk meant
but she pushed it away for the moment. Too much to
think of in the present tense.
Silence. Why did she just say her husband is not
possessive? She wonders. How did that come about?
But it's a bit late for rational thoughts. Something
in the boy's languid presence hypnotized her. She's
already asking questions just to hear him talk. In that
near Southern drawl masking a faint German accent,
with his mild manner. Blushing occasionally under
his golden locks.
—Do you need references?
—No. I am satisfied with what I see.
Her response struck him. It was from a world of self
confident assertion he hadn't inhabited yet.
He likes it, he takes the room, she waves bye bye
from the doorstep, she returns. Time for wine. Calling Chubby Sticks.
—Hi, honey. It's great, I've a tenant. That problem
out of the way. Of course, not over for me. Trouble
just starting. Ah, thanks, honey, you're sweet. Too
sweet, really. Chubby, but sweet.

And then the evening comes and she sleeps, and everyone sleeps, and dreams fall like fairy dust over every town in the valley.

Except Daniel. He can't sleep. He won't admit to himself, but he feels like he made a catch. And while entirely feeling out of his depth and surprised by the success of his operation, he also feels entitled to it somehow.

When Julianah's wispy hair flutters in her own snoring breath, he turns around, and hides his face in the pillow. "Hero level 1.2". He feels something slightly wrong, but he tells himself it's OK. He's just after the company of the smart woman. No connection to her looks, and their chemistry. He shrugs it off and refuses to allow his own conscience to bully him. He's a good man! He's a kind fiancée! He sacrifices for women, and cares for them! It's just that it's closer to work, and he's tired of this damn commute. And it's all for Julianah's benefit, doesn't she see it?! So he's less tired when he's home? He's deep into a decade of breadwinning for her, after all. What, is she blind? Enough. Let's sleep. And he falls asleep in a foetal curl, imagining the glamorous lady hovering above him with a seductive smile. Eyes glimmering more than her many jewels. Skin translucent and smooth like a soft pearl shell. Waist thin, breasts firm, spherical. Perfect spheres, perfect size to fit a delicate male hand. He dreams.

CHAPTER III

Notwithstanding the enormity of the news circulating worldwide, life still goes on a bit as normal. Sure, a death here and there. An unfortunate "cold" that feels more like the lurgy. Images of people collapsing on the street and being carried away in secrecy by Chinese doctors in hazmat suits. But news pick up a more hysterical step. Still, the government lagging behind. Not very bothered. "How's this different to the seasonal flu?"

On her drive back to Belmont, Eris had lots to think about. She knew she was Daniel's focus of attention. She sensed he was transfixed by her facial dominance during that chat.

He felt weak and ready to give himself but also strong and ready to take on the world for her. His little world.

She guessed that much and that combination captured her instantly. This was a shy boy but not a weakling.

She recognized the utility of this situation to perhaps attempt to shame her husband into losing weight.

—So I met this young lodger in the end..

— And?

— Well, he's... and she huffs her lips. He's very hot, Stan.

— Ah. OK. He says absent-mindedly, burying his head back into his paper.

— He looks a bit like me.

— Good for you, hun.

— Aren't you jealous? She arched her left brow high up, watching him sideways.

He repeated the word "jealous" absent-mindedly a few times while deep in thought about the content of the article. He'd usually put people's words in a waiting queue on the surface of his mind while finishing the thought in his head. Priorities inwards, like a ruler of sorts.

He finally paid attention and tore himself from it. Looked surprised. Like he'd just woken up.

— Um.... Jealous. What? Why would I?

— Because I get to spend all this time alone with him, young beautiful male...

— But he's got a wife, right?

— Girlfriend.

— And you a husband, right?

— Almost.

— Cool then. Nothing to worry about. And he buried his peaceful, chubby head back into the obviously more captivating paper.

What a solid waste of intellect, she thought to herself of her dutiful husband. To be so deep and thorough but assume people can be victims of vows they've taken at a previous point in time, with less information. She almost took it as a challenge.

— Look, my darling. Heart wanders. Heart knows no rules or bounds.

He ignored her. Suddenly the ticking old clock sounded very loud and looming. The flies swarming outside in the sun suddenly fell very heavy.

She waited.

— And... I can't help sexual desire, you know.

Suddenly he lift his head up from the paper like a rabbit in the headlights. Of this he was very insecure. He knew their love was deep and unshakeable but he had a mirror; he knew his belly the size of a small town and often felt inadequate for being such a fluffy teddy bear who couldn't please this goddess of a woman before him. No energy, no desire. Not for her. He did have a secret penchant for women of the pornographic realm—let's say, women of more slut factor. "How can you compare to them?! they're sex goddesses!"—he would say. To which she would throw her purse at him: "you do realize I am a sex symbol to millions, right? Just in a more elegant way, which you're blind to". And then the Chubby Sticks would point to his crotch helplessly: "I don't make the rules, darling. It just responds to things."

But on this eerie afternoon, her words finally cut. Panicked, he said:

— And so? You want to play with him for a while, yes? And he looked wounded like a little animal, but resigned already. This mountain of a man looked adorable and vulnerable for a moment and she found it irresistible.

— Yeah, maybe. Why not. She walked over to the kitchen and shouted from there. A girl's got to live. I have needs you know. Five years no sex, I am young, in the prime of my life. I gave you enough.

She gave her little speech from the kitchen feeling powerful and imagining his crushed face in the living room. She was smiling and relishing the moment. Silence from the other room meant defeat. She was ready to walk over and find him begging on the floor.

She walked in with a coffee pot in hand, ready to comfort him.

He was still, at the table, furious at what he'd just read in the paper. Having fully forgotten the exchange, he slammed his fist on the table.

— Treason! How dare they interfere with my practice like that. Have to call the Mayor immediately. And he left the room, furiously grabbing his phone. Huffing and puffing, a picture of clumsy anger.

She felt empty. Not less love, but less romance. This carved an empty slot in her and for the first time she felt a longing for Science boy. Maybe she was too silly and frivolous, not sure. But it's hard to be the wife of a busy pillar of community who lives for the tribe. And she was younger. Much younger. Hadn't lived her life.

She sunk to the table drinking her coffee to the sound of Stan's angry call. Pacing up and down in the inner yard shouting so loud that the whole neighbourhood knew the exact details of his controversy with Town Hall over health and safety measures. His impressive weight and height a fearsome spectacle.

Not like that delicate docile boy. Not like his ready cheeks and sweet availability. Ah, that boy could live FOR her. Could be hers.

Cinco is sitting in a club, beautiful bodies in hot dresses passing him by, dancing, knocking into him. "Too much stamina for my taste", he mutters to self into his glass of Jack Daniels. "They just need a mortgage or two and they'll settle in to a more decent pace of living."

—Hey, meet the doctor! Says Abe, close friend of Eris and Stan. The party's getting bigger, music louder. Eris and Stan both shake the doctor's hand and both pretend to not understand the name:

—*Circo?* Eris asks over the music, eyes wide and innocent.

—No, Cinco! Cinco!! Five! And he puts his hand up, all fingers. Eris looks at the hand and high fives him, amused. He rolls his eyes, flustered to be misunderstood by the beautiful lady. Stan just rolls over like a tank and shakes his hand, no introduction. Tries to say something over the DJ, but weird phenomenon: the louder his booming voice, the less he's understood.

—Cinco, tell him about the virus, old man!

The what? Ah, yes, Eris moves closer. "Can't hear, though! Come to ours tomorrow and let's talk!". Cinco accepts, but he forgets to take her number.

Abe grabs both his friends by the waist and dances around. Drunk again, but so sweet. He's more biting when he's drunk.

—Hey, darlings. You know, you two, you're the definition of energy conservation.

—Oh, how do you mean?

—Well, weight stays the same in the pair of you. One shrinks—and he digs his fingers in Eris' waist, close to her bra—and one... expands!! And Abe points happily to Stan, who nods embarrassed, but with such bonhomie, that no one can resist him. In fact some younger ladies with daddy issues circle him on the dance floor like he's a cuddly teddy bear. Eris likes to watch that kind of stuff. She encourages it. It somehow reassures her that despite the fact she's not got the hots for Stan's now rotund shape, other women still find him hot. A weak, pathetic consolation. She tells self.

—Have fun, darling. Want to take one home to the flat? she says. Stan looks confused. He doesn't hear very well.

—What!? He shouts so loud, the DJ almost stops.

Seriously... Eris leans into his ear, speaking straight into his brain. "I bet you can't take one of these girlies home. I know you want to. I see you. But can you attract them?". Stan shakes his head. He's not entirely innocent. They've discussed it often before. In fact, it was his idea, long ago. "One woman is not enough for a man", he said. It's not his fault that men are wired for quantity, he would say. "Biology dictates that a man spreads his seed wide". "I only love you, my Queen, but sex? Sex is a game of numbers. And it means naught to me. Naught! Mechanics, gamete expulsion."

"But, Stan... Eris would ask sarcastically. How does God feel about that?". Ah, don't worry. "God understands men. He's one himself". And Eris used to roll her eyes and walk off. He was just silly, everyone said. No filter, they claimed. But heart of gold. And indeed he was.

Heart of gold with bullet holes through it. Or something like that.

Everyone crammed into Abe's car on the way home, but Stan. Who left with a twenty year old bartender.

—It's OK, I had Red Bull.

—I'll drive, Abe—I'm just on mocktails tonight.

—No, no, I am fine. But—are you really not offended, Eris? Abe interrogates her in the rear view mirror. Not that I'm against that, God forbid. I'm a fan of quantity myself, and he coughs with meaning. But you... I mean it's a bit weird, no?

—I don't know, Abe. Stan and I have not had sex in years. Perhaps it's a good idea to let the man roam free, earn some confidence. We left it open, you know? I mean the relationship.

—And you're not bitter about it?

—Yes, I am. But what can I do?! I've a life. I have a great relationship with him, just devoid of sex. And sex doesn't really matter.

Abe is a bunch of neuroses and drunken biting wit spurting at people like a centrifuge. Offending people with the skill of a professional offender. But he cares about his friend. He leans in and asks her quietly in his educated English accent which only starts to falter after perhaps 5 drinks. "Are you really happy like this? You're a young woman, you look great. You can have anyone. What's wrong?"

—Don't know, Abe. I don't know. The truth is... I don't think it's enough either. But I owe this man my fabulous life. He makes me happy: he's funny, kind, he believes in me. My seven years with him are the best of my life.

—Darling... You have a duty to yourself. Not him. He helped you grow, yes. But he benefited too. It's not like he gave anything up to make you happy.

True. She says. But she doesn't want to think about it. It's wrong. Stan is family. He's home. He's the only home she's had.

When she finally got home, after cruising more cocktail bars, more laughs with Abe, she unlocked her door. Late night. Threw her purse, her heels, her dress on the furniture as she walked to her bedroom. No plans but sleep. In her bed, Stan was sowing his wild oats with the waitress. Her bed, her house. Her idea. In the bed where she, so often, tried to seduce him.

They didn't even notice. So she went back, put her dress back, and thanked the Lord for Albion Cottage. In her car she jumped and once more drove through the mountains, to be away from this. And think. Blasting Billy Idol, defying the awe of the mountain road, once more over the shaky narrow viaduct.

What a great place to feel fear and awe, away from her increasingly oppressive nest.

In Dahut, in front of the door, key in hand, she hesitated. It felt like a door to something better. Something just for her.

Oh, how happy she was to see Daniel's head at breakfast. He tidied up the place. Offered her coffee and croissant. She wasn't used to this. She wasn't used to the low decibel in the morning, and having a subdued musical voice asking her gently about her work. She felt a soothing change from having to explain her life and success away to the religious husband, who judged her romantic books, her champagne habit, her luxury expenditure. How refreshing to be admired for her refined ways, as "sophisticated"; to be watched with close curiosity as a sort of exotic butterfly, by an inexperienced geek who obviously hadn't gazed much at the world beyond his computer.

Important Daniel. There was no time in his life for love. And relationships... everything had to be attentively portioned and metered. To function around his whims. To be cheerful when he demanded, and silent when he had important thoughts. He had through finance and gently firm behaviour moulded his girlfriend to be that perfect shadow, light entertainment on command. Teddy bear to hug for comfort. Cook and clean. Reflect his own round face back at him, pour compliments when needed. It was a comfortable life, designed for his success. But now he had grown dissatisfied with the shadow he moulded for himself. Ready to molt his exoskeleton and fly off. Now he felt he wanted more. But he wouldn't admit to himself. Much of his self image was crafted around his domestic stability, "marital" respectability. "I am a loyal man"—he said to colleagues.

Now he had a project. The Eris woman. Shiny, full of life. "She's so independent. A strong and independent woman. Bet she even has her own bank account". Pragmatic sort of being, he even saw advantages in the fact she was, unlike his dutiful fiancée, a woman of independent means. Destabilizing scenario, but exciting.

He watched her discretely as she walked in, threw her keys and gloves on the side table. Her trench coat and bag. He'd never seen such dainty silk shoes, such thin defined legs, such immaculate skin and ordered facial structure. Afraid to be caught staring like a school boy, he'd side eye her from every corner of the large living room as he gave himself chores to do. She existed in a world of her own, always connected to her mobile device. Always chatting to someone, laughing out loud in crystal tones. He felt as though he was skating on the cat eye contour of her makeup, breathing in and out with her. Her skin so soft, her silhouette so perfect, like she was a large porcelain doll. But when she spoke, she sounded like an eminent scholar, he thought. She knew everything, she taught him things he had no clue about. He wanted to be so close, but knew not what to do. And feared her indifference. His small efforts to catch her attention fell on deaf ears. She said thanks for the tea cup then always returned to her work on the laptop, typing away with perfect posture, back at him. He felt ignored. So he upped the efforts. Made himself more useful. Day after day after his work, rushed home to do more subtle gestures of kindness hoping she'd observe.

To do things for her, was a compulsion. Wanted to throw himself in being useful to her. Anyhow. Anyway. To fit in.

—Did you... Did you just wash my dishes?! She said incredulously, from the kitchen.

His heart stopped. So she noticed. He blushed.

—Well they were in my way. If you want to look at it that way.

She looked at him with piercing eyes. She thought about that later that evening.

Their bedrooms were right opposite each other. It wasn't unusual for them to wake up and slam open the bedroom door at the same time, thus surprising each other in a sexy mess. Her in silk striped pyjamas, and tousled hair—him, black t-shirt, black underpants. A litter of sparks between them, before she'd find her authoritative voice and say:

—Good morning, Daniel. And she over-calibrated the formality of voice, to compensate for the over-intimate meeting.

—Good morning, Eris. He answered. But his voice, while formal, wasn't deep. Nor authoritative. It was melting into the air like ice cream in August heat. His eyes like saucer plates yelled vulnerability. She could read that language. She had seen boys like that before.

One night they sat at the table drinking tea and discussing his field. She couldn't understand a word, or just bits, but she was transfixed by his arguments about physics. To her, it sounded like philosophy but with more maths: of philosophy, she was fond—it was one of her favourite subjects with Stan; but maths was her Achille's heel. She could swear literal stars emerged off the boy's head as he described the physical universe. It lasted until 3am. When she closed the door to her bedroom she felt a pang. Dismissed as nothing.

Eris was often found in various places round the house dreaming, or reflecting, on a topic often related to Daniel. His modest black jumper did a very poor job of hiding the contours of his beautiful torso. And there was something particularly seductive about the proportions between his curly head, broad shoulders and thin waist. And how his movements seemed elegant, like a naturally poised young man. His hand gestures flirted and said things his tight lipped conversation didn't. And when they did, his cheeks turned pink. Eris took it all in with that smirk. It felt like she was talking to a high school boy.

So it took long showers for her to suppress, not entirely successfully, that... Well, that she was attracted to the boy. Seriously drawn. Tidal waves knocked at her door and she still held it shut by a hair. "No, no, no... No." And she then she called a friend. Abe.

—Blue Balls? Yes he's in his room. No, he can't hear me.

But the boy could hear, even if not her words. He heard "her". And too well.

—He's in the other room, just in from a run, freshly showered. Crossed paths on the corridor. And he looked so hot.

—Girl!! Go get him. He's there. Take it.

—No, no. I am married.

A deranged laugh cut her ear drum in slices, so she had to nearly throw the phone. What's wrong with you, Abe???

—Well darling, tell you what's fucking wrong. You worked that out with Stan? You clarified?

—Not yet.

—Your relationship is... Where do I bloody start?!... The effeminate tones of his British accent could affect fake outrage better than genuine anything. It was a gift.

At that point Daniel was heard outside the door so Eris walked further into her bedroom, to hide. Even covered her mouth.

—Your marriage is a game of football, if you like. Yeah? Stan scored. Ball is in your court. Your turn. Don't let him lead!

Now it was Eris' turn to explode in contemptuous cascades of laughter, so witchy that Daniel froze beyond the door as he was weaselling back into his bedroom half naked, again. She shared with her pal the gift of sarcastic laughter. A laugh that cut a room in half. You didn't need to be insecure to take it personally.

—Come on, Abe. Seriously. I am not like that.

—Darling, we're all like that. Nature is like that. Take the boy. God sent him to you. Don't give yourself blue balls no more.

Daniel was putting on layer after layer in his room. Open window, breeze through his long hair. No one made him feel so much like he had a purpose. He had to be ready. What for? No clue. But he had to be ready, clean, available. He knew with his unimaginative scientist mind that, however, he was already knee deep into a story, something about to happen. And he was eager like a school boy to do good, to please.

He set the table, like he observed she wanted it. Fine chinaware in the right order. Silverware for 3 courses. When she walked in, he froze and hid his face under his hair.

She circled the table a few times pretending to be looking for something, all the while looking at him faffing about with the table stuffs. He felt watched. Got clumsy. She stops.

—Hey listen, Daniel.

—Yes? He cut her off with sweet anticipation. Heart beating like a drum.

—Did you have any expectations when you moved in?

Oh my God. Daniel's little tweety heart yelped like a mouse. She could swear she heard it. Daniel sunk deeper under his hair. Silence deafening. Tic, toc—the sound of the grandfather clock in the corner of the large living room. Where did aunt Ely find her antiques?! The whole theatre of this evening of many evenings was a museum. A set someone pieced together through years of careful loving acquisitions to make a sumptuous setting for exactly what was happening. Aunt Ely's never-lived dream of romantic love.

He finally looked up. But not at her. He couldn't. This was it. What he hoped for was happening. He felt unready. Cheeks burning.

—Did you? He gasped.

—Say again?

—I don't know, Eris. Did you? Now in audible volume.

—No, of course not. I think you did.

She felt the room change. The dance began.

They sat down and tentatively looked at each other through bites of a Mediterranean dinner. She played chamber music from her phone. Harpsichord, for some reason.

Resisting a strange new magnetic field in the room kept Eris tense while she explained the basics to Daniel; Daniel was happy to hear, because, he added, so was he. Would you believe the coincidence.

—I'm in an open relationship. She starts. Memories of the waitress writhing in her precious, hard earned silk sheets. Under her chandelier purposely brought from Venice to cast atmospheric shadows over her own sexual sanctuary, to benefit her. Her. It "benefited" her once. In the form of Stan reaching his fat fingers to feel the contours of yoga muscles then fall asleep to general stupor. Once. But good thing the nameless faceless waitress got to enjoy her sexual sanctuary instead.

—Yep. Open. Re-la-tion-ship. She articulates with sadism while her fingers choose something soothing from the Sonos playlist. When she lifts her forlorn forehead, pretty shy Daniel is already talking with his delicate fingers. And unusually vivacious too. What's gotten into him? Eris a bit slow on the uptake.

—Me too. Me and Julianah have been in one from the start, ten years ago. It was agreed for her, she asked for it; when we met, she was popular, I was just a geek... I went along because I could tell it was good for her. I wasn't really... a stud. She was active in the kink scene.

I never really used it. The.. openness. He stops. Looks searching for eyes. His eyes swim to hers and meet in the middle, among the candles. Such perverse words from this innocent flower, she thinks.

—What, so you're like a virgin?! She explodes in jovial laughter. No doubt enhanced by the sweet Valpolicella she so eagerly savours. Glass after glass. After bottle.

—Almost. There was heavy expectation in his "almost". They looked at each other. Their souls were dancing musical notes, climbing, twirling together on the stave of the song. And a beautiful song it was, thundering through the rooms.

—I think we should satisfy our urges with each other. Our partners seem... otherwise occupied.

—I mean, they're good solid, relationships...

—Exactly.

—But...

—We can live a little ourselves.

—Of course.

It was agreed. Sealed deal.

O Phile Pai! She realised she had to play the role of the femme fatale here, and nurture this young man into the realm of sexual maturity: she would play *erastes*, him *eromenos*—the ancient Greek erotic dichotomy of ...gay love. Here it was, her dream of having a Greek statue. Antinous, Adonis, Apollo, ...perhaps Narcissus.

Not a role she was fond of on paper, but something she was naturally inclined to fall into since she fancied these paragons of virginal athletic beauty: belated erotic dreams of teen Eris that still haunted Ms Clemens. The shy beauty of the young male in that thin stretch of time before he ripens as a man. Timothée Chalamet. The boy in Death in Venice. Whose blond wavy hair invoked in her ethereal romance, poetic dreams. And also some fears but let's not think of that now, she said to herself while swimming in Daniel's anime eyes.

And she played "Eyes Without a Face".

—This still Billy Idol?

—Yes. You like it?

The boy spoke softly. He was all hers.

—Yes. I hear you play it sometimes.

Something in the boy's vocal tones spoke to her of an abandonment so deep, expectation so large, she shuddered. Its lure of power could not be resisted.

Then she stood up to bring desert and the boy sat down watching her carefully. It started to feel like a movie. Connection established, like two Bluetooth devices pairing. And she held the reigns. She was going to lead this dance.

Next day when he left for the weekend, he left a hand drawn smiley face on a yellow post-it on her laptop.

Mornings, Stan always spent hours in bed doing nothing. Or nothing that could be described. But this time it was different. He nudged the young woman in the direction of the door as politely as he could. Then ran away to the corridor to grab the big phone. Searched for the number of Eris' cottage in Dahut, flipped through papers, searched his phone's memory. Eris wasn't picking her phone. He was scattered and afraid. What a tragic misunderstanding. Finally, Abe rang. With relief he gasped "where is she??". Truth is Stan loved Eris very much. She was the absolute center of his world—*axis mundi*. Grumpy sort of fellow, though surrounded by people at all a times and regarded as a bit of a community leader, he remained a misanthrope at heart and let no one in his heart. Few people saw the real Stan; they got a PR version. Only she did.

—She is at her aunt's place.

Stan froze. He wasn't dumb. He may have played dumb for a number of years ignoring Eris' pleas about the more terrestrial aspects of the relationship, but suddenly he started to pay attention. Like a hare in the wild, his ears popped up to pick the danger signal. "The student".

—Is he there?

—Is who there, rolls of threat-heavy syllables pour out of Abe's sly mouth.

—THE STUDENT!!

—The what now?

—Please don't pretend you don't know. The student? Her tenant? I advised her to get him. I am not sure it was a good idea.

—You mean like it wasn't a good idea to bring home a waitress? Ah, but don't worry. He's not a student. He's a lecturer.

—How does this make it better?! Who cares? Student, fludent, schmudent.

—Yes, he's there. Not sure how long though. Apparently he's married.

—Yeah, and so is she.

—She-who? Abe's dead set to sabotage the course of the conversation.

—Eris, of course!! Stan's forehead drips over his phone into his clenched fists.

—Look, man. You have to chill. OK? Whatever you've done, it's your business. Apologise. Send flowers. Anything. Just don't project.

—Ah, so you know.

—Of course. She tells me everything.

—No, she tells **me** everything.

—Really? Has she told you about the Christmas tree story?

—Yes, of course she told me the Christmas tree story. When she got stuck on a tram with the tree?

—Ha. No, old man. Do you ever hear what she says?

—Have you got her number at the house?

Stan gets dialling to get hold of the lady of his dreams. The woman he devoted himself religiously to. But neglected terminally. And his prayers unanswered. Left to cook in his own juices, he rolls into the sofa. Puts his

dirty shoes up and breaks a small vase. A favourite of
Eris, some find from her European trips. One of those
one of a kind things. Hand painted. He doesn't even
notice. He reaches to the end of the sofa into his bag and
starts absently stuffing his face with chocolate. It is here
that he parks his fury, and night falls and finds him here.
Inconsolable but a few hundred grams fatter. And here
is where he watches TV and falls asleep. Ringing every
half hour hoping to reach her. Texting long passionate
misspelled apologies and explanations of the confusion.
Wishing he'd taken down the address when she was
talking. But he wasn't, except to say from time to time:
"how is this not trivial, darling?"; "How does Ha-Shem
regard the futility of your cottage interior design? Does
this frivolity help your soul?".

"Material possessions are decadent, you spend too
long focused on them. Aesthetics etc."

"Ah, but not when your enjoy mine, in my house?
What does God say about that?"

"I enjoy you. It's about you. Your mind."

━───❦❦❦───━

She had a bell. Found it round the house, an old bronze
servant bell. She would sit at her desk in front of the
laptop, typing furiously. And when she yearned for tea,
rang the bell.

Daniel barged in. Stood respectfully before her, and
looked eager to please. She liked to order him about, and
reduce him to a state of mental and physical undress.

"Stand there. Look in the mirror. Turn around."

And he did it all. He warmed under her commands,
like a toy that's finally found its purpose: being used by
the Goddess of strife. She caressed his contours, dug
her fingers in his flesh. Hurt it a little. Checked the
merchandise. It was fun to squeeze a reaction out of him,
so sometimes she'd say harsh words like:

—You like being my puppy? You're nothing but a puppy. I've a husband.. And a puppy. And she walked behind him, observing his reaction in the mirror. His brief flash of pain. Mental pangs of horror, under the surface of his doe eyes. Then she'd grab his hair and pull his head down towards her. He was taller than her on heels... But somehow it felt like it was him smaller. Between her hands, his flesh, his feelings, became clay to play with.

—What will you do to me?

—TO you? I don't know. I don't know.

One day he was gone for three days back to the "wife", Eris still rejected Stan's calls. She spent them on the sofa day dreaming with the music blasting. Her incoming tidal waves of desire hard to control, steamed windows through which the world disappeared. She texted him: "when you get back, remove your clothes and wait for me in the living room". So on his train journeys from Julianah to Boston for work and back home to her, his heart beat like a caged animal trying to get out; and she danced through the house to appease the tension. Passion making her dizzy with the lust of the kill; she felt a ravenous desire to take, to consume. Violently.

These soul dimensions were in her before, but not like this. Something like a vague feeling of feline predatoriness; graceful internal lusts. But this boy was catnip. Thoughts of his docile Prince Charming silhouette were a red cape to the beast within. Incensed and alive. Fireworks exploding, constellations of lust configured in her mind, impossible to resist. Luring her on a path of delirious excitement, a tunnel. And she knew it was wrong. But she was on an island. At the edge of something. So it didn't matter. You don't say no to these things. You'll lie on your death bed sorely regretting if you do.

Meanwhile, the world was turning. Really through the ignored old television sets in the house came news of an upcoming apocalypse. A bit of this, a bit of that. More deaths. When Daniel arrived, before carefully undressing and folding his garments in a neat pile next to the sofa, he texted Eris that university was closing down. Eris got the message from across the wall in the bedroom. Shrugged it off. Somehow reality wasn't very real. The murmur of evening news was more like a prop in her theatre of Eros.

He was a flower that blossomed just for the right girl. She was the right girl. She played Pulp from her phone while he waited the living room. English band, 90s indie songs of love and despair and all things lurid and romantic.

In the other end of the valley, Julianah was browsing the shelves of her local supermarket. She dragged a basket bigger than her, filled with elements of a feast. She was preparing for Daniel's return: "I'll only be a few days", he said. She was apprehensive. She had perused his laptop to Google the new illustrious flatmate of his half week over the commute; and immediately went to the bathroom to try vomiting. A visceral panic gripped her. She said nothing though. Wanted to stay cool for the man. And then she upped her offerings the way she knew how: by cooking him a feast for when he returned. She stood in front of the kitchen tool isle. Above all colourful kitchen paraphernalia was a big, shiny kitchen knife. What made it special was its handle in the shape of a unicorn head: pink, lilac cuteness to sustain the lethal steel blade. The kind that will slice a big juicy steak in one swift cut. Her man liked a steak from time to time as a special treat. Which man didn't? And she liked to make it for him. She came closer, fascinated by the knife. She grabbed it. Watched it mouth open, in a trance: "The Uknifecorn"—cutesy merchandise of an anime company. Threw it in the trolley. Walked around. In the toy isle, she saw the stuffed animals. Hid the knife under a whole pile of stuffed unicorns and puppies. Threw a rainbow garland on top too. "He'll like my new décor; things need sprucing up". She stopped at the till. Handed a card, looking a tad scared. But the card was declined, said the lady at the till in a bored tone.

Julianah felt the hairs on her arms lift. She scrounged for her vintage pink phone in her large hobo bag. People grew restless behind her, and she acutely aware, nearly growling like a cornered animal.

She rang Daniel. Tried to look away from the people around her who must have been watching the scene. She was red in the face, scared. A scared little animal feeling like she's been caught stealing. She rang. Daniel didn't answer. He had purposely left his phone in the bedroom while attending to Eris' demands in the sitting room. Instinctively, he knew to separate the two worlds.

The earth was shaking underneath her feet though it felt rather tritely stationary to the rest of the queue. She looked at the lady, panicked; why wasn't his card working?? Did he limit her allowance? But it always worked. She didn't have her own, but he set up a common one for her to use. She scrambled for some cash, anything, in her bag. Nothing. Something snapped inside of her. She found some coin. Threw them aggressively at the lady at the till, shouting.

—This is what you want, right?? Take what you want, bitch! Take it!! Bitch!

And she ran away, limping, leaving her shopping by the till. Her naked legs stumbling against each other as she tried to cover her bum with her hands because the mini skirt was wrapping up.

But this dimension of reality was paling out of view for Daniel.

He was more captivated by the anticipation that gripped him near the bay window of Eris' house. He thought he should kneel. There was something of a knight in him. Or so he liked to imagine. He thought of himself as a knight who fights for and protects women, and pays them true respect; not like those other oafs, who don't treat them right, and make vulgar jokes in their presence. He saw inside their soul, and gave them soothing gentle sounds. He saw Eris as a Queen, the Queen that made his latent male heroism possible; for her, he could be a hero, he thought. He felt he can drop to his knees and put his male stamina and intellect in her service. He never knew what to think of his own gifts, and career. And his titles. Finally they all made sense. He instinctively felt like there should be someone in this world, someone else than Julianah, who could guide him in the right direction, tell him what to do, where to go, where to sell his gifts. How to achieve greatness, by following the right directions. Julianah had fulfilled that role once, but he long outgrew her and his mind vaguely felt a vacuum. An Eris shaped vacuum.

CHAPTER IV

Stan was waiting for Cinco to come in for a chat.
Agitated and gaunt. Cinco was the leader of the Belmont Hospital, and through their common friend
Abe, found it was probably a good idea to chat to this
respected pillar of the community about the incoming danger on everyone's lips. The Corona Virus.

—Is it really true? I was cynical for a long time, to
be honest. Stan serves his opinion like a tennis ball,
while grabbing a Coke from the other room. He puts
one in front of Cinco, who shakes his head—he never
consumes sugar, he says. By the way, it seems things
like this make matters worse.

—Matters worse for who, in what? Says Stan who
downs a whole can in a second. You could like hear
it gurgle down the ample guts and a smirk of drugged
satisfaction appeared on the rabbi's face.

—For the virus!! Cinco shouts. A neurotic, pale
man, acutely aware something's happening.

OK, I tell you, don't dismiss it. It's everywhere. It is
bad. I work in the hospital, Abe told you. I have seen
it. I know it's real. I have seen people die, OKAY??

Stan's eye widen. Die of what?!

Corona virus. It is a mutated corona virus.

But Stan interrupts, he always does. He always finds
what he has to say more important:

—But corona virus is in cats, right?

—This is different, Cinco becomes impatient. He is not allowed to speak, he can sense. It is from China. You have seen the stuff from China??

—Of course I have, but to be honest I just assumed it is propaganda against the Chinese or similar. I didn't pay attention, have some personal issues.

—No, it's not. Cinco stands up. Starts to pace around, slightly correcting the orientation of objects dotted around Eris' large living room. So they align with the edges of the furniture. Just a little OCD, which no doubt serves him well in his work as a surgeon.

It really isn't. It is real. It's not your regular virus, flu or whatever. This ravages people, It kills in a matter of days...Destroys the lungs, attacks internal organs. I saw many cases. I saw them... And he stops, looking haunted.

—Saw them? Stan cuts the silence with his barking tone.

—Die. Saw them die.

Stan starts to mellow. Grunts, furrows his brow. His face retains the youthful look of a man with no vices apart sugar, and a good heart. His blue eyes are piercing and impatient but also deeply human. So hearing about the gravity of the situation, he sits down.

—You're right, I have heard people in my congregation, come to me with these videos, this Twitter stuff... I tend to dismiss, but perhaps you're right. Should pay more attention to it.

What do you want me to do? He asks.

—Well, perhaps we can arrange community help. There isn't much guidance from the government. No one knows what to do. But of course we must do something. At the minute, ill people are told to self isolate. Stay home, quarantine. Yeah? Someone needs to take supplies and stuff to these people. Someone needs to look out for the ill, old, disabled... we can't just let them die at home. But there aren't enough spaces in the hospital either.

—Wait, what?? Not enough beds? How come?

—Stan. you don't get it. This thing is huge.

Huge. Resounds in Stan's head. Alarm bells finally ring. Oh wow... OK, let's discuss.

Night falls over Belmont, and Stan lies in bed, that bed, texting Eris.

"Why are you still at mine?" She replies furiously. "Don't you have a bachelor flat?"

"Of course, my darling, but I like it here. This is our home. I can feel your presence here. Plus it's nice and clean. And looks nice."

"Thought all that's trivial."

"Well, a bit. But I like it."

"Well, I'm not coming home yet. I like it here."

"I bet.. Satisfies your urges :-). We're even now, you can come home."

"But I am enjoying the views, the house, the quiet. The space without your loud calls."

"OK, bunny. I love you very much."

"Good night".

The little hamster was checking out the new wheel. It had dropped from the sky in his roomy cage without a manual and the little guy wanted to explore. So he hopped on. Started walking in it. Noticed a change. Good, he's getting somewhere. This must be an awesome ride, he thinks. So he runs, descends again, looks left, right... hm. Back on. He runs, harder this time. Comes down again, looks left, right. What the fuck. I am exactly in the same place. He seems to say to self. Looks more depressed. Does it again, same result.

That was the end of it. He never tried to ride the mouse wheel again. Far too smart for these scams. What, a ride that doesn't lead anywhere? What is he, an idiot? So he just went back to his little hut and lounged, no doubt thinking of the mysteries of the world beyond.

And that's when Eris, leaning forward to see the mouse creature, became convinced he was a genius among rodents. Whatever Ely called him before, she would call him Napoleon: master of escapes. This rodent was too smart for the caged life. She respected that. She hated cages herself. Real or abstract. In fact, she was rather proud of her life's trajectory that managed to ski cleverly around them. Being her own boss, a life free of most things people call problems. Of course, not fully free. But enough. Enough to have the time to stoop down at hamster level and meditate about its noble character.

—Napoleon, can you tell me. Have these pains in my stomach. Do you think I am ill? I think I am. And she decides to lie down on the sofa to enjoy the bizarre pains that feel kind of sweet. Some would call them butterflies.

—God, they better be a stomach bug. Was there something in my coffee? You think I got roofied? Then she felt her forehead and became convinced it's a fever.

After hours of this, she dragged herself to the laptop. Gazing through the window, she gathers her thoughts. She always kept a diary. Since a girl, the diary was her friend. In an unfriendly world, with testing circumstances, she kept her calm and carved a confident path through life by every day performing therapy on herself on these pages. Always tried to dismantle any bad programming from her parents or other factors through ruthless self analysis, cold self criticism. And it worked. She made herself into a self vigilant work of art. Not in a shallow way, although that too. But the circle of good people around her found in adult Eris an oasis of wisdom, a reasonable and wise friend. She was really enjoying her current inner peace and exterior success, avenging a turbulent youth.

Then the diary keeping stopped in the Stan years. It was just too happy, stable. He was a very good confidante. A father figure. The diary was forgotten.

But now she smelled an emergency. This wasn't stuff to confide in bunny. So she began.

February 26, 2020.

"His girly, ephebe charm; a flower kneeling on the floor yearning to be plucked... hiding in the folds of his shoulders and behind his ruffled blond locks I just pulled. Blushing, warming up under the abuse; coming alive, coming undone, flowing animalistically now that I've given him carte blanche to be himself. Never did a boy slip so comfortably and naturally into the carpet, kneeling, as if to refute the artificial pretence of having to act equal. His lips, his cheeks, his dark eyes invite in... seductively like a secret harem wife.

Blue Balls has given himself to me this week. All I had to do was ask. My question sunk in his flesh like a knife in lemon curd. He was anticipating, already trying to get under my skin by what he carefully observed in me these weeks. The subsiding of my blue balls was only temporary. I found that as he lay on the floor softly I couldn't bring myself to violate him just yet. It was too soon, too much. A lifetime of pent up lusts wasn't easy drawn out. Explosions that happened for eons inside my head lack the tangible bold definition in real life that I anticipated in my dreams. It's simply been too long. Decades."

And she listened to "His 'N' Hers" because Jarvis Cocker's desperate voice explained what she felt so well. And she told herself that what she felt was sexual desire. She insisted that this boy is a disposable lover to fill in the holes of her perfect marriage. And by saying it many times in her diary, she thought she was safe. A further insurance policy was texting Daniel to say that too, in a dialogue peppered with a bit too much contempt. The boy took it and said nothing.

Images of Daniel possessed her brain. Political interests, current affairs, art... all concerns that left her brain to make room for the new obsession. She thought she recognized him from the sumptuous galleries of the

British museum and the Louvre. Often visiting those museums she felt a strange affinity with the statues. Busts of beautiful Apollo and Dionysus, she could nearly make out with. Those statues felt more real than life itself. What she felt then looking at the heroic bodies and elegant faces in stone she now felt in a side glance at him. Just injected with more soul, more vulnerable emotion. She always knew she was a bit different. She used to like to be mean to be boys. She liked to be cruel but also gentle. Take them. Beauty had a very strong effect on her. Once upon a time, Stan had had a pretty face. Too bad he decided to pour disdain on the body, like a medieval catholic monk, just in the other way—excess of consumption.

Instead, Daniel was young. His features spelled "Adonis" in capital letters all over her brain. The longing was too much, too much. Like a cruise ship approaching Venice menacingly... its shadow larger than the whole island... she felt the encroaching presence of something new, and big. Caught between the desire to take and be bold, and the captive feeling that what's happening is a bit inescapable, like any force of nature; like a Greek tragedy. Powerful and powerless at the same time. But so damn alive. It was a bit dangerous how alive she felt, because—she guessed, everything would seem dreadfully boring from now on, compared to this.

When she walked in the sitting room that evening, after a tortured weekend without him, the music was blasting. Tragical melodies infused with heart rending romance. Walking through it, towards him, she approached him. He fell to his knees. Head into her. She held his head. The floor started to spin.

—So why are you eating... that? And he pointed to her plate full of a clear soup with a few carrots floating in it.

—Haven't I told you, I am fasting? Or rather, fast mimicking.

—Like a monk, you mean? His eyes widened like that sweet emoji he painted on her note.

—No. Like a person who believes in longevity. She guessed this needs explanation, so she continued. You know how we have all this technology today? I like it very much, it's very promising. I am not like these people who think it's bad etc. I think it's the best thing that ever happened, the natural direction of history. But of course.. and she paused for a sip of tea. And by the way. Green tea enhances longevity—prevents the shortening of the telomeres.

—Yes, I know. The Japanese drink it a lot and they're very healthy.

—In short I think this technology should be applied to the medical research of longevity. You know professor Aubrey de Grey? He shook his head. She continued. Anyway, there's a cohort of professors in California researching the many branches of life extension. Mostly biology. Valter Longo another. David Sinclair here at Harvard. Seems to me like the most worthwhile aspiration for people nowadays is this, everything else pointless in comparison. Why the fuck would you care about more gadgets, creature comforts and going to Mars and not prolonging your youth, your life? Preventing your loved ones from a slow painful decay? Saving your parents?

Daniel thought for a bit.

—I think you're very intelligent.

—But?

—No "but". I mean I don't think it will be achieved in this lifetime, but it's of course a good goal to have.

—Anyway. Fasting is shown to extend life by a bit, and it also makes me feel great. It gives me a high. I can go without eating proper food for five days, at the end I feel like I can take on the world, take anybody and smash them against the wall.

—What day are you on now?

She counts on her fingers.

She puts up four.

He nods: smash me against the wall?

She wants him. He wants to be wanted that way. But nothing yet happened that night. Just a dense tension building, atmosphere so red hot it was one spark from a supernova explosion.

Next day, he stood away from her, listening to her cryptic warning. "You know, it's a bit dangerous what we're doing. Just a warning. People often don't think long term." And she threw him a meaningful look, like an arrow. But he didn't receive it as a warning. More like honey. He said nothing, and waited to be dismissed. She turned back to the work station. He stood several more nanoseconds to take in her look. Her magnetic field did something to his insides. The pull was more than any living creature can fight.

So on finishing her work that day, she pushed the lid of the laptop, stretched and texted him to get ready. For a hot evening. She had planned it all day.

Eris was aware of her looks. She saw how people reacted to her. But she didn't do much with it. It played a role in her career—she was a package of wit and glamor. She liked to be that sex symbol and most of all, enjoyed good genes and good health and a disposition for adventures that kept her looking like a dancer. So far, though, she didn't feel beautiful privately. Stan often emphasized she's not voluptuous enough; wrong hair color; too focused on the superficial things, etc. She was confident enough to take that in stride but secretly she would have liked her beauty not to be wasted. She would have liked a lover who trembled exploring the silk of her skin and played with the sumptuous, splendid festival of feelings and natural drugs that only a young healthy body can elicit.

And here he is. That person. And her, captivated back. She spent an hour getting ready. She left her bedroom glammed up like a Victoria's Secret model of their heyday.

Musical riffs travelled among the many candles in the room. Only light in the room came from candles dotted around various laptop screens and a rosy lamp projecting shapes on the high ceilings. Almost a religious atmosphere with all the sober portraits on the walls who watched upon them with severe lips. Outside you could see trees fretting in the wind like they wanted to say something. Maybe rescue them from what was coming.

He was lying on the peach sofa, still. Naked. Hair framing his face. Lax, ripe for taking. He was ready.

There was something magical about her walking to him looking like that. She reached her hand. Put it on his face. Grabbed his head by the hair and pulled him into her. And the little back and forth would take hours. Without ever becoming boring. Because it was something dreamt by both over a lifetime spent trying to push it down and compromise.

And then she threw him against the door. Slapped him hard. Consumed his neck like fruit. Slapped him again. Struck by a sudden awareness, she took a few steps back in her heels. To take in this immortal picture. This picture was too good.

She stood feet away from him, in the chords of a hysterical indie song (Pulp's "She's a Lady"?); her eyes burning the matter between them, and his burning back. Who knows how long she stared at him like that? Maybe in a parallel universe they're still locked in that eye contact which birthed galaxies. They recognized each other and used all their self-control against the magnitude of emotion or they'd burst through the ceiling like astronauts in a jetpack.

She burrowed further into his eyes and said in a deep voice she didn't recognize. A voice she didn't know from where it came, like some higher force speaking though her:

—**You'll never be able to get over this**.

And he said nothing, but melted more. He parted lips, head tilted into the door, too heavy for his neck. The scene travelled through him and made him a slave. He would never be the same again. He stepped into a myth and she was the Goddess he never dared to dream would exist.

So she punched him hard in the guts. He kissed her hand on the way to the floor.

She wrote before bed:

"My body enlivened, my mind in agony. My body trembling, alive with desire, pulsating, lithe, heart thumping. Young and ravenous. But my mind brooding, let down. In panic. Trying to piece together a battle plan. Trying to arch my back and escape the cage of my fallen shoulders and sullen head. Trying to curb the high. Natural drugs are more potent than I. Who has ever hacked them? The scariest drug of all."

The sweet boy walked in the kitchen, at 4am, because he heard her. He wasn't asleep. He lived in wait. And he ran through the corridors but when he arrived at the kitchen door he stood there shyly, not daring to approach. Not knowing whether to collapse at her feet or grab her hand or jump and kiss her. Letting the contradictory impulses go through him and flutter in his chaotic bed hair. Hugged the wall to his right to occupy his hands that wanted to wrap around her. She turned around. Her gaunt face enlivened. She smiled happy to see him. Flushed. So he finally garnered courage to take those two final steps and awkwardly but passionately grabbed her in his arms. Two impulses giving conflicting orders in his blood: one was follow; one was dare, and take everything. She saw all this and was amused but most of all was happy.

Lying in the dark at the end of a week of no food. Her nightly nightmare usually started around 4am. Waking up with the awareness something bad's happening that threatens her world order, then a longing for the boy sleeping next door. Wanting him so badly. "Wow, never knew sexual desire can be this bad". "I must really be horny". "Really need some sex about now". "I'll go to his room later, need a snack". She needed some calories for she was wasting away feeling half dead. Having to feel so intensely and battle so many demons and think of the occurring apocalypse was already too much for her 500 kilocalories a day. She dragged her feet along to the kitchen, slightly touching his wall with her fingers... felt her thin stomach with her hand and caressed her own cold shoulders in the dark. The semi dark of the kitchen washed in the moon light. The moon light was so bright. And she said she would go to his room after this snack. To have him, sexually. She planned her moves.

"A good thing I didn't take him to my bed. It would have been so wrong. Eugh, who wants him there?! He's not a lover, he's a toy.

A fucking delicious toy".

And then she didn't need to go because he was in the kitchen.

In the morning she beckoned him to her baroque sofa, draped in a red kimono and asking for a cup of coffee. But feeling so much longing melted the resolve to treat him like a serf. He served her, then sat on the floor. He looked desirous and young, much younger than his 27 years. And his skin glowed; he liked being semi naked. He finally found someone to appreciate his many hours of bodywork. Now he knew what he trained so hard all his life for.

She yammered about her business. He listened, juicy lips parted. But she couldn't focus on her words, since a torturous desire for his lips took hold of her. So far, she had told herself that it's okay what they're doing as long as they don't kiss. As if the forces of nature could be held at bay by this one gesture—or absence there-of. She suffered in silence for a few minutes, while he obviously waited for something. His naïve eyes pulling closer in expectation. She finally lost her temper and jumped straight for his face. Fully unannounced. He didn't expect it nor reject it. He became incensed by it, but with little display outside. Like that, this Goddess from the sofa reached her hand down to him like God in Michelangelo's painting on the Sistine Chapel—and made this human an equal. His head spinning, mouth grinning.

—Eris Clemens isn't your real name?

—No, it isn't. Mine isn't very palatable to American audiences.

—Why?

—Well, because it's Romanian.

—What's that? He frowns.

—I am the daughter of immigrant parents from Romania. I was born there. I've an unpronounceable name. So I chose a fake name for my work. It works! And she turned around smiling.

—But you can perfectly let people be tortured by your foreign name as a flex, you know, he jokes. What I do with my German name.

—Maybe. But I also like to make it easy for them.

—You never told me about your parents.

She looked away. Not her favorite subject.

—... Well, very typical immigrant story. Dad left me and mom when I was a kid. New family, new kids. I didn't fit in his new life concept, so he cut contact. We worked hard. We're fine now.

He was sorry to hear. He told her his sad dad story. It was sadder almost.

—Well, I told you when I moved in I have a complicated family story. But basically my father never left me, he did worse.

—What could be worse than abandon?!

—Rubbing in our face for decades that we're not as good as the other family; he lived a double life.

Eris' jaw dropped. So sorry, she said. That does sound fucked up. She felt pity. She recognized her mother instinct lunging to protect the hurt child in Daniel. She guarded herself against such thoughts. Old enough to know many people in life don't deserve the purity of maternal affections, which are dangerously selfless and she was "professionally" selfish. World weary enough to know that kind of feeling was the building block of both love and the kind of dynamic they had.

—Come on, tell me something about Romania.

—Well, we have the greatest poet that lived and the world doesn't even know it.

—I am not going to accept that statement without evidence, he flirted.

—Fine, she said. She walked over to her suitcase in the other room and emerged with an old leather bound book. In a language he didn't understand. This, she says—I carry with me everywhere. My favorite poem in the world is "The Northern Star". "Hyperaeon". It's ... and she searches through the pages...

But he brings up the poem already on Wikipedia and reads off his phone, sitting on the sofa, legs folded like a girl:

—*"One in a "constellation" of poems, it took Eminescu ten years to conceive. During this creative process, Eminescu distilled Romanian folklore, Romantic themes, and various staples of Indo-European myth, arriving from a versified fairy tale to a mythopoeia (from J.R.R. Tolkien: myth-making, creating mythology); the poem is a self-reflection on his condition as a genius, and an illustration of his philosophy of love.*

The eponymous celestial being, also referred to as "Hyperion", is widely identified as Eminescu's alter ego; he combines elements of fallen angels, daimons, incubi, but is neither mischievous nor purposefully seductive. His daily mission on the firmament is interrupted by the calls of Princess Cătălina, who asks for him to "glide down" and become her mate."

Wait, what is this? Hyperion? Hyper Aeon?? He stops himself reading, and demands enlightenment from her, looking up and beyond.

She laughs, good-natured.

—Well, you know... something, something, beyond time. Fancy Greek words for his immortality.

—Why's he immortal?

—Cause he's a genius, genius.

—But genius also dies.

—Well, yeah. But the products of the genius don't. It's a form or immortality, the best one we've had. So far.

—Oh. Gasps Puppy Eyes.

She drinks the moment through her voracious mind and feeling. She continues imparting wisdom:

—In fact there's more to it. One day there will be more ways to not die than having babies and being a genius. A third path. Which, of course, will also only be available to genius.

Her words, said in callid didactic tones, while playing with his hair—hit a wall and bounce back into the room, falling flat. The Bluetooth connection temporarily disabled.

Daniel gathers his confused gaze and continues with the more clear task at hand, reading words off a page, for which he's trained, academically:

—"*Cătălina is not interested in acquiring immortality, but asks that he join the mortal realm, to be "reborn in sin"; Hyperaeon agrees, and to this end abandons his place on the firmament to seek out the Demiurge. This requires him to travel to the edge of the Universe, into a cosmic void. Once there, the Demiurge laughs off his request; he informs Hyperaeon that human experience is futile, and that becoming human would be a return to "yesterday's eternal womb". He orders Hyperaeon back to his celestial place, obliquely telling him that something "in store" on Earth will prove the point. In his brief absence, the Princess is seduced by a fellow mortal: the page Cătălin. As he returns to his place in the sky, Hyperaeon understands that the Demiurge was right. it's better to remain "immortal and cold", separate from humans and their temperament."*

Silence. Silence during which each digests the meaning in their own way.

Daniel looks back up to her while she puts the book aside:

—Sounds interesting. Why don't you read it to me?

—I might. She, for the first time, blushes. I took this little book with me everywhere since my teenage years. I always wanted to share with someone...

—So share with me, he offers, radiant.

—Oh, okay. But what's the point? You won't get it.

—It's fine. I will read you Goethe in German too, he chuckles.

—Is everything this simple to you?! She laughed back, incredulously.

It was the sunniest, mildest winter the earth had seen in a century.

They knew outside the house a world was crumbling, but they didn't care; they had their enclosed ecosystem, their little, fresh world in hues of rose and burnt orange; all was comfortable inside. Through every window and every computer, phone or TV screen rumors of the developing crisis tried to reach them. Outside: Australia burning, corona virus, panic, strikes; inside: a love story. But being caught up in each other, they ignored it all. It simply sounded like background noise. Just walk from room to room, entangled, following each other, and just switching off televisions, forgetting phones in the bathroom while friends' notifications rained in warnings. Switch off news notifications popping on their computer screen. Looking at the window towards a golden landscape, not answering the doorbell.

And it was bathed in the sunshine of a miraculously warm winter. Birds singing outside windows earlier than usual. Golden light creating shapes on the rug through lace curtains, misshapen with age. So much light. So much consistence and color to it, like honey was pouring through. And they just liked to lie in it, holding each other, kissing, watching each other across the room.

—This is quite intense, isn't it? She would say, holding him. Taking a break from passion.

—Yes, it is, he murmured.

—It's quite deep, isn't it?

—Yes, it is, the answer came with a firming of the hug. They were doped. Brains injected with the fatal opium of love, to which no living creature can resist.

One day, he was sat looking at her. "Will you use me and discard me like a toy?". Eris was caught by surprise; his honesty gave her a sharp pang. She didn't yet know what it was. She gave a little speech about decrease of marginal utility in time, terms she remembered from her economics course in university days. "The more I consume you, the less interested I'll be over time. You know?"—she tried to make a femdom joke of sorts. It didn't help anyone. Daniel's face went a bit gray.

Say something to me in German, she prompts. Pushing him into a corner of the kitchen. Again she feels taller than him.

He utters with abandon:

—Das Universum existiert nur für dich allein.

—What does it mean?

—The universe exists only for you.

She says in her drawl:

—You love me, don't you? He hides his face. Admit it! He whispers "I love you". They faint into each other.

On a walk, they found an old church. They walked straight to it, as if beckoned by its neo-gothic arches. And in its yard, in the shadow of very old trees, a wooden bench. There they sat timidly next to each other. Eris had never been shy. She was now. She felt his presence like a huge magnetic field and zeroed in on his hand; she wanted to hold it, but not sure whether to take it yet. It had been so easy to rape him, but this other layer of teenage romance yet another forbidden frontier. The erotic violence hadn't truly broken the ice for them as lovers. As she thought of all these things, his hand touched hers.

—Look, I'll leave my door open. If you want to sleep in my room tonight, just come. He said, sweetly.

Her heart fluttered. Surely he knows what this means. They're no longer just fucking. Gate after gate was opening to that higher-most castle of the sublime, "love".

—But should we? She whispered.

—That's why I am leaving it open. If you want to come in, just come.

She liked to watch him work on his laptop sometimes. There weren't many times. He postponed everything for her; with uni closed, no work pretext kept him there. He hovered in this suspended time and space to live the magic. She observed how sometimes, focusing, he pursed his lips. Other times they opened like flowers. One day, he held her in front of the mirror.

—Maybe I can be more passionate too. Maybe I can be more active, Daniel whispered in her ear, grazing her neck with his breath, her back with his fingers.

She froze. Something announced itself. Something she wasn't ready for.

—Sure thing, darling. Go on, play at being a man let out of the box. I'll push you back if you stray.

—Yes, but. I am like fire. You can contain it but it might get out of control.

The fear. She disentangled just one millimeter from him. What, these stages have to run at her like this? Can't she have some normal pace of life, digest each broken frontier one by one.

—Well, then good thing I'm a "homo sapiens" who's learned to control fire.

And she left the room, smiling as she punctuated by slamming the door. He stood there suddenly alone in front of the big mirror, watching himself like a goat trying to understand French. But he felt a bud of power. And he guessed the re-flux in hers.

"David's Last Summer" was the last song on the Pulp album she'd been playing on repeat— the savage guitar riffs were cutting through an unusually hot afternoon.

Eris danced around. Felt like the resolve was to use and hurt. Squeeze the juice and discard. A temporary cold voice inside her head pronounced itself against humanity, against caring, and against weakness.

Everyone knows love is a weakness. One she wished not to have again. She thought she'd surpassed. Pained teenage loves ended in nothing... no more, she decided ages ago. She had mature love at home. The room was now spinning. And her head with it. Who's she lying to?

Her plans to break his heart, which had never been broken, would and could turn against her. But for the time being she just enjoyed power. The power of seducing two objectively remarkable men who had no choice but to accept each other and all the rest of the compromises, because she was who she was. And none could recover after having tasted heaven with her. She held them both in a power-lock. But she felt the tension herself. The developing poison. So she danced hard and loud to chase that threat away. Until the song ended with a really poignant riff, and she collapsed on the sofa.

—You're mine, she says, hand on his face.

—I am all yours.

—50% though. She said, and he watched him wince but not as much she expected. He didn't seem as bothered as her by the statement.

"Just become mine already!" She'd have loved to scream. But she couldn't. There was no way. No inroad into the complicated ways of this boy and this situation. His mind seemed sealed off, only his adolescent body on offer.

—You need to know something about me. He said sweetly. You'll never drop below number three in my life.

Then he looked at her stunned face.

And no one will ever make me hurt you. No one can force me to do anything against you. It's a promise.

She looked at him questioningly. Took in all the contours of his face. "Why is he saying that?" merged with "Ah, isn't he sweet, the little hero; my German knight,

Teutonic Knight". It warranted a warm hug. Hugs discharged so much electric power between them.

On the floor, entangled, Eris on top like a predator, him a dying gazelle. Taking, hurting, feeling his young flesh. And his eyes slanted with abandon but a sweet abandon that looked way past sexual and into romantic territory. It wasn't really his body this boy was handing over to her on a silver plate; although a beautiful lusting body it was; it was his soul he was longing to give. And there was so much to give, she was in awe at the gift.

The pangs of love circled her closer and closer. Fear like a dark cloud. Almost made it all more exciting and dark, like an 80s' psychological thriller. This was meant to be a sexual liaison to refresh her soon fading youth. A swan song of sexual desire. A little entertainment on the side. Convenient and easy. And she lifted her head from their embrace, it was so heavy; the magnetism of his face, his angelic head was so heavy it almost hurt physically. But she tore herself a little, stood up and walked off. For a moment, to cool off. To look at herself in the bathroom. To ask what the hell is going on here. She was with husband, he was with fiancée. They were solid, unshakable bonds. What is this, how does this fit in anything?

And then she looked in the mirror to him walking towards the door, standing in the dark. His eyes glimmered with a sweetness like she'd never seen before. An innocence out of this world. Like ready for her, no matter what. His body like Michelangelo's David but with her bite marks on the pectorals.

—Can I help? Can I do anything for you? Like he guessed she was in turmoil. Like he really cared.

Like a current went through her and she jumped, kissing him hard on the lips. Grabbing his head with both her hands, violating his mouth. Once more, a border trespassed.

But in his lips there was something celestial. Once more that pull. Like she could drink his whole substance and become one. Dizzying and spectacular.

Shaking her head in bed at night. Wet sheets. Unease. Guilt. SO MUCH GUILT. So much confusion. What was happening? The fabric of her settled life, unravelling. She couldn't sleep, again. Never happened to her.

Sitting up in the dark, thinking, contemplating, feeling the pull that told her to go to his room.

She left her bed, naked. Put some lip gloss on and ran her fingers through her hair. And opened her bedroom door towards his just across the narrow hallway. His door was wide open. Slammed open, possibly more than 90 degrees wide. He didn't leave the door open as much as ripped it out of the laws of physics.

"Wow, Puppy Eyes really wants to allay any availability ambiguity... "—she only had time to say to herself, briefly. Before she launched from the doorstep straight into his bed, almost flying in. Like the Incubus her favorite poem inspired from. Landed on top, encapsulating him with her arms. He looked like a scared little animal who was at the same time excited to see her. Of course he had been awake. Of course.

In the dark, there was nothing but the moon coming through the window, leaving shapes through the blinds. And in the dark she grabbed his head to look intently in his eyes, to see what's there. To see, what is it she's feeling, and for whom. And what's going on.

His green eyes had a potent, fascinating mix of Bambi like candor and masculine resilience. Not seen before. World operates on caricatures. Boys are boys, girls are girls. But this boy wasn't any caricature. The simplicity and determination of what he presented was deafening yet the words on his lips sparse. The silent depth scary and captured her focus like laser point a cat. It all came about rather easy. She had to do very little. The seduction had happened before they met. The bits of her Creation, thrown in the ether like a smoke signal in hope someone able to grasp... they landed on him like pollen finally finding pistil, after riding winds across internet meadows. And her photos, videos all over the place. Her content fertilized his mind. He was prepared. She didn't lift a finger. What a natural flowing rapport it was.

It was the fourteenth day of their time bubble. She dressed up, as usual. There was wine, there was music and sunshine. She paraded on the corridors and rooms in lace and heels; head heavy with a clean natural desire. Her catch sitting down, watching her, tension building up in his Teutonic features, like arrows shooting from under his eyebrows.

He kissed her neck; it became rather passionate. Her breathing intensified. He pushed her on the white sofa, feasting on her all of a sudden. She had question marks popping out of every pore but it was too hot to resist. It was insanely hot. Fear and lust. She remembered she was supposed to be in charge. She shoved him forcefully towards the other sofa, where she became aggressive, gasping for air. Ripping every bit of fabric left on his body.

But he wouldn't have it. The fire now out in the room, consuming it. He threw her on the other sofa, again. The boy had manly eyes. He knew how to grab, how to possess. It was a festival of lust in which she stopped resistance with anything but breath. Heart rate rode high.

And then it rang. The phone rang. It was next to them. She looks sideways. "Stan", his smiling picture on the screen. She ignores. But it keeps ringing. She can't be bothered with this. She's got no breath left to talk on the phone. Daniel doesn't stop feasting on her neck, but the phone keeps ringing, loud, overtaking the music. The most grating alarm she'd heard. Like post-war nuclear threat sirens. So she stops. Daniel walks off, warning: "watch out; your breath". She lies on the sofa trying to

wake up from what just happened and cool down so that
she can ring back.

—Yes??

—Oh, hello, darling. Are you well?

—What happened?

—You haven't watched?

—Watched what? Eyeing Daniel, irritated.

—The president's speech. It's **lockdown**. Everyone
has to go home.

It was like the sky collapsed. From the high temperature of a new earthquake, to the hideous blow of really bad news. Daniel looked back, worried. They knew
what it meant. Cold shower of reality.

So he packed his bags and decided to leave next day.
Him to Julianah, of whom he never spoke, her to Belmont, of which she always did.

It was hard. Waking up was dreadful. The last minutes
before departure he started crying.

— I will never forget you, Eris, I don't want to! I
won't!! He repeated through tears as he raised his arms
in despair. She held him closely. No one knew what to
do.

When he left, she watched him leave. Tear forming on
her hot cheek. She did something she had never done,
that she would never understand. She ran to his bed and
hugged the sheets. Rolled around, in a fit of tears. And
put her head against his pillow. Inhaled his scent. And
cried.

He walked through an empty town, a deserted train
station with military guards making sure he's actually
going home.

Heaven was dismantled, like a circus tent after the
show. She packed too and left. The drive back was gray.
No music this time, not even over the viaduct. Uncertainty and panic supreme. So much happened so fast.

PART TWO

THE CHESS GAME

CHAPTER V

25th of March. The apocalypse begins.

It was the first day of lockdown and earth suddenly changed shape. So many people who'd been encouraged for decades to go out and spend their pennies in places where other people also spend their pennies, were now told to stay in, away from everyone. That's it, no more drinking out, concerts, events. The world stopped. Suddenly less cars on the road; it was beautiful. Helped by this unusual mild winter. They said it was a bad thing that happened. Bad deaths and never-before-seen medical tragedies, but that was all out of sight; what the average person saw looking out their window was a fresh new, quiet world. It was eerie. But they had the internet, so it wasn't truly lonely. And it's OK, they still had online shopping. So was it really that bad? Some thought so. The official bodies of authority finally acknowledged that the new virus needed measures of quarantine. It came like lightning. So, from indifference and an unabashed embrace of the Darwinian method—almost outright praise of the virus for culling the population of its "unproductive" elements—we were now onto a new chapter: FEAR.

By magic the news changed tone and pumped fear through the television; and all the screens people had lying around which were more of a reality than any non screen objects. You couldn't be lectured by your socks or forks, but this cute little device with moving pictures—everyone's best friend, and foe—the phone, could hypnotise you with an endless stream of information. If you wanted to call it that. It was bytes, for sure. Bytes of godless data falling upon us like acid rain.

First, it was important to blame the crisis on a suitable entity that fit into with the rest of the narrative that supported our times like a skeleton. These invisible narratives oddly prop our times made of oil and lithium as much, if not more, than hard won hard matter itself; funny, life. Had to make it clear who the bad guy was in this Western paradigm. China. It came from China. Those barbarians eat disgusting things and don't wash their hands or something and look what they did. With their slimy culinary habits, they got us civilised folk infected. It might even have been true. We don't know. How could anyone know.

That's perhaps the magic of the whole 2020 landscape: invaded by so much data, yet no one knows anything for certain. Or at least not with their own computing chip. Medieval peasants watching sheep on the hills of Transylvania would have more of a genuine idea of what is going on, based on their own stream of thoughts and deductions, than your average British or American person. This side of the fence, people were astute and fancy white collar professionals, with professional tones and thick rimmed glasses of knowledge, but most of the verbosity in their mouths came ready made from a dichotomy of the Guardian—Fox News. They just chose one ideological factory over another—like supporters of football clubs. Frequently dismissing the reality of their senses to subdue their conclusions to those coming from trusted sources. And the new apocalypse, a strange world-uniting disaster that made life stop and could make people think... would instead make people navigate even farther in opposite corners of an artificially generated dichotomy. Almost like pawns in a game of chess. They don't choose to be there. Fighting each other. It's the hand from the sky moving them to guard a Queen and King they haven't even seen. Nor need to see, in order to offer their lives for them. Such beautiful dedication. Such self sacrifice of the pawns.

Eris met Stan years back in a political meeting. She heard him talk, nodded a few times and that was it. Their bond shared a central column that mattered to them more than anything; bit hippie, some might think. But not the worse thing to care about in life. Social justice. They spent many hours talking and agreeing with each other, helping out in camaraderie. Eris was a bit in love with the sound of her elocutions, and to be honest, Stan catered to that a bit too well. He was the cheerleader she lacked. Harsh he could be, too; but when "she wasn't wrong", by God he poured applause on her. He liked her audacity, her eloquence in political passion. And her nature, quite fond of admiration and superlatives, lapped it up. Maybe that was a central thing that tied them together: support Eris gloss on the continental map with her speeches and books, and speaking passionately with her hands. But now, she climbed a step higher on the ladder of needs and wants. She had grown her own legion of half loyal fans. Was Stan's role to be re-negotiated? Was the central column anchored deep enough? But, of course. She had no clue these questions were configuring on the horizon of a particularly unusual year.

She came home. Literally, her soul home. It was here. She was very confused. Apprehensive, she opened the lobby door. Still held her tummy to quell this constant "digestive upset" that had grabbed her since early February. Or whenever Daniel moved in with his hair.

Oh, no. She opened the living door to a mini apocalypse. In the midst of chocolate wrappers, and Coke cans, was an enlarged Stan that had unified with the sofa.

—Fuck's sake, Stan!! What the hell is this?!

—So happy to see you, bunny!

—Really? Well I am not happy to see this... she advanced into the room shocked at the state of things. Worse than ever. Collects her broken vase and instantly anger shoots up. She throws it at the wall while Stan hides, taken by surprise. Then anger shoots up another level and she also throws her pearl bracelet. Pearls explode everywhere, seeping it into nooks and crannies. Standing in the midst of the explosion Stan understands he'd done wrong, but vaguely.

—Bunny... come on! What's the big deal?! Let the cleaner handle it, it's why you pay her.

Stan shouted too. He felt he had a right. They spent the evening sat on the sofa next to each other, grouchy. Both diving into their phones. On hers, sweet words from the young lover. His, news, politics, that kind of stuff.

" You have set quite high standards in what is possible to expect from a partner". Daniel types with a winky face. He felt confident that was the wittiest emoji he could top his remarkable statements with.

Eris understood this new chatbox would be their lifeline from now on, for God knows how long. And she knew that she was now condemned to a double life. Before, she lived a slice of heaven, divinating clouds on the horizon. Now, she lived under them. The purity and romance of the previous stage of their new love was a gift of fate that would never repeat, sealed in its perfection and floating in the air to taunt her, meanwhile she had Stan, unkempt, hostile, to feel tied, somehow obligated to. In a fight, she would call him Stan. In a neutral disposition, "Chubby Sticks". In a semi romantic mood, it was "bunny".

—Stan! I am off to bed. Too tired, sorry.

—So, no movie? We wanted to watch something.

—No. Hard day. Good night.

And it wasn't a good night. She exchanged more love texts with Daniel, while a new sordid feeling of guilt and secrecy descended upon her. She felt a prisoner. She dreamt of an angelic boy who waltzed in perfect harmony and synergy with her—captive to vows of loyalty to an oaf who made a mess of things. Enter the real apocalypse.

On a parallel timeline, half of the bubble of magic that love created was also returning to reality, in Johnnyville. A reality that looked him in the face from just below his chest level, with adoring eyes set in a donut-shaped face. He was on auto pilot to be nice and kind to the lovely lady. She kept a bit of distance because, well, he had travelled, he might carry the virus. The virus of Eris' presence she could smell on him.

Julianah was a bit concerned with the pandemic. But really, she was much more concerned with this evil witch that was trying to steal her precious treasure. Yes, she had suggested and even insisted and even benefited from an open relationship years back; when she met Daniel; he was a shy inexperienced young man, and she was a world weary party girl with boys on her tail. Bit of a goth rebel, bit of a catch for a pubescent Daniel. Ten years later, he was still an inexperienced young man, and she was an experienced housewife. They both told each other sex doesn't matter but their kind of deep loyalty and teamwork beats everything. Yes, she had lovers, and liaisons, and developments. But this was different. Eris was more of a threat to them than her lovers were. A lot of the safety of their bond was predicated on poor loyal Daniel not having grazed on greener pastures; not knowing there is better because he'd always worked too hard to look left-right; work hard to scale the tough ladder of bourgeois success. Predicated on his extreme dedication to be loyal to just one girl, his entire life, in order not to be his dad or men in general. She lounged happily in the artificial comfort created by Daniel's complicated psychology. But if he was to see there can be better, then she would be in trouble. If he found that he doesn't need to settle, now the new star of Eris high on the firmament.

So that evening Daniel was fed a juicy medium rare steak and a luxurious home made toffee pie. And she observed carefully how he also disappeared in a world of his own, with her ten inches away on the sofa.

"You have set quite high standards in what is possible to expect from a partner", he types.

"I bet", Eris typed back with a wry smile emoji.

Eris and Daniel were like angels cast off heaven, suddenly aware they're captive.

"Careful. You know what happens if you get too close to the sun."—were words of prescient Eris that rang in Daniel's mind a lot, these days. In his mind's eye, he saw her standing, flirtatious smile in a vintage dress, sunlight bathing her like a cosmic spotlight. The world her stage. And he clearly remembered the crystal of her warning seeping into his ear, its meaning dismissed by the many explosive emotions of love, drowning everything, making the world spin, creating an internal music he was all too happy to live to the rhythm of from now on. Secretly.

Cinco just wanted to help. It was a new virus with new symptoms and much more lethal and contagious than other corona viruses, but after all it was a respiratory virus so knowledge from other such viruses could help. It was hard, at this stage, to imagine a solution to the extreme ends of the illness, and he had seen them in hospital. Like a horror movie. But the least you could do, he said, is manage the early stages. Stop it from getting to the stage where you need a respirator. Intubating patients with oxygen was devastatingly hard for the patient and a drain on hospitals, because there simply weren't enough respirators around. Cases still under-reported. So he gave an interview where he advised people to take vitamin C. Supported by 30 studies, most of which coming from the US military—the mother of all research. Links and everything. The science was sound, and he

was a man of science. He told people to take large doses
of vitamin C to keep the virus at a benign level. No one
claimed there was curing it; the idea was to stop it spread
to the organs—where it behaved like an unpredictable
bubonic plague and killed fast, and with a lot of pain. 10
grams or so if you have it. 4 to 6 grams maintenance, to
prevent. He indicated other vitamins and supplements.
This was hardly controversial stuff, and no side effects
were known for the innocent vitamin.

But the Gods of internet disagreed. At first, the interview went viral. Cinco was in his crammed office when
pings on his Medium account started to create a techno
music of sorts. It was encouraging. Lives could be saved,
he told his nurses. The hospital applied the wisdom.
Success was measured. That day, less lives lost.

But by evening, Cinco's entire web presence had been
censored. The papers reported he was a "quack doctor"
and a lunatic who via his dangerous misinformation is
trying to kill people. Death threats followed.

Anonymous egg accounts on Twitter told the director
of the Belmont hospital, a surgeon, that it was "ignorant
people like him that cost thousand of lives with his
unverified herbal remedies".

—I don't understand. Don't they even read the links??
That IS the science. They could at least bother to open
the links. It's fucking vitamin C! Even if it was fucking
"herbal remedies", who was in danger?! This virus kills.
What is the problem with taking some tablets we all take
anyway?

His nurse, half convinced, nodded. She knew him for
ages. But to her mind, all those people online had a bit
more authority, because they had the power of numbers.
And to her, numbers outweighed the simple common
sense spouted by the educated mind in front of her.

But the other nurse, Jenny, was older and the opposite. As she strolled along the doctor through corridors
filled with ailing people overflowing, in their masks, and
makeshift hazmat suits, she vocally agreed. She believed

in Dr Cinco no matter what. Not because she'd read the 30 links. But because she was the loyal old dog. The world needed people like her from time to time. As long as they were loyal to the right doctor. And to be honest.. with so much suffering around, you'd have to be a heart of stone NOT to try anything, anything to reduce the pain of these horrified patients that didn't even have beds to suffer in. She said with a hand on his back, as she slalomed through their writhing limbs.

By the evening, the Doctor's face was on the news. His reputation and credentials wiped off the public mind, his entire web presence now red-lined with the scarlet letters: "fake news". It was judged in absentia. His CV re-written; the angle was "unscientific homeopathic advice". The social media companies did it, after hundreds of people flagged it. It was the new way. Considering the traditional way would have been to burn him at the stake for witchcraft, this was progress.

—Don't mind them. And post elsewhere, under other names. Said Stan, the solution man. So Dr Cinco did. So in a small act of revenge, the article flew again, under various names. And then other accounts would post again and again, until it was impossible to censor. The fractal internet.

—Just hope they don't wash down all that vitamin C with a vat of Coke. That would *slightly* undo the benefits.

———— ❧ ————

In his little cage, Napoleon was doing what he did best: try to escape. When Eris walked over, or sometimes Stan, the little man didn't feel safe. He felt, like many creatures justifiably do around huge things they don't understand.. scared shitless. The cage was torture. He was a wild animal. He wanted to roam free in underground galleries in green pastures, adventure, store groceries, create engineering works and enjoy the delicious art of taking complex decisions; what he was evolved for. But no such fate for him presently. He had a little nest, and a little wheel he ignored, because too smart to run to nowhere. And every day, he hatched plans. And every day, he jumped high trying to burst through the cage's lid.

It was here, before her rodent cell mate, that Eris sat on the rug and texted Daniel. Her oasis of illicit privacy in a married house.

"When I'm away from you I feel like in a mental cage. And I'm so happy when you come to that cage and give me some attention".

His text like a romantic arrow. She played his melliflu-ous voice in her head as she read feverishly.

Her heart jumped now when she had a text from him. She was an opium addict, and the opiate came in small doses from her phone.

But she, looking around and inside herself, felt a great wave of defence of the greatest period of stability and happiness of her life. A new concept kicked in automat-ically: "duty". Faced with this crisis, she simply defaulted to the familiar. To her family.

"Just want to make sure, Daniel, I know the situation will lead to hopes and expectations. I love you, but I have to make sure you know I have a partner for life, and based on what I see, I doubt that will change."

Daniel had been floating on a dream bubble since Albion Cottage happened. There was no clear thought inside himself about complicated things like the God-dess and the future, as he lived in a state of charmed ex-pectation like a passive receptacle: she was the emitter of his reality, and his duty was to accept and reflect back the created magic and happiness. Did she not say she would take the lead? He had not stopped to *think*, but he had often dreamt. Dreamt of Julianah elegantly stepping out of the way with a handshake; about parading through town in a gilded carriageway, generously waving the crowds with the Queen in tow, to military fanfare; he was great and this new woman could bring him to even greater greatness, even Julianah would be happy to see, as she no doubt was selfless enough to care more for his happiness and ascension in rank; ...she herself had told him that true love was selfless.

So when Eris' text came out of the blue, in the first day of their separation, its cold shower dashed his daydreams.

There were two vectors at play: one slightly descending curve of a very long and real love, with deep healthy implications, which, while descending, still had levels higher than your average relationship. And this crossed on the graph of Eris' emotional life with the new, and vertiginously rising curve of romance for the young man. She sat at their precise point of intersection and from where she sat, they looked equal. But she knew better. In metaphors fond to her: one was a tall glass of red wine, the other ephemeral champagne foam.

"Then you're not as smart as I thought. I thought it would be obvious to a brain like you that with my intellect and career I deserve to be number one". She couldn't believe what she read. He couldn't believe what he just sent.

From where she sat, she saw the levels shared with Stan as more substantial than the fireworks display suddenly born in Albion cottage. Stan was older, wiser. He fit her soul like a glove. And Daniel... he was belated teenage passion she didn't expect; she welcomed its late and awkward arrival in her life, but she didn't recognise in him the deeper things that make for stability once hormones wane. She wanted to take her lover down easy. But she had a temper. When Daniel took the insult route, she became incensed. So instead of easy, she took him down a road to hell.

"Look, I know you can't comprehend at your frog level. But what I share with Stan is sublime. The chats we have, unbelievable. We mentally share philosophical terrain. We sit and watch the Big Comedy of Life sharing popcorn. It's a marvellous feeling, one you wouldn't understand. You're young and limited. You're smart in your bubble, no doubt. But who are you outside your bubble? You go to work and follow orders; you are a good obedient serf and don't disturb anyone. You and your girlfriend watch Marvel movies on the sofa; me and Stan speak on stage in political debates. We're not the same."

Daniel felt the blow destroy him internally. The woman of his nascent dreams thought so low of him. His ego had never been challenged thus. Could that be? He was a successful man of science... it wasn't enough? It had never occurred to him it mightn't. In his small circle, he was undisputed Prince of everything.

Then he needed to be with her for whom it was.

For the first time in days, he turned his head to actually see Liddel. She sat there dotingly, waiting to be seen. God, he felt guilty. He also felt lucky to have her. He put his phone away and hugged her. "What, Eris doesn't think I am good enough? Well here is a wonderful woman who thinks I am the world". It felt soothing. As they held each other, disappointment pangs dug a hole in his soul but couldn't tone down the huge excitement of recent Eris experience. As Julianah's body heat helped his cortisone levels settle, he thought: I am not giving up. He will try again.

Back to the phone keyboard, typing furiously.

"Let me explain this in detail: Your intelligence is hot. Very hot. Your apostolic following of your partner's intelligence, however, is not."

"My god, kid, you're ego tripping. Can't you see, considering the happy marriage I am in, you should count yourself lucky to have my love?!"

Another arrow in Daniel's heart. Another hug session with Julianah's portly bosom.

—You're so good for me, Liddel. I am very grateful. This is really real love, you know?!

A lightbulb moment tears him from the cuddle. Another battle plan.

"Yes. It's frustrating. In January I was discussing wedding plans with Julianah and now here you are."

Eris slow on the uptake:

"You are getting married?"

"You've not noticed the engagement ring?"

"I thought it was a vague plan?..."

"Anyway, we've been engaged for eight years. We were discussing her dress before this damn pandemic hit."

Eris went quiet. With it being a WhatsApp conversation, she had the freedom to abscond her reaction or pretend life took priority, away from keyboard. But it didn't. Daniel was the absolute priority of her emotions, even if not her mind.

"It hurt when you said you are getting married. Does it hurt you that I am married?"

Daniel smiled. So ... it worked.

"No, it doesn't. Why should it?"

"Romantic love is possessive."

"Yes, it is. But we have been in love for so short. The rational part of the brain comes in. Although I would love to have you 100% I could not be responsible for you losing somebody who is proven very important for you for years.

Will I think of it differently in one or two years? Quite likely. Do I have responses for the obligations we feel towards our partners? No."

And with this swoop fell, a time frame for their torture was drawn on the calendar.

Now it was Eris' turn to hurt him a little. Since this was the dance they were dancing.

"How wise", she texted back. She was nodding approvingly while her heart sank.

"I think we think very similarly about it, or don't we?"—he is testing.

"Well I am glad you ask. Because this really brings us back to what I've been trying to tell you all day. I am pretty certain that my long term feelings for Stan will stay. I am very worried that my love for you will fizzle out like all my teenage loves, but not yours for me. Call me a bit of a fortune teller. I don't want to hurt you. I would still like you in my life in some capacity." She didn't want to say "as a puppy" anymore. Those times had passed.

This was not what Daniel expected. He emphatically put the phone away. Another cycle in Julianah's bosom etc.

They spent all their waking hours either texting or thinking of texting. Trips to the bathroom phone in hand became customary for both. Making coffee with one hand and grabbing the phone instead of the sugar bowl with the other, also. Yet most of the content of the texting was focused on this warfare. A chess game. What do I offer, what is he offering? How do I calibrate my offer to theirs? Assessing carefully what there is on the table to make sure none offers more. Two hurt egos in love. Starting to defend their existing partners in a psychological sparring game. Using them as leverage in a jealousy game.

"Why are you at war against me?!" Eris exclaimed once, exhausted.

"I'm not at war. But if I seem so, I'm fighting for my love to you."

The earth started to spin under her feet. Her mind entered damage control. Mind games on opium.

"God, modern Romeo & Juliet, huh?"—her mind checked the watch metaphorically, certain this teenage effusion of erotic obsession would wane any minute now. Give it a year. Or two. She's seen this before. In books and movies at least.

But her heart disagreed. Her heart entered a tunnel where Daniel was the angel in the silhouette, a magnetic field so powerful no cell in her body could resist. Her heart had been wrong before, and fixed by the solar presence of Stan. So the heart was sent to fuck herself, while the mind woke up every morning at 5am to check for new messages from the boy, only so that she can then tell him how much better Stan was.

It wasn't all a chess game across the digital medium, nor merely spiteful psychodrama. Sometimes they let go and enjoyed their sweet, pure love. And then it was rather beautiful. Surrounded by panic, closed indoors, aspiring to each other like their life depended on it. Lockdown psychodrama.

She had to find pretexts to go out. They weren't allowed to go anywhere. It was all shut. The only thing open was the supermarket. So long daily trips to the supermarket were suddenly very important. "Bunny! Need to buy... olives. I am out of olives". With a mask on, she wandered sunny streets and thanked the Lord it was a hot March and that her bunny hubby was too absorbed by his work. On these trips, she lived in symbiosis with her phone.

"Sometimes you say such romantic things you sweep me off my feet. Like last night. I don't even think they're true, but the precise way they're ordered, the logic behind them."

"You don't think that what I say is true? Why not? Everything I say to you comes from my heart."

"Because being in love gives superlative proportions to things that once the love is past, seem more trivial."

"How do we know that the trivial but not the superlatives should be true? Aren't we more honest when in love, more eager to find the words that truly describe it rather than lazy?"

"Perhaps. Permit me to be cynical after many failed romances."

And he texts back:

"I hereby grant my written permission.

Anything else you want my permission for, while already doing signatures?"

CHAPTER VI

Meanwhile life was quite good at the Eris residence in Belmont. One day, to spite Daniel, she tried to do something from ancient history: fuck Stan. It started innocuous in the chat.

"You're gorgeous, darling. The earth should be an "Eristocracy"."

"Come on, Daniel. That's too pompous even for first stage romance standards. What's this clumsy portmanteau of my name and aristocracy?"

"It is a thing actually... look up discordianism. They made up a religion around you. You are famous! See?"

"Ah, I see. You've been reading Wikipedia. Those famed PhDs research methods of yours, then?"

"At least some of us have one."

Eris is taken aback. She's not accustomed to this interplay of idealisation and devaluation in the space of five minutes. She notices how every day the boy shaves off inches of the plinth he'd previously put her on. She resolves to deflect with humor for the time being:

"What are you talking about? I have one. PhD in Insultology. You simply won't find a better insultologist around!". Giggles, etc.

Daniel, no giggle.

"Yes, I have noticed your colorful insults. Sometimes they're funny. Sometimes not. Your "funny bunny" takes them better. Maybe you should spend more time with him."

So that was the end of that exchange. Fine, she said. Bring it on, bitch. She put the phone aside and called the funny-man to her bedroom. He comes in. She throws him on the bed.

Eris climbs on top, starts dry humping.

—Ah, feels so good to have sex again, bunny, whispers a neglected Stan.

—Sex? This isn't sex. I am just riding you because this is a suitable means of transportation.

Laughter explodes through both. She continues within the joke:

—Are we anywhere yet? Looks left, right, throwing her hair around.

—Nope, let's continue.

And she rides aggressively on top of an elated Stan who feels as though he won the lottery: she wants him again.

Yeah, but. She said during lying down; projecting ardent images on the ceiling, of her and Daniel entwined, like PTSD flashbacks.

—See, bunny, doesn't work. We've too good a chat, and it's too funny for sex. Sex probably works between people who have nothing to say to each other. Good sex is between people with no shared sense of humor. You need a dose of dimwit to take its ridiculous workings seriously.

But the fun wasn't constant. Another day, Stan tells her of a plan. But Eris was absorbed by a tense chat with her toy boy.

The word poly was being used. Maybe even agreed on. Polyamory seemed like a good definition for them to temporarily park their semi-illicit romance in. So she didn't really hear Stan detailing this trip to the hills, because good weather etc. She apparently said yes. Because next morning, when Stan turns up ready backpack on, Eris is a bit shocked. Freshly woken up, cup of coffee in hand.

—Swear, darling, this is the first I ever hear of this!

Slowly, Stan picked up on the necessity to improve his behaviour. He might have even told himself the events of February were good for them, as they nudged him in the right direction. So, one day he offered something big. He vacuumed. Eris inspected behind him and arched her eyebrow.

—What, no good?! Exasperated, he asks.

—Sorry, pal. Do it again.

—Thought I got out but they pulled me back in—he says, in a pretend forlorn face.

—Oh, look at you, the dignified selfless hero who vacuums once.

She started to fancy the idea of two lovers. There was division of labor between them. One was the funny-man, the other was Prince Charming. One was for rational talks like adults; the other like an emotional labyrinth of captchas when all you want is to log into your porn account and wank.

She used to find Stan hilarious. And indeed, he was. Making her laugh was his passion. But recently, when he took long to say something, or just answered a simple question in an overly complicated manner, she felt less entertained and more like spreadsheets chock-full of useless data spread out of his mouth and hit her over the head. There's only so much information you can take on a simple yes/no question.

So, what's this mean? "Do I just love the boy then?" And she asked questions. But no... no, no, no. She was as frightened as her new pet. Cage in a cage.

As she asked these questions, Daniel starting asking them the other way. And he started having nightmares. In the hypnagogic state between wakefulness and sleep, his imagination went wild and produced these complex plots.

For instance, one day he dreamt he met her in a café. Life back to normal, after the apocalypse. He saw her at the till talking on the phone. Happy. Him, crushed. Turned pale. Who was she talking to? Gesticulating.

He hid behind a tall plant in the café. Heart pounding wild. Saw red. Breathless. She even see him? Suddenly she looked around like she felt something, scanning the whole room. But then, the voice on her phone must have said something funny because she burst into laughter. It felt like an eternity. Waiting there. Trying to decide what to do. In the end he walked to her. Felt kind of like he was swimming. Legs seemed to go the other way but he pushed forward feeling he's going to the slaughter house. Appeared before her at the counter. Like he was just casually there. He still had that self control. Utterly inscrutable.

She saw him. She looked a bit like something familiar but alien was looking at her. She was confused.

—Yes?.. His heart died.

—Hi, Eris. Been years. How are you?

—... I'm... Okay, Daniel? She seemed so calm, so utterly unperturbed. Like he was a forgotten acquaintance. He tried to find something casual to say.

—Are you still with Stan?

—Ah, no. No, we split. Didn't you hear. He's given up his practice to teach maths in Canada now.

He wanted to make small chat etc. But he couldn't.

—Are you with anyone? He said breathlessly cutting straight to the chase. But she seems unfazed. His determination no longer the opium it was. If anything an air of coldness passed her face like she was put off.

—Yeah, I am. Nothing serious though. I'm enjoying myself at the minute. And you!? He sunk again.

And that was it. His nightmare. Clear cut, simple. German. No crazy stuff. The crazy stuff was in hers.

Like one night she was trying to direct her own hypnagogic dream—in the semi-wakefulness before sleep; at first it was delightful. Atmosphere of intense romanticism. Daniel and her, princess and prince. Magnetism. Bright starry night sky like a Van Gogh painting. Encircling them. Pulsating hard like their hearts.

At this point she'd have fallen asleep and her dream was an actual dream. He leans over as if to say the most romantic words ever spoken. She blushes in anticipation. Him in a flat anti climactic voice: "you're not too bad really". "Actually.. you're not ugly". " I want all my women to be not sad"; "I have two great women"; "I had to ask myself how you rate next to her and vice versa"; "she's better than you in some ways". Quotes from his WhatsApp chat of the past month, the first month of lockdown, and the first month of separation. She opens wide eyes and stares at the ceiling, horrified.

But later in daytime... his sometimes romantic words projected onto the same sky of her imagination... "You are the brightest star on my sky". "I am in love with you, circling around you like twin stars do around each other". She carried that in her soul when she went to the supermarket. The vegetable aisle particularly became an epicenter of romantic thoughts. His dollar store poetry managed to scrape his insulting "pragmatism" off her short term memory of love.

She got back listening, on headphones, to the music they had played together in March—mostly Pulp; by the time she entered the lobby she'd play it on the home's sound system so there that would be no interruption in the soundtrack to her internal "movie of love". She threw her sunglasses on the side-table and called Stan.

—You'll have to accept Daniel, Stan. I don't know what is going on yet but he's very important to me. Maybe he is the vehicle that will correct the insufficiencies between us. I think, maybe fate sent him to save us! She tried to joke.

—But we are really good for each other and I'm working hard to make us work again.

—Yes, mentally.

—Everything but physically!

—Domestically you are only a fit with, like, rats. She throws with contempt.

—I think the rats might throw me out! They both laughed. He was such a kind man. Never shying from admitting his own faults. She walked over and caressed his head, and arranged his Kippah.

"You're so German", she texts Daniel, one of those many sunny days in lockdown.

"Why?! Only in name. I was raised mostly here."

"Because I can see you control your emotions in that robotic manner. I think you love me more than you let out. You want me, you want just me!!". She is tripping on her fresh power, the power of having two men pursue her. The power of seducing this young man and playing with his mind.

"I need to control my emotions when you tell me that I can only be number two, for self-defence. How can I unfold my emotions when I know I have lost, when I know all I can do is come with a cavalry against tanks. Shall I ride onto the battlefield and die?!"

His words reverberated in her. She felt teetering on the edge of something, something about to change. Once more his vulnerability seduced her. Mother instinct etc. There was, she told herself, a screeching sincerity in him. The irresistible lure of vulnerability.

She would write love letters that she never sent. One of them floated in the wind for an hour before it ended up in gutter with a rain-shower. The red ink of her handwriting bleeding until nothing left to read.

"I didn't know I needed you. Such a revelation. I didn't know there was more to need, to want.

Now I can't live without the rigorous phrase structure of your desires. Without the math in your romantic thoughts. The answer is always love. What is he? I am not fully articulate in my definition, but the answer is love. Why is he so fascinating? I don't know but I have to have it. What do I do about having two partners? Love. Close to my chest."

Over the mountains, in Johnnyville, Daniel sat as usual at his desk working. Several computers at once. On one his chatbox with Eris was opened; he'd just sent her big emoji hearts. "I love you, extremely".

Julianah, who gravitated perpetually around her prince and saviour, walked in. She saw the letters. She saw the big heart emojis pulsating in the chatbox, threatening doom, inducing nausea. Her shriek woke him up from a programming trance. He immediately saw the screen, realized his mistake, ran after the girl. She sobbed inconsolably in the garden, grabbing her head with both hands, throwing objects. Eventually settling in the grass, yelling at him.

—I knew it, you found your whore, you'll abandon me! Go back to her! I am going to Alabama. She pretended to browse plane tickets, glancing at him; eventually dropping the phone in the grass. She had no money anyway.

But Daniel sat quietly, with a guilty face.

—Don't worry, you are my true darling. Yes, I tell her I love her, it's these games we're playing; but that doesn't detract from my love or you. How can she compare to our ten years? You have been behind me for so long. She... I basically just met her. There is lust, and he gesticulates in the general direction of the mountains; and then, there's love. I lust for her. But I love you. And he walks and hugs her.

And this little dialogue reiterated until sundown, when the two sat embraced on the porch, streams of tears, her reassured. He caressed her.

—But you know, darling. He goes. You did want an open relationship. You used it too.

—But I didn't move in with them!! I didn't tell them I love them!

—But it doesn't take away even an ounce of the love I feel for you. You are my fiancée. You know how loyal I am. Ten years of soaring together. I wouldn't be the man I am now if it wasn't for you.

—She just wants you because you're so loyal. She wants to steal my precious treasure!! Her fears explode in tears mixed with snot.

—She doesn't want to steal anything. She's married. He said, bitterly, looking down. He caressed her. He again felt the healing power of her body heat. And there was a lot of body.

—I won't let her anyway. You are so much better than her. You know me so well.

—I am. I am modest and kind, and selfless. I am superior. You just use her for sex.

In the night, he texted Eris. "Sorry, but Julianah saw the hearts. I cannot text all the time any-more. She is right. Since coming back, I've been ignoring her too much. You told me I am not your number one. It's time for me to start acting like it, and focus on my partner."

But it was too late. Eris was in too deep. The lockdown month of April 2020 was a long descent into hell. She may have said what not about Stan comparatively to Daniel; but she opened the door wide to Daniel. Albion cottage was there, waiting for them both—empty. Offer was rejected. Now Daniel was reverting back to status quo.

She felt her power, which had diminished considerably in the past month, decrease to the size of a pea. She was in love with the toy boy.

They were playing a game of chess. At first, he moved. She positioned herself to defend the "king". He withdrew. Then she was on the offensive. He moves to defend the "queen in Johnnyville".

Days became crying festivals. She was tortured by the absence of privacy, so she finally sent Stan to his old bachelor flat in the outskirts of town. She wrote down in her diary.

"I didn't feel you were number one in Albion. It may have felt that way because of the setup. But I was still in love with Stan. I actively felt it. Which is why I avoided sleeping at night with you. Which is why I wasn't as wild and forthright as I'd have been had I felt you were number one.

But I did feel the threat. Hence the sleeplessness. The worry. I felt the powerful draw towards you. The terrible frustration that I can't have you. The cutting feeling when you said you were happy we both had relationships. I didn't really guess then, when you were in Dahut, that you felt that strongly about me. When we had the world's hottest make out session during the president's speech, I felt overwhelmed. It was incredibly powerful.

Then when Stan rang, interrupting, I felt the pangs of terror. I knew what it meant that I didn't want to pick up to him and he was calling desperately because he felt what was going on. It felt like the jungle and that the fittest male won. And I felt crushed, for him. The fittest man was enjoying his prize and my heart sank for the omega.

While I was enjoying the hell out of the winner. The bunny is now paralyzed with fear. He's afraid to speak. He's infantilized. Heart-breaking. Lives up to his bunny status. Bunnies are prey animals. He's just sitting there waiting to be skinned alive, not doing anything. He's even stopped running. I want to talk to him but I'm afraid. Every day I hope there's a way out of this. That something will happen. A magic solution. That something will fall from the sky and I'll be able to end amicably and he'll see the light too and say, ah yes, makes sense. No hard feelings, pal. And we'll shake hands and move on. Every day I fear the horror. I am standing there knife in hand. I know I have to cut. Slice open. I shouldn't feel guilty. Every day I tried for seven years. Gave my best. But feelings are feelings. Attachment runs deep. Into your guts. Your memories. Like water, it's seeped into so many aspects of your being. I can find traces of Stan even in my pancreas. We've identified with each other, each other's dreams. Excising that is aggression against parts of me. Violence against the parts of me that have become him. Which put up resistance. I am fighting him first internally before I fight him outwardly.

I love him so much. I loved us so much. I just want to make sure he's okay".

—————❧———————

Though he wasn't there, she felt Daniel's presence. Sometimes she lied in the sun and felt his eyes, without a face, hovering in a dimension of pure love energy. So sunny it felt like nuclear radiation. It was too much to bear, and she was tortured by the feeling. It was the fire he threatened with. Now spreading in space, hypnotizing her. Despite herself.

"When do you think uni re-opens? I hope next month we can see each other", she smiles into the typed word.

"I don't think so. Realistically, maybe September. Could be later."

It's like he electrocuted her.

"Baby... that is utterly awful. Can't we nip to Dahut for a few days? I miss you like crazy. I don't care what Stan says, he has to accept it. I want to see you."

"That's not wise. Let's see. My situation a bit different."

"Meaning?"

"Meaning my partner not as understanding as yours."

"So? I thought you were in an open relationship. What happened to that? Don't you miss me?"

"I do. But it's hard here."

"Baby.. Let's live a little." She pleads, already not a trace of the emotionally sadistic Ice Queen he met in winter.

There is a pause. And then there is a delivery.

"I wanted to "live". But you told me someone else is number one. You told me to wait. So I am waiting."

"But I never said let's not meet each other in the meantime. Besides. You launched the idea of "one, two years". I remember clearly."

But her words were wasted.

Daniel turns his ripe apple cheek to the buxom lady in his living room. She cries, again. He feels a duty of care to ask what is going on.

—I just watched some of your bitch's interviews online.

—And?

—And how can you like this Botox Barbie?! She's full of herself. Who does she think she is?

—A successful author, maybe?

—It's just because she looks like an anorexic whore. I am far more beautiful than her. Men like real women, like me, curves and everything.

—You are a kind and wonderful partner, Julianah, he says. That's what matters to me.

—No! Her money, her fame matters to you! You used to love us, value real values. Now you want a cheap bitch who knows how to seduce you, because you care about sex and money? You lost your way. You're becoming like her.

—No, I am not. I am here, aren't I? Am I with her?

———— ❧❧ ————

And then one day. Back to reality. She was washing dishes. Sun through the window. Music in the background, something chill out and plain. Relaxing beach music. She looked at her hands like it was the first time. Like nothing happened.

—You look so pretty, bunny! I mean pretty ugly!! And he roared like a school boy making his belly fat roll with him, to the rhythm of his laughter. Tapping his feet in delight at this rambunctious attempt to tease her. It's like he was Peter Griffin of Family Guy.

It's like his familiar voice woke her up.

"Maybe this constant horror dilemma is solved. Fuck the boy, I am home."

She just looked behind her and there he sat, with his big blue eyes and confident grin. His face quite sexy. Surrounded by computers and books, in disarray. Big hair up all ways. Bit mad, really. And she felt the old familiar love for him all over again. All the comfy teddy bear love with its deep security. And bunniness. Oh, what a comfortable return.

—Ha ha, shut up, fat man!! She quipped back, jovially. The laughter travelled across the room like sunshine. It was a golden room with yellow rays of sunshine reverberating between her and him like a magic fog.

Gone was the torment. Two months of stalemate. Inextricable chess positions, endless erotic stratagems. Gone was the wild dream. The unbearably high altitude of romance interlaced with wild promises and desperate efforts to make it work. Too much beauty, too much elegance, too many efforts to make it work.

She blinked a few times trying to remember, she knew there was something to remember, but it was out of reach. Daniel's torrid memory with its orgasmic altitudes fading into abyss, losing definition. Who was he? What happened?

The chubby S.O. had been there all along, knowingly waiting for it to pass. His confidence an unwavering stone. He had guessed what was going on. He had never doubted. Never despaired. His love unflinching. Just waited for the girl to live out her madness, sow her wild oats. He was there to welcome her back.

The memory of the boy a faint dream. Like a relief, that all that incredible emotional roller-coaster was gone. Looking at the face of the mollifying husband, with his vulgar jokes, his bonhomie, his chubby cheeks and unkempt figure—felt a soothing familiarity. A lack of pressure. No intense chess. No more daily desperate efforts to appease a jealous, weeping boy in love. No more sneaking, guilt, lying, brushing teeth for half an hour so she can type to Daniel in the bathroom.

Ah, the distant memory of that volcano.. the soothing sea absorbing her temperature, cooling her off... washed ashore on the calm of chubby Stan's blue smiling eyes.

She'll never forget the home that those eyes felt that day. Knowing, confident eyes with superhuman patience. He had let her do everything. Never insulted anyone or barred anything. Bit of jealousy here and there, understated, under mature control. She sunk in those eyes with him. The chubby imperfect feeling of being home.

A pang of terror woke her at night. It had been just a domestic dream. Sent to her from a future she hoped for as desperate solution. She was still in the trenches, knee-deep in conflict on two fronts. The promises... the grief... She was sweaty. An internal scream. She jumped up in bed but Stan wrapped her in his arms, lovingly. While being asleep. Even in his sleep his automatic reflex was to soothe her. So she wiped her tear and sunk deep in his arms, crying softly and trying to heal.

It was the birth of the Zoom era. Eris and her leftie friends naturally moved their long debates online.

Suddenly everything was on Zoom. Work, social life. Now everyone could be a TV news host. Host of their own show. Daniel frequently had that excuse these days to avoid calls or loving chats. Zoom calls with other scientists, students.

She was broadcasting herself in a large group of activists, musician friends who were in a band, various party members, do-gooders. A nice selection of the more thoughtful part of society.

—Basically this entire crisis is evidence capitalism doesn't work—says one activist while caressing her cat in bed. The cat's purr drowning out her own voice.

We all see its failures to deal with the deaths.

—Yes but guys, have you seen how the lockdown brought nature back to life? We have all seen animals re-appear, river waters clear again. Have you seen the pictures from Venice? The canals are clean! This is what we could have if capitalism stopped!

Eris starting to get irritated.

At the same time, she was texting Daniel who was also in a zoom.

"Why don't we do this sometime? I mean zoom. At least silently".

"It's hard." he says. "I have someone close here".

"Come on, can't you hide somewhere? You don't even have your own room? It's your goddamn house".

"It's not your business".

So she catches fire and takes it out on the zoom audience with a rapid fire rant.

—Look, people. It's not as easy as that. I know, it's nice, green grass, clean air. It's not as easy as kill all capitalism and go back to nature. We're enjoying the fruits of capitalism right now. How do you think you'd like to live in North Korea? We do have the virus, yeah maybe some economic factors, military research, yada yada, had something to do with it. We just don't know. But the fact is we have the internet to keep us connected and informed and that's a product of capitalism.

You all dream of communism. Well do you really know what that is? Do you think communism is anything but an ideological fabrication, a dream born out of the free time that only capitalism created for a little middle class? Had there been no industrial revolution, there would have been no wanky middle class intellectuals dreaming up an utopia based on equality. Well that equality doesn't exist in nature. We are on a planet evolved BECAUSE of inequalities. Inequalities are the motor of evolution, therefore life. Innovation, competition, technology, art ... all come from the fact that we're all wonderfully different in different ways. And we want to out compete each other for various spoils. To survive. Not everyone is a genius. To the genius the spoils.

I know we have too much capitalism. I know that now we live in the era of too much competition, so much that basically that's all we do. There should be a carefully calibrated balance between competition and cooperation, not only one of the two. Cooperation alone doesn't work, doesn't exist. Look at nature. And competition alone is kind of where we are, also nuts, also unstable. Rats in a race. To the bottom.

But, please. Let's not throw out the baby with the bathwater.

She said that all in a breath. Gazing at WhatsApp every ten seconds. The camera recording her love-injected eyes. The delivery of the speech fuelled less by political anger and more by Daniel. Daniel, oh beautiful, unavailable Daniel. Who belonged to someone else.

Next day she got an email from the debating group. They threw her out. Her ideological objections to communism and exaltation of genius unacceptable to these gentle lefties—seen as unkind and un-comradely. "Cooperation, yes, but only if you obey our ideas"; "debate, yes, but if you agree"; "no one is better than anyone, we're all equal". But she didn't even care, barely even noticed. What she did notice was the fact Daniel accepted a zoom call. But silent, he said, with a sad emoji. His home office had thin walls, he explained.

He agreed to read her latest love letter on camera for her.

She turned on the camera. She walked to her laptop in her finest silk pyjamas, diamond earrings. Bit of understated makeup, hair a deliberate mess. She made sure to sit in the best light, and bit her lip with delight when she saw the pretty head, once more, after so long. Three months. Agony. He was smiling. Radiant, fit. How sinewy his athletic form. Reading her love letter, he blushed. She hid behind the tea cup lest he sees her blush too.

Butterfly torture. Like trains derailing in her stomach.
So tiring, yet so sweet.

Then... he looks back, surprised. Quickly clicks
around on his desktop, face like a Russian spy. She sees
Julianah's neck-less head advance slowly in the frame,
staring straight at his screen. She had the intuition of
wives; she guessed something going on and came to
inspect. Her thin hair in a tiny bun atop her head. The
face... possessed by rancid jealousy. Eris froze.

When you see fire you should run for your life, but
something beckons you to sit and watch this fascinating
force of nature... So you sit there while it turns matter
into ash, progressing towards you.. to make you also into
ash. Eris felt those moments a slow fire. She blinked, she
recoiled. But couldn't tear herself. As if in slow motion a
tragic movie was playing on her computer screen.. with
her love in it.

She also noticed Julianah's kyphosis; it was the first
time she saw her competition.

Daniel's eyes went back to the computer pretending
to be working. Julianah hovered right behind him, staring carefully at the screen. Pretending to have business
in a drawer behind him; with her eyes glued to the
screen in a hateful scoff, her hands navigated in the
drawer until she found a pair of stockings which she
took a single look at. Then she says something. But
Eris couldn't hear; it was a silent video call, for stealth
reasons. Stealth which failed.

Daniel turns to her; jumps on his feet. His moves
graceful, his body so fit. Too graceful for a man, Eris
always thought. He hugs Julianah, as if to comfort her.

Eris's heart dies as Daniel kisses Julianah, and she puts
tiny hands on his ass. Squeezing, dotting circles. It seems
to last forever. She has to see her love entangled with the
woman he puts above herself. The tableau is a new low
of life Eris can't process. So she ends the call. Disappears
into the depths of her house, cleaning and organizing
and exercising vigorously to process the anger. She did

80 push-ups that afternoon, listening to select French songs of electro despair.

Daniel calls. He feels guilty. She refuses to talk.

That night Eris seeks the comfortable embrace of a devoted Stan. Stan maintains that she is the best woman in the world and he would never put any other woman first. How does he know? She wonders. Sometimes he knows so much. "But he hasn't guessed I love the other". And she falls asleep crying. In Stan's arms. A new kind of torture. One of many nights. Months.

This was her life now.

"Daniel, I am really curious? What do you think is so valuable in her, that you risk us for it? I mean, sorry but from the outside it doesn't look like you have yourself a good deal there."

"You cannot talk about her like that". And he ends the chat.

But comes back fifteen minutes later to say he loves her.

"But I have two great women in my life and it is really hard they don't like each other."

"But darling... can't you understand the conflict it is in the situation? A situation that naturally places all of us four in competition. I know you said let's have poly and all..."

"Actually you said that. We live in a world created by your facts in March."

"Whatever. No. We don't. But surely you realize jealousy is a natural emotion in this, and on top of that, I am puzzled at your choice of priority."

Daniel insists it is a situation Eris wanted and he's merely adapting, doing the right thing for himself by upkeeping the emotional support of the dedicated Liddel, the emotional rock of his young life. He insists this is poly, but Liddel doesn't know, she's not been made aware.

—Look Daniel. All I am saying. Expect hard emotions. I miss you. I am not seeing you because this woman has you by the balls. If it was me I would be in my car asap, in Albion. But you refuse that. I don't understand it. Expect jealousy.

Every one can be sweet at the start. Then ugly survival and competitive instincts take center stage when stakes run high and you run against those sharp edges.. the cutting edges of conflicting interests with people you might otherwise like.

—Don't lie, you don't like her.

—What's to like? But in general I don't hate her.

—You do. You want to kill her.

—I do?? How? By wanting to see you once in a while?! So wanting to see the object of love is such an alien feeling to you, that the only possible explanation is my hatred of her?! Where's .. your logic? Your mind on va-cay?

—What can I say, darling. It's the lockdown. Uni is closed and this is where I live.

—But you can drive your car.

He stays quiet. She cries into the phone.

—I miss March. She says in a faint voice.

—I love you, he says, robotically.

She continues.

—I miss that paradise time. I call it "*illo tempore*"—a sacred time before recent history, the history of prob-lems. A mythical primordial time of perfection. We'll never have that again. Now it's knives out. Toxic. Every-body in a fight for survival. Now everybody has been made everybody's enemy by the situation...

The Daniel has no input but a mechanical "love you" and some basic guilt tennis which he's very good at; for decades he's disguised his propensity for it under a meek tone and external motions of care.

His intellectual efforts on the chess table of their re-lationship are invested in keeping the stalemate, as it's a stable power trip of a situation. He internally admires his own skill of serving guilt to both love-locked women. He checks the term she introduced, jealous of her linguistic proficiency: "illo something, time". One more thing to emulate. He goes to Amazon to order the book by Mircea Eliade, the Romanian author from whom the concept originates. He will, if needed, outdo her in this also. He can outdo anyone, in anything. Eris elicits his love for combat. He thinks this is love. Quick glance over his trophy shelf in the tiny living room.

Later, Eris cries in the shower. The shower becomes her sanctuary. There she listens to synthwave, raining soothing sounds over her burning forehead, while tears cascade down in the gutter. She looks at her body in the mirror. It's a very hot body. Thin, yoga sculpted. But Daniel prefers to shower across the mountains with Julianah's rubenesque folds. They're also mixing tears with shower water, but it's reconcilement tears.

Eris throws the soap at the wall. Rejection. Once more, her old friend rejection. She thought she'd left that behind.

Suspended in the summer of 2020 was one declaration that she never regretted but she soon disconnected from. One of those afternoons. She was in queue at the supermarket. The queue was huge. Everyone masked. Life was weird. A weirdness she could brush aside because everything had become an annoying distraction from her real life, which was Daniel; but not Daniel himself, his WhatsApp avatar. She was impatient with people, with life. Life was something she wanted to scroll through to get to Daniel's bytes of cryptic love.

It was obsession.

"I feel my feelings are river water about to break the dam. I am not sure I can control what will happen when they do."

Nothing felt more deafening than his silence after this statement.

Things changed after this moment. Again the chess pieces rearranged. Now she moved back to protect the "king"—Stan. Having lost a lot of pawns, but not the core of her stability. Was the piece she re-positioned herself

to defend, the Burger King? Stan's proclivity for rotund cheeseburgers.

It seemed so, as they sat on a bench in the sun.

—You can take the burgers out of the man but you
can't take the man out of the burger joint. You are an
American doofus trying to swim his way out of a deep
frying vat, eating fries to save his life.

Stan laughed jovially. He was the definition of jovi-
ality.

—Stan is eating fried chicken like a caveman on a
park bench! Eris admires her ring fingers.

—Come on everyone looks like a caveman eating
fast-food on a park bench!

—No, bunny, not every body. Some people sit
upright and chew normally. But you... you had to
roll your shoulders forward, make a protective space
for your food, looking ferociously left and right for
predators who might want to steal the rotten carcass
you're chewing like a hyena.

—It is not a rotten carcass. It is fried chicken.
Should try some sometime. Won't kill you.

—Sorry, I don't consume peasant food.

And like old friends they went on and on laughing
at each other.

—I'll do anything to improve, I know I failed you. I
am horrified. I neglected you.

Eris looks ahead, bit absent. Stan cries. She hugs him.
She's there in hug, but her soul has a hole through it. Stan
is hugging a corpse; her soul had deserted the hug and
is floating in a fictional Albion cottage in the sky, where
hers and Daniel's eyes burn each other for eternity.
At least Stan can cry. She can't, with him. She has to
offer support to a wounded soul while she wishes she
was with someone who also prioritizes another wounded soul over them. Her mind went in circles trying to
understand. But it's the damn chess. Competition etc.
Four unfortunates stuck in a quadrant. No one making a

move. "It is what it is"—as Daniel liked to say, in a faint German accent.

"I think I'll always have many men on my tail. I'm a bit voracious. And too beautiful to be monogamous". Read her diary of late June 2020. Death of dreams of being with Prince Charming of Johnnyville in a pure lock of eternal monogamy.

—Oat milk decaf sugar free hazelnut syrup latte, please.

Stan was standing there like a giant school boy, eager to please.

—Okay, hope I remember that. And he repeats to self on the way to counter many times until it becomes: Whole oaf caffeinated cheeseburger. Please. Lady at the counter is a bit shocked. He turns to laugh at Eris in chummy bonhomie. But nowadays everyone too easily shocked. He grabs the latte. It was hard to find a park bench. Even cafes were take out only. Fifth month of a preternatural lockdown, and there was now even a queue for a free park bench.

She sips and sips until finally a message from the boy. "I booked a train on the 27th of June. I can only stay a day. Work is hard". She felt a mix of irrepressible joy, butterflies and also disgust. She recognized the lie. It wasn't that work was hard, it was all he was willing to risk with the Queen of Johnnyville. The work excuse worked both ways and stretched only as far as 24 hours in Dahut.

The Goddess had been demoted to mistress, but even a mistress would get more than that. No trace of a capital M mistress either. Pang after pang became a daily pain, and she had her bunny to contend with. He sensed the problem but was nonetheless happy to contend with the crumbs from the other table.

CHAPTER VII

Funnily enough, later in life, and that year, Eris would always remember the lonely days of lockdown spent in symbiosis with her phone as more real than the one day of summer Daniel actually visited.

That week no one spent more time or effort getting ready for a 24-hour date.

Tooth bleaching. Hair dye. Body hair removal. Manicure, pedicure. A selection of fine clothes and seductive undergarments. Endless yoga and push-ups in her living room—since gyms closed. She had the house deep cleaned. Albion cottage was a love theater that needed to be perfect. In the bay window she sat crying before she went to collect him from the station.

It had been five months. The most intense love of her life. A Greek tragedy of a love affair. The biggest historic event either—this strange lockdown pandemic thing..., but she wasn't really present in that. All it was to her, an obstacle in the way of seeing Prince Charming. She felt quite healthy and invincible to the virus but consumed by love. She reflected bitterly on how much indifference she received from the boy who once put himself fully in her hands. And how he managed to seduce her back to this love story, as soon she periodically tried to check out; with his mellifluous voice dosed in measures allowed by Julianah's sparse trips out of the shared Johnnyville home.

She loved something solar, something hurtful. She started to ask, is she an emotional masochist?

There, on the train station escalator, looking devastating. But no high glamor this time. Except her head—but she wore jeans, and a Nirvana t-shirt. Naturally she chose all black. It had been a summer of mourning. She dressed in her high school clothes. She realized the change in her but too busy loving him to meditate on it. She wore a mask. She was going up. He appeared at the top. Going down. In a mask. What a symbol of their continually mismatched timing. Her mind caught fire. It was him. Even more beautiful, more mysterious in a mask. They crossed eyes when they intersected, eye contact like thunder through their blood. She was going up, he was going down.

When she descended back to meet him, standing there, she expected to run into each other's arms. But he said no, we can't kiss here. It's forbidden. He stood glacially apart.

And then she drove in the night, her catch on the seat next to her.

Was this the most surreal 24 hours in the history of love?

She could distinctly feel in meeting him there was an invisible presence either, one she couldn't name... a load of other considerations, silhouettes... was it the phantom of the bunny? The phantom of the girl in Johnnyville? The things this boy wouldn't share because "it's not her business"? Was it global warming? Maybe the Christian loss of the soul.

Whatever it was, it made longing for him worse even with him present, as though not even his presence could satisfy her need to have him.

Daniel saw the Goddess and realized... well, not much; he wasn't one for a lot of conscious thoughts. He just felt enormous love. Or so he thought. It was an amorphous ball of sensations and focus in a mirror hall of flattering reflections and ego-tripping elation. He felt like kneeling next to her and putting his head into her lap. Once his favorite medieval knight aspiration. But of course he didn't. He sat naturally next to her on the pink sofa, and she straddled him like the old days. But instead of slaps and thunder, she laid the most gentle kiss and brushed his cheek with her lashes.

And the magic was re-activated, like their Bluetooth connection.

What she was struck with more than anything was the unusual purity of the connection. Pure to the deepest corner of their souls. Gestures functioning in unison; a certain economy of words and movements because they just understood each other in silence.

"It doesn't matter that we argued and bitched at each other all summer; it doesn't matter what he did. What I did. I love him. Life with him is a height I cannot fathom elsewhere. Anything else compared to this is boring. I want to live in this space forever".

He sat on the sofa, in her robe.

He had long golden curls framing a sensual face, but searching eyes. "He's got deep eyes", she said to self, fixating on his plump pectorals. He wore her white robe, half opened. His contours showing. She had never seen such a beautiful animal on her sofa, ready to be taken, or take. Just exerting an enormous amount of charisma coming off him like steam off a forest at dawn. She sat on the other sofa, in his navy robe. Half opened. Hair a mess. Delving into the deep waters of this eye contact that would come to define the Everest of her psycho-erotic life.

Every minute counted, so they didn't sleep that night. It was a rare gift from a world in lockdown to see each other at last.

They took a ritual walk to their bench. Now in summer. They sat holding hands. It was strange, but she missed him while sitting next to him. He was taking it all in, bit happy, bit sad.

And she now had a new image burned in her.

Whatever else happened in those 24 hours was lost on her.

He left, and he later told her he inquired about their odds of being together and she had said she can't leave the bunny because he would die.

She didn't remember this. She wasn't there when it happened.

Did he really ask? He never asks anything clearly. She realized he candidly navigated through a labyrinth of remarks carefully laid out as a data fishing expedition. There was no question. It had been a labyrinth, and she just shared her view honestly.

After that day, a new stage of grieving began. None of the two were in possession of reason. The longing too strong. Brains cancelled.

The 24-hour meeting just confirmed they had chemistry, but each went back to their status quo. Made no sense.

"It's not fair that life stopped with this lockdown and all I have to focus on is you."

She whispered to him, but not him on the phone, or in reality. A him in her brain.

"I am going to my mom's for a while". She announced. Stan was sad. She was hollow. Her life before Covid Sars had been full of travel. No reason to stop now. More bureaucratic hassle now, but no big deal. She wanted to escape. If she had a choice, she'd have flown to him. Straight to his bed in Albion, like that mythical night. But he sad no. So she flew to her mom's in the countryside. It had always been healing sitting on a porch in the rural sun.

And there one day, lounging in the sun in a rocking chair, sharing red wine with her mom. Out of the blue one of those notifications on her phone. Reaching to it lasted a century. She had a bad feeling.

"Sorry. We have to break up". Daniel typed those words, then went offline.

She dropped the wine. Her mother rushed to help. The world sank with a loud cracking noise. The Rocky mountains split in half.

Daniel liked to be fit and he took great pride in his body. So ever so often he went for a 6 mile run. He did other things too, often in the mirror. Asking Liddel to record him. Sprinting in the hills around his house, he found a bit of solitude away from the doting woman. Nothing wrong with escaping her sphere from time to time.

He left his phone at home, of course. He trusted Liddel... "my little, darling, mini girlfriend". He trusted her with his life. And now that he sort of sacrificed his passionate new love to stay with her he thought he'd downright deserve a medal. Only Julianah didn't quite see it that way. He was on his phone so often... She hated his phone. She was convinced every time he picked the phone, which was often, was to send more hearts to that whore.

That day as the sun set in rainbow colors she used the password he so kindly had shared with her from the start. She went straight to WhatsApp. She looked at the first conversation on top, of course it was the bitch. God, she hated her. Too much chat, thousands and thousands of hours of pointless chat, so she went straight to photos.

There was from 27th of July a selfie of him and her, naked. Happy. Too happy. Her heart split in half. He had never seen Daniel this happy. A wide toothy smile from the bottom of his heart, naked next to a naked Eris who looked tired and happy.

Julianah snaps. Her sweetheart she lived for. Why?? Why??? Darkness descended. Hate, rabid righteous hate was the color of her blood.

She did not recall how she entered in possession of her favorite knife in the house but she did and then she stood in the garden, phone in hand. It was a large kawaii knife with pink and purple motives on the handle in the shape of a bedazzled unicorn: "The Uknifecorn".

Despite its cute decorations, the blade—the horn, razor sharp and heavy; too heavy, too large against her tiny hands with long painted pink nails. Also bedazzled. Her black makeup dripping around the corners of her down-turned mouth.

Daniel steps in happy, glowing after his jog. But he sees her. Sees the phone. Heart stops. Panic. She shouts like a hurt ox.

—I saw!! I saw!!! There was no more decibel to hold the pain of the girl. And in the abyss that formed around her she lifts the knife and reaches to Daniel gesturing: break up with her, now! Do it. Do it. Do it. Do it. Do it!!!!!!!!!!!

Waves of cortisone and adrenaline wash over his forehead and his quick calculations say, yes let's do it, yes, OK. "Save the relationship"—the default of his mind. Save the sinking ship. "Keep the status-quo".

He sends the message to Eris.

"Sorry. We have to break up". Throws the phone over his shoulder, in the grass. "Keep. The. Status. Quo".

He reaches to cuddle his girl, to take the knife away from her, to apologize, to kneel and ask forgiveness. Frankly her rage was like nothing he's seen before.

She tears away and runs to the end of the yard and puts the blade on her. We're over!! I hate you!! He stays silent but pleads with his eyes and cries and she melts down, melts into him and then punches him repeatedly.

Waves of guilt wash over him and in that moment Eris doesn't exist, just this girl who suffers, and he has to save her. Save her, save her no matter what. Saving the girl is frankly the very definition of his identity. From himself. From herself. From life.

They walk in the woods talking and she has many things to say and in those hours, four, five, ten, he has no thought to communicate to Eris what happened.

So in the other end of the country Eris is attended to by her mom with Valerian pills and other herbal sedatives.

The ever-thinning formerly glamourous woman sinks into a deep gray state. As she hovers from toilet to toilet between vomiting and fainting she has a thought. "It was her; it couldn't be my baby. My baby wouldn't do that to me".

She types that in the chatbox, but no response.

And that's the episode on the chess table, and that's her stand.

—What do you think, mom?

—What can I say. He's weird. But I get where he's coming from.

Eris too upset to inquire and open a box of historic explosives. But her mother goes on:

—I told you: you have always been far too generous to that fat Jewish oaf you married. You make more money than him, you do more, you look better. You converted for him. You provide the house, the car. Is he even a man?! You deserve better. Perhaps this boy is it. I mean, an MIT academic?... Very respectable. I am sure he's got a fat salary. But how can he be for you when you cling onto that loser?! Of course he upholds what's his. You caused this.

—Mom... which side are you on?

—The side of the truth like I've always been. And the mother drinks from her glass, measuring her property with an intake of prideful air. Her property measures acres of well maintained land. She worked hard for this. Not like her frivolous daughter with a questionable occupation; a pretty, empty head she's only partially proud of.

With a tall glass of Pinot Noir Eris washes off some nagging ghosts of childhood, under the shadow of her mom, Callista. Disbelief; but what wins is the Stanian method of compassionate understanding, which melts her filial frustration. Stan had taught her to apply a filter of religious kindness to things she otherwise would have raged against in punk fashion. "It's not their fault, bunny; they just don't know better; feel pity for them."

—Why is this white horse standing in the garden, mom? You know him?

—No, I've never seen it before. Must be the neighbor's.

But the poor horse, morning after the Hiroshima, was standing on three legs, looking pained. This was the strangest horse she had ever seen. In the steaming dawn, cool refreshing air that washed the apocalypse away, the horse stood there like a bad omen. Pain visible on his poor horse face.

—God, it feels good to be away from Stan and his incessant demands for affection, she said. Couldn't cater to him now.

—He is suffocating, the Mother said. A man shouldn't be so emotional. Weak. No pride. Daniel... now that's pride and dignity. Hard to get, knows his value. But then Germans are real men. She adds with a slight burp. She stands up to pick the litter off her farm animals.

Eris stares on, grey in the face. Numb.

—I don't understand the horse. Hours since he's been frozen there three-legged.

She gazed at him until one time she turned her worried head towards the screech of a crow and he vanished.

Something extraordinary happened that summer. And it was wasted. People relaxed and had some free time, but what did they do with it? Lament about some statues and post pictures of home-made bread. The discovery of bread endearing, but a bit redundant—homo sapiens having already made that discovery in Sumeria, some 13,000 years ago. Shall the world wait, breathless, for the lockdown invention of the wheel?

They could have rustled their chains. Dance a bit more. Meanwhile, some corporations got very rich and honest small business owners got bankrupt. Like a heist by the already big, inverted Robin Hood in the sky… or rather, inverse Robin Hood in government computer servers.

If you went around the earth a few times you'd find the same story. It was apparent how no country was different any-more, all united in this process. An upwards migrating tendency of wealth and value, streams of money liberated by fear to flow upwards, unencumbered. And for the first time in history the small and the brown and the yellow and the colors of the earth and the continents were united in how much they suffered alike under, not just the virus, but their governments' measures against the virus, which seemed to be as much against the virus as against themselves.

Not just lockdowns which made people go nuts and poor; but were somewhat perhaps medically necessary; not just not having work, which is not all that bad because most people work too much anyway and never ever even contemplate there might such a thing as having time for idleness or to think. Having time to just think seems a remote concept for people in general. And not even the forced idleness of lockdown awakened in them the need to just sit and think or any desire to discover and explore with their minds or souls. Most really just felt like aimless ships without a captain putting their doe eyes out there on the internet. "Help". "I had breakfast with two eggs. Here it is." Waiting for likes, in their robes. In the poor lighting of their devices. Strangers' approval of inane habits. For commands, for a structure to fit into like the incomplete pieces they are. Freedom an alien burden to them. The emptiness was clear like a freezing winter sky. The people had a newfound freedom they couldn't cope with. Without the rigorous structure imposed on their lives by work, they acted like zombies.

But of course Julianah was a stranger to all this as her life had already been always idle, grace to her generous hubby to be, who believed in her artist star and said she is best not harassed with notions of productivity. So this summer wasn't hard on her because of that. No. It was hard because of the romantic threat and her instincts correct.

She had insecurities that hit hard even when no threat present. Once, in the cafeteria at MIT when Daniel said hello to an older female colleague, she shouted: "who's that fucking whore". He, he thought her jealousy a mark of his intense desirability.

To her the presence of Eris was a mental breakdown waiting to happen. And the threat to, not just her romantic love, but her breadline. Her everything. To their mutually agreed idea that she was the definition of feminine desirability, the standard of a good woman; that what she offered (pie, steak, unconditional admiration) was better than the Agatha Christies, Marilyn Monroes, Marie Curies of the world. The women who did? Of course they got there through sex—this theory allowed for sexual appeal and success itself to be presented as bad—whereas her artistic in-success and sedentary lifestyle to be cast as a triumph of honesty and the vague "being yourself"; of course the self-made women out there were selfish and self absorbed, even narcissistic, to get where they had—of course they slept with the right people to get to the top, and who the fuck did they think they were anyway? Definitely no better than her, honest Julianah—that's for sure.

To her there was no life outside Daniel. And with her persuasive little hands she had poured the idea in his brain that this was true love and saintly devotion, not dependency. That it was noble to abdicate life for the man. And this idea suited his egomania very well: a comfort wife devoted only to his service, but by a stroke of luck, no stench of patriarchy, because she had always been the sexually liberated one? Bliss. People lauded their progressive, open minded relationship. Young kinky goths shifting into petite academic bourgeoisie, a most respectable trajectory. All it took for the theory of their exceptionalism to be real was utterance—they both believed their shared fantasy, verbally enforced day after day even as reality sent contradicting signals every morning. He was one of the greatest scientists in the world, she was the most amazing partner. It was an age of wishful thinking, where people often replaced grim reality with rainbow unicorn fantasy right out of Disney. Until the bubble burst.

She snapped. She in her imagination licked the knife before plunging it into Eris' neck. But in Daniel's presence she had more success running it along her wrist. A gesture she learned to do early on whenever he gently tried to suggest "that maybe you could get a part time job because we're not doing that well financially". And with that simple gesture the pressure would stop.

Daniel devoted his waking hours on August 18th to the girl and her knife. Took days for him to reach to Eris with an explanation.

Eris' stages of disintegration manifested in the chat in unanswered texts. She could see him read them; but no response. And when he did, the stupid love in Eris answered before the brain could.

"Get out of there, Daniel. It's not worth it. I say it as friend."

"I cannot. I have to make sure she has a good way forward. I cannot lose half of my life".

"She would really kill herself. I had to stop her doing that for now."

"I stay with her for now because I don't want worse things to happen".

"She gave me the phone and told me to type it. I thought you would understand".

—Understand how?? You saw my rage, my despair... in my texts, the hours after. You KNEW I didn't understand. Were you held hostage?? Really, the American football player, by that five foot gnome? You just didn't care. You forgot I exist.

—I understand why you're this way. He was strolling outside to take this call. Liddel's irate behaviour had earned him additional calling rights; he was quick to capitalise on her guilt.

—You even said you... do you remember? When you sat on my sofa in Albion and told me you won't let others hurt me?? How fucking prescient you were. I didn't even ask you anything. You just said it yourself. I didn't pay attention at the time. But you betrayed yourself. You did what you promised not to do.

She asked you to plunge the knife into my heart, and you didn't hesitate; you did it. And then let me seethe for 48 hours. Until I was a pale copy of myself.

Dump me through a message, that you say you didn't even mean. To save... what? And how can I trust you, ever again? How can I see you as anything but part of a psycho tandem from hell, out to hurt me, betrayal behind every corner? Every time she has a meltdown, you throw us into the abyss to soothe her? Are you a damn masochist? You must be the absolute emotional masochist.

—I understand you're angry, you have a right to. But you can't talk about her like that. She's not psycho, she's understandably upset.

Silence fell like a ton of bricks. Eris blinked a few times. And again.

—So... her knife wielding behavior okay... the problem lies with me using language to accurately describe it? You are fucking gaslighting me and you know it.

Things didn't arrange chronologically for Eris any-more. There was no more meaning. She knew the boy was bad, and that pain would be a given and a constant with him; she now held in her hands the proof that the purity she felt was an illusion, a fantasy fabricated by the belated teenage lusts and aspirations in a non experienced man. It only felt pure because he was an erotic blank canvas. And a consummate manipulator.

But life painted a Dorian Gray picture on that canvas, and that was the opposite of pure.

She knew she stepped into something bad. But, too late. She couldn't fight it. She was a prisoner. This time, she didn't feel a prisoner to Stan's affections and the status quo of a golden past age.

She was now prisoner to the horrid fluctuations of a love that was nothing but psychodrama. She was captive to love someone who was prone to periodic betrayals. She saw into the future and it wasn't bright. She was not just captive to the lockdown, the marriage, the economy, the physical bounds of her body.

She was now captive to her biology; parts of it that aspired to the erotic opium of a teenage love that couldn't be. Life smelled of tragedy.

And the cracks began to show. Holes in her self image; why, she worked hard her whole life to be an invulnerable, aloof Ms Flawless. Career, success, work and a tough skin. Now errors turned out underneath the surface. Demons of yore resurfacing. Lonely youth, sexless marriage... While she cultivated a sex symbol look, her life had been too long devoid of sex and passion. And she was a passionate soul. An unfulfilled romantic potential. You create lacks, pent up yearnings, that, under a calamity like this, grow deep as the Marianna trench. Crumbling, her flawless picture. Her ice queen composure. Here she is, melting for a boy. Feeling unwanted. "Where did I turn wrong at Albuquerque?".

In the days that followed, his excuses followed. Never with any logic. She listened and said her opinion.

—You tried to lead the ship but... You weren't up to it... half a soul looking for a master.

—I am just afraid to completely crush her.

—So it's okay to crush me instead?

—You're stronger... she is weak.

—Is this always how you make choices in life? You know what your future looks like if you donate your time and energy to the fatally weak?

—I can't cut out half my life.

—Then Daniel.. explain to me... what do you want from me?!

—I want to be friends with her. I don't want to throw her in cold water. But I love you.

—Doesn't make sense to me. None of the things you do, you say.

And when she managed to fall asleep, she'd have this recurring dream. A tragic image of the couple in John-nyville drifting on a raft in the vast ocean, copies of each other... Scared, helpless, weak. Two handicapped souls, one slightly better than the other... the blind leading the blind... Drifting alone into the sunset, not understanding what is happening but congratulating each other on be-ing "beautiful and intelligent". Two round faces, forlorn; confused by the complexity of this monster called life they were merely floating on like lice in a dog's fur, di-rectionless. Direction dictated by their animal instincts, raw and unfiltered. Chaos of the subconscious.

As for Daniel, days after the night of the knife, he sat there in his garden; in the fuming ruins of his relation-ships. He tried to chase two rabbits and now they both got angry at him. He felt misunderstood—he had tried to give so much, be so kind. Yet everyone upset with him, but why? All he wanted was to love and care for the two great women he had in his life.

This is his pay-offs? How unfair. He felt a huge vac-uum, disorientation. What a loss, losing half of his life. Julianah was the face that accompanied him everywhere for ten years. The family he chose for himself. Her self-less kindness his oxygen. How could he function with-out her? And now she split up with him. And yet ... she was still there. He heard her faffing about in the kitchen, with pots and pans. There was nowhere she could go.

—Won't cook for you or do anything for you from now on. She announced, standing in the doorway.

He looked up. The sun was washing her silhouette in rays of psychedelic gold. As she announced her verdict, he felt salvation. So she will stay. He can cook for himself, no matter. But she stays.

And with the other... he performed damage control over a few furtive calls he managed to steal on walks on the meadows opposite their abode. Which would be interrupted by Julianah chasing out of the house, hands on hips.

—Talking to that whore again?

—You can't tell me who to talk to. He managed to utter, with newfound authority. And Julianah didn't like what she heard, but not much she could do. They both had each other by the balls. She left the porch slamming the door.

That night she cooked for him. They ate in silence. Talking about his work.

"So you are staying with her, then, Daniel". Eris typed furiously with anger in her throat.

"No. I am just making sure I am putting her on a good path for the future, independent of me. You know I love you, you are the Goddess".

"And that has to include sacrificing us for her?"

"You want me to throw her on the street and that just won't happen. "

"That's not what I said. Coming to see me doesn't have to mean dumping her on the streets. No sense in what you're saying. Give the girl an allowance, I don't give a flying fuck. But if you aren't seeing me to not upset her, then it's clear."

"You have your "bunny"."

"But I was more than willing to leave him in Belmont and spend all lockdown with you in Albion."

"Our relationships very different, sorry".

"Maybe but who cares? What is the goal here? I put us first. Why do you tell me you love me "extremely" if you put someone else first?"

"It is difficult. Why is everyone angry with me?! It seems I can do no right. Sorry, I have work now. Bye."

"For a guy who wanted to elope with me after a few weeks, it doesn't feel like I'll ever be more than number 3 or 10 for you."

But the last sentences remained in the chatbox with two gray ticks, unread. For hours, hours in which Eris tried to asses which spot in the house is best for crying uncontrollably.

And then in the evening he checks his phone. Brows furrow and fingers type fast hiding his phone from Julianah's vigilant eye-line.

"How can you compare to ten years?! Ten years of harmonious relationship."

On her computer screen there was this little comedy clip from Stan. He always sent her funny stuff. Cats, memes. Then he would sit opposite end of room watching with an anticipatory grin. "You like??". He knew how to make her laugh, heartily.

"Guy posts selfie with latte on Facebook: "So I just woke up, what is this about black lives matter? Update me plz".

Officer immediately arrests him for "white supremacy/racism". Evidence taken in. Analysed under microscope in a lab by scientists in white coats. "Yep. Traces of subconscious racism in the pancreas". "To the gallows!" —it's decreed. Person hanged. Officer on the street again. Sees Jeff Bezos in a rickshaw pulled by orphan black kids. Officer dips hat respectfully."

Eris reads, smiling. She is willing to laugh, to relax. But the image of the scientists in a white lab coat reminds her of Daniel. Though he never actually wears a white lab coat.

So she cries instead, holding her head. Stan, surprised, walks over and asks, "what is the matter, bunny?? Please tell me. I am sorry, I just wanted to make you laugh. Sorry". And he holds her.

She allows the hug but looks at the wall behind Stan's back and projects a bitter movie. The horror movie of her failed love with the boy, a love that cannot be, but won't go away. And she feels cursed.

"We will never get over this. But we will never be together. We're doomed."

She wants to launch her text at Daniel like a missile but she knows pre-emptively it will flop on the grass like everything she does or says.

"Don't be so negative, darling. Daniel texts back. I am sure we'll find a way. We are meant to be. Our love is celestial—do you remember how I used to collapse at your feet?".

That evening, Eris sits Stan down and serves champagne with a light supper. It's what she has. Not what she wants. But what she has. She so wishes that was Daniel sitting opposite her. Exerting his animal magnetism, turning life into a movie.

—What does he do that I don't? That I won't give you once my efforts are complete, because you know I am trying hard. I run 3 miles a day now. I starve myself. I try, and very hard. I will be fit and good for you.

—Don't know... he does romantic things that you never do.

—Example?

Eris doesn't really want to go into it. But she feels she owes the husband a bit of truth. He has been so kind. The two of them always had a very open conversation about everything.

—Well, for example. He sometimes grabs me in his arms and carries me to the bedroom. He can be quite the knight. Like, classical chivalry ever so often wins over a girl, you know?

Stan nods. Cogs turn in his head.

Yep, Daniel seems to put on that European sophistication. He only has a hyper rational Jewish bonhomie. He always thought the latter trumps the superficiality of the former, but hard times beckon reconsiderations. And if he has to perform silly teenage gestures to gain back his woman, he will, goddamn it.

So after dinner, Stan lifts her up in his arms. Slams her into doors on the way to bed. She screams and beats him over the head. Then he awkwardly drops her in bed, almost slamming her head against the bedpost. He leans into the wall, breathing like Darth Vader.

—Bunny... you're heavy!!

—I am not, doofus. You were claiming I am too thin. It's you.

—My arms are made for thinking, not heavy lifting. He blurts, defensively.

—Well, have you considered thinking with your brain instead?!

—I'll improve, you'll see. Just you wait. He smiles to self.

———✦✦———

—So all I need, to have both, is convert to Islam, get gender reassignment surgery and then I can have my harem?!? She laughs in Abe's ear on the phone.

—Then why do you complain he's got a wifey thing?

—Well because.. and she loses her train of thought. Well because I opened the door wide for us too. I offered some 50%. He offered me zilch percent. I am not even a mistress.

—Well, cupcake. Life is hard. If you can't give him 100%, he's got a right to give you nothing. You're like exact mirrors of each other.

—Not true. Why doesn't anyone get me?! You're on his side just like mom. I mean, it's like you all band together against a poor poly girl.

—Yeah. Listen to yourself. Why doesn't he drop his entire life to be your plaything for a few months until you get bored?! And throw the used toy into that trash bin of a relationship? Entitled much.

—It's just this fucking pandemic. If everything was normal, we'd have our half week together in Dahut, under the guise of work—it wouldn't force dramatic choices and or separation. The pandemic created this melodrama.

She hangs up the phone, turns on on the computer.

—Imagine if human relations were more like the free market.

She says to a zoom audience. Fellow writers and journalists, only half listening in the group video call as their food cooking in the background or kids screaming for attention. The thumbnails of the video streams forming like a panel of windows into people's real home lives in 2020 in a way that had never happened before.

In a strange way, 2020 felt like year zero for a new eve no one could define yet. They all felt terribly caged, in their home arrest; it had now been six months of this, some people dropped at the edges like flies; pushed to madness or depression by isolation. Some quite the opposite, used the new setup to do new things, to read more, run more, to explore the medium of Zoom. But to the defeated and the thrivers, the magnitude of the experience didn't elude them.

It was a strange new era and the internet made this horrible experience feel somewhat cosy and connected. They weren't even aware. They constantly bashed the internet for horrible things like Kim Kardashian and TikTok and conspiracy theorists. But they did this "on the internet", while enjoying its warm and instant convenience. It's like people saying they don't care about air because they're not conscious of breathing—so it mustn't matter.

Eris continued, admiring her own face in the Zoom stream. "Needs a bit Botox top-up, soon as clinics open"—she tells self. "This broken heart aged me".

—Companies pay good money for focus groups and customer feedback. And that feedback very important to their growth. You don't think of companies getting offended. "What, so you mean you didn't like our morning cereal? That's mean. You just say that cause you're jealous". I mean, can you imagine car manufacturers say "you're just jealous" when clients complain the brakes don't work 100% on a model?

Instead I think we should import this model in relationships.

People could give each other customer feedback forms at the end of a relationship, you know? That's the kind of feedback I'd really appreciate. Help me grow, you get me? I mean —come on! I've been a bastard, I need to know!! Maybe I was tired after a booze bender and I said something dumb. Give me a chance, let me know. How can I improve my services? Maybe I wasn't tough enough?

How pleased are you with the levels of violence in this relationship: a. Pleased. b. Could have been more. c. For fuck's sake, you barely beat me like you didn't even love me.

Some chuckles cascaded from the various thumbnails but it was mostly some men who found her attractive. Stan was listening from the other side of the room.

—You're marvellous in ways the vast majority of people cannot detect, bunny. You're worth every penny, every minute. Every day without food. Every 5 mile run. And every tear. I know how superb you are.

She heard the words and so did many on the zoom. Some embarrassed silence and grunts were heard. She felt this immense love and devotion more like a burden, sad not to be able to reciprocate anymore. Tragic that they came to her as through a fog, and she wished hard it was Daniel saying that, feeling that.

—You're a very kind bunny, bunny. Why don't we use the lockdown restriction lift to go somewhere? Let's enjoy ourselves a bit, worry free.

Easy said and done for Eris and her persuasive credit card. The European thermal baths open vastly under their nose, full of socially distanced people. They are very privileged to enjoy this when the world in lockdown; to have an oasis of relative freedom. A Mediter-

ranean country that is more desperate about lost income in tourism than lost lives to Covid. So, hello, and
welcome, American tourists.

People still masked left and right. But allowed to
mingle in the stadium sized pool, in the sun. She is
wearing a sexy swimsuit, Stan wrapped in towels to
hide his shape now he's a bit self conscious.

He again is making her laugh, and she laughs, bit
absently.

At the same time she and Daniel pour their love
down their phones to each other. Sometimes she can't
hear Stan because she's listening for pings from her
phone. And they do come, often.

"I love you tremendously, Daniel. Like a fire that's
slowly burning everything around it. And I can't let it
out outwardly so it consumes everything inside."

"I love you too. You are amazing. Have to run, sorry.
Julianah broke a nail."

"Oh, fuck you right back". And she puts the phone on
airplane mode.

Grabs Stan's arm.

—Hey. Stan. Know what. I like you. Your head is
like a box full of jokes rambling around. You shake the
head, you come up with a joke. You're Mr Joke Jukebox.

They walk into the vast pool, nearest people five
feet away. She looks dazzling, sadness imparting her
a dignified look. Crammed many gold accessories and
sparkly things on her person to distract from the pallor
of her cheeks, sunken like she's terminally ill. With
love.

—You OK, bunny? He asks, all heart.

—Well, you know, I am not in a great mood. I'm sort
of in love with a douche. Romantic love can be hard.
More like limerence, in this case.

Stan takes the remark like a sucker punch. But he
keeps his calm.

—Ah, yes. Love... I love you the right way, bunny. She
just goes:

—Love is a mental disease. It breaks people. But me and you? We're solid: we're based on hate. And she laughs a little, not with her eyes.

Standing and splashing around in the tropical-themed pool. Mariah Carey's "Emotions" comes on. They dance.

—Come on, bunny. Let's have fun like it's the 80s. Second or third generation peasants ever with disposable income, living the life, petite bourgeoisie luxuries like these. Our parents protested the war in Vietnam but we don't care. Nicaragua ain't shit to us. Let's bounce to this 80s pop frazzle and pretend like it's all good in the world.

PART THREE

ROOMS ON FIRE

CHAPTER VIII

At night sweats in bed. Another one of those dreams she starts awake as fantasy that go haywire into their own direction when she falls asleep.

At first she lay there imagining herself getting married to Daniel. She liked to see herself in a Vivienne Westwood wedding dress. Looking fabulous together like princess and prince. Their bodies such a good fit. Entranced by each others presence.

Then it turns into nightmare. They're not there to become a union, the priest says different vows. "And like this, Eris, you vow to leave Daniel and forget about him until death do you apart". And then people sitting down, eating and celebrating their divorce. With little speeches from the crowd about how "I knew they were never a good fit and they would never do".

Then Julianah strangely there in the crowd for some reason with a bosom full of hand knitted socks for Daniel stands up and pick up the glass...

And then she wakes up, scared. Alone in a house that's cold. A house that isn't Albion cottage. She goes to the bathroom, rubs her eyes. Time to pick herself up from the floor, and live, goddammit!

There she is. Dancing at one of the many illegal parties of late lockdown, in a denim overall, big colorful scarf tucked in. Here no one asks for Covid passports and vaccination, and masks are even sparse. She's even more slender, hair fluffier. Earrings more bombastic. Spaced out. Eyes like black holes. But dancing wildly like she wants to shed Daniel off her cells once and for all. Young men drawn to her. She was having fun.

Stan here too.

—Why are you here?!

—Because I want to gift you my presence!

—But really if you love me, give me the gift of your absence!

Stan pretends he's not heard, he's happy to see her.

—Can I kiss you?

—No!! She screams and hits his arm with her purse.

You know, I think I'm going to kill you. I'm going to tell the officer, "his bashed head is just a new Coronavirus symptom, trust me officer, he died of Covid", I swear!

—But you're my wife! He says with his most heart wrenching doe eyes.

—We're in crisis! We are like separated!! I am in love with another man!!! And Stan finally relents and walks off, really sad. If only he liked to drink or anything. But not even. Now, not even chocolate. As he's trying to lose weight for her.

—I am going to fight for you, he comes back to say. This guy isn't treating you right; you'll get over him, or he'll fully return to his missus. I'll be here when that happens. He doesn't deserve you. I do.

—You had me for umpteen years, Stan! Do you really need a reminder of all the bad things you've done that got us here? Her eyes popping out of her head. Do you need a reminder of how you rejected me, cheated on me in my bed, used me? You willed this into being. Had it all, and pushed me in the arms of another man!

—I was wrong. I was deeply wrong. I am so sorry.

—Well. What can I say. I am sorry too. We now live in a world of consequences. Of your idiocy. And she turns around and gets a drink; starts to mingle with the young people.

It's fun out there, for once. She hasn't been out in so long. There is a sense of great celebration. People now actually grateful to socialize after being trapped indoors for so long. These young people feel a bit more invincible in front of the virus—to them, the problem is not risk of illness as much as not living.

—Anyway, he sounds like a high achieving loser. Good on paper, with his titles and pecs; more of a wuss in reality.

—And you? What are you? A low achieving winner?!...

—I've had small successes...

—Yes. Small successes, or by their other name: FAILURES.

Abe comes along, glass in hand—"Hiii, sweetcakes! How are you lovebirds? I am living my best Covid life!!" and he twirls around, drunk.

He's always drunk, this one.

—You know, Cinco. Eris shouts in the doctor's ear, over the music.

British people need alcohol to mate. Even to socialize. And she gestures towards Abe who's filling the dance floor. They don't meet people otherwise! They can only mate by clashing into each other like electrons powered by the charge of booze. Otherwise, it just doesn't happen. They just sit there.

But no reply from the distracted doctor.

Eris leans over into Cinco again. He looks sad.

—Cheer up! She elbows him. Aren't you glad we're out? Look at this!

—I am, I am. But I am also not.

—Oh?

—Well... Bad stuff at the hospital.

— Yes, I've heard.

—I can guarantee you you haven't heard of this. This is... secret.

—Oh?? Tell me, tell me, and she kicks him, delighted to get the juice.

—No, it's not like that. Eris, it's serious.

—I am listening. Want a drink? I'll get you a drink. And she gestures the bartender, she's thinking, information extraction justifies any means. Top shelf liquor if need be.

What do you want...a Jack?

The bartender, a young girl with beautiful eyes, stares at her like an angel. You can only see her eyes under the mask. Eris feels protected by this angel somehow. It's the angel that pours booze, maybe that's why. The bartender smiles and fixes the drink, only delicately eavesdropping.

—So... basically... Cinco finds it hard to gather his thoughts. Basically, Eris. You know this virus attacks strange organs and does strange things. Well, organs destroyed. Lungs etc. You're not going to believe this. Turns out ...

—Yes??

—Turns out..

She's angry. Fuck sake!

—It eats the brain! He shouts simultaneously.

—I am sorry?

—Yes. And he looks dead serious.

Eris can't help herself. She lets out such a sardonic laugh, the whole room goes quiet for a bit.

The bar angel definitely widens her eyes a bit more. She heard. Not funny.

Eris stops for a second and frowns.

—Wait, it's true? What do you mean! Cinco, what do you mean???

—Swiss cheese brain. Dead or alive, the brain is fucked. Bits missing.

—But they recover mental function, right?

Cinco shakes his head slowly, grim.

Suddenly the room full of youth writhing next to each other feels more like a horror movie. "I am not afraid of a cold, me!"—she hears the late teenagers chuckle at each other with vodka in their hands, and she immediately recoils.

In the little house in Johnnyville, Julianah is arranging her poppets on the sofa. They all look more or less like her, with beady eyes and lots of girly frills—but skinny version. There is among them a princely poppet too—a Daniel.

The murmur of evening news is offset by loud typing from Daniel's desk. She stops every other minute to check him out, gazing at his phone. She walks over with her hands together, smiling cutely: want to watch Netflix?

She fondly remembers a time when her presence was enough to light up his face, and her helpless cuteness triggered that sweet fatherly tone. She wanted it back. But he doesn't stop typing and absently utters "maybe later". She looks at his screen, make sure it's not WhatsApp. But it's not. She doesn't have any information from him, but things have settled as of late. He's now more available, less focused on his phone. But he's also more emotionally distant. No more talk of weddings, that's for sure.

"Maybe it's all over, he is over the bitch; back to mine, like it's always been".

—You sat through my adventures, I sat through yours. Now we're even. It's going to be OK, you'll see. We have each other, we're strong. These were her words of many afternoons, her fingers reaching up to his hair. He usually murmurs "yes, darling", offering body heat; but moves his lips out of the path of her kiss.

She goes to take a bath. In the time it takes her to remove her beads and necklaces and undress in the mirror, the water overflows. She walks back to the living room in Hello Kitty panties to take one more look at his screen. He doesn't even notice. She walks back forlorn, but when she gets back to the bathroom, she lets out one of her screams.

—What?? With one jump, he's there. Says nothing, but takes charge of things and clears up while she cries violently on the hallway floor. He wears the situation with solemn tolerance, but until when does he need to tend to this perpetual child?

—Have you applied for any jobs yet?... he says, delicately tense. Her cries intensify. She leaves slamming doors, seeking refuge into her poppets. He goes back to the living room to find her, mascara dripping down, gathering in her double chin; she doesn't want to leave this status quo. She's not ready to be an adult. She thought she had heaven and a warm nest. Why does evil Eris want to rob her of this?!

—Go back to your whore!! I hate you! Go back, why are you here?!

—Well, frankly, because it's my house.

She's audibly crushed.

Hours later, when things settled, Daniel checks his WhatsApp. Stuff doesn't come up there anymore. In days, maybe weeks. Eris didn't block him. But she just doesn't communicate anymore. He sees her social media posts every day, pictures, selfies, her daily musings. Her fans interacting. He is shun out of that. It tortures him.

He breathes in and texts:

"I want to come to you on September 27. Please text back Y if you agree, N if not."

She is online. Takes minutes until she types something. Then, nothing. Then offline. His stomach is churning. This thing called love... much more beautiful than this called duty. But also much harder. Duty is just exerting inertia like a beast of burden, no decision, autopilot. Love... it takes balls.

After forever, she comes back.

"Oh, you let me know your arrival date, how generous of you. His Imperial Highness descends upon my modest abode at his convenience."

"I just want to see you."

"Aren't you with wife?"

"... you know things aren't great here. Tough on all fronts for me."

"But why? It's what you fought for. Enjoy it. The two of you make a stable pair."

"Please, stop being cruel."

"I am not cruel. I am giving you reality.

I am only saying things as a friend. But with such a weak mentality the friendship won't last long either."

"What is this, a threat?"

"Look, Daniel. You are still dancing completely to her worldview, a worldview that is weak and will drag you down. Day after day since the Night of the Knife, you are displaying a unity of values with someone whose value system is exceptionally fragile and self defeating. A person who's trying hard not to drown has shaped your ethical beliefs. And sacrifices."

"Actually, you're wrong. I have learnt my mistakes. I want to come to you."

"Why?"

"Because I love you."

"Not as much as you need to sacrifice us to save your little damsel in perpetual distress. You fucking white knight."

"It's OK, you don't need to tell me. I know you love me too."

"OK. I love you too. Unfortunately. Not sure for how long though."

"Not unfortunately. It's a magnificent thing that happened."

"Is it?"

"The Universe wants us together. We will triumph one day."

"Bombastic nonsense. Who the fuck has time to wait for "one day"? I am getting old here. Come off your clouds, Dan boy."

"You're not getting old". He adds. "You are forever young, like Marilyn Monroe."

"You mean because your love will kill me young, at 36 just like Marilyn?"

"No, because our love is divine and eternal."

At this point, Eris wriggles her elbow from Stan's firm grip who sat next to her on the sofa in Belmont.

Across the mountains, after typing these news, Daniel also withdraws from Julianah's firm grip on his shoulder, on his sofa in Johnnyville.

"You're beautiful. How do you look so strong without a backbone?".

These are the words an inebriated Eris types furiously in her diary that night, looking at her lover's photo with knives in her heart. She is not a religious woman, but she worships at the altar of Dionysus: the power of raw emotions, lust, freedom, creation and heightened states. Usually, life is seen more honestly through a glass. Or two. Vintage red.

"But those moments... just perfectly choreographed by me. I fell in love with a fantasy I created pre-Covid in Ely's house where he was the poppet. I moved him from place to place, ignited him. And he delivered. I fell in love with my own creation. With Pulp the soundtrack to our liaison. And every tortured conversation I was puzzled at the contrast between this magnetic incensed image in my head and the wooden monotone in front of me. Yet that couldn't stop me. Because such is the power of nature and the unconscious. And a hot body.

Until you meet Julianah, you might fall for the carefully crafted mythology of Daniel Graf. The world class scientist with a big heart, a hero for women, a success story. A jock and a scholar. A made man.

She is the physical embodiment on the outside of what he is on the inside.

I feel I am someone else with him. Some sex Goddess. A fantasy ego, waltzing with his fantasy ego. The Teutonic Knight he thinks he is, he sacrificed us to be. The Knight protecting the feeble female. Or rather, like they say in pop psychology: a white knight. A Teutonic hero with the saviour complex, who needs a victim to sacrifice for. Sacrifice our love for the needy. He's also the ridiculous Black Knight of the Monty Python sketch: "it's just a flesh wound", each time he loses another limb to the King he fights, pointlessly. We laughed together watching that sketch.

He's all three. He's the little boy hidden beneath that façade, hating me occasionally for lifting the curtain."

She jokes with him, trying to extract some reaction, confront him with his demons—maybe he grows, like a hero in a fairy tale.

—Are you the Teutonic knight, white knight or black knight?

—I'm the zebra-colored Teutonic knight.

—I guess that's all the self awareness I can hope for today.

This hero doesn't grow.

As she closes a first lockdown chapter, her heart thaws. She knows this will be a new episode of love, probably the last. She dislikes him. But the memory of spring still strong. Anticipation builds.

Day after day, she gets re-addicted to the heroin he drips. Love returns with the thunderous power of the largest organ in the continent of their roots—Passau Church in Germany; 17,774 pipes thumping in her chest cavity at once. The kind of moment when one takes a sip of chamomile to chill, or a bottle of wine.

—Red, please. She'd be heard every night of that week in an assortment of bars that were advertising "last orders" before the new lockdown measures upon Belmont and the country, coming up in two weeks.

Everywhere was just another place to think of him. She graciously shunned young male flirty attention while lingering her gaze on them for a second to see if they remind her of him.

And everywhere, people lived with this notion of the clock ticking over their fun. Tic toc. TIC TOC.

———⚬⚬⚬———

"At first, no one loved me. Now, too much love is killing me". Dum-dum-dum—the starting notes of Law and Order.

This was the funny joke playing in Daniel's head a lot that summer. And if he had any friends, he'd have said it as a joke to make others laugh at his situation too.

He remembers a time when he would have to beg girls to look at him. Ages ago. Then he found Julianah, who swore life long devotion in the first five minutes of their online chat on a goth forum, pre-Facebook era.

Now, he was suffocating under the impression two women were fighting for him. At times it even flattered him. Moments of elation, often.

Often times that summer, he didn't even understand himself. What's to understand? His four ventricles, his phantom sexuality, his obsessive neurons belonged to Eris. The way she made him feel. She had irradiated his brain, and re-ordered his whole existential picture. Triggered some big re-evaluations in life. Like, he started drinking full leaf green tea because of her. He grew ashamed of his simple clothes. He envied her large social media following.

Sometimes he'd spend long hours (or until Julianah burst into the bedroom, suspicious hands on buxom hips)—projecting a solar ball on his ceiling; half asleep, super high on love. A ball of white plasma with enormous magnetic pull, an entity of pure light and energy that his biology told him to follow to the end of the world. That was Eris to him. And then he orgasmed.

He didn't recognize the feelings happening in his body. He liked to savor those in his head. Probably liked to live in his head a bit much. Crushed by work, and duty. Captive to an artificial, mechanic self. And this damn lockdown. The lockdown, especially—the German voice inside his head would say: it rrruined him! Everything would have been so easy, had the lockdown not pushed rash decisions and choices and separation. Had it not blown the cover of his double life.

Lockdown forced decisions and loyalties too soon; aborted the serene paradise progression of their love in the idyllic house in Dahut. It brutally forced them apart. "But trains are running, dear"—she'd say to him.

His mind internally belonged to Eris; he was obsessed: he even spoke to an of her inside himself; came near to feeling he WAS her; ...separation? What separation? She lived in his mind. That's how he couldn't understand why Eris was complaining he's a vegetable on the outside; in his inert actions towards her.

"Some plants have more personality than *some* people I know. Take nettle. Strong personality."

—... Do you mean me?! Nettles are stronger than me?

—Of course I mean you, you fucking lettuce with a saviour complex!

He thought he was on a good path. He thought he was doing the right thing.

But he saw the developments. Since the "Night of the Knife"—as Eris liked to call it, to twist the knife... things went on a major down slope. Gone any dreams of juggling two women like a King. Now both relationships in tatters, and Daniel scrambling around to rescue the pieces. They were no longer fighting OVER him; they were both rejecting him. And that, well that was pure agony.

How could he dump Julianah like that? Since a child—late teens, she had been his rock. A life lived for study and work and her the only warm bosom to give solace and company. He couldn't just drop her into the abyss. He felt he owed so much to her. The successful man he'd become. Why, she only followed him to Boston **for him**—that's the sole reason she was aimless and professionally unemployed. Because she, heart of gold, sacrificed herself for his trajectory to rise up. She was an angel. The face he grew into a man with. The face he used to go to rock concerts with and get drunk together, and grill marshmallows over an open fire in his garden on a summer night. His glorious self image depended on her exquisite adulation.

He thought that was the height of life before. Before... Eris. Now life had these strange high arches of glory, like moments of wonder he never expected. Hot, sexy, raw athletic curves and her bone structure like a Disney princess—all in love with him. The dominant magic of her black eyes, the unusual energy that made her dance around from room to room. Strong and independent, a life and money of her own. A sort of strange music and tunnel vision played every time he remembered Eris. In a way, he felt it was too good to be true.

Too good. For him.

Looking besides him, he saw Julianah's hunched back and rolls of chins full of passionate obedience in a Lolita dress... it felt familiar, real, secure. Rehearsed cuteness bursting at the seams on this body and face crushed by stale misery.

Solid. But Eris?... That was the stuff that dreams are made of. It felt too perfect, so it scared him. She had options, she wasn't trustworthy.

What if she realized she, Goddess of Olympus, has fallen for a mortal, and shall cast him in the abyss? She will, no doubt, one day. He thought.

And what? She wants him to not even have his loyal girlfriend when she does? To be left with nothing to fall back on? No. He shook his head. Weary with so many thoughts, and calculations and attempts to read the future. Eris was a dream that was too good to be true. He was grateful to Liddel for being dependent and therefore

dependable. Optionless and therefore reliable. Penni-
less so unlikely to leave. Unattractive so would regard his
majestic physique as the ultimate stroke of luck. She'd
never be able to attract anything close to his caliber at
this stage of her life. Grateful.

"Maybe I'm just a dream. But my life has been affected
by it"—Eris would usually say in chat, as if reading his
mind. She was so good at that. She was too good at it.
That's why he had to usurp her powers by contradicting
everything she said, and always putting a front. It was
hard labor, that. A hard labor of dignity, he told himself.

Take now. He was on a train to Dahut once more.
Heart beating loud. Heavy head leaning into the glass
pane. Heart like a scared rat.

And... he was convinced he was going there to be
dumped. Certain she'd end his tenancy agreement.
She'd stopped talking. She had a life he followed like a
fan online. She looked great. She smiled in her pictures
on Facebook. He saw her in a swimsuit, in a Mediterranean spa. Champagne in hand. He of course deduced
who took the picture. Who was the invisible spectrum
that haunted him, the threat. The competition he sort of
decided to not fight.

He was a victim going willingly to the slaughter. His
face pale, a sadness that became him.

Yet he was going anyway.

"Why? I don't know. I am going to her."

<hr />

*"He was leaning against a pole in front of Brown's,
backpack on. My heart recognized him but I controlled
my emotions very well.*

*Had resolved to do fluffy, jovial conversation; put on
a warm funny front. But arms length. He had love in his
eyes and leaned forward for a hug, which I gave him.
But a friendly one. Bit neutral.*

We went to Brown's where a drunk man gave us shit for sitting next to him: "I've been here since 1pm!!". Good for you, pal. Not sure that's really the criterion of you now owning the place. I looked elegant, but purposely dressed youthful, in a burnt orange linen skater dress, back-seam stockings, 70s style sandals. I was wearing glitzy makeup, did my hair. Blow dry. So I made an effort.

Him? Well, he was shaven. Shy, sad, his face looked older. The staff told me they're closing soon so I took him and my bag in search of elsewhere.

We walked in the night, quiet Monday evening. I laughed, asked about his uni etc. He went along with it though obviously taken by surprise. Probably the last he expected. he thought I'd be sad and resentful. We found a place in the Northern Quarter, I ordered a large and expensive glass of wine, him water. He sat next to me. I felt it again. His presence unsettled me but I went on with the chirpy neutral conversation. I would take a deep breath and relax my fake smile as soon as he looked away. It was hard work.

His physicality had an effect on me. I felt that strange draw, that I can't fight. Something so weird. Finally he got a bit bored with the fluff so he took the conversation towards physics. It was a brief but interesting exchange. I always like to let him shine in his field.

We agreed to walk home. We like walking. As I got drunk, I started being more personal. I confessed to him old stories from my life. I don't know why. Something in him invited that intimacy, that confessional tone. I felt what I used to feel when just friends, before the pandemic: that his silence speaks volumes of understanding and respectful curiosity. I remembered how I felt when we were friends, before falling in love. The tension building up, the tone friendly, the mind wandering. The suppressed tension. It was beautiful, poetic.

We got home. Daniel was unloading his luggage and making the bed as usual. Took a while for him to join me in the kitchen, where he pretended to have business in his cupboard; confused, defensive, scared, but warm and polite—it was all in my hands. Felt like the ambush evening of long ago, that started everything: "Did you have any expectations when you moved in?". I got my powers back. Powers stripped off me by the long distance.

He was taken aback by my cheerful behavior. I sat down on the pink sofa, him opposite. We fluffed a bit more. He looked tortured, eyes like sinking ships of despair in the midst of his deadpan face. It was painful to see. I saw so much love in his eyes. I ask something, like, "are you happy?" Yes. He says. "My sister just submitted her Phd thesis last week. I am therefore happy." He was lying. Avoiding. The face looked sunken.

So I took a swift decision. Move to the other sofa. I sat down, one foot from him. He was apprehensive, bit shy, sad, looked more like a man, less like a child. I always thought his face had that Marilyn Monroe style childlike vulnerable joy blasting from within, high wattage; not now, now the lights were off. The face I had loved for being an anime cartoon image was now inanimate. Without the glow, he wasn't even beautiful.

I felt such a pull. I knew I was fucked. I knew Abe was correct: all my pseudo intellectual scaffolding of disentanglement collapsed. The programming I had performed to excise him out of my mind had been just repression. The love was there, blasting, just buried deeper, temporarily hidden. A volcano waiting to irrupt. His vulnerability ignited it.

I knew it was all up to me. He was passive, a flower. Like at the start. Injured, waiting to see what his destiny is decided to be. Waiting for a death sentence. Rolling his eyes in those of his executioner; resigned. I gazed at him with that passion I had suppressed all night. I couldn't hold it in any-more. I felt the most intense pull of my life, bursting out of me, violently. Like all life's aspirations, desires, questions, everything, in that pull; how could I resist it? My eyes heavy, and so were his. And then he lay his hand between us on the sofa. It seared through me. I hold holding hands sacred, and with him it's always been an earth shattering experience. I touched his arm with my finger, playfully. I think he reciprocated. Then I couldn't hold it any-more, I brought my face close to him, as if searching for a kiss. His eyes burned me. So much emotion. So deep. My face flew over his, but his lips stayed shut, and only his eyes burned.

I went back, I waited. The silence deafening, in the dim lit room. I played Byron, the Romanian band. I think it worked. It reached him. The album "Nouă" sounds like such a soundtrack to our story. Another soundtrack, for another chapter.

I touched his hand. And then the earth started to spin under my feet. I held his hand, he held it back. He could barely look at me. I held it like my life depended on it. Our hands told everything our words couldn't. The intensity was enormous. Then he grabbed my hand with his second one, and caressed it passionately, looking at it, focused, on it. Passions now swimming on his face. It's like the world ceased to matter and it was just us alone in the universe, our sofa floating in thin air. My heart wasn't just a pump, it was an explosion pit.

Breathing very hard, with deep slow breaths that sounded like the Big Ben, we were still and silent. We hugged. It was surreal, I felt dizzy. Our temples rested against each other. Our eyes crossed and burned again.

"A man of silences", Abe would say. "He speaks more with silence than in words".

We re-found each other hug after hug, and the gaze reactivated the love, multiplied it. I was fucked. Dishevelled, I didn't care. I couldn't resist him. Resist anything but him. The territory defined by his chest, arms and hair was where I wanted to drown.

I started to think of bed. He said it out loud, like nothing ever happened, and like he was saying in the good old pre-pandemic days: "let's go to bed, baby". So our *being over was over. At least in this suspended moment. So we went to bed. We circled each other fondly in our arms, close. It was heaven. I was once more swimming in us. If I twisted in bed and changed position, he would come and spoon me, search my hand. With the hand that set my soul on fire. His beautiful hand.*

The love that won't go away. That can't be fulfilled. But won't go away. And every time there is tragedy, it comes out again, strengthened, undisturbed. With our souls in broken glass around it. But the love itself, rises high like a beam of light. That can't be captured, controlled, enclosed, cut. Because it's light."

CHAPTER IX

The two lovers stepped in a myth, beyond the mirror. They were finally together. He didn't come on a return ticket.

They managed to go a restaurant or two before it all was shut down again for the second lockdown, as strict as the first.

They were spending lockdown in Albion Cottage, having nothing but each other and home office.

The days became one. This was it. After long absence and psychological torture, they were together in love. They were happy. They were always aware of each other, a domestic love story laden with surreal magnetism. It was almost fortuitous that this pandemic happened and forced them indoors to get lost in each other. Always aware of each other's presence. No work, no task could remove from each the awareness of the other's physicality. Following each other from room to room. Eyes burning across the room. Shy, intense.

One day they went to their bench again. She didn't recognize it now, in the fall. Instead of chirping nightingales and blossom trees, there were gray branches sticking out like soldiers who'd lost limbs in war. They sat down. The cathedral bell rang. They held each other. She grabbed his hand and whispered something sweet.

Her fingers felt something so sharp, it burnt! Pushing down her horror pang, she knew what it was. It was the cold silver of his engagement ring.

—Why do you still wear the engagement ring, darling?

Isn't the girl supposed to have one? Oh. I forget. You are the girl in a romantic relationship. She chortled, head back in delight at her own quip. Flash of power.

—I don't want to talk about her.

She felt an iceberg dropped from the sky next to her and sat cross-legged on the bench and there was nothing she could do. So she remembered the summer and things and felt better about having told everyone she was in love with an asshole. She was admiring the little pigeons quarrelling on the side when Daniel grasped her chin and kissed her deeply, all of a sudden. He had his ways.

She was smitten. Any notion of five minutes prior was erased from her head. She wrapped herself around the ice block and told him "let's go home".

And they did.

Julianah and Stan were entities that disappeared from their lives. Long streams of their partners' texts appeared on their respective phones, to be gazed at and forgotten before they found each other' eyes again.

Eris decided to make the home arrest fun and exciting; she ironically dressed as a housewife, with hair on rolls and vintage 50s underwear. And ironically baked a cake. It was the lockdown thing to do. Daniel helped. Their hands together in the bowl. Kissing each other to the rhythm of the music. He brought German precision to the recipe, she brought improvisation and boobs. When she bent over to take it out of the oven, Daniel grabbed her in his arms then thrust her across the room to the nearest sofa. The fire was out, in the room. The shy flame of the passive boy was extinguished—through sheer force of her hotness, he had become man. And she hid her extreme excitement under her hair and lashes.

That night they sat across the large table in candle light; not so interested in the food, eyes sparkling, conversation tense. The pull was irresistible.

—I am an awful cook when you're around, she chuckles. Even blushes.

—Then let's go out for dinner, baby. I invite you.

— Oh, darling... I am not used to being spoiled! Except by myself, of course. I spoil myself A LOT.

In response, he stands, surrounds the table slowly, gets behind her, gently encircles her neck, taking her breath away. And in the few moments he feels her Disney princess cheekbones and hairline, she nearly faints into him. Leans her head back to look at him.

—You're mine, he whispers.

—I want that. And she puts her cheek against his hand.

When they danced slowly in the vast room, semi naked, in the large baroque mirror she could see his princely torso and flowing hair, their heads heavy with so much love and desire. Gleaning dark bits of each other's eyes in mirrors and windows dotted around the place, spinning slowly. She played him "My Legendary Girlfriend".

Outside, a world gripped by the pandemic.

Here, a paradise for two young bodies that finally found each other.

As she melts into his arms, her mind is shipwrecked on the shore of his otherworldly halo that she doesn't comprehend. His strange emotional intensity. That for the first time in her life, she has no words to describe.

———⊗———

There were, however, clouds. One evening, as they sat on the sofa teasing each other, his phone between them. Julianah's texts pouring in. He ignored them for a while. Then Julianah rings. He panics.

—Shall I respond?

But Eris stands up and while wrapping herself in the velvet robe she shrugs. Walks to the window where she fixates on the darkness, eyebrows pushing against each other. Stubborn not to let another tear out.

Daniel jumps to his room in two steps. Eris could hear Julianah's shrieks like a dying animal, in the call. She felt pity and horror. Fear. She texted Abe back and forth while frozen in the window.

She was there two hours later when Daniel came back. She was afraid to look at him. He looked absent. She made a joke. He didn't hear. So she decided to go to bed. Her bed. Daniel didn't acknowledge her, lost somewhere else. In a sofa in Johnnyville, where his heart belonged that night.

Like something died inside her, she brushed teeth, stomach in a knot. If only she had those Valerian pills her mom gave her. Her usual anxiety medication—red wine, was insufficient this time. Shaking. She walks through the corridors like an undertaker, cheeks sunken. And after what feels like an eternity, Daniel texts her.

"I am sorry".

"Well, fucking come here in person and say it."

She barely hits send, he's already in the bedroom. He stands in the moonlight, she finds him so hot it's painful; and so cold, it's torture.

—So? What's the news? You're going home to save the girl?

—No, no. He softly says. She just.. I told her I am not.

—She must have taken it well.

—Actually not. She said she's going home to Alabama. Then she said she's killing herself.

—Oh, then you must go! She throws sarcastically, throwing a pillow against the wall.

—No. I am not. Can we sleep together?

—I don't know, ask her for permission.

They slept together but this became a thing. Twice a week there was a mini nuke through their romantic evenings when he would disappear into the bedroom to video chat to the... whatever Julianah was for him at that stage. "I will wait for you", the kawaii enthusiast had sworn; patient in a purgatory between ex girlfriend and future wife. Eris was convinced she was developing a tumor or similar, with all the pain she couldn't solve, or extricate from. Because as soon as she saw him, the attraction was stronger than anything. Even self esteem, it turned out.

The calls, the ring still on his finger, the occasional coldness were clouds that hovered. And Eris was pragmatic. Impulsive and total in her belated teenage love, but still an adult underneath it all.

She had ignored Stan's desperate pleas to return. But one day she sat down at her desk with thinking pen and paper while Daniel was in his zooms; she took the decision to give Stan some visitation days, since Daniel had long video phone calls. It was a bomb to be saved for later, at the next transgression.

For now she still wanted to enjoy her domestic bliss. While it lasted.

Sometimes it felt like their erotic back-and-forths were a theater beneath a whole symphony of clocks; under the threat of Time at all times. Even the grandfather clock chased them, tongue out, aggressively, down the creaky hallway; they were persecuted by the loud tic-tocs, every minute a gift. "Time". This mass murderer.

"You will use me and throw me away".

"You love me now, but for how long?"

These sentences often came from Daniel's lips in his down time from being a confident lover. These moments he became the boy again, haunted by the reality beyond their love bubble.

She enjoyed their time together which became months, months of fire and bliss and torture into the guts of winter. But sometimes she had PTSD flashbacks from a summer spent crying, reaching her hands to grab a lover that wasn't there. Dreams of her stretched hand gasping for his, finding blood spurting cuts instead. Blood filling the floor. She remembered that he wouldn't come, to save something else, something that was sinking. That he chose her pain over Julianah's. She tried, but she couldn't forgive.

And he could tell her mind was in an area hostile to him, even if she said nothing. And he feared. Hid in bed, duvet over his lips.

"I am always between faint hope and bitter disappointment. That is the rhythm of our relationship—the two poles, the options. Give me something else!!"

But he had nothing to say, just hold her, bathe her in his Bambi eyes. Touch her with his silky skin.

And then they'd seek solace into each other again. Their naked bodies could reassure each other in a way minds couldn't.

<hr/>

She played "Rooms on Fire" by Stevie Nicks.

She was getting dressed.

He was too, in the bedroom opposite hers across the hallway. From time to time he came to her room, teasing her, pretending to play with her lipsticks and things. Kissing and hugging furtively, then hiding. He was such a flirty laugh sometimes.

They laughed like children. Standing in their respective doorways ready, they looked at each other with gleaming faces of bliss and desire: they both looked hot. She wore a green lace dress, long legs in heels. He had a blue tight fitting shirt that showed his healthy outline. She grabbed him by his slim waist and threw him against the wall, violating his mouth.

For a while, he's breathless in the candle light with beautiful parted lips as he sinks into her, giving his soul. But then an electric jolt runs through him, he immobilizes her as if he'd just recalled he does after all have more muscle. She puts up a fight.

—This is a fight you want to lose, he whispers with a husky voice straight into her brain.

But they dust themselves off, dishevelled and longing, as they have to continue towards their restaurant booking in the nearby town.

And when they get there masked, holding each other, everyone steps out of their way with a complicit smirk—they look like young people in love. They are. Their eyes burnt shinier above a masked face.

She barely eats. He tries to take photos of her looking more glamorous than ever. The restaurant is glorious, ceilings high to high heaven, art-deco mirrors to multiply their burning eyes, glitz and glamour, gold chandeliers. A setting just right for her, he tells her. Her vanity slightly flattered. She agrees. They are entranced with each other. Other tables gaze at them, remembering fondly what it was to be in love.

After dinner, they walk to the bar, where she sits with a glass of champagne, her fur hanging over her elbow. She is pushing herself into him, listening, making him talk about the stars and the electrons and everything he's an expert in. And uranium. He likes uranium.

As she watches the strange scientist talk in his Southern drawl with German affectations, stars shoot out of his curly hair, filling the high ceilings... sparks between them.. they're flying. He speaks calmly and confidently, observing her transformation into shy girl with muted amusement. Another picture of romance fixed in time for them to return to like victims trapped in a time loop. Because what's the point of living on a continuous timescale when perfect moments like this merit revisiting forever, time and again?

Her agent Martin phones one day. Socially distanced book event in the middle-of-nowhere town. Important. He said. She was used to it and she liked being on the road.

Yes, she loves the golden boy and they're welded at the hips; but she also likes to take flight alone, those nights alone in hotels are good for the mind. Meeting people, reminding herself why she's good at what she does—which stopped once the apocalypse started. Missing being the center of attention in a state of relative indifference where she owns the room, all eyes on her.

Less of that extremely high temperature of love. I mean, it's fabulous. What movies are made of. But who wants to live in a movie script all the time? Sometimes it feels too perfect. Sometimes too much lovemaking in every corner of the house. Too much tension and lust. Where's the simple fun? Where's the cat videos, the laughing out loud in pyjamas, that deep belly laugh that clears the air? Not much of that with her perfect lover. Too movie-perfect. She's sick of makeup and lingerie every evening.

She leaves him at the door. He stands tall in black, supportive but sad. The wind blows his gold locks into his rose lips.

—It's only a few days, darling. He watches her get in the car and drive off smiling. He stands there forlorn but understanding.

Goes back to his work. His work a good refuge. Work had always been his best friend. Even he enjoys the solitude a bit. Also, what a good time to check on Julianah.

His texts arrive like arrows into her tranquil day. He's out for a stroll through the deserted town. Sending her selfies of him eating ice-cream, playing with puppies.

"Have you noticed how empty everything is?? It's a whole town to myself. I am loving lockdown now!!".

And he sends cute selfies of his hair in the wind, against the mad trees; posing with his café latte on a park bench. He likes to objectify himself for her digital consumption, relishing this new feeling—bit like a trophy wife. Her attention caused him to blossom like a ripe peach, in ways he'd not known before. His submissive cuteness his own delight at discovering his desirability, playing with it. Autoerotic manchild.

Now that the world in home arrest, Daniel's princely silhouette haunting the vacant fall town, kicking golden rusty leaves, feels like a scene from a cheesy film. She orders him to go there, do that. And he complies. Something in her melts more.

—Have you read what I gave you?

—Not yet... was busy taking selfies for you.

—But darling...

—OK. And he goes off for an hour. Then comes back to say:

—OK, now I know why you like the Morning Star. It's about us!!

—...

—So obvious: I am the star!! I am Hyperaeon! You, the beautiful girl Cătălina, ask me to descend from heavens for you: which is when you beckoned me to Albion; so I ride to the edges of the Universe, and ask for permission from the ultimate God to gain human form so I can be with my sweetheart but then...

—I wouldn't call Julianah the ultimate God.

He's knocked off his playfulness. Frowns and pouts.

—What?... Voice dropped a few octaves.

—In your pathetic example, Julianah is this ultimate God? Hyperaeon asked for permission for love from the supreme God and you from Julianah. What the fuck.

—No. I never asked her for permission for anything. And no. That is not what happened. I offered you my love in spring; and you chose the page as your long term number one. You betrayed me, the immortal, for the page. Hmpf.

Eris arches her brows and says menacingly into the phone.

—Who is the "page", little darling?!

—Isn't it clear?

—Actually not. Is it Julianah by any chance, and you're talking of yourself, not me?

—It is the vulture that always haunted us; that I am afraid of. That we both know you will return to one day.

He pauses. Her pulse is off the wall, she's shaking. She is clutching the phone angrily.

—Stan. He says through a clenched jaw. I can't imagine what you see in him. It's not like he's my level. I mean... I am one of the greatest scientists in the world.

Takes seconds like eons for those words to reverberate their full meaning into Eris. This little numpty really thinks he's the Genius in the poem, her the lowly mortal, and that interfering in someone's marriage gives him **victim** status. Staying loyal to her own husband is cheating on the newcomer. Her face winces under so many irritating simultaneous errors and delusional entitlements.

So she simply flips the table the way she knows how to, and also because it's true. The mirror hall of their relationship rather a masterpiece of symmetry.

—Daniel. Please listen to me well. Cătălina, that's you. When people read that poem, they all want to think they're the immortal. The genius. The star. That's the mark of a great work of art, everyone can identify with the hero.

But here, the Morning Star is me. You didn't find me cheating on you with any low rank servant. The parallels are clear. You had access to the hand of the immortal Goddess, who descended from heavens at night straight into your bed, flying; just like Hyperaeon, remember that bit? Remember how I came down to you and took you in hand? Weren't you the shy passive wallflower waiting to be plucked? Didn't you tell me you would be my apprentice, in life and sex? That you wanted me to be the dominant partner? And with cold hands I showed you a superior kind of love. Like Hyperaeon.

And you... **you** let the "page" knife us both in the ass, you left me alone for the whole summer in favor of a ...

—PLEASE. Stop. Stop. I can't take this anymore. Why does everything go back to this? I just wanted to share my reading of your favorite poem. I was happy, for once. How silly of me. I know I did wrong. I can't hear this bullshit story of the Night of the Knife any-more. I am going!! Speak later, "Hyper-Fucking-Aeon-Genius-Ass". Julianah was right. You are a narcissist who thinks she's above everyone else!

And he switches his phone off. Purses his lips, tosses his hair and lets out a small tear. A tear of remorse, a tear of agony. Like a feeling of having broken something precious, shame at having been stupid, but a tragic feeling that... well, there was nothing he could do. It wasn't his fault. It was the circumstances. His hands tied, he did the right thing.

And he rocks back and forth nearly crying—absent tears—whispering to self: "it was the right thing to do". "It was the right thing to do".

In half an hour he's back into the chat with little heart emojis and words of love. A crafty apology.

But Eris is now ushered in by her agent. Martin. She greets her fans in a mask that has Botticelli's Spring printed on; she has thin leather gloves, and a beautiful blue velvet dress with a large white lace Victorian collar. She radiates a warm smile to her fans who while in lockdown came in small numbers to meet her; with masks on. Lively, curious people fretting about. Excitement in the air.

She gets lost in chatter, she likes talking to them. She mingles.

—Hi, a pleasure meeting you, Madam. I am Lucius, huge fan. I would like to invite you to a small socially distanced gathering of fellow artists and writers. We're all Covid tested and safe. I guarantee an evening of intellectual delights and wonderful company. And good cheese, wine and eclairs!

The young man with a moustache chuckles. Her love of eclairs was famous. He held her gloved hands with both of his, and was dashing and bold. Nice suit in an updated Ivy style, check shirt and Nantucket red pants.

How charmingly quaint on a fresh face like that... born in the 90s? She wondered.

—Ah, you are very kind, Lucius. Very tempting! And she wiggles her finger with a smile that flashes her pearly whites and rosy lips. But I have to excuse myself, I am very tired tonight. Perhaps on my next trip!

Said with her down turned eyebrows, after which she taps the man on the arm and walks off. She sits at the table ready for autographs.

Life is exciting. Daniel is far away, but look how great life can be.

Daniel is far away.

This one fan of Eris drools a snail track in approaching her desk, saying lasciviously, like a sycophant:

—I am very much a fan of yours, Miss, I read all your books, they're so erotic.

Eris nods to him absently while memories of last nights pierce through her. The emotion of last night's lovemaking lingers on her face, mistaken by this man to be fascination for his words. So he feels encouraged.

—Ah, daughter of Zeus and Hera, antonym of Harmonia, Goddess of strife and discord, you who by a mere vocal differ from that other real deity you elicit in men... Eros... — he leers in high pitched tones, an overly thin older man with a beak like nose, who follows her around for autographs in every city.

But Daniel is far away.

She looks at him witheringly. There it is, the eyebrow. This time bit jaded. Her left eyebrow nearly touches her hairline and then she takes someone else's phone off the table pretending she's got an urgent call.

—Thank you very much.... Alfred? How wonderful. Enjoy your copy. Copies.

She steps away from the table. The room feels heavy so she throws them all a brief defensive cornered look. Suddenly that Lucius guy's party invite doesn't seem so bad. Leans her forehead into her agent Martin, nervous, huffing into her bejewelled fist:

—Look, can you get in touch with that guy, Lucius. I would like to be out of here. Tell him I am going to his party, but a bit later. Ask him about the eclairs. I want eclairs.

Martin stands on his toes to reach her height. He feels self conscious which accentuates his blushed cheeks. But he's eager to please, so his ear literally reaches as close to her lips as possible without being in her face. Have to watch out for these things.

She makes her way back to the table, grinning widely to an impatient masked crowd.

Alfred stands in the doorway of the library, while elbowed by hungry fans still making their way to the table. His dry lips wet by a worm-like tongue. The air-conditioning howls loudly over the library murmur pumping too much heat for November, so he has to fan his eyebrows with Eris' volume of "The Lively Egolympics of the Post Human Mind". As he does, the book cascades open and his eyes stop on a paragraph he's not seen before:

"Love is for idiots. Nature made it to make us replace ourselves. Have kids, love the other unfortunate cell mate you reproduce with; then kids shoot off, you are left alone, the love wears off... You die. After a long withering last episode of life when you sit remembering the jollies of love, weak and impotent. Love is an evolutionary trick. The real Darwinian thing to do is dispose with it. Live for yourself. Fuck the kids. Fuck replacing yourself with a clone. Focus on your life. Living. Survival of the fittest 1.1. RE-PROGRAMMING."

"Hmm...". Alfred isn't the most perceptive of perverts. But somehow, after just looking into this woman's eyes, those words don't ring true. Not for her, not right now. Eris wasn't a woman who appeared to be above romantic love. He felt very clever, like he stumbled against a hidden treasure. But who was he going to say this to? Who would listen to him? Who cared?

She spent most of her brief time at the party gazing obsessively at her phone; no reply from her love.

She couldn't feign any significantly deep enthusiasm for the pleasant Lucius and his interesting acquaintances, as much as she liked their ideas and dress sense.

—Perhaps this global pandemic is the beginning of the end of Time! A tall woman laughs.

—Perhaps people will finally pay attention. It's been totalitarian to the point where even the most obedient will raise an eyebrow. Says another, an Italian. Her remark welcomed by a choir of "of courses". In that sense it's good, because people who never questioned authority are now forced to.

—Seems like you want to kill grandma, Lucrezia! Lucius adds, nonchalantly.

—Yep. You caught me.

Another woman interjects:

—But grandma would be far better off walking in the sun. We do have an immune system. This madness makes no sense. The measures will be condemned by history, as much as they bully us now. Lockdown, tests, and soon vaccine mandates.

—Hard agree, hard agree, Eris quips.

She doesn't have context, but she feels a certain haunting presence. She can sense the girl in Johnnyville move slowly in the frame, eyes on the capsule of magic that is her and Daniels' love... with spite. And of course the poor girl can feel nothing but hate for them, but how tragic, that something so pure and wonderful has to be shadowed by so much unhappiness and hate around them. She imagines love triumph through it all like weeds growing through cement.

In the dark of the night, exhausted from a full day, Eris is hypnotically drawn to her phone, because Daniel was in it. All day she waited for this moment, to hear his voice.

So she rings. She wants to share her day.

But what she doesn't know is that Daniel spent large part of his free time from her arguing with Julianah, such that at 12:42am he was tired, his mind empty. Fruitlessness and despair with the whole female gender.

—Hello?

She blushes, even on the phone.

—Yes! Comes his irritated answer.

—How are you, baby? I miss you! This is your compulsory sort-of-boyfriend end-of-day call, when I share with you my adventures at work.

—Oh, I see.

His flat voice sends a cold shiver through her, cold shower over hers, flirty, happy.

—Oh, so we're not doing girlfriend boyfriend things? Not even sort-of-girlfriend sort-of-boyfriend things?

—I don't know. Maybe. I am sort of tired.

—I see... everything is "sort of" for you. Shall I call you Mr Sort-Off? Sortoff. Like a Russian aristocrat—and she tries to giggle, to thaw the ice man.

Quiet.

She sits down because it hurts.

—Are you okay, baby?

—Yes. Are you?

—I wanted to share my day—so much happened, I met so many people... wanted to tell you about this guy called Lucius. I... missed you like crazy..

—Won-der-ful. Listen. I am very tired. Speak tomorrow.

And then that's that. A beep.

Her brain makes like an audible click; something split in half.

That night, she has that wedding dream again. It's a wedding high on some rocks, with storm incoming. She feels cold but she turns to him enraptured, to say yes. And he says:

—Actually... Julianah needs me. She can't fix the faucet in the bathtub, and it's late. Love you, babe. You're amazing.

She wakes up with shivers. Checks the phone. He's not there.

Those dangerous curves around the lake gave her just the right thrill; she needed this. It was thrilling what she did.

It felt wrong but in a really confusing way. She couldn't tell who this felt wrong to.

Night before, after Daniel hung up, message popped on her screen.

"My love for you roars inside me at a deafening volume. I find its scale incomprehensible, vast. Vast like standing on the moon looking up at the vastness of the Universe in the absent atmosphere. It calls to you.
-S"

Who could stay cold before such love? It made Daniel's sound like a squeak.

What she knew from Abe and Cinco, like echoes from another world beyond the mountains, which she swept away like unwanted fall leaves, was... Stan was withering away. To regain her back from the arms of the young lover, Stan had starved himself.

People, scant as they were in lockdown days, were shocked to see him. He started running every day.

He was physically better than ever and sworn to never be with any other woman outside Eris ever again, repenting for his slutty ways. Remorseful pleas had poured from him in chat day and night but she liked to push away the phone, a story-line, an arc she couldn't cope with. While drugged on love in hot and cold Daniel heaven. No room for that other story, she was in this romance.

But that night, she felt duty. She felt... why reward the boy with so much love? When the boy treats her this way? Why not reward with her brief company and care the man who devoted his life to her, day and night? Who, even hurt and abandoned, doesn't say a bad word. But with dignity he suffers and pushes himself heroically.

Do anything to be good for her again. To undo the mistake he knew he'd done.

She didn't feel lust or romantic longing; but a deep sense of care, deepest human care for this loving man she left for that fickle floozie with the oiled chest and whiny psychology.

She pushed the pedal and drove faster.

She knew for a fact that Stan, no matter his state, no matter how betrayed he felt, would sit there and patiently listen to her stories about Lucius and Martin's mates and the lights and glamour and sales and marketing and every little thing that ran through her mind and into her vivacious words. Perhaps the litmus test of real love was, will the other be there to listen to your adventures at the end of the day. Maybe this constant storm of butterflies in her belly for Daniel was in fact just illness, and not love, after all.

It felt a bit guilty, but also not. It felt a bit like the right thing, and also like a disaster about to happen.

She knew he was there to listen. She knew he was there.

CHAPTER X

Eris arrives in Albion. Shopping bags in hand.

Her mind full of Stan's tragic circumstances. She had found him in squalor, but emaciated. Anxious, ranging from frantic, to impress her with everything he'd done, to deep depression and bouts of crying.

He was doing zooms with congregants, warning them in mysterious tones of the darkness of their times. The poor people nodded in approval, thinking he meant the pandemic. With no clue the progressive rabbi hid soap opera levels of romantic dramas in his soul.

It was excruciatingly hard to look him in the eyes and say she was going back.

—What?? He irrupts in tears. I thought you'd come to stay... I thought you've come because it's over between you and him, you're done playing with your boy toy... We have a future and high goals together, bunny... Please tell me it is so... please.

Her heart was stewing, torn between going back to her fragile bubble of beauty and love, and the duty for this kind man who gave her the best years of her life.

So she resorted to shouting.

—Don't I have a right to live?? I gave up enough of me for so long. I have a right to be happy. I am not your prisoner!

—But he doesn't make you happy! You cried all summer!

Stan broke down and sat on the floor, crying deeply, rocking back and forth.

She sat with him, gave him a blanket.

Then left.

Behind her, something was sinking. A planet, something. She wasn't entirely sure.

"Daniel better be fucking worth it"—she thought to self starting the engine. There were clouds at the other end too.

As she unloads the trunk, in front of Albion cottage, Graciella makes himself heard in the next yard. Looking like a Salem witch, making old-fashioned soap in a pot over fire. Eris' eyebrow pops up like a question mark.

—What you doing, Graciella darling!

—Soap, my dear. Real soap. With caustic soda so do be careful.

—What you going through all that trouble for? You can buy artisanal soap at the store for five bucks. They've got them in all flavors and shapes.

—Nah, m'dear, it's no good that stuff. And he smirks wisely winking. This... This is real, pure soap. Washes your skin, nourishes you. No toxins, no baddies. Washes your soul.

To hear that last word, Eris winced. It cut through her. Graciella saw. His skin like melted wax but his eyes steely.

—Okay, Graciella! Eris shouts, fakely amused, affable. Good luck with that stuff!!

—I'll bring you some when it's over, my dear, and he smiled wryly again.

Eris was prepared to dismiss the hunch the first time around but now she became convinced Graciella knew.

—Alright, Graciella, why not. We all need to wash our sins, don't we!

Hello, Cătălina! She shouts from the main door, grinning.

He runs to greet her, engulfing her in a torrid embrace.

—You are Cătălina! He laughs. I am the Morning Star! Worship me, he says with a sweet smile, mocking authority. Though too sweet to be authoritarian.

She quiets him with a deep kiss, grabbing his head by the hair.

—Shut up, Cătălina.

—How was it out there?? The world in pandemic?

Strange, she says. So eerie, all closed. Many businesses out of business. Although, that's not all bad. Like some of them deserved to go. Thank fuck. If this pandemic is the price I have to pay to see these bullshit businesses go bust then it's a price worth paying. Survival of the fittest etc.

I mean if you make bath bombs and moustache gel and gold-leaf-covered chicken perhaps you deserve to go bust. Who the fuck needs bath bombs?? There is war, kids starving in Syria. And you want... fluffy bath nothing?

He laughs with her:

—So you propose corporate Darwinism?! The pandemic as Evolution for business?

—Well, yes! Fucking make something useful, you know?

—Like... lingerie?! He says looking through her shopping bags, taking out strings of lace and bows that he struggles to grasp how and what they do.

She grabs them off his hand.

—Yes. This is essential. She leans into him. Essential business, you understand.

He understands. He kisses her lips so hard, she nearly faints into him, forehead in his neck. She breathes him in, he inhales her.

—Your silk is very skinny!

Question-mark eyebrow pops up.

He blushes... I mean your skin is very silky.

They laugh. He whisks her to the sofas, their playground. Of many days that winter, late 2020.

Wrapped in golden sunsets, dancing to soulful synth-pop. Magnetism so strong and dense you could cut it with a knife. And in fact someone did. It felt like borrowed time. She'd hide her agony face in his childish curls. She didn't know why, but it felt it would be taken away from her.

Maybe one or both their "satellites" would force them back, maybe it will wane like steam when'd lockdown over. Maybe this love a mere survivalist fantasy of the pandemic and when life returns to normal... maybe they both die with the corona-virus, entwined in the remote house in the hills. Graciella will find their bones and wash them with soap.

It was a gloomy cloud of fearful uncertainty, always there above their love. Sometimes she prayed it wouldn't stop. To some god. Her favorite, Dionysus. Red bottle in hand, flute in the other, dancing to exhaustion in a dim lit sitting room of concert hall proportions. Him, sat, face flickering with the candles, regarded her as a Goddess. Felt the magic of these borrowed moments. Felt the ticking clock in his chest. He felt—despite his flimsy reassurances to self he was marvellous—that she would dump him; soon, any day now; very soon. Tic. Toc. She has to. Too good to be true. So hard to have both the best of life, and be pierced with agony knives from time to time. There was the parallel heaven they were writing together on the blank sheet of each new day; starting with late brunch. At the white table, between flowers. She liked fresh flowers, roses and peonies. Drenched in the East window sunshine. Coffee, blue Araucana eggs, boiled. French cheese, roast Spanish peppers and Californian avocados. Their robes like curtains waiting to be pulled aside for the show. Holding hands in silence.

—Why are you looking at me like that?

—I want to capture your face. Forever. Photograph it in my mind. Because your beautiful face is like a painting. And he reached his other hand to gently touch the contours of her face. They both sat in silence with messy hair until they decided to exchange the breakfast table for dinner and start walking around dancing, watching stuff. If she went to get an oat cookie, he'd follow and envelop her in kisses. "Where did you go? I missed you". If he went to get a piece of dark chocolate she'd ambush him and steal it from his mouth. They unwittingly sent electric sparks to each other while trying to work on their respective computers. She would sometimes sit in the bay window among the cushions. Play with her playlist. Watch him surreptitiously in mirrors dotted around the place.

Sometimes it was him sitting there in lotus position. He looked so radiant focused on his geeky work. She found his numbers fascinating.

The sexy scientist, robe undone, hair in his eye, rotund pecs of porcelain. Lost in his laptop world.

When they first met she'd dress a bit 50s. Pencil skirts, elegant suits and a severe updo. By summer the pant suits were cord velvet and hair, down.

But now, she was full on late 90s style. Teenage fashion. Her favorite accessory was a black velvet choker with a gold and rubies pendant she had custom-ordered in a matching pair for them both; she wore it with a crop top and high waist trousers, showing off a well sculpted mid riff. The seed pearl pavé of the pendant surrounded a gold smiley face, set with three heart-shaped rubies—the in-love emoji. One of their most often-used emojis, in 18 Karat gold. It did after all start with his happy emoji post-it on her laptop one day, long ago—pre-apocalypse. Months of romance then juxtaposed love hearts over the smiley, red and sparkly. She loved the pendant. She found it cute and satisfying to manifest the online symbolism of their romance with this precious metal embodiment in real life, close to her heart, always. Often felt it with her fingers. He didn't really wear his.

She liked to dress up at home. Life hadn't ceased just because the pandemic pushed it domestically. It just became more intimate. Not house arrest. Domestic bliss. Better the world was shut. Who needed it anyway? Lovers didn't.

He tried too. By taking off his shirt and sitting up in the good light by the bay window. Waiting. Every day was a celebration.

—I think you just want me for my body. His words come when she's "testing the goods"—his body, in the window against a spectacular sunset. They enjoy this view over the river each night, lounging embraced.

—Look at this splendour. We are having the best apocalypse ever!! You can't even see the apocalypse from this window, she laughs, nuzzling him.

But he's serious. She reassures him:

—Ah don't be stupid, darling. I love you. Can't you tell?

—Ah, yes, you love me because you love my body. You want me for sex.

—But what is sex? I don't want sex for sex. I don't think it works like that. I am deeply romantic. Can't you tell, by the way I look at you?

Sex isn't sex.

Sex is like a core of everything, a secret code of all our lusts and desires. Easy to dismiss it as a low cheap thing. Horrible how it's disembodied and sold as a hollow commodity nowadays. It's actually if done correctly quite divine. And to do it correctly means to not dissociate it from the heart, love, intimacy, deep human connection. Commitment. It tells you so much about a person.

When you do it randomly, it leads to the Christian loss of the soul.

Do it right, and it's the key to the pearly gates.

But we're not quite allowed to live it like that, the sublime way. The adoration for the other, giving-your-soul-in-a-kiss. That's way out of fashion, verboten these days...

—Why?! That sounds crazy. Who doesn't allow you to have sex with love?

—Well, society. In a deeper way we're not supposed to fully enjoy the full spectrum of divinity we can through our biology.

A lot of the forms of connection we have as animals have disappeared since we traded them for comfort and technology. We've become "respectable", and lonelier. Disconnected. Sex was a supreme, divine form of connection. But not the only one.

What people would see as the orgiastic drunken cult of Dionysus, that was more us. It was a clever thing, you know. Much cleverer than other religions.

—Ah, so when you drink, in fact you observe religious ritual... and I thought you just liked to get drunk—he smirks.

—Yes, pretty much... I am not even kidding. She says, laughing.

—Really...

—Really. We used to be more free before the advent of agriculture. But agriculture and civilisation took it away from us, by and large. Then Christianity worse.

I have only seen this in three forms: Romanian peasants' circle dance in the mountains, full of joy—when you feel a divine sense of joy and unity with other human beings, no competition, no nasty. Pure joy. Music. Group ecstasy. Hard to believe today, but that existed for a long time.

The hippie movement of the 60s and 70s. The electronic music scene of the 90s. That was people rediscovering what they thought they had lost in 13,000 years of agriculture, of slavery.

—Wait, how was agriculture slavery? Isn't it more, like, agriculture freed people from the pursuit of food? Don't go full conspiracy theorist on me.

—No, it's just history. It really didn't. It created surplus, but also tied people in socio-political bondage. You read books, you should know.

Each revolution domesticated us further. Agriculture, industry, digital. We become more and more enslaved, further from group joy and free lust. More isolated capsules of individualism, competition.

—But aren't you Miss Competition?

—Pardon?

—You always say competition is good, you thrive from it, etc.

—Of course. But it like all things has an ideal plateau. Needs careful calibration with cooperation... Modern life is **all** competition.

But he stayed quiet, so she went on. Doing her robe up as the sun drowned in a spectacular light show.

Well, because agriculture didn't domesticate plants and goats. Really, agriculture domesticated us. And some serious core aspects of the human experience were eradicated from our soul. A certain lust, joy, freedom, idleness, creativity, wild release of the subconscious with drink and drugs and dance. Community.

An ecstatic experience.

Idleness, she repeats nodding, looking deep into his eyes. Not this tyranny of productivity.

People always long to return to that paradise lost. *Illo tempore*. A time of innocence. Because hunters and gatherers, pre-agriculture and settlements, were free, like free animals; their lives hard, but also freer; they had no master. We still have that in us. Sometimes when we gaze from our modern luxuries, there are unknown sectors in our soul, that long for that, and we don't know what it is. I think sex is a window into that.

And in the '90s it looked like now might really be the time. "Look we endured 13,000 years of slave farms; but now is our time; we have plenty, we have surplus, we're liberated form the pursuit of food—we can have a party for the end-of-history! Celebrate". And.. it didn't happen. It did for a few years, but humanity didn't get free. It got worse.

—But, darling. You haven't explained why sex isn't sex. Why do you think primitive people didn't just have casual sex.

—I don't know. Sex shouldn't be divorced from love. They evolved together.

I mean sex isn't JUST sex. Sex is our personal evolution, our intimacy. A code of all our lusts and longings. In our age it's been dissociated from the love aspect and sold separately. Like sugar. Sugar was a compound in fruit we evolved to lust for because it came with the good things in fruit. They discovered processed sugar and sell it separately without the good things. Same with sex. With love, it's divine. Forms connection. Satisfies deep corners of the soul. Creates allies. Separate sex and sell separately? Casual sex with random people? And like they do in porn? The most mechanical exertion of it, like it's just a sport? No emotion? No trust, no respect, no care? It's god-damn awful. Why so many people are broken and jaded today. Single and depraved.

I think primitive people... before civilization... they had more human connection. I think when there are fewer people around, you do. I think things were more sacred. Meaningful.

—I am sure ritual sacrifice and rapes were very meaningful.

—Yeah, but when you are more real and free, you have both better good things but also more raw bad things.

— I see... he looks at the river as night sets. So you mean... I should rape you? So it's more meaningful?

—Ha! As if you could, young man. I gave you delusions of grandeur, I made you a man! And now it went to your head—she says launching a cushion attack on his nude persona.

But he stays calm, takes her weapons off her one by one, gently envelops her in his body mass until she melts and curls into him, happy.

—You are my baby. You always will be.

—Until someone holds you hostage, then you forget, she interjects.

He pauses. Holds her tighter. You can feel his love like a silent force field, a monolith filling the room in a wave yet unidentified by 21st century science. She's hazy, eyes half closed.

—No one can hold me hostage, he replies with sweet conviction. No one can make me hurt you.

———⋙⋘———

Eris curses at the windows in Albion. Not good for selfies. The way the light falls, not the most flattering for someone in her thirties. She waltzes from window to window phone in hand trying to get the best shot. She usually does get a few good shots in. They go straight to her social media. It's an industry. She creates these video reels with witty captions, the follower base gets to live vicariously, everyone happy. Daniel is sat legs folded on the white sofa, lazily scrolling through Facebook at the end of the day. Eris' happy video post with light washing behind her is lovely, but it feels like a personal affront somehow. His dim silhouette just visible in the background as she swirls. So he objects, in typical mellifluous tones. Sweet choice of words, even sweeter meek voice—almost singing. Easy to drown harsh words with a voice like that.

—Think of poor Julianah. At least make it friends only. His pretty face pleads, looking up to her.

It's like something grabs her unannounced. Her smile turns to lemon sour.

—What, why?? I am in my home, in the one spot with good light. A single video frame happened to have a faint suggestion of another person in it, only visible if you freeze-frame. I've a public facing persona, this is part of my career. My career is very image focused and I'm stellar at it.

Daniel is taken aback. He takes seconds to think. He usually does.

—My God. It wouldn't hurt you to be more modest.
You'd make less enemies that way.

As soon as he says it, he understands what he's
done; he triggered one of her buttons, so he prepares
for storm incoming, regretful.

She continues.

—Modest?? I'm sorry? What has modesty ever
brought you?? Does modesty make the world spin?
Invent electricity? Go to space, put satellites in the
sky? Modesty is a code word for failure.

Why do you want me to be modest? Not know
where I stand? Act humble and fake? I look good.
I've a nice life. So I flaunt it. It actually pays my bills.
Your missy, if she doesn't like it, she has two options:
improve her own life and stop blaming others for
her failure or she can, you know, stop parking her
neuroses on my social media. I definitely didn't invite
her on it.

—She's not a failure, Daniel mutters through gritted
teeth.

—Oh, really? Does she have an Oscar in home-mak-
ing? Daniel already fuming through his ears. Pressure
cooker. License for Eris to continue. Point she needs
to make supersedes his delicate sensibilities in impor-
tance, and she's going all in. To teach him a lesson he
needs to know, that life hasn't shown him yet.

She takes off her pearls, suddenly feeling their
weight. She takes off her shoes, suddenly craving
comfort. Circles him like a headmistress; or a lioness.
While his body crouches even smaller in a perfect
golden ratioed snail shape into the cushions. Once
more hiding under his hair.

—I actually have a career and still I'm a better
home-maker than her. She just uses her failure and
lack of aim to glorify doing fuck all. Things we all do
as part of life. Maintenance.

Time to wake up, cupcake. You want success, you
have to confront reality. I'm fighting wars here, and sor-

ry, but part of my warfare is looking good for the camera. Live with it. Or not.

The tense air becomes lead. She thinks she's triumphed, made her point. Who can not be seduced by such life-affirming words? But she looks at him off the corner of her eye, and sees him clenching thick jaws in a tiresome repression of painful reality.

—You're really mean, you know that. Finally, he speaks. His voice guttural, deep. So unlike him.

I think we're happy here and she's alone there, no point gloating, shoving our happiness in her face. Eris quickly cuts off:

—And if I was going to post a portrait of us two tongue kissing, I'd agree with you. But this is footage of me. No one looks at faint blot in the background and says: "aha, she's flaunting her new catch!". My followers are used to me posting content way before I learned there was a Julianah on Planet Earth. If she can't cope with that she can't cope with life. And that's not my problem. Survival of the fittest etc. Daniel blinks. Thinks. Purses lips. Nails deep into his fists.

But not much of a rational retort to that. When she's right, she's right. He hates it, but what can he do. How to escape. So he resorts to what he does best. Flicks his hair, jumps to his feet, grabs the door and slams it.

—Bye. I won't even dignify you with an answer, when you're like this!

Ten minutes later he scrolls through Facebook from his bedroom. Stares at her post. Tilts his head. "Oh, well, maybe". He goes back to tens, hundreds of posts back to make a comparison. The lady of his dreams smiling, or pensive, in all of them—the same way; different settings. Zooms in to see himself, a blob in the background. She looks radiant. Happy. Like she always does. You can fault her for being image focused, he thinks. But she's always like that. He used to like that in her, now he's insecure.

Unless she's using next level subliminal messaging, there is no outright offense. No daggers aimed at any particular rival wasting away in a Johnnyville living room.

He walks sheepishly to the living room where Eris on the same page interacting merrily with friends and followers. She likes the excitement. At least for a bit.

Daniel advances to the foot of the white sofa. Looks at her, eye behind blond curls, lips bitten to the blood. A tear on his cheek. Doesn't even know why, for whom. He's just confused, he wants some kind of release, anything. For lack of better ideas, he curls at the feet of his tormentor, one he resents, but cannot help but feel beckoned by the steel logic of. At her feet, he hugs her knees. It hurts him, she hurt him, her—his protégé, and it, through a feedback loop, comes back to hurt him once more that he adores the giver of pain. Febrile thoughts and impotent raging fists can't work this out. So he resolves to park his exhausted inner conflicts at her feet, massaging them. Meekly. Hoping she looks down. Heart racing. And she does. Arched eyebrow, launching a look like a school Mam.

—You chill yet?

—What? He murmurs.

—You calmed down? He's ashamed. "Yes". Looks down at the floor. She grabs his chin. Won't let him down easy. Not her style. Before he can react she flashes the camera before him, to immortalize the moment of defeat on his face. Laughs in a satanic tone. Cascades of sardonic laughter fill the room. How could he possibly resist them?

CHAPTER XI

They heard conflicting stories on their daily walk. All was shut, so human contact consisted of lone people on a park bench who longed for human company so much they struck a chat with any passerby.

And people usually wanted to strike a conversation with lovers in smiles. One lady told them of illegal parties down the road, another man told them he'd lost his entire family and he wasn't even allowed to watch them die by doctors in hazmat suits.

One day, a man in old fashioned clothes carrying a suitcase down a back alley looked drunk; they approached the strangeness and they saw a horrified face in a black mask, hissing them away.

Terrified, they looked at each other. The man in his trilby looked barely conscious anymore. Feral, in agony, struggling to breathe. But loudly struggling on with his little suitcase. Then he disappeared.

They started to fear.

He was worried for the vulnerable Julianah, in the overweight category the virus seemed to have predilection for; Eris for Stan, with less of the same problem now. But they couldn't talk of these secret worries to each other, lest they hurt and offend more. They had to dance around this box of explosives. Mentioning the "satellites" could ruin an afternoon.

They were too tired of these explosives, so they made great efforts to avoid all their memories of a long life shared with other partners; which required quite some mental push-ups.

—Yeah, I visited Venice too, with ... umm. It was lovely, yes, when I visited Venice.

As they walked into ghostly late November streets, cuddling into each other, even shop windows were unlit, only takeaway cafés open. You had to queue outside in the cold, far from other human beings.

It was clear the fun part of the lockdown was over. The cool feeling of novelty, the unusual sunshine and everyone's excitement with Zoom and the return to nature because of the halt in industry.

Walks in the park no longer an adventure—a boredom of death. A pet stroll round the cage.

It began to feel stale and oppressive. People dropped like flies. Some died of loneliness. Some because they didn't have Covid—so hospitals turned them away. It became clearer and clearer to Eris that her aunt had died of the virus. Stories like that popped everywhere.

But there was nothing you could trust.

Some people said it's all a scam, to sink them into deeper state control. Globally. And you couldn't deny that control increased tenfold. Some people thanked the government for the lockdown, for they might have been rescued from certain winter death.

—Now is the winter of our discontent.... Made hideous winter by the virus of Wuhan.. said Martin to Eris in a dim Zoom call that fell through every 5 minutes. Even the internet suffered with the virus.

I am suffering terribly. He said among coughs. She really really saw the face of Covid then.

—Take care of yourself, please.

—I will. But the loneliness is hard. I can't see anyone, everyone I know is vulnerable. Haven't seen family since ... it started, in February.

Daniel's Zooms were more perked up by their Gung-ho work content; draining, but kept the illusion of life going on in a form or another. He took one on a walk to town one day, camera off. A peripatetic work Zoom—he felt personally victorious against the tyranny of work through these little cheat code codes. Eris was quietly holding his hand, which still felt divinely romantic.

She stopped in front of a lit panel in an art gallery. In the deserted town, with barricaded bar doors and dilapidated shops, this was unusual. A very large manipulated photograph of a Kim-Kardashian-esque figure meets Miss Piggy, in a luscious pink swim suit, too small for her overflowing curves, holding a phone in hand, taking selfies. Duck, inflated lips.

Title of work: "Silk Purse", caption: "Here is a Portrait of Sow's Ear".

Took Eris a few moments to get the joke, and when she did, she chuckled, and shook his hand. He put his hand over his mic and gazed. Didn't get it.

—Well, it's a... she rolls her eyes. So like, this is a quite ridiculous narcissistic woman, who doesn't look great—"Sow's Ear", making herself look like a "Silk Purse"—something fancy: see the glamorous air she's putting on. It's a phrase, to make a silk purse out of a sow's ear means you make something attractive out of low quality. Take this Instagram generation, with their lip fillers, their overly sexy clothes, their filters. They take something mediocre and try to pass it off as high value.

Ah, he says, absently.

—She still doesn't look good. Grossly overweight.

Eris throws the arrow through her teeth:

—But I thought you liked overweight. Isn't your missus...?

Daniel at first doesn't hear, focused as he is on his online meeting. But then he replays the words to himself, the words hanging in the ether. And he immediately becomes incensed. Withdraws his hand.

—I won't allow anyone to talk about her like that. I wouldn't allow anyone to talk of you like that.

—Well you wouldn't need to, because I am not like ... that, and she points her finger to the light-washed panel.

Daniel walks off.

—And to think I left her, for you, came here, on a one way ticket. You could at least leave the poor girl alone.

—You did? I didn't even know you came on a one way ticket. I didn't quite get why you came to me in the first place. Why, Daniel? You talk to her a hell of a lot. I didn't get any videocall rights back in summer when I begged you to give me a day out of five months. You fucking wear her ring; you defend her like mad, saintly, major abnegation. She is Holy Julianah the Great. As far as I am concerned, you asked permission from your handler to come live your sex fantasies with the mistress for a while. Not with a capital "m".

He doesn't answer, just walks off. Shakes his head. She chases after him, grabs his arm.

—Well??

—Well, what? He says calmly, coldly. She can't stand the coldness in his eyes.

—Why did you come here? What do you want from me?

—Well, obviously, to be insulted and mocked. I must be a masochist.

She isn't getting what she needs, what she wants. And she's not asking correctly, but the barrel of TNT is lit. Her furious temperament hard to control even in normal times, let alone in the double, triple quandary they're in.

—I am certainly glad I also went to visit my "satellite" day after my work trip, and didn't fully dedicate myself to a "married man" who declares love to me but has loyalty elsewhere!!

A menacing silence drops. Silent streets, now frozen. Daniel listens to the bomb, looking down. He takes ages to react. She looks at his face become pained, she regrets launching the missile. She takes a step back. But she has no clue just what she triggered. She still thinks she will sort this out with kind words later.

He finally looks at her, lips tight, face grey.

—You know, I had a hunch that day that you went to see him. I had a feeling you were lying to me about staying on the island with your new friends and Lucius bullshit. I didn't quite get why you were telling me about Nantucket pants hunk. It was an alibi. I said, no my baby wouldn't lie to me. But my baby did.

And he walked off, alone.

Earth sinking. How many times can the earth sink beneath Eris and Daniel?

"—Descend upon me, sweet Northern Star,
Down a beam you slide,
Conquer forests and my heart,
My fortune set alight!

He trembles like in times of yore,
Betwixt high trees and hills,
His shine impressing tides
Into the solitary seas.

But no longer does he fall
From heavens into sea for her;
—What difference to thee, face of clay,
If you love me or they!

In your shallow human sphere,
Onto Fortune you must hold,
Whereas in my world I stay
Immortal and cold."

He looks at the piece of paper in her handwriting, prescient, or sinister. Covering it with lipstick kiss marks didn't make it less so.

—Take back your "love card", from your favorite poem, that confirms what you told me in March and showed me all along... That I am not good enough, that you will always return to your real love, the guy who "gets you". Who is "better than me". Like a religious simpleton could possibly be better than me, an elite scientist!!

By the way, you're not the Morning Star, seducing a mortal; you are Cătălina, I am the star. Just Google our respective names, see who's got more cache. And now, I am off; I'll be a shooting star.

He flicks his hair like a raging sissy.

She stands, shocked.

—Baby... it's not a love card, it was a joke. A cruel joke I wrote after the Night of the Knife... But I love you. I only performed a duty of care, like you to her... I am sorry.

But his voice was weak, his mind broken. He cried, and felt utter despair. Unbending in his path.

The year was harsh on him. He lost his emotional rock, whose longstanding adulation had gifted him stable success. He left her, to be with this cruel creature. For whom he never was allowed to feel good enough. Lockdown, corona-virus, the leaden shadow of other partners, everything was standing against them, he had carried so much pain secretly, he was about to break. Perpetual injury of the self.

So he went to his room to cry.

Eris chased after him, standing in his doorway.

—I left that poor girl for you, I am here!! And you go back to him?! The young man cried, like a little boy.

Eris was apologetic, she didn't know what to say. Once more attack was the best defence:

—Look, you never said how and why you came. If it was a real rupture back home. I told you my fears: I think you are still trying to live your polyamory fantasy. I don't think you are able to leave her, as demonstrated by this summer. So of course I also checked on him.

But if polyamory is what you want, then be honest. Please. Your ambivalence is a huge mindfuck. What do you actually want?

Among tears and choking, Daniel muttered, destroyed internally:

—I always loved you more than anything. I had big dreams. I could have given you everything. Yes, it was hard, I didn't want to destroy her. Had to do it slowly, in stages. But unlike you. I never had any doubts. I always wanted you. I waited for you to see us. At the start you didn't.

—But baby... and she sits next to him. Did you actually share these big dreams with me? You kept saying you had a great relationship at home. All summer you banged on about these "two great women". The facts... ambivalence. You want a domestic slave there and a sex Goddess here. You want your cake, and eat it.

—Defence to you!! I had to defend her against your jealousy. I had to defend myself, when you said you're not leaving your guy for me. I didn't want to be the third wheel.

I had checked out of that relationship long ago, I just didn't want to destroy her. Now you destroyed me. And I destroyed my life for nothing!! I feel like an idiot!!!

—You don't think it was more damaging to keep her as leverage if you don't love her anymore? To extend her pain, knowing you'd leave her anyway? Isn't that selfish and dishonest?

Daniel didn't answer, head buried under pillow, sobbing.

—You came here wearing her ring. You constantly think of her, call her. It must be some fantastic kind of true everlasting love; the bond between the two of you is toxic but it runs super deep; what can I think when you say she is this amazing woman? She isn't all that, really. She's your perfect doormat and you like that, you need the total abnegation, it defines you. That to you matters more than the objective qualities of me or other women.

It irks you I am independent. You love your lasso around her neck.

Daniel pokes his head above the pillow, sober, frowning like a threat. His growl, his words emerge through gritted teeth in a baritone this effeminate boy never capable of:

—You will never understand how deeply and utterly dignified she is!

Heavy emphasis on each word.

—Dig-ni-fied. He repeats, pinning his lover down with steel eyes.

The other side of the mountains, Julianah, fused into the couch, is watching "Twilight". Surrounded by vats of strawberry ice-cream and bags of Cheesy Puffs, some of which drop down between her boobs, down into the folds of the blanket; she bows down to pick them, in doing so, the ice-cream vat rolls over and drips. On her knees, she collects ice-cream with crisps and licks it, there, on the floor. Standing back up takes a while, so she eats another bag to gain courage.

In Dahut, the lights flicker. Eris grabs a cardigan. Stern but haunted by love.

She reached out to hold him, but something was broken. Her caress can't prevent disaster. Hours later he announced, coming out of the shower with red eyes, that he's going home for Christmas.

That's when earth really sank. All the tectonic plates crashed, cracked, with a loud boom. They had two weeks left. Arrangements made. It was over. Their "trial" was over.

—I need to go away. In a place where nobody broke my heart.

—... back to her. Eris whispers, looking down.

—NO!! I am going back to my PLACE. Where I can lick my wounds. You want me to go live under a bridge?!

—Please stay, darling. She was pleading, paralyzed heart.

—For what? For an adventure, some fun? I wanted you forever, but you never offered me the long term.

—I offered you the only thing anyone has certain: the present.

—Was it the present you offered ME when you went to him?

"The proportions of your face are the Bermuda triangle of my ego. Better drown there, than exist freely anywhere else. With my eyes I search, and find, a magic realm defined by your body. I feel, enhanced. Everything is enhanced. With my lips, I mark the silk of your skin. I kiss it once, it's mine forever."

These were the words she wrote in her diary late night, after he'd gone to bed.

They had two weeks left. A death sentence. It was hard times again, and the diary her best friend. Especially since she started being too embarrassed to assault her real flesh and blood friends with requests for advice on the never ending story. Some people (her mother) would call daily to ask for the juice, the gossip; the newest episode of the love psychodrama.

—So, mom, you tuned in for your daily "The Young and the Restless"?!

—Yes!! Your life is such a soap opera—Callista laughed in cascades that brought temporary joy back to her house.

Abe was particularly generous with his insight.

—So, Eris, are you recycling your daddy issues with Daniel, who's leaving you for your step mom?

Eris gasped like a deer in the headlights; taken aback by this brazen insight served cold. "...Am I... a fucking cliché?!".

Abe would chortle.

—We all are, dear. Don't worry. I got daddy issues, you got daddy issues, Stan has daddy in the sky issues. And Blue Balls.. the mother of daddy issues. Or is it mommy issues? What do you think?

—Yeah, you, normies, have these issues, maybe. I was supposed to be aloof and perfecty-perfect.

—Hmm. Abe thinks before he speaks—a first for him. I'd say specifically THAT attitude is your battle to overcome. Maybe Blue Balls' been sent to knock you off your high horse and make you human and flawed.

—God help you, Abe, if you think I'll let this or anything make me a victim. One way or another I'll come up on top.

Her pal served pure essence of harsh British wit, putting the finger in the wound with his diagnosis, no care in the world. The situation brought him amusement.

But she was lying here in the ruins of what she'd done to betray the love. She hadn't seen the boy give her everything like he claimed, she saw his duality in clear colors, and she cared for the other, her ailing abandoned husband.

She'd not betrayed Daniel, she couldn't feel guilty. But it was clear she'd done something wrong. Because he was leaving.

—Look, I want to show you you are important to me. You are not my "boy toy". I've invited our neighbor Graciella for dinner, so I can introduce you as my boyfriend.

Graciella came and went like a giggly charm bot. But Daniel didn't flinch, and kept going on about being made to feel unwelcome, which is why he had to go back to his nest, where he had always been the undisputed King of the abode.

Another time Eris tried again, harder:

—Look, I have built a fort on the sitting room floor for us. We can lie there under blankets, with our laptops, and watch movies. And drink tea and wine.

She was making peace offers day after day, squeezing the juice off days left until his departure. By now she was already dressing like a pre-teen: lilac dress with large Victorian collar, pink bow in her hair... Standing before him with wide open eyes trying to hypnotise and melt him. He was sweet on the surface but didn't relent. But at least accepted to crawl together into the fort.

Where they watched a Japanese movie: "Love Exposure"—which reminded them of them, which is when they looked at each other with meaning and hugged each other's fingers; their fingers made love while stony faces looked forward. Then "Metropolis"—which prompted long intellectual talks.

—This is so powerful, isn't it? Not much has changed in 100 years. Shame about the ending. Feels anti-climactic.

—Yes, I know you're not a fan of happy endings.

With the grandfather clock in the hallway ticking like a bomb timer, days passed slowly in a haze of love and lazy; each day closer to the inevitable. After discussing movies together, they'd fall asleep on the floor. Holding each other's hands and feet, drunk on love. Semi naked bodies glistening in many screen and rosy lamp lights.

Somehow, despite recent blows, love grew. Because with Eris and Daniel, no matter how intense and incessant the mutual blow-torching, regardless how great the disappointment, love knew only one direction: up.

Terrorized by the ever-growing loud tick of the metaphorical clocks, hanging above them, Poe's pendulum in "The Pit and Pendulum". A symphony of ticking clocks: 3-2-1 days till separation.

Eris' last diary entry of their troubled honeymoon period was left open on her screen the day he left. They walked together to the station.

"*Morning with Daniel.*

I sit up in bed, clutching his head into me. Then we start kind of wrestling, I am aggressive, quick. He looks confused, shelters his head into his shoulders, defens ive... escapes, then I regain control. Lock his legs into mine climbing onto him. Use my elbows, push his face. I am very quick. He immobilizes my hands behind my back. I escape. He looks weak for a split second but he's thinking. Of how to attack.

Then he does an American football style grasp and employs his whole body weight to push me down. That wins it for him because ... well, double my body mass. To feel that grasp and his body finally being used like a man makes me ultra hot. I breath like a marathon athlete while I succumb to his embrace and his passionate intense kiss on my neck. My neck is being bitten to shreds. I melt. Then there's that eye contact. God. God. He looks at me smiling, calm, gentle, but confident. He whispers something in my ear. The fight is over, he won.

—Did you fight me to trigger this reaction? Almost effeminately he asks.

—No, I just feel aggressive, I attack, I enjoy passion either way. If I win, I enjoy the win. If you do, I go with that. I don't care. It's the intensity of the fight I'm after.

The locked eyes and bodies last minutes but it feels eternal. I sink deep into his soul. A caress on my face, calling it beautiful. Goddess etc. A moment of sublime romance. He emulates fucking me but doesn't do it really, just the motions, while I am under his splendid body and surrounded by his blond locks, my body writhes, I clasp his back fiercely, scratch him, plunge hands into him, drown my face into his neck; his hair, his body create a space of wonder. I have never felt such ecstasy nor did I think it possible. Looking into each other's eyes again, I am more and more feminine but I am not ashamed of it and there's nothing weak about it. It's enjoying male strength but for us, I stir it, I elicit it in him, but it is for me, for us. It is team play, not a competition, anymore. I turned the boy into man.

His long lashes. His smiling eyes raining gentle love and confidence, lips gasping "you're mine", "I am inside your mind". He is. He is mine too. So intimate. So into each other. Perfect. Sensual woman with a God complex, and explosive strength, succumbs to the beautiful refined German male with a white knight complex, with silent strength that attacks like a submarine. But who has succumbed to whom? Who wins? Whose curls haunt my dreams forever? Who will never find a creature like me ever again?

Then he climbs off. I am left there, still breathing hard. This is the flip side of the coin to his passion. It starts things then walks off. I am feeling jilted, still flush with eroticism, longing for his mellifluous voice in my ear, his delicate touch.

—What happened, stupid?

—I ...remembered. He wraps self in bed sheets. Meets my gaze and clarifies: our problems. Him, my erasure...

—I remember too, you know. No one chasing you, by the way. You decided to go back. I remember the dark bits all the time. I didn't forgive you, you know? But I want to live. We have the love, it's a certainty, why squander it? I want to conquer all obstacles and have this unbelievable feeling forever. Don't want to let it go. I am a fighter, not a loser.

I continue, sitting up wrapped in bed sheets like a toga:

If winning was easy, if anything was easy, anyone would do it. Then what would be the point? It's meant to be hard, for the good to rise on top. Victory is hard and bittersweet and also fucking spectacular. I know how being a loser feels like. Now I want to know winning!

—Yes, win. Don't you think it's time for us to concentrate on our respective battles? Our "love experiment" failed. We each go home, fight our fights alone.

—But you are my battle, I say, painfully.

He grabs my hand, looks mournfully through the wall. The child feels. He's stubborn.

Then we talk about gods. He says I should be a cult leader. I say that's for idiots. I say science is the new kind of religion.

—I have a theory, wanna hear it?
Yeah, he whispers softly, not so interested.
—I think the brain is more complex than the lucid mind can grasp. The use of drugs has a sacred quality; natural and not, booze and love included—the best drugs, in fact; it's the ritualistic joy of diving into your lower layers of consciousness where you can shake off lies imposed to the self, and rejoice with the subconscious of your peers. This meeting of subconscious matter is divine. This is probably how the notion of divine must have first occurred to the cleverer monkeys. I am sure that's how your monkey brain expands and looks at the Cosmos with the intention to grasp; and you can't, because your brain doesn't support it, so you imagine. And out of the first metaphysical efforts of imagination came the idea of God and Gods. A silly, rudimentary idea from our vantage point. But a beautiful thought at the time. Prehistoric cave dwellers with the revelation to share must have made a killing at the tribe gathering over fire. They received privilege and resources, sacrifice and status, and called themselves messengers of God—the priests. To the Neanderthal mind, this must have been as metaphysical and avant-garde as Einstein to the 20th century. They were illustrious leaders, those who, using the metaphor of an imaginary omnipotent anthropomorphic existence–i.e., God/Gods, gave in fact form to the idea of the unknown beyond our perception. They were seeing into the future. They were subconsciously guessing that's the future of the species. We will become gods.

And that includes leaving death behind, the main condition of godliness.

They were daring and innovative and I guess, primitive religions must have also been fun. For all we know they celebrated sex, rather than shame it. They used mind expanding substances, experiences of all kinds, to transcend, and to live outside the banal. They did not worship an anthropomorphic man in the universe;

they worshipped their future, the fact that their evolving brain was curious about the skies, the universe; set to conquer all; an exciting cosmic adventure started then. What we now entrust with the likes of Stephen Hawking. People we worship with muted 21st century jadedness on TV.

When did all that splendiferous religion go downhill? It did with monotheism. Religion to early settlements, like fossil fuel to us industrial and post-industrial societies, was a survival and civilizational tool. That's what humans do, they use tools. The problem to early people several thousand years ago was scarcity of population. Although smarter than animals around them they started to exploit in farming, their condition was still frail. They were still in small numbers and at the mercy of elements. Hymns and poems were told about tragedies they did not understand nor control. Lo and behold! then, a small tribe—the Yazidis?—comes along, tells the beautiful story of human enslavement through agriculture, in metaphorical terms, as an intelligence unequal to its goal does when it lacks a scientific/exact set of concepts. They told the story of creation. The story of the Garden of Eden: man domesticates wheat, which is given to him by a snake god. Which later turned to something completely different, a cautionary tale against knowledge: the Old Testament lifts this story from Yazidis, and the wheat becomes forbidden apple of knowledge. The serpent God becomes evil. Religion no longer fun, it's now a matrix of mind control. But the discovery of agriculture did solve the problem of food scarcity, and nomadism—settled, humans now have an identity, History begins. The invention of agriculture was immortalized in this proto-Bible.

The most beautiful story of monkey turned city dweller. The story of how civilization came along. How you, sordid hairy homo sapiens of the cave, left behind your spear and built a hut to grow grains and have loads of children. Children that live. That story, my friend with benefits, is the story of everything.

But those first people? Their tales, their Gods?

They saw into the future, inventing those Gods that personify things that are natural for a big brain to dream of, to defeat limits of their station.

The first humans guessed we will become those Gods. We will. It's where we're headed. That should be the new religion.

Is this the cult you mean? Then yes. I'll be the cult leader.

I finish my speech waving arms wrapped in a bed-sheet toga; waiting to have dazzled, and I... meet his slightly bored gaze instead.

He says stuff I've heard a ton of times before, that dinosaurs could have ruled the world. Humans won't become gods, they'll likely perish, likely soon; their dominance an accident. I cringe internally but outwardly:

—No, dinosaurs couldn't. They had size, but no tools. It was an evolutionary dead end; evolution tested size as an evolutionary advantage and it led nowhere. Size doesn't really offer supremacy. Neither does flight alone, that's why their successors—birds, never became dominant. Smart, agile, but not smart enough.

—Yeah, but they could, though—Pretty Face objects—because they fly, etc. They can grasp things.

—No, genius. The birds did solve the problem of distance and navigation. They are evolution figuring out **that** *problem, for us to emulate consciously with our technology. All science does is consciously reproduce stuff evolution solved through slow trial and error in a six-billion-year-spanning scientific test, to solve various problems life forms have, that makes them less successful. That's the purpose of birds.*

That, and chicken soup.

They could never be dominant.

To be dominant on planet earth you need to have this height, to be a biped and have this size and a large brain.

And capacity to process food so you don't spend all your time grazing so you devote more time to the next level of problem-solving, that makes you more sophisticated, and in constant progress.

He goes quiet, a bit overwhelmed. Suddenly his body mass seems less imposing. Rotund muscles seem to merge together in a puddle by the bed's headboard, under a golden haystack of hair.

—Look Daniel, the path of humans is to become Gods. And they will. Isn't that Zarathustra's prophecy about the Superhuman? Nietzsche gazed right into that abyss, he had the correct intuition.

That's what all this is. In the childhood of humanity, those people had this intuition but they knew not exactly what it meant. Greek Gods were Marvel heroes. Technology shows it's going that way. But most people will be slaves, serving those Gods. A chosen few will become gods merely by virtue of solving the problems of physical vulnerability and time that makes them mortal. We already have some superpowers that make us look like Gods to ancestors. But the big thing is mortality.

He stays quiet, mulling. Curls bounce over his rosy lip, bitten hard in mounting sense of frustrated confusion.

I step towards the door: Look, I am disappointed in your pathetic contributions. I am going to write down this insight. You stay here, mull your tepid philosophical problems, yeah?

—Ha, ha, I love you, baby. I really do. You're wonderful. And he appears cheerful, watching my legs as I drag the silk of my kimono down the corridors."

PART FOUR

ERIS IN SIRIUS

CHAPTER XII

So that's when they announced the coming of the vaccine; that sounded to people like the second coming of Christ. A whole nation, whole peoples sighed a deep diabetic sigh of relief: see? They never needed to give up their double-decker cheeseburger with triple fried fries, and the caramel ice-cream bucket. It can be solved with a magic pill, from the angelic pharmaceutical industry, who always has our best interests at heart! And with childlike docility, the public reached their hands to pray for the vaccine.

Meanwhile people who dared to say online that perhaps the data of the pandemic shows a correlation between a thick waist and fatal or long lasting complications from corona-virus, were expunged from public opinion, expunged from their jobs, expunged from life. And these monolithic publicity panels were erected in town centers, with size 16 or 20 models in skimpy clothes trying to preach at lowly ant people in its shadow this is the new healthy; the new beautiful. That excess is good; that decadence is by no means correlated with ill health and a tired mind and body. That if you happen to develop ill health and a sad mind, it is to be fixed with more shopping, more food, more pills, more, MORE. It was like a new religion, where up was down, and left was right; a religion of excess, people victims of their own evolutionary success.

The two lovers left Dahut in opposite directions, opposite to the extreme magnetic forces that drew them together. Two arrows on the map shooting outwardly from their love nest. Took silly superhuman determination. Rational minds fighting every cell in their body, a fight meant to fail and hurt.

Both convinced the other betrayed them. Both with devastation yet hope in their hearts. The house remained locked like a museum of love. Their love had impregnated the wood; their ghosts entangled, left to dance on the halls of Albion cottage forever on a parallel timeline.

There is so much unacknowledged beauty in the world; so much inconsolable suffering. So many people who need to hear they are beautiful, they're appreciated; whose silent struggle supports the world, like bricks in a castle. Their lives a dignified sacrifice.

Like the beauty in the face of a lavender farmer in Provence, smiling at the sun and passers-by, with quiet appreciation of life's hard-won gifts. All serene, the wisdom of romantic poets naturally inhabiting the brown of her eyes:

> *"Time will come and time will go,*
> *All is old and all is new,*
> *What is great and what is low*
> *Ask yourself and think it through;*
> *Desire not and have no fear,*
> *Things which are like waves will pass;*
> *If they rush you, if they call you near*
> *You remain as cold as glass."*

There is so much unacknowledged beauty and suffering, like the nurse whispering soothing "last rites" to the dying patient, in the night; an angel. A voice from Heavens, taking on the suffering before her night after night, releasing the poor soul into the abyss, in a furtive hand hold.

And many of these souls dropped into the abyss every day, with body parts devoured by the virus that no one understood.

Industrial scale murder of humans by the microscopic creature. Outsmarted for once, in this age of supreme intelligence everywhere. Industrial killings. And for most people, it was just statistics communicated on evening news by a lady with good hair and very white teeth. People die all the time. No one cares. You have to make sure you live, running on the cold streets from the big hairy virus chasing you with knives in its octopus hands.

Likewise, hearts break all the time. It's a whole industrial process out there. One could imagine huge hangars of broken hearts like defective steel mechanisms just coldly loaded by crane into a crusher. Nobody cares. All these dead loves. Who cares. People bleed and stop breathing. Just statistics.

Hearts, lives, beauty, sacrifice, light, all crushed by the Giant Car Crusher of Time. Made into an amorphous paste that is oil fuel for the next unfortunates of the next cycle. And so on.

When Eris drove back into Belmont, the world was different. It was no longer a lockdown with happy quips about the quirks of Zoom life; how everyone's life became a tiny TV broadcast with makeshift set design; the excitement of seeing inside the abodes of rich people as they were imparting important TV opinions from home. This was all small change compared to the rising problems. It turned severe. It was no longer through hearsay that people knew of the Covid. No, this was a world ravaged. Streets looked putrid. No signs of life. Broken shop lights hanging in disarray. Malls, abandoned.

Gaunt figures wandering the streets, avoided each other.

It was eerie, but the landscape outside matched that in her soul.

Sometimes, large men and women who barely breathed, dragged their feet along the pavement, pained. Blood dripping from their lungs and guts into the mask. Why were they out?! The mandate to stay in hadn't permeated through these poor ailing souls. Almost like they were beyond any mandate, any human attempt to reach them.

One was slowly going down a slope street in his mobility scooter as if by mere inertia. His void eyes, gray skin frightened Eris who had slowed down. He noticed her, so he tried to angle his vehicle towards the Tesla. In a split second, others like him came towards her car, surrounding her. On foot, on scooters. They all had gray skin, but she could only see their eyes; and there was nothing there. They seemed to see something in her. It's like she gazed back into something primal, a reduction of humanity to the most feral. Competitive clock mechanism instead of a heart like a broken software running on empty and awry.

As they surrounded the car, her engine stopped. She couldn't start, so she started screaming. It's what the beasts wanted. They started to bang the windows, to ask for something. What?! What were they asking for? What did they want?

Why did they bang pots and pans?? Why did they pick on her?

Finally the engine started. The creatures jumped off her path, frightened. She was breathing like a marathon runner, eyes frozen ahead. This was no longer her town.

"Finally, an apocalypse; finally, something bad enough to take my mind off Daniel".

Even as she drove straight through every red light like any notion of traffic police waned, irrelevant in this landscape—she clasped her necklace. The ridges of the pearls and ruby stones brought her back to the sights and scents of paradise behind her. Which she quickly shook off her head, as she was going back. Back to her

life, her... broken marriage. Her house. Back to reality.
How disappointing, reality.

Interesting, every corner and nook of her Belmont
residence had a gilded nest to the best years of her
life. But it all seemed alien now, as she clasped the
door knob to her flat... stepped through creaky flo
ors... walked into her rooms to find an eerie air, like
she walked into a freshly unearthed pyramid tomb.
Ancient history smelled stale.

—Stan?

Walks twice.

—Stan?? ... Napoleon? She realized there was no
one in. The pet not in his cage.

Strutting through rooms searching for signs of life,
she heard a rustle in the kitchen. Puts her head
through. Napoleon—her late aunt's hamster—on the
table, with a big load of food in his cheek pouches.
Frozen in fear—he also heard her. The little man
was in the midst of a transport to his "galleries", like
hamsters do in the wild. As Eris approached, he froze,
trembling. He never recognized anyone as an "owner",
he just wanted to be free. But under the kitchen sink,
there was a nest made of colored paper and plastics
the little man had fashioned into a bed. A round straw
Chianti cover he chewed off a bottle was the nest's
centrepiece, decorations all round. She was astound-
ed, moved, but also sad: she'd have to be the agent of
the little man's incarceration after so much fun.

He knew this too. As he stood there frozen with
loaded pouch, fear showing in his cute features; he
knew the presence of the very large, other hamster
meant he needs to go back in the cage. And that just
made him ... well, hardcore depressed. Jailed.

Eris took him back in with love and promised to
self she'll get him a larger cage; but really, what the
poor soul needed was freedom. And where to let him
out, in this landscape? Certain death outside, certain
misery inside.

The predicament bondage of domestication. You're no longer fit to roam free with the wolves, not quite yet adapted to this apartment cage business.

—Know where he is, Abe? I need to talk to him.

—Mah dear, I don't know... he calls me with updates of his running routes, he...

—Yes???

—... sounds a bit mad, really. I worry for him a bit.

—I don't know what to do. We should get ready for Hanukkah, I am back home... I wanted to end it with him, but...

—But?

—But Daniel sort of dumped me, without dumping me. And here..., Eris cried.

—Meaning...?

—Meaning, Abe... he left back to his missus. No plans together, no future, nothing. It was left at "we'll see". Well, I can't cope with that!

—Babes... you have to do things honourably. I kind of understand your boy. You need to truly part ways with one if you want to be with the other. It seems like you juggled to keep both.

—And he hasn't?? No move to formally split from her. No move out of that stupid flat. Nothing. I am the mistress he kept to play with while always plotting to go back to the respectable wife. He's spending Christmas with her!! Me, the mistress. Her, the respectable wife!! I am losing my mind.

—Well, she has been there for him for a long time.

—Then what does he want from me?

—You two are the same. Trauma bond.

By now, Eris was a crying mess. Stuff ahead needed planning and there needed to be a rescue mission for Stan the missing. But she could no longer function. Not even the greatest crisis of her life, of her century—the Covid pandemic, wasn't enough to plug her back into this reality. This, here, in Belmont. Her mind was tuned to the rosy evenings of dream and wonder that bewildered her mind with maths and physics she didn't understand, and circumvented around her Ice Queen defences to degrade her to the lowest, simplest and yet happiest reality of life: childish abandon in the arms of an adoring lover. A sweet, tall lover, with beautifully formed shapes.

⸻ ❧❧ ⸻

Walking back from the train station, with his backpack, spring in his step no matter how heavy his heart. He was impassable, Daniel, and not even this blow lead him to despair. He was already working out that evening's menu, his route via the supermarket, his choice of wine.

Maybe that is exactly how he processed heart break. Get lost in the exact mire of organized tedium that his life had to be, to keep him stable and satisfied. Heartbreak—something debatable, abstract; but satisfaction? That was real and paramount.

Apprehensive, he touched the door knob. Something sounded like danger. When he walked in, he knew why. Smoke came from the back garden. And his whiskey collection finished, bottles thrown around the place; the goth girl turned domestic who had made it her life's mission to be a housewife to a German scientist had left the place like it'd been hit by Hurricane Katrina.

He walks slowly and carefully towards the back garden dropping his things with typical care, each in the correct spot.

In the midst of skeletal unkempt bushes and trees, in front of the fire, Julianah stood with a large bottle of bourbon she drank from. She was wearing a white short wedding dress, long train sweeping the yard. As if to celebrate. She had white plastic flowers in her hair. But when she turned his face to front him, her makeup had dribbled down her chins again, and she looked positively irate, ready to burst. He was afraid.

In the fire, it was his clothes that were burning. It took all his Teutonic self control to stay put.

She saw him. A primal rage shot though her. So she smashed her bottle against the nearest tree, then proceeded to walk at him with the broken remains in her bleeding fist. The jilted bride to be was living her moment. This was it, the revenge against her parents, every judge on every show that had shunned her act, the world; her revenge against stupid beauty ideals that said you have to be fit to be attractive; against any idea that hard work and ambition are the key to success. Any idea that personal responsibility is somehow relevant. Against any idea.

This was her moment of revenge. She shone, and she walked in both utter loss of composure as well as the dignity of a victim finally taking a stand. History spoke through her.

He drew small steps back; but he didn't think she'd do anything yet. "This is the woman I trust with my life!"—he remembered shouting at Eris day before he left; the memory torturing his ear like tinnitus. He remembered Eris warning him, in her usual confident sarcastic tone he sometimes took as a personal affront: "Look, I can sense, I can guess—call it female intuition, though it isn't; it is just observing, and thinking, and pattern identification; please be careful; she will do something against me, against us. I need you to defend me from her. Keep her from doing us harm". He saw the film of that last Dahut afternoon, now hovering like a golden painting in his scaredy head, playing in both slow motion then sped up within nano-seconds; he had left the room, uttering words of loyal defence for the woman he had held in high regard for ages, merely for the merit of physical proximity. He heard himself slamming the door on Eris, in the same moments he watched Julianah's bleeding angry face walk at him with glass shards; violence in its raw form threatening to end every film playing in his head ever again.

"She would die for me!!!". He remembered himself shouting over the sound of slammed doors in Albion cottage; as Julianah walked in Johnnyville, ready to off him with his disused Jack Daniels bottle. Had time to notice the other sad Jacks lying in the grass.

Before he had time to calculate his moves, she struck him hard with the broken bottle. Luckily it just touched by his arm as he ducked with the agility of a football player; still it opened a gashing wound; and Daniel the athlete, stopped her hand and removed the weapon from her hands. Then she fainted in the tall grass. Unconscious, portly and bloodied in her wedding dress; game over. This round.

So tragedy truly had begun.

This silent, book mad, shy polite man of science wasn't equipped to deal with this. He stood there, kneeling, among the ruins of his life. He couldn't comprehend. How was this possible. How did it get so bad.

Mysteriously decided to text the woman he loved: "what a mistake coming here".

But decided to not give more detail.

What, the pandemic?! That was nothing compared to his bleeding arm, which he had to handle himself as no ambulance would turn up to his doorstep in Covid times unless he could prove the wound had Covid.

Covid had nothing on the fact his life had just become a horror movie. And he had no one he could call for advice. The one person he loved in the world, he wanted to stay mad with, for she had betrayed him. As he had so firmly convinced himself in insomniac nights, wrapped in check blankets chez Eris' love cottage.

So he decided to suffer alone.

He also decided to forgive.

To forgive Julianah for slashing his shapely triceps and trying to kill him; not Eris—she had cruelly forsaken him in visiting her ailing husband for an absent minded visit. To Daniel, this rage was what real passion looked like.

He couldn't admit to himself, but its theatre pumped drama into a bland academic life.

Hence in the coming days, and up to Christmas, he nurtured his fiancée back to life. He gently held her head over the toilet as she vomited her way through the hangover. He spoon fed her depression medication. He cooked for her. Bought her Christmas decorations, set up a Christmas tree. Presents, toys. Baked his German grandma's cookies. He was now, not just her Prince Charming, white knight and prisoner; but her Santa Claus and mother too. He was grateful; she was too. He called her Liddel once more.

He switched his phone off to not have to talk to Eris.

He said to himself, now he's home. This home never betrayed him. She didn't try to kill him—she was "putting anger into the knife"; it was all understandable, she was hurt, poor thing. Abandoned for months. She did it for love. She did it because she really loved him.

His own forgiveness made him proud.

Look how much she loves him; doesn't even go anywhere to see any other man, because there isn't any. In a twisted way, he saw Julianah's violent meltdown as a courageous proof of love; fear turned into respect. He felt important, even flattered, to generate such strong reaction in the diminutive woman. He lived off the dopamine for days.

And as days progressed, and Julianah regressed back into her obedient wife role, attention fully on him... he started to remember what great times he had had with her. Not because he was exhilarated by her. But because how her attention and care made him feel the absolute unquestioned center of the universe, and she knew when to go quiet, so he wouldn't need to interrupt his academic endeavors. His football watching either. She had been properly trained in the art of being Daniel's silent sidekick over a slow fruitful decade. With her, he didn't feel challenged; no more difficult conversation. No more having to be witty and sparkly on command.

And never, ever, having to impress. No more feeling inferior or asking self incessantly, "am I being desired for my body? Am I a toy boy? Will she abandon me?"; no: with Julianah—he was the scintillating brain and provider of the home, a sort of mythical God of everything. She would never leave him. She would rather die than do. How deeply nourishing.

No more challenging post-coital conversation in bed. There was no coitus. There was no conversation.

Ah, he could relax. Now he could use the events of his return night to put her further into her place. Which she did: she apologized, mentally on her knees. She felt genuine remorse, for in her life was so kind as to return. So she bled tears of remorse, saying she didn't know what possessed her. They were slipping back into themselves as a couple.

They slipped back into bed. She once more put her tiny hand on his buttocks, and they fell asleep in a hug.

Not quite the extreme passion of Eris' hug, and it suddenly felt different to feel his girlfriend's voluptuous forms into him like a warm duvet as opposed to the energetic outlines of Eris' athletic body. But if felt refreshingly cuddly. More "huggy bear", less Ice Queen Bitch of impossibly high standards; a cosy home. And he liked the absence of love drama and high temperatures, and this little nest reminded him of many years of success on his path as an MIT scientist. It was a hard path, and he had to work hard, and much of that would have not been possible had there not been a loyal woman behind the man. Who swallowed her own ambitions in order to mold herself into the perfect shadow for the career man. It was a marriage made in patriarchy heaven. Which is weird, because it started as the opposite... but nature found its path, worked its way. Nature does.

While ignoring the torrid aching messages of love coming from ignored Eris on his WhatsApp, he fell asleep in relative comfort and peace.

But, alas. It wasn't that simple. Nightmares woke him up at night. And he had to stroll all the way to the sitting room, to find himself, in solitude. Wrapped in a blanket looking at the ceiling.

He was haunted. And because he had resolved to tell himself Eris was just a bad woman he didn't need... he couldn't quite work out the source of the haunting misery. His repression mechanisms were generating errors, and his scientist mind too dissociated from realities of the soul to gather; he liked to write off emotional realities as unimportant, not as important as the secrets of the universe he had made the subject of so many a successful research grant. It was easy in the world of grants and research, robotically easy. In matters of the heart, it was not just complicated, but distasteful; it didn't align with his vision of his noble self. Floating above human weakness and "emotions". So he had to dismiss everything that didn't align. Like the Eris affair.

Mind going in circles night after night. Until it was Christmas eve, and he even spent the night on the sofa in the living room, in the pulsating light of the Christmas lights, finally admitting to self he truly loved Eris and the girl in bed next room felt remote and toxic to him.

I mean, how many times did she take out the knife on him now? How long until she actually did it... kill him? A rare occurrence of his survival instinct finally piercing through the sophisticated scaffold of interdependent duty, juxtaposed with terrible fear of abandoning anyone, even someone as violent as that; fear of being abandoned. A rare burst of truth from a more animal sector of the Doctor in Sciences, finally gnawing through self imposed layers of deception and notions of self sacrifice combined with levels of traditional male calculations of benefit. A rare glimpse of light. Kept him up all night long. His furrowed unibrow and his bitten lips proof.

The invigorating instincts of survival. They had the bad habit of being exhausting, urgent and scary, as opposed to the cosy nesting lies of numb domestication and dulled sense of low expectations, lulled into a mental torpor not unlike that of sheep placidly grazing on the pastures of their butcher.

But by now, on Christmas eve, it was Eris who stopped responding to him. Tired of being ignored, she blocked him.

Not without sending a long winded letter where she explained she needs to take a break, to regain composure. She liked letters in Word format, sent as an attachment in WhatsApp.

He fell asleep crying on the floor. Had he made a mistake? Had he chosen wrongly again. Out of fear?

"She posted another selfie, the scrawny bitch; what do you even see in her?!"—Julianah's voice came through the afternoon, waking him up from day dreaming while doing a bit of home office. When Julianah was found going through his laptop and phones again, to make snarky comments about Eris' social media posts... Daniel felt trapped.

His little nest built over many years as a proud academic suddenly felt like a chintz prison.

Once, he looked at her dolls, lined up on the sofa. They stared at him. He shuddered. "Why am I here?" He looked at Julianah. Her submissive smile, that used to feel cosy, the best home he'd ever had, suddenly felt deranged, threatening.

His cold-sweats followed him everywhere.

It was a true horror movie. And the damn scar on his arm wouldn't heal. It just didn't want to heal. It was weird. Every day it bled. Every day he looked in the mirror, trying to search. Find, what he was. Was he the white knight that Eris said? A guy whose identity addicted to saving the damsel in distress? Was she right? Slight regret at how he'd always dismiss her observations, always bitch back every time she tried to play Dr. Freud with his pretty head. Digging through his brain with her insensitive remarks... who did she think she was?!

Maybe she was correct; maybe he was weak. He definitely didn't understand himself. What was he even doing here?! Why was he here against his heart? So much of his life he told himself he was defined by his courage. Where was his courage now? Was it the courage to fight for something great, or was it the courage of withstanding endless bad?

Anyway, he guessed it was a bit too late now. So he didn't do anything. And you can't do anything on Christmas anyway.

Eris saw herself become a Queen on the Chess board of their relationship again. It was a lonely and dark chess board but she felt the thrill of the fight. She couldn't even see what, who she was fighting for. Except it was now clear the pieces changed meaning. She said, "it is my turn to do a move; I must move"—and this thought chased her every day. She loved, and she wanted to be with her love. Obstacles, problems, unanswered questions paled in comparison to the power of the emotions felt together; she left behind a space of wonder and she wanted to do anything to get it back.

Most people imagine paradise in Instagram pics, or dream a five-day vacation in Italy is it; or their retirement; or the lost glory of their childhood. Everyone has an image, which either powers them to go forward, chase a carrot or a chimera; spin endlessly in a hamster wheel; or wilts them slowly with the unhealthy conviction that paradise is a lost point in the past, sealed in the black hole of Time. While life propels them away from it.

But she had a vivid image of paradise, she lived it. Was within reach. It was the sweet cohabitation with the autistic words of a childish German Adonis who, in a chemical reaction with her, created magic, constant magic, on tap, by mere proximity. Simple life things like breakfast and walking to the supermarket together—the only place they could go together in the late days of the second lockdown—were somehow intense, life-changing, world-stopping experiences; full of surreal fun. Just seeing his face across the shelves was exciting. Seeing him pick pears in his mask, blond hair framing his wide eyes, anime pair of eyes powering animatronic head moves; so alive, so full of emotion, so weird in the way he shows love. The way she'd poke him to talk about science, only to be left befuddled that she doesn't get much when he explains about uranium and electrons.

His image reading machine learning books, half naked on her baroque sofa, gold hair curling down, Adonis body calling like a siren, mind elsewhere. Did he even know the signals he was emitting?

Those were days of paradise, and she now knew it existed; so it was just a matter of getting it back. Thinking of those days felt like atrocious punishment, now he left. And she wanted to hate him for leaving, but it was hard.

When she walked into the communal garden of her building, on the overcast late December day of her return, her resolve got slightly dented by the view before her. Stan, emaciated, in a wheelchair, sitting, enjoying the fresh air.

Her heart sank cutting through her guts, she went through her pillbox for a calming pill. Guilt, agony. Despair. Hate, love, all at once. A life that's always had challenges was taking her next level. She wanted to run away from this.

Stan turned around in his wheelchair. He saw her. His eyes lit up in superhuman joy. It's like he had seen her inside himself all this time and was now seeing her externally too.

—My angel!! You are a bunny angel, and you have returned!

And his hands held a little winter rose, he had ready for her. By the look of the garden, he had picked one every day waiting for her. Approaching in his wheel-chair, he reached out to her, pushed the floor with help-less limbs.

He smelled of tears. His weight loss was incredible.

Eris was taken aback. She touched her abdomen, then wavered. Then reached forward and held him, just to save him falling. He was overjoyed. He cried with joy. The flower dropped and they stepped on it.

—Why are you in this chair?! What happened?

—I don't know... I fell one night and they put me here. I was running a lot. I ran for you, to get you back. To demonstrate I am young and pretty for you. You see? Like you want me. But you are back. You love me after all. You are my angel.. he was sobbing. His kippah was down the side of his neck.

Eris pushed the chair back up in the lift. He stood by the staircase and dragged himself up, his legs frail. Everything, frail.

They went back into her home and that's where Eris knew she had to be the butcher and she hated the feeling.

Stan was overjoyed she came back. He wanted to hug her all the time.

Air by Bach seemed appropriate, though not quite sad enough. But she had time to parse through her playlist now.

God, it was hard. She fell asleep on the sofa. It was like a nightmare. The world outside, the shattered glass inside. And you couldn't set your foot anywhere, be-cause it'd set sirens of wailing agony, souls hurting left and right. Her, the unlikely agent of pain and Decider. She didn't like this. Selfish hellish screams inside told her to fuck off and think of herself. She'd always lived life on easy mode in a sort of cheerful selfishness; but now it was adult time. Voice of duty kept her trapped in a binary of hell. What on earth to do with this weird unwanted power in her hands? A lose lose situation.

—Stan.

—Yes, baby bunny? His blue eyes lit smiling. Mismatched tweed clothes too big now flung on his tall frame like old blankets.

—Look. We'll spend Christmas together.

Stan's faith rebelled in a swift arch of the brows unleashing round moist eyes. But bunny...

—Yes, bunny, shmunny. I grew up with Christmas. We have done what you wanted all these years. I changed my life too much for you. Hanukkah, not this year. This year I celebrate Christmas. I miss my happy childhood space-time.

Stan looked crushed but lacked energy to oppose.

—I guess I should be grateful you're here, at least. He muttered. Your presence, that's what matters.

He clung to the crumbs falling in his lap off the Daniel table, with saintly gratitude.

—Oh, and bunny? Thanks for taking care of me. I know it's hard. Thank you. Eris tried to smile but the corners of her mouth ended downwards. "Yeah. Hmprf. Welcome"—only grunts came out.

<hr />

The table was set with scintillating Christmas decorations, a music box playing quaint Christmas carols. Red globes burnt everywhere with passion. The fir tree smelled magical, the candles burnt slowly and the whole Belmont flat was a picture of the cosiest American Christmas straight from the mythical 50s.

Foods and presents and sparkly things all over the place. Eris wore a red silk velvet dress, with a single large geometric sleeve; red rubies hanging in a chandelier waterfall off her earlobes; but most importantly, her fingers always went to caress the seed-pearl-framed emoji gold pendant.

Eris' mother, Ms Clemens Senior, was throning over the festive table. Quietly enjoying her daughter's bubble of success, even more quiet about the complicated love life that clouded her. She was well skilled in reserving her objections for one to one coffee chats.

Eris set the plates: one, two, three. Large Wedgwood porcelain. There was barely any room for cutlery among the many dishes, pheasant, roasted quince, Panettone, Cointreau, French eclairs flown in from La Durée in Paris. Turkey inside Romanian *sarmale* cabbage rolls to bridge two worlds.

It was a beautiful Christmas in lockdown. On a superficial view.

And then the guests sat for a pic. Stan awkwardly grabs the camera and photographs mother and daughter in a warm hug, over and around the decorations, the splendor. Wide smiles and warmth.

Eris ironically plays "Santa Go Home" by U.S. Girls, an anti consumerist anthem. No one appreciates her humor but they sip the wine.

Stan sits down. They all laugh, eat. Eris bit testy with Stan, who she interrupts often. Feels him a burden. He feels it and is broken but puts on his best face in the circumstances. They exchange quips like old friends. Callista feels a tad left out.

Not even finishing her plate, Eris walks back into her bedroom. She checks the phone, leaning exhausted against the door. Nothing. She sends another sad emoji.

Chat looked like a one sided list of all the sad emojis.

She leaves the bedroom, empty... when... a ping. She looks, in her rush, the phone drops. She crouches, and there on the floor, she sees his message. From him. The Daniel. He got the presents she sent. Melting into the floor on the cold corridor, in her elegant dress, she watches the video he's sent. Unwrapping the presents. He's got her Kintsugi crystal heart in his palm. A heart made of pink crystal, broken and fixed together with gold paste—symbolic craft from the masters of symbolic arts and crafts and all things hipster, and Daniel's favorite country: Japan. "Kintsugi, to fix pottery with gold—the golden strings add to the character, history of the object, which becomes better for having been broken and fixed". What a concept. What depth. He says. "You always have such excellent taste". She tries to fix a broken heart so he can put it on his desk and lie to Julianah it's not a gift from Eris, so she won't slam it against the wall. And then other gifts. Trinkets and things. A fanciful bow-tie. He gushes on camera.

Is this some kind of reconciliation?

So, of course, Eris runs away in the guts of the house and calls him, leaving the other guests alone to awkwardly make chat at the Christmas table, pushing cake round their plates with a silver fork. Her mother not a fan of Stan's direct, no-bullshit ways. She was more on the Daniel team: the fifty shades of bullshit.

December 25, 2020, Eris logged this into her diary. It obviously hadn't been a very fruitful video call:

"I love a Greek statue. Literally and metaphorically a statue. In beauty and in being an inert block of stone. A block of stone haunted by feelings which cannot move him physically in the 3D world, so he's condemned to feel them stationarily."

Eris liked to upload her nice pictures to social media; she'd always been a bit of a show-off. She loved the spotlight. Got used to being admired. If she could move with a stage-light at a flattering angle anywhere she went, she would. What is the point of having a picture perfect life if you don't show it off? If a tree falls in the forest and no one is around to hear it, has it even lived and loved?! What exactly is wrong with documenting your life, at its best? Renaissance merchants and popes did it, it just took longer to paint a church wall than snapping a phone selfie. The Dutch bourgeoisie had painters create masterpieces showing off their pheasant too. And they're hanging in museums worldwide, people gasping in cultural admiration. But when Eris does it, it's "that self-absorbed narcissist"!—words of her critics reverberating in her skull, lately.

"But, Daniel, it's not really narcissistic if you also have other interests and care about the world at large; it's only a problem if that's all you do". She explained to the Daniel in her head—he was somehow part of this chorus of negative feedback floating in the air. She just felt it. Paranoia? Could be. Ancient mental demons came flooding back in this heavy crisis, so she wasn't sure what in her circular thoughts was paranoia, and what truth. People eagerly throwing digital manure at others' display of joy online was a real thing, anyway.

With nonchalant grace and her pianist-like fingers, she uploads the beautiful portrait of her dining with her mother—over the nice festive arrangements. At the other end of the world, Daniel, who was following her every social media post more than he read her texts to him, saw it instantly.

Daniel was an astute man. Very observant. His eyes would take in tons of detail much faster than your average person. He liked to observe often like a fly on the wall, and mistrusted everyone, so that this kind of meta intake of information far more precious to him than any information given to him directly by people in his life. "She's saying this—but why is she saying it? What does she really mean?".

At first he saw a beautiful photo of the woman he loved and her also beautiful mother. He smiled. He was proud. Then, he counted the plates: one, two, three. Three. THREE.

Waves of electric currents passed up and down his face while his jaw made a few clicking noises. Then his teeth started to screech.

The phone dropped. Julianah—always nearby, on standby—gasped:

—What's going on?!

The last thing the busy man of science wanted to deal with now was the hysterics of his sort-of-ex-partner-not-quite.

His Christmas was officially ruined. He was lonely. He went out in the cold, put his hat on: had plans of a long walk. But then he remembered and went back to withdraw his phone from the floor he's dropped it on. Just in time as Julianah was slowly shifting position in the room towards it herself. His hand intersected hers under the table. His eyes rolled with silent anger.

And he went out in the cold.

* * *

It was Execution Day, 27th of December 2020.

People's Christmas celebrations had been nuked. Most people not allowed to travel, sitting obediently at home and only seeing their family in bad Zoom calls with audio failing and cats and dogs and kids flying in view, interrupting or knocking down the computer.

Eris grabbed Stan by the elbow and took him out for a walk. His attempts to hug her every five minutes had been hard to fight; a hard fight with someone you don't want to injure too much, but also slap over the head with a rolled newspaper.

—You know, bunny, I am really glad you invited me here for Christmas with your mom. I think it was really good for us. We should plan more of these things, to re-find each other.

Eris stops and looks ahead, bewildered.

—Stan... I don't want to be a cruel psychopath but... didn't I say I am not sure about our future? Haven't I said repeatedly that it's not working, my heart isn't in it any-more?

I am sorry, I know this hurts. I even said it would be the same even had Daniel not been in my life.

She pats his back, she feels compassion. But she goes on:

—I regard you as very important, you are like family to me. But the heart wants what the heart wants. I am still young, and I don't have those feelings towards you. Anymore. She looks away, she takes a deep breath. She knocks pebbles on the road.

—What feelings? He answers, tortured. He looks gaunt but still quite a good looking man, with very youthful eyes. He combs his unkempt hair with his yellow comb, then uses it to gesticulate, like an orchestra conductor. I tried so hard to be better for you, I have entirely dedicated myself to it. Of course it's also helped by the pandemic, not much else to do in lockdown. But run and diet and work on my finances. I love you like no one else, I love you more than life.

Eris grabs her head with both her hands.

—Do you understand?? I know you do, it's noble, etc. I feel for you. But it takes two to tango. And I am very sorry; very, deeply sorry but I just don't feel the same way!! I don't!! Do you understand? I can't be your prisoner any-more. I care for you, deeply; but I have a duty to care for myself, and I want something else now.

Stan cries, loud harrowing sobs. His chest collapses, like a giant dejected kid.

Eris looks with compassion but she has to plunge the knife:

—Stan. I am sorry. I am filing for a divorce.

He stops in shock; he shouts the loudest "no". Repeats it. Cradles back and forth. "NO-NO-NO!!!". For him, life was over.

And she walked off, her posture hunched over, for the first time. Forehead wrinkled, jaw tight. It was a nightmare. As she walked home alone, the desolate winter streets reinforced further how she needs to get out, escape somehow; no clue where, but escape. At all costs.

CHAPTER XIII

Daniel was trying to enjoy a fruity cocktail when his heart fluttered as he heard the unmistakable text ping.

The cherry on the toothpick fell into the glass, splashing alcohol into his nose. There goes his dignified composure.

He took a deep breath. He knew it was her. Who else, on the third day of Christmas?

He wipes his nose.

His love. He liked to dream of her, being together one day, maybe even in a house with their other partners. But them at the center. He wanted her, but he couldn't cause more pain to his current flatmate. As proven, her pain would become his. Quite literally.

He thought he understood Eris, and himself; and Julianah too. The only person he didn't quite understand was his competition, the strange progressive rabbi who shared his taste in women.

But then, there were probably very few men who didn't, so not much in common. He thought Stan primitive and unworthy of a woman such as Eris. Daniel, a man of science, scoffed in contempt for what he perceived as a mindless religious man.

Not a suave, sophisticated gentleman and intellectual, like himself.

But he also held an unwavering confidence in his decisions and presented his victims with a unique combination of patient compassion for their rage at his own actions and yet, standing by the decision.

"I did it. I left him". Eris' text forms on the screen with dizzy letters.

Daniel's iris grew like a saucer plate. Then his otherwise very stolid heart grew a bit agitated.

Like it wasn't enough, new ping:

"I am filing for divorce".

His agitation turned to rage.

He typed without thinking—atypical of him:

"I am sorry to hear that. It must be difficult for you."

"That's... all you have to say?"—she replied right away.

"So? What do you want from me? You expect me to jump on your command?

As predicted.. I have to chose today because you chose today."

Immediately Eris irrupted in a string of furious messages.

She wanted a call. Daniel texted back:

"Sorry, I am with you know who. Can't exactly call."

"Isn't this important enough for you to move your ass and call while pretending to go out and buy olives or something?!"

"Not a good day to call. Too cold".

Eris broke down at the other end. But Daniel didn't waver.

He brought out the heavy artillery.

"Listen. You have some nerve. You spent Christmas with him. I saw the plates. The THREE PLATES! You broke it to me via public media that basically you went back together with him, that he's family, and did it on social media, so it is maximally painful. Sorry you broke up now but it doesn't make any sense. This is too much. Just don't expect me to jump now, after all you did."

"Excuse me?? What business have you who I invite over for Christmas, since you left? To be with her?"

"I left to **my house**. Remember what you did? I had to go somewhere, since I didn't feel safe with you. My house. Or did you want me to be homeless? Julianah happened to be here. You had to **invite** him over to spend Christmas together. He had to walk from his filthy flat across town and sit at your table. And now I have to go. Sorry. Someone you don't like prepared dinner." She types back in a state of shock.

"Can I come see you? Please. We need to talk."

"What? In Johnnyville? You want to kill Julianah?! What am I going to say? "yes, darling, you know that woman you hate, well, I am going to town to meet her"".

"...Kill... what? I want to talk to you, I want to clarify things. I want to be with you. You said you loved me. What is going on?!"

"Listen. You can't hold me to ransom."

"... Hold you to ransom?! Because I want to be with you?! You told me you want to be with me. I left my husband for you. This is the answer? You can't even call, because it would hurt her?! Remember when you told me she's your ex? Fine, then stay with her. But then... why tell me you want to be with me, all of 2020? Is this some farce? Am I on a prank show?!"

"I understand you are emotional today. I am there if you want to talk about your divorce pain."

"My divorce pain?! My pain is you. The way you react."

"So I can't do anything right. Anything I do, I type in this chat, is wrong. I will take a break, this is too hard for me."

He puts the phone away. He's offended.

After 45 minutes he thinks maybe he should say something to Eris, who keeps pouring messages of hurt he ignores.

"Yes, I went to spend Christmas with her after seeing what we had in Albion was a great time but it didn't feel like you wanted only me. I was a fling. The thought that I would spend some time on Christmas alone was a nightmare. The thought of what a monster of former partner I am while you take care of yours..."

He looks at Julianah. His head spinning for Eris, but the gravity of his life, the grounding force is here with him, at the table, serving him sausage. He says to self,

he is doing the right thing. What Eris did, unacceptable. What Julianah did... also a bit unacceptable. But
it's not like he is with her. He is with her, but not with
her. But at least not with Eris. Who he wants to be
with. But can't.

There are layers and layers in the brain; frequencies
and narratives of desire, sometimes conflicting, life of
their own. In an abstract way, on the firmament of his
soul—he longed for the magic carpet adventure with
Eris; it possessed his longing quarters of the mind,
the knots deep in his gut; but here, this 16 stone of
feminine abnegation before him, felt secure and vali-
dating on a deeper soul level. Anchoring his feet deep
into the ground. Julianah couldn't hold him to ransom.
She had nothing, and no Stan of her own. Julianah
wouldn't challenge him. Safety. The evening served
him sausage and safety. They fell asleep watching the
Disney channel inebriated on Jegermeister. Interrupted by her occasional burping, which he'd meet with
affectionate pats on her hunched back, automatically.

<hr />

When she left Stan in the park like that, it was agony
for her too. But she just felt it was the right thing to
do. Powered by love, the strong belief that despite
problems and betrayals, feeling so much love meant
she had to fight for it. She was almost religious in this
pursuit of Eros.

It was odd how much his image burnt in her like
a Christian icon—despite all the data looking grim,
and betrayals coming in periodically like clockwork.
Betrayals, mind games and gaslighting.

But now... it felt like once more, skies fell, earth
opened. She felt before she was pushing Stan off a
flying plane without a parachute and stood there to
hear the screams.

Now, she felt she had been pushed. And it was even hard to get a clear answer out of Daniel: what was it that he actually said. He never said it clearly. It took a team of psychoanalysts, doctors, agony aunts and others in her circle to constantly decipher the cryptic communications and gestures of Daniel. They were all tired.

But one thing was clear. She was now free. And he wasn't interested. And free fall started.

But first, she had to attend to her mother during the Covid-Sars holiday season. So she did. She made sure her mother had a marvellous winter season despite the limitations in going out and places to go. Why, online deliveries still worked, so they home delivered luxury and they had it all.

Daily walks in a quiet winter town; Belmont museum, from the outside only. Walking together uphill to the hospital, short of breath; meeting Cinco, who kissed her mother's hand but soon apologised and left.

After she put her mother on an empty train, back to the car, Eris had a mental breakdown.

And this time, her long-standing best buddy, the person who she always sought and found great emotional support in, was no longer accessible. Because she had left him. It felt strange. She always, always, had picked up the phone to ring Stan to discuss anything, seek advice. How could she seek advice and help on this matter? "Well, Stan... I left you for Daniel; and Daniel sort of said no. I mean, I am not sure what he said; can you advise?".

She felt stupid. Very stupid. Lonely in her big pathetic house full of nice things that are now useless and shallow.

Her diary read the next week:

"I am OK. Really. I have to weather this with courage. Enjoy every little last drop of pain. It is life. Bigger than us and what we want. Hijacking body parts for its goals, not ours. Discarding us like used toys when her goals done.

And I have to be strong and weather it."

—Well, there are things, hopeful things... like there is an experimental pill, ... Stan in typical fashion interrupts:

—What's it called?

—Not sure, Cinco thinks. I'll look and tell you. Funny thing by the way, the way these things work... apparently it is rendered ten times more potent by interaction with NAD. If one can find that now, just found it interesting.

—What is that? Stan impatient.

—Ah, just oxidized nicotinamide adenine dinucleotide. Stan explodes in laughter.

—"Just"?! Speak English, pal.

—Right—it's a coenzyme produced by the body, involved in anti-aging, anti-inflammation, that sort of thing...

—Ah-ah-ah, I know! Eris always goes on about how much of that her body makes, because of her fasting, I recall now. I guess you guys would have to buy it in pill form.

—Ah, Eris... well... suppose her blood makes a lot of these... hm.. "longevity" compounds, hmprf? Cinco suggests, chortling.

—What.. I am not following?

—Well, she's Romanian, isn't she?

Silence. Silence Cinco is determined to pierce with his punchline.

—Vampires??

—Ah. Original, pal. Yes. Never heard that one before. And by the way don't mention it to her, she doesn't take these clichés well—in fact she gets very irritated. She'll probably tell you they don't really have vampires in Romania and "Dracula" wasn't even written by a Romanian.

—Right, Stan, good to hear you're well. Keep me updated.

Cinco circles the table like a vulture. Abe just merged with the sofa in a cloud of alcohol vapors.

—Where's this magic cure? The vaccine? Is it here yet? No? Then, let's continue what we're doing. Cinco says. His thick-rimmed glasses tremble, his hands fumble.

—Doctor, you're tired, you don't think straight.

—Really? I was on the front line from the start. I think I know what I am doing.

—All I am saying, it's going to be over. With the vaccine arriving, it's going to be over. Abe says, clearly inebriated again. It is that time of the day for him: something o'clock.

—Is that why you're drunk?

—No I am drunk because I am ... Ah, no, right, yes, I am celebrating.

—And last week? Also that? What good news was that? Cinco says, jaded and sick of it all.

—It was celebrating lockdown. It's been good for me.

—How??

—More free time, time to enjoy myself, learn new recipes, new plants in my flat—I have like a garden in my living room. Even cultivate my own tomatoes. It's fantastic.

—Abe, this isn't the idyllic return to nature you think it is.

—Come on, man. Everyone knows you think like negative Nancy.

—Negative Nancy??

—Put such a bad spin on everything.

—Everything?? This is probably the worst time of your lives, hundreds of thousands dead, if not millions, more poor, out of work, lives destroyed, freedoms lost. We don't even know if the worst isn't yet to come. The lockdown itself destroyed lives, society, small businesses. Society as we know it is going downhill, and fast. We're going to wake up from this bad dream sometime next year or in a year and two and everything will have turned to shit. Life as we know it is being ripped to shreds, potentially for good. What do you think comes after this? Economic crisis, social crises, an epidemic of loneliness, teenagers that will grow up with trauma. It's fun now. You have your pleasures. Your parties. Your "drugs". When the high is over, you'll open your eyes to see we stepped into a full nightmare. And you stepped willingly, cocktail glass in hand.

And you reel here, celebrating because you learnt new cookie recipes and picked some flower from the park. Millennials, man. No sense of reality.

—I don't know that you should talk to me that way. You should have a bit more respect. Offending people all the time won't get you anywhere. I do think this is precisely why all that bad stuff happening to you at work.

—Telling the truth ain't offending!! We live in hard times!! We need the truth, not lies!! What comfort is a lie to you, if you end up a corpse in hospital like those poor people I nurtured into death in my own hospital?? Thousands of them? This is life and death Abe, this isn't happy hour at the cocktail bar any-more.

—Wow, you really are negative aren't you!

—It's a pandemic!!! It's dangerous!! And you're having fun!

—Ah so? Why can't I have a little fun? Why can't I have my bubble of happy? To forget about the world? I mean, I am not ill myself, so...

Then the bell rang. So Cinco picked up the delivery. It was a frozen DHL man handing him his shopping. He looked so sad and overworked he wanted to give him a tip or a hug or something. But he settled on offering him a mask.

—Come on please take it, why not? It helps. Saves lives.

He hated his own meek voice saying that. What a pathetic thing to offer.

The man muttered in his chin and reluctantly put on a grateful smile while sinking deeper into his bitter day. The world now relied on people like this driving across state to deliver things, and ring the door each time in hope the air coming off the house wasn't poisoned with evil Covid. They did their jobs with fear, "essential workers". With very non essential wages. Lower wages than middle class homeworkers who just crafted a nice home office in their living room, typing away on their Mac, while cashing in furlough checks.

The doctor's flat sound system played some quaint tunes from decades past, the languid happiness of which seemed now an intangible dream. How can anyone dream of getting that life back??? The freedom of getting around? Those things in the songs, impossible. Getting around, sitting in the sun with fellow people, drinking overpriced beer in a smelly bar, rocking your ass off on the dance floor with sweaty people, paying an extortionate price to see a tepid band... All that stuff. When is all that stuff happening again?! People longed for. Cinco longed for it. Even his meager whiskey glass in discos with young people he didn't understand.

—Abe, knock the booze off, please!

—Why? So I can cope with this head on? Let me float, man. Let me live my best Covid life. And with that, Abe checks out, head first on the table. Cinco pushes a cushion under his head and just minds his own computer business. He is used to his friend crashing at his house. Why he's got the car parked on the street to drive him home when ready. Like a good pal. What is a world crisis without a good pal?

———— ✖ ————

—Graciella, Graciella... How silly are you. So silly. Don't do this, don't do that. Don't do anything.

He stands in the doorway with a water pot, overlooking his rooms. His wig has rolls on, and the robe is half undone—who cares? Not like anyone here to see any-more. Robe he inherited from his dead mother. Much of his journey of self discovery into sort of womanhood was re-enacting his mother; turning into a living monument to Ms Graciella Sr. was his life's work. Down to the solitude in the semi rural house he inherited from her, shared with plants and cats—also of the old lady. A loss Graciella never surpassed. The loss of a mother who was the only soul to grasp his complicated ways, even before he announced himself a "she"; she cultivated then understood why Graciella was that way; and then she died, leaving him alone to fend off a world he did not fit in.

He had been trapped indoors forever and even escaped the plague, though many of his friends died. Like in AIDS times he had also lived through with stoicism, some people on the fringe were more vulnerable, more isolated, more prone to desperate unprotected parties to fend off solitude. He wept for all and isolated more.

—Graciella, Graciella.. What are you doing. And he went back to the sink, absent mindedly changed the water again.

—Hard times make hard men. Hard men make good times. Good times make weak men. Weak men make piss-pot tea.

Granted, he made little sense, as he'd been talking to himself so often. He watered his plants with love, caressing each one of them.

—How are you baby? You lost a lot of leaves didn't you? No sun, no people, no fun. You'll recover though, won't you sweetie. You're strong. You've lived in a pot all your life and look at you. Doing better than most. If only everyone was as strong as you. We'd be somewhere. But we're not, are we, darling, sweetie.

He lovingly picked dead leaf after dead leaf, then lift chin up to gaze across the lawn to the neighbour house.

They weren't here much any-more, were they? And the old crossdresser touches his wig and brassiere with faint longing.

They used to be nice... Ah, youth! Maybe I shall water their plants. They look a bit wilted. Like me, he chuckles. Self conscious, but on a good mission, Graciella puts on his shoes and walks across the lawn to late Ely's Albion Cottage, now sitting empty like a love mausoleum. Graciella still remembered seeing them; nights, as they giggled and embraced in every window of the house, with no care in the world, young and happy. Often naked. Graciella was there trying not to look from the penumbra, but looking nevertheless, chest heaving, living vicariously, tear in his cross eye. Following the film of love as each episode played from one window to another.

Now, he gazed inside as he watered the exterior plants.

—Ah, those plants in that corner need some care. She left them like that... Tut tut. He pours and pours over the geraniums while the water overflows and his memories keep him warm. As if before his eyes, Eris and Daniel dancing with bodies like Hellenistic statuary, always in candle light, always listening to synth pop or Stevie Nicks or this or other heartfelt song.

He used to recognize the song and murmur to self in the dark, "ah, yes, that's a good track".

—She left everything so neat, though... But as everything was orderly and put away, Graciella recognized the signs of love: a sonnet book here, a fluffy red blanket there, on the bay window reading nook, a half used candle, and a tea cup with lipstick on. A yellow post it with a smiley face attached to the bureau in the corner, strange addition to the strange anachronistic design of the room.

—Ah, well, darling, let's go back and make some tea. Tea will make everything better, won't it darling, Oh yes it will. And he hobbles back into his corridor where he suddenly weeps like a sentimental old mother whose offspring fled the nest. Everything, everything was dying and lost in this damn pandemic. Getting darker and emptier.

On the walls, dozens of drawings. Drawings he made in better times. Of nice places, far off, he'd never seen. Venice, Paris... The good stuff. Now he was convinced he'd never get to see anything either.

"I am afraid this is the end, my friends"—he posted on Facebook that night. Next to a photo of him wearing his mom's favorite dress, a tea dress with little blue colors.

Over Dahut, a mist was descending. It was the last days of January. After a gruesome Christmas spent mostly in solitude or via Internet with family and buddies—for who was lucky enough to have them—this was the anticlimactic end of this side of the pandemic.

Like the sun over the hills in the morning, vaccine era soon upon the nations. All of them.

It was close to a year. Of the pandemic, and of their being in love. Daniel was very sensitive to these cyclic celebrations, or pins dropped on the time map of their relationship. As the earth spun into space, they touched the same spot again. "I've been here before, but it was different...". Google photos reminder nagged him each day: "1 year ago on this day...". Seeing those dates again on his phone every day, he felt the buds of incipient love and incipient world crisis all over again, like he did year back. He did love her, he told himself. He just feared her. Feared abandonment more than anything. The words said at the start of it were burnt into him. "You'll never get over this". And two black holes swirling at him atop a Goddess figure in red lace lingerie.

But we weren't at March 25 yet. This was just mid February. So every time he gazed at the date on his phone lock screen, or the calendar on the wall of his kitchen, his heart fluttered. It was as if he was there. In the beautiful rooms. So much sunshine pouring through. The film of their love. It gripped him so bad. Little shown on his poker face, but all felt within. Torturing him, eating tunnels through his brain. The best moments of his life. A perfectly choreographed theater of love, where all was perfect. He had time to think, with this new reality of working from home, and the time gained by not chatting to her as much as they used to. And he realized that early month before apocalypse hit was a lost paradise, they'd never have again. No abject scenes from jealous partners yet. No awareness of the complications of this damn quadrant. No rejections, perceived or real. No, it was perfect then. As he gazed into the calendar, regret and nostalgia tore through him. And a bit of hate. He hated her a bit, for destroying the dream. And when he finally went to her on a one way ticket, she destroyed it again. Then the *coup de grace* was the THREE PLATES. Who would forgive that?! It was a heavy instant of hate lulling on the edge of an abyss, and he faltered ready to fall. But he invoked the torrid film of love once more and came back. It warmed his heart, finally the main character of his own movie. He'd found his center. His center was her. She was his *axis mundi*. She had done wrong, he hit back at her with distance. Maybe it was time to find his way back to her. At least talk a bit more. Ask her for an apology. Ask for more.

Julianah walked in the room, knocking him back to reality.

—I've got everything ready for you, lollipop. He didn't hear for a second. He still heard Eris' voice in his skull. Her seductive, confident, sweet voice. She was there, in the calendar, dancing sexily. February 10. The first time they talked long into the night.

—Hey!! Julianah elbowed him, annoyed. You don't even hear me when I'm talking to you?! She walked off, furiously.

So he walks after her to the living room, sitting, waiting patiently for her to initiate the proceedings. They're doing a little arts and crafts project together: mending hearts. Kintsugi. She likes her crafty crafts, pink and flowery things. Unicorns, rainbows. They... soothe the soul. Relax the mind. She knew how to do that: relax his busy mind.

But the girl seems lost in her phone. Suddenly, she looks up at him. She puts the phone down. He glances: it's Eris' social media she was looking at. Eris' prolific media.

In the last video reel, she was dressed to the nines in another tweed waistcoat suit and rust red tie; while her pearl earrings and hair overflowing. Rolled white shirt sleeves to reveal arms forming a question mark.

—How do you even like that cheap slut? You betrayed us for that?

He takes a deep breath. He's been here in this scene before. Always the same.

—No, you betrayed us. You had it coming. And I won't have this discussion about Eris.

—You always defend her! I mean nothing to you!

He replies, articulating words slowly, with weight.

—I also defend you from others. I don't allow anyone to say anything bad about you.

But it doesn't satisfy the girl.

—And what could they have to say? I am the victim in this. You all did this to me. How did you and Eris not think of me??

—Look, darling. You wanted an open relationship. I used it. This is what it leads to in a person like me. For me sex leads to attachment. Love. Shall I remind you of what you've done since?

He looks at her gravely.

—What?? And she clenches her fists, eyebrows pushing into each other. An altogether furious looking demeanor contrasting with the Disney faces stretched over a large bosom—her pink tee.

Daniel goes quiet for a bit. You know well what you've done. And he gestures to his left arm with his jaw. The never healing wound. His face forlorn, but calm.

... She thinks. Waves of emotion cross her face in quick succession, shame quickly chased by ever more fury.

—So??? You did that to my heart!! You swore to love me forever.

Daniel finally puts his tools aside. A quick gaze at the pieces of broken glass glued together with gold suddenly wakes him up, transport him elsewhere. He remembers something. He looks towards the one hidden drawer he managed to hide the gift from Eris in. A certain Kintsugi heart. With real gold, and real heart. So.. he feels once more trapped in a surreal situation. Dissociated from himself. Why is he doing this, now with Julianah? Whom, he moreover accuses retroactively of bringing this upon herself? If that's correct, then why is everything a pile of burning trash?

Who even suggested they do that glass heart thing? Isn't it a bit romantic? Was it her? Him? He can't recall. If her, then how come... what a coincidence, if him, how shameful.. he thinks.

He corrects himself out of his dissociation. He is just kind, that's all. He is kind to poor Julianah. He is also too kind to Eris. He is too kind for his own good.

—Look, schatzi. I am very forgiving and kind. I am still here to offer you moral support. Despite the fact you brought this on yourself with your early and many mistakes. How many times now did I say find a job, we both need to carry our weight? How many times did I ask you to clean after yourself? How many times did you go out with other guys while I paid the bills, because I wasn't man enough for you? You made this happen. And despite it all, I am here for you.

Just ...not all of me. Not like you want. We're not doing only what you want any-more.

Julianah shoves the contents of the table across the room. She grunts and charges at him with her fists:

—Then dump her! Never go see her again. Cancel that contract!!

Why are you even here if you still plan to see her?! If you love me, dump her!!

He calmly grabs her fists and hugs her. She sobs.

He caresses her head.

—We'll see. I care for you. But considering what you've done, you have no right to tell me what to do there. If I want to spend a few weeks a year for work when work comes back, that is my decision.

She sobs more, with squeals that would make a dead man cringe. He consoles her into him, while pouring guilt into her ears.

Finally after a good spasmodic cry, she feels secure and powerful again.

—Leave her or I leave you.

Daniel acts surprised. He is always surprised when his careful labyrinth of psychological arguments fail to achieve the desired effect.

So he says in quite a cold voice:

—I thought you already left me. I thought we already broke up.

She is confused. Looks up at him.

—Then why this?! Why cuddle me?

—Because I care for you. I will always care for you. You are half of my life. But you broke up with me.

—I was just angry, I was angry... don't you understand I love you?! She pleads, blinded by her own tears. Voice breaking under a strain she can't bear any more.

—Burning my clothes and slashing my arm was quite the love statement, dear. I got the message.

—Because you left me for a month to be with your whore!!!

—You left me years ago when you refused to get a job and stop seeing other guys.

Her mind breaks. The screech irrupting from the caverns of her broad chest is enough to pierce eardrums on the far side of town. She sees red, tears and agony ripping through, and through, with no consolation in sight, no way out of his maize of arguments, guilt, and hot and cold showers. No success in her own traps and pleas laid out with all the power of her aching, loving heart.

She runs out of the room, slamming the door; goes to sob quietly in the other rooms, rocking back and forth, trying desperately to contain her circular thoughts, soothing herself with her ventriloquist dolls, clutching them to her chest, drowning them in sour tears. She tries to etch a plan, but all she can come up with is more images of knives, blood, smashed glass, she wants destruction. Destruction is her safe space. If it didn't work on him, against him, maybe it will against herself. She wants to perform the supreme act of self mutilation in front of him, to melt him, like she used to.

—Could you get a job, dear? I mean, something related to your arts, but something, anything, to contribute; also to get you out of the house, have normal relations with others. Do you really just want to be a housewife? Was the usual plea from Daniel's lips over the years; from the mist of time, many times, coming back to her febrile mind.

—I can't, I am depressed! You don't want me to cut myself, do you? And she would flash her scars, on her breasts, her thighs; it was her biography in scars. And this little chat would repeat itself through the years, and she always melted happily in his resignation, his arms. Her hero, her prince. Who rescued her. Why wasn't it working now?? This faint memory, played to self like a sweet film of romance, had yellowed round the edges from so many times she played it in her mind in hard times, and it was so many hard times. She thought, time for it again, he will melt again. She stops sobbing. She crawls on the floor towards a drawer, a specific drawer.

Her kawaii knife. The one with the unicorn blade. Cute but lethal. She found solace and an eerie calm in the solemn proceedings, like she was performing a religious ritual. She held it in front of red eyes; when he stepped into the door frame, looking calmly at her. He stood there, judging. She felt fearful, and yelped. Dropped it. Dropped her head down. He left.

He walks along the corridor, desperate he has no place to go. It's fucking lockdown. Pressure cooker household with the ex-fiancée-friend-flatmate. Cell-mate. He stands there until he remembers there's the piano. Upright piano leaning against the wall, now used by Julianah as storage for her many things. He sweeps them all off, sits on a few books and plays.

And his fingers run along the keyboard with all the passion his words can't express. He plays Clair de Lune. The dark corridor fills with music, and romance. Romance the girl on the floor next room hopes is for her, but knows is not. He plays, his tears finally come out; over the fingers, into the keys; fuelling notes of silent, mortal despair.

CHAPTER XIV

"Turnips, squash, shallots. Turnips, squash, shallots. T
urnips..."

She said to self. In front of the cat food aisle.

She moved an inch, surprised the shelves presented
no turnips and shallots.

It took a good five minutes to realize where she was.

Her sunglasses and her mask covered her face entirely, and she liked it that way. To make it even more
dissociated from physical reality, she had synth-pop
blaring on her headphones. Securing an impenetrable
head space where she just lived her emotions. Revisited
the same thoughts, over and over again.

In a derelict landscape, with life at a standstill, Eris
entered a relationship with her diary. Now that the husband chased away, she had her house to herself. Now
that she had cut off communication with the boy, she
had her time to herself. So her day routine involved,
like everyone else, the ritual walk to the Mecca of groceries, and then, unlike everyone else, long hours pars-
ing through diaries.

Dreams, nightmares, crying in the shower.

Music, dancing, collapsing on the rug crying.

She had her crying rug. A vast, fluffy woollen rug. Felt
like cuddling a sheep in there. Good for melting into it,
crying. Surrounded by tissues. An ocean of them.

Sometimes febrile calls with a vast network of friends
and advisors. She would seek them out by the mood of
the day: if she felt more favourable to Stan, she'd ring

Abe or Cinco, or some of their other mutual friends. If she felt more inclined to favour Daniel, it was her mom, her childhood friend, or other female friends who called the German scientist "The prince". No matter how hard he erred, he was young, he was inexperienced, it was a pandemic, and he was shy and soft spoken; readily offered apologies in meek tones and sent roses.

These gestures and this cocktail of features melted the hearts of the females; Eris would thank for the advice heartily but press end call with a raised eyebrow; something was off.

Oh, dear. The huge traction of the surreal love for this ethereal boy in abstract corners of her subconscious; battling her own rational scaffolding of decades of intellect and self assurance and wisdom about relationships. It's like her brain was hijacked.

Like, how can you trust a man who'll put an abusive partner on a pedestal? How can you trust a man with secretomania? How can you give your heart a guy who says one thing to you, then shows you another with his location choices?

I mean, come on... you understand he felt crushed and ran back to his nest, for the perceived one night betrayal during their fall paradise. An imperfect paradise. But surely, the statistics were grim: one year of love, three months physically present. She walked to the kitchen calendar pen in hand: drew little hearts on the dates together; black crosses on the rest. These numbers in threes always on her mind, floating on the surface of her consciousness like a nagging wife.

Yes, you could pardon the boy if there was one disappointment, for one perceived betrayal in favor of the competition—her existent husband of many solid happy years.

Once, twice.

But now she looked back at this year, and it rang more like, Daniel naturally gravitates back to Johnnyville independent of external factors, AND her actions, non actions or words more a pretext to serve her in cold tones as post priori pretext; surely, if the man was determined, as his passionate words claimed to be, as his kiss said, as his burning eyes did... statistics would paint a different arithmetic of hearts versus crosses on that calendar.

So she walked off.

The situation was a Pit and the Pendulum predicament bondage type conundrum. If she used her many spare hours to re-program herself with indifference and contempt for the lassitude of the boy, then she'd suddenly find Stan better. Not hotter, no, no competition there.

Creatures in the maze arches of the mall meandered, sloppily, with take away coffees in hand. The one thing left. Some breathed really hard behind oversized masks in mobility scooters, threatening. Some went out of their way to avoid Eris as she walked round with hollow yes for fear she might be contagious. It could be thought she had the plague, but no, it was love that did that to her.

In one archway, a girl like her—dressed up with no where to go, coffee and shopping in hand. Beautiful and sad. Eris searched her eyes; signs of love, a soul, anything. Then the girl lifts her brow and exchanges electricity; yes, love. They understood each other with a glimpse, and smiled bitterly. Then walked off. Secret solidarity of broken hearts.

It was convenient she lived not too far from the nearest shopping super-mall. Ideal walking distance to take a surreptitious call from him, if one offered; or think of him, over and over. Her mind was heavy. Same thoughts aching like an overused path, or overstretched muscle. This was not the Belmont she knew. This was darker than usual, quiet, empty. She knew she had to stay away from certain alleys and certain hours—when a certain breed of "patient" would come out and hover towards her menacingly with God knows what intent.

Intent to die in agony before her? Take her down with them? She sometimes still heard their gruesome grunts—gruesome not because so much pain, but the absence of humanity in them. Covid ate through their brains like pudding. And they wandered the streets against any directive in revenge for what's occurred to them, hoping to take others down with them; some autopilot of some animal part. Nothing but the worst basic instincts.

When she approached her house, she stood there for a second. So many times she'd be back at the door, breathless with guilt and excitement from a fresh call with the unattainable prince. Ready to put on a face for the dejected hubby. This time, no hubby, no prince. No call.

Just her circular thoughts and she was drowning in them. She needed to open windows and let fresh air in, but no reality anywhere as sweet as him. Forever, however, him.

But a full surprise. Alas, her open door gave way to two simultaneous sights she had to take in with tired eyes: Roses, roses everywhere. Beautiful splendid red and pink roses and every shade in between, with thorns, and in the midst of it all, Stan.

Stan, a picture of defeat and despair. She could smell his tears. A terrible scent.

—Welcome home. He said, with smiling eyes, like he'd seen God. She saw the emotion but could not reciprocate, which caused pain in her brain.

—Stan... Did you ... Bring all this? And she gestured with her right arm while dropping bags with the left. Taking layers off herself and stooping to inhale the flowers like the requested breath of fresh air.

Until she sees a note. Not a small note. A big rectangle with cursive letters in it. His writing. HIS. "My dear Eris, I miss you, deeply. Will you talk to me again? Life without you is a bit hard. Please accept these flowers as humble sign of the intensity of my love. I hope they speak better than my pathetic words can do".

Tears, tons of tears flushed her eyes, she had to drown a sob. Why'd she have to find these with Stan around? She swallowed tears with monumental willpower, sharp breath intake, turned around:

—Why, what's going on, bunny? Are you well?

—Yes I let myself in, hope you don't mind. I missed you. You disappeared on me.

His voice hung sweetly in the air while she felt tiers and tiers of emotions for the other, absent lover; Stan's sweet words felt like bullying background noise because she had other emotional emergencies to process. Which she wasn't allowed to let out. Eyes glazed in tears, she reaches to Stan, mechanically hugs him.

He hugs too much, too strong, Presses on her body until she suffocates; a squeal escapes her. His love is strange, she wants to run away from it. She wants the other's love, who isn't here. Who is never here.

—So, these from him?

—Yes, she harks on defensively. Something you don't much like to do.

—But didn't I do other things, like care for you?

—Yes, she mutters while taking flowers and putting in vases... Bit too much even.

—What?

She shakes her head, too tired to repeat.

Stan's just nagging noise pollution over the torrid love film in her head.

—Why are you here anyway? She blurts. Sorry you have to see this. I guess it hurts. I should have been here to find this alone.

—I didn't know. I told you why I came. I miss you. You never took away my keys.

—I am needing space a the minute. Heard from my lawyer yet?

—My God. You sound so cold. Jilted Stan steps back, legs melt.

—I am sorry. But her voice doesn't say she's sorry; her voice sound like tin.

—I am sorry. I shall go. It was wonderful holding you for a minute. I shall go. And he motions towards door waiting to be stopped. His eyes fill with tears, but unlike her, he's no good at self control. Like a giant toddler, explodes in harrowing crying, convulsions and all. Eris feels torn between pity and disgust. At the end of her wits too, nerves stretched thin, she has no energy to assuage the pain of this man.

—Oh my god, Stan. What do you want me to do?

—No, there is nothing you can do.

—You want to stay a bit longer?

—YES!! I don't want to go!! And he cries more.

She turns around arranging her shopping, rolling her eyes in secret.

—You know I am the man for you, Eris. you know no one will ever love you this much.

Deep sigh. Eris hates her life. She sinks into sofa.

—Stan... This is matters of the heart. I can't control my heart. I gave you mine for far too long. You cheated on me, you held me back.

—I know!! I am tortured by guilt! Do you think a day goes by that I am not wrecked by guilt?? What's the purpose of reminding me again and again and again, to twist the knife? I know. I will never do that again. I was stupid. I neglected you. I always regarded you as the absolute number one in life, but I was careless. Mistakes, but honest mistakes, deep down there's an abyss of love. I will do anything, anything you want!!

He steps forward, shows her his clothes, his weight loss, wants to take shirt off to show improved figure. In a fit of panic she shouts "NO.. I have seen enough."

He cries more. Face drowns in hands. He is zero resentment, all despair/remorse.

Begging desperately. The other is all resentment, zero remorse. A hole in the ground opens for her. She wants out of there. She runs towards her bedroom door, but he grabs her head like the Abominable Snowman in a clumsy attempt to kiss and hold... but it ends up being too forceful so she shouts, hits him and slams door in his face.

He cries loud, alone in the room, crushed, he takes ages to gather his things in a bag and stands there for minutes thinking. There was never a sadder man.

—I even come to you on Shabbos! I didn't even care about that. Nothing matters but getting my bunny back.

But quiet follows. He stands a bit longer hoping for a reply.

But Eris' loudly disintegrating neurons don't make a sound, on the outside. They just feel deafening on the inside. She presses her ears to silence the strain, the despair. Block things out. The truth is she needs to reach out to Daniel and she just desperately wants Stan out. She feels sorry for him but heart aching.

He sent roses. She unblocks him. She doesn't even hear sobs as Stan walks away. She feels a huge wave of release, a fresh lease of life: waiting there by the phone, serene. To speak to her baby. After weeks, months without. She can tell the same circle of hell will be ridden, their mutual accusations, their inextricable differences in respective guesswork into the timeline of cause and effect of this disaster; but she is willing to brave one more episode, like survival depends on it. Truth is, she loves him. Sometimes she loathes him. But the love is stronger. Stronger than anything.

Ping. Ping! Ping!

The music of the spheres. He's elated. It can only mean one thing. I mean, there are other people who also manifest a tepid interest in him semi regularly via these digital channels. But it's really Eris the Goddess that he expects all the time to ping in his pocket. He always hopes. He trusts she'll come to her senses.

He patiently waits for her godly fury through punitive silence and WhatsApp blocks to wane, lets her ire unfold then chill; he will be there when she forgives. To give his dulcet tones apologies, explanations and soothing meek promises.

He walks to the window. It's a February mist of almost snow and almost sunshine. No one knows what season it is any-more. Not like the first year of the pandemic, when spring was summer like a consolation prize for staying indoors and not going to work or restaurants.

He reminisces. He touches his tousled hair. He's not aware of his Adonis charms but sometimes remembers she's fond of them and that makes him feel good, so he wants to be pretty if it brings him her. All for her, on the inside. Every thought. It's just on the outside that it looks different. "Autistic, darling?' He hears her crystal laugh. No. No. Frowns, looks down. "I just can't express myself". Checks his pockets. One thing he needs to stop is talking to her and his memories out loud. Dangerous with that other girl around.

Twists in the window, shelters the screen in his torso. Reads in this little capsule of privacy just created, ray of blue sunshine on sullen cheeks.

"Hello".

Goddess said hello.

Shot of blood through the brain, his everything. How fast it all flows from high quarters to basement, in the body.

It's like God reaching his finger to Adam again in Michelangelo's masterpiece. He connects. Looks up, hope forms on his furrowed brows.

Goddess said hello.

So he quickly types hello back, with a smile.

The smile he left on her laptop centuries ago before they were cast from heaven.

"I love you tremendously, Daniel."

Messages pour one by one, slowly.

"Like a fire that's slowly burning everything around it". "And I can't let it out outwardly so it consumes every-thing inside."

"Will I ever lay your beautiful head on my pillow?

The kind of magic we feel together, the intensity we find in each other, just makes the rest of life utterly boring. Everything is comedown after you. And yet, I have to pay for those moments in so many tears. I don't know how much more I can take. I know we clash emotionally, mentally, in big ways."

"So what shall we do, baby? what shall I do?"

"I DON'T KNOW."

"I know. I don't know either."

"You're the best thing alive, and a danger and a threat. You're the man of my dreams, you're a natural disaster. You're so good and so bad you scare me."

"I want to be good for you, baby. You are the best thing alive, not me. You are the woman of my dreams and as intense as an earthquake".

"And the negatives?"

"Maybe good things are exhausting."

"Wrong."

"I just want to love you and leave all our problems behind."

"How can you be so optimistic when we've been split up for weeks?"

"Neither of us wants to split up. And you already mentioned "let's just be fuck buddies" not long ago."

"Sarcasm. People who are this much in love can't really just be friends with benefits."

"Then let's continue to have this pain with benefits... because you as the benefit are worth any pain."

And with this exchange, the ice is thawed. The dance begins again.

His words minimal, pour like exact drops of lust on the screen between her fingers. She once more doesn't understand how the inexperienced boy knows her so well, just what to say.

Lulls from sofa to chair to bed to kitchen phone in hand, robe undone, cooling down with champagne in dainty glass.

It's not lascivious, it's luminous; he talks of touching her lips with his piano playing fingers. He talks of undoing her robe in a corner, engulfing feminine curves with athletic muscle. She feels the ethereal eye contact across the mountains like he's there; she needs his eye contact like life support. Like primordial fire burning matter, elevating it.

Hundred miles apart, but their souls dancing in the sky, hanging onto every thread of the myriads of digital connections between them.

She lies down imagining him wrapped round her legs, on the floor. Head in her lap. Vertigo unites both in embrace. Then, he looks up. Languid abandon gives way to ravenous lust as he meets her gaze. His eyes dance around the contours of her face. He feels heroic and male.

He jumps to his feet, grabs her, her head into him. She looks up. A kiss of some kind is consumed.

He lies down, imagines her on top of him. Covering his face with her hand; teasing, hitting him playfully on the arm. He leaps up and entraps her below. A capsule of love. Hips into hers. Vertigo unites both. They feel the same earthquake shake the bed into the stratosphere.

His lips ravenous, bite into her neck like fruit. They hungrily search each other's mouths, they breath hard. Sinking into each other, silky skin against silky skin.

She holds onto him like he's a lifeboat, as they both sink into ecstatic lust. And despite this intense lust, they both perceive the other saintly somehow. Glowing in spirit, in purity.

A passion that elevates.

Their fantasies align even when they don't text online. Sometimes they just text telepathically.

She can't get his curly head out of her mind; he can't get over the delicate chin and long neck. Lust does wonderful things to their faces, they still remember. Sometimes they even video call each other.

Days like this pass. They needed it, after so the post Christmas calamity.

Slowly the grey in her face wanes. His frown melts. They start smiling again.

They talk, they talk all the time. Text while brushing teeth. Text while shopping.

Wake up at night after the first slumber and text.

He puts a languid hand on the Muriel—it's the wine they used to drink together. They had dozen empty bottles of this Rioja lined up out front porch until someone took them. He downs the glass, sensually. Wine recalls her to him. He used to lick it off her lips.

Fingers hover over the fork; he looks at the bowl to re-memorize their favorite dish; they used to cook it together, in their kitchen. Cooking together more a pretext to horse around to loud music, play wife and husband like little kids playing mom and dad. Those were the days. She would wear vintage lingerie on purpose, drive him mad trying to undo the straps of the suspenders while pasta boiled. While vegetables steamed, he would lift her up and carry to the living room. Then, a perfect scientist, he'd then return to kitchen just when the alarm went off on the hob and all was ready. The halloumi would sometimes end up burnt in the oven. All fixed with an excess of fresh garlic they pressed together, to mask the other flavors.

In drinking the same wine and cooking her pesto pasta, he invoked those days again. Docile boy paying homage to Gods, sitting put hoping to be beckoned to celestial gardens. If you perform the right ritual down to a tee, perhaps you invoke the golden days again? The mythical "illo tempore"?

He sat there, silent. In expectation.

Over the mountains, at her sumptuous table, Eris moves bejewelled hand in white porcelain towards the tall stem of the wine glass. On the bottom, few drops of burgundy liquid: their own Muriel. She tilts her head back as she waters her buds in the precious elixir. She feels him all again. She sees him, animated, like a child. Trying to dance for her.

Then she grabs the fork and attacks the pesto pasta.

Like repeating the combination plays out the scene again. At their table, in a house of love tucked away; she sees his golden head again before her, through narrowed eyes. Their laughs intertwine, it's like he's here.

rs form and drop in her plate.

Like a tribute to what was, she repeats all the little things they did together; and the bigger things.

They're stuck repeating heavenly gestures to invoke the golden age. A year has passed, spring is coming—the time they met. A time for remembrance.

Of course, Eris isn't satisfied with merely this theater. She's a woman of action. She wants the real thing.

Days become nights and then there is dawn again.

—So when can I see you, darling??

He can't come yet, he says. Something, something, dentist. Work, business. Julianah etc.

—Oh. I can come to you. Want to?

There is a silence. One of his silences that speak; but she's momentarily deafened by love.

So she puts up Google on her large screen; flags up two or three of her favorite hotels right down the road from his house on Johnnyville. Shares to him with a click:

—See? I can book right now. Alive and excited, she waits for the response taking impatient coffee sips. She understands online chat an asynchronous form of communication, he might be elbow deep in grading student work.

Night falls. Coffee cup empty. Eris arches her legendary left brow. Maybe no response means something, in the cryptic style of Daniel.

So she reluctantly types again. Hello? I could come tomorrow. She glances at the room mentally packing already, choosing a suitcase and an outfit.

Daniel typing.

She gets excited.

He plays with the mobile at his desk. Papers, pens, laptops, tissues, in a mess.

Looks out of the window, his only oasis of privacy. She—Julianah—can't control his gaze. She controls everything but not the inside of his head, the direction of his eyes.

Something disturbs him about Eris' message. He should be elated to see her; it's been long. He's sort of getting ready to go himself. The natural way is for him to go to their shared nest. Why does she want to move towards his nest with Julianah?

She's a threat. Like a submarine, she wants to approach to attack the poor suffering girl.

Julianah has ballooned to sumo player size. She's sitting on the floor with her dolls. Grown some more wrinkles. Her white Lolita dress rolled up, revealing her hello Kitty underpants. She has the same ponytails with pink ribbons and overgrown black roots, rolling head side to side, in the faint rays of sun coloring the rug. She caresses the rug with her tiny hands, towards him. Discolored pink nail polish, tattooed fingers that stop when he stalls in being aware of her. She doesn't know what else to do. Tried her usual charms. Daniel is lost in his little world.

—Hunny?

Nothing.

—Hunny!!

The nothing deepens.

She throws a doll at him. The doll kicks cup of milky coffee over his papers. Success. Daniel is rudely awaken from his daydreaming. But he's not happy.

—What is this, darling?

—Well, you weren't hearing me.

He tries to clean up and rescue his papers, morose. Thoughts reluctantly elsewhere. Revolving around Eris' long neck and cheekbones.

—Why are you doing stuff like this, all the time, Julianah?! When will you grow up?

She goes quiet, scared. She didn't expect this retort. He's usually so much more patient with her kid antics. She knows what's up.

—You been talking to that whore, again, haven't you?

Blood shoots to her brain, clouding her vision.

Gets worse when he doesn't answer. That's really what she hates the most.

The Fury visits again. That fury. The destructive creative fury. Her shining moment of feeling alive and vengeful for decades of self repression and being Ms Nice and Kind.

Then comes the growl. A deep, animal growl. From the bottom of her being. She throws her rubenesque folds at him, shoving him into his desk, disturbing the already wet papers, brown sticky liquid everywhere.

—What is this, Julianah? He blinks, impassively.

—Don't like it here?? Then why don't you go to your whore, in Dahut?! If she's so much better than me?

His face is numb. She takes it as an invite to go on.

—Well, why don't I tell you what's going on.

I am tired. Sick and tired.

You manipulate me, make me feel guilty when it's you, you all along. You live in the slut's depraved world of fakery and bluff. She is obscene, yet you seem to like it. I am 100% natural and authentic and dignified, modest and wholesome yet you prefer her!

Her books are porn, she looks like a porn star! She is just a prop enabling your false mindset, your toxic world. It is destroying me and I happen to be worth saving and protecting.

You are not my Daniel I used to know; you forgot real values and started seeking these sluts because I am not enough for you. You selfish wanker! You used to have values, now all you care for is sex and money.. and she gives it to you...

I sacrificed myself for you, gave my whole life... you used me now you throw me away.

Pang stops her. Breath stops, voice breaks. She irrupts in violent sobs. Punches him with tiny fists.

All this while he's stood like stone. Impervious to the outburst. In contrast to the hysterical energy of her outburst, his tone is deep and calm.

—Many wrong things there, darling. One thing though: it was you who wanted an open relationship, who needed more men. I never wanted other women but after 10 years of abstinence I tried something entirely in the terms of our open relationship, something you used against me to cuck me with from day one. Sorry I fell in love. Couldn't be controlled. I unfortunately correlate sex with love. I'm not like you.

He says it all while looking out the window, then hands her a tissue. Swift hand gestures and the mess sorted on the table, with a click of his heels he's out of the room. Pulls a coat on, twirls, exits into the darkness.

On the porch, in the cold, his fingers hover, type the beginning of a word. But his mind goes blank.

Looks left, right, crosses the road. Commences a long nocturnal walk to clear his tired soul; maybe answers will come.

He looks up train tickets, he mentally packs for the journey. Maybe take his car? He has to go, not now, he likes taking things slow, but soon.

"Oh, Eris.. Why, oh why did you have to go to him? We could have been together happily. Why did you have to invite him for Christmas? Your choices show me he's your number one time and time again; they align with the horrible things you said at the start. If you want to constantly torture me with the primordial doubt you seared in me with your March 25 words, that's the way to do it. And you did. Forever keeping me insecure, a boyfriend in waiting, a ... mistress. Oh, Eris... If only... It could have been heaven. The heaven that is rightfully ours."

He looks at the sky. He knows somewhere, up there, there is a happy ending for them.

She takes minutes to sit up from a harrowing crying fit, mucus and tears accumulating on her chins. Helping herself against the floor while lifting her bum in the air, stumbling, finding balance in nearby furniture. Her pink phone, bedazzled, hangs from her neck. She dials the passcode and selects her friend's number.

—Hello, Julianah, you okay??

Her friend shifts worried in his gamer chair. Frets and toys with the crumbs of a few packs of crisps lying around the computer.

—I am not okay!! Look at her, go to her social media now. Take a look and tell me what he sees in her. She's just a mindless slut, but that's what he likes now.

Jack brings up Facebook and immediately opens Eris' latest post, an interview.

Sat in lush decor, sun on her cheek, Eris gesticulates with gusto:

—No, I frequently employ the dichotomy of Apollo and Dionysus in my work. I am fond of both, I don't personally identify with one or the other. They are there as existing polarities in reality and as artistic categories which to me are equally important. Yin and yang, if you will.

They both represent values to pursue: one is diurnal, rational, elegant flight of reason... The other is lust, subconscious, creativity, romance. I don't see why one should chose one over the other. The key is in the balance. Too many people want to live on extremes of a binary; happiness, progress is... in the middle. In the balance. Carefully calibrated balance, exerting self discipline, being true to yourself.

Eris stop for a second, looks down and pushes hair off her face.

Jack pauses the video there:

—Yes, I see what you mean.. She is ... Well, she is a bit pompous, you mean?

Look. I am very sorry this happened to you, Julianah, it's horrible, you didn't deserve this. But then no one does, he adds fast. In the same breath he bends over to collect some chocolate sauce off his Converse shoe, and licks it.

—You can't see how ugly she is?? How empty? Julianah shrieks.

Jack feels sad for his friend; so he answers with compassion, not with his mind:

—Of course of course!! You are very special Julianah and...

—And did you see what nonsense she's spouting?? Like who does she think she is??

Jack scans the web page with his geeky eyes and shoots automatically:

—Well apparently a writer? I mean I see what you mean but what she's saying isn't... Like... Let me check again perhaps I am missing something.

Eris looks into the camera, smiles enigmatically:

—I am a firm believer in the unity of beauty of the physical body as a triumph of nature and on the other hand, the beauty of the mind; the flight of the mind elevates the body and vice versa. *Mens sana in corpore sana* etc. I believe in letting forces of the subconscious, lust, beauty—these forces roam free, as it were... And she smiles in a near flirty way to the camera. Her megawatt smile adds some kind of hypnotic emphasis to the argument.

I think that's healthy, she continues. But I also think they should be controlled and disciplined by the rational part. No excess, you know?

"So it's not just that you love a good booze-up!"—the interviewer quips. She bursts into laughter, electrically. No... no, bit more than that, I am afraid.

Jack pauses the video again.

Julianah's sobs rip through. He changes the phone to the other ear. Tortured silence.

—Julianah... you will find someone some day. Don't... don't destroy yourself for this.

—Did you see how ugly the bitch??

—Well, ... she's not like you, of course. You're absolutely amazing.

Minutes later, Jack is alone again. He brings lube and tissues, places them carefully by each side of the large monitor frozen with Eris' picture. She is wearing her large pearls and a Victorian style velvet dress. Buttoned up.

With one trembling move, Jack presses play on the interview and unzips his pants.

———✤———

Daniel, striding along the dark streets. Lockdown colors them greyer than ever.

What is the thing that irks him so?

He plays her words again in his head: "I can come to you, I can book this hotel close to your house". Threat alarm. Doesn't even know why.

Vaguely, something from the long dead decades of his childhood down South plays in his head. Almost the same words. What is it? He stops. Frowns, looks down. What is it??

"I have booked a hotel near your house for us. Daniel won't see us. His mom won't know. I can come to you".

Oh. The words of his dad's mistress. He was a child. He heard them on the phone in the big house.

He hated her so. He turned fully to protecting his mom. That was his childhood's cross. Now, Eris was the dad's mistress. In a deep drawer of his mind, the overlap was exact, hence the reactions against his lover. He wasn't even aware. Kick her like a startled horse, ask questions later. In those moments, he ceased being Eris' lover. In those moments, a deep animosity directed his hand.

Panic washed over him. He felt protective of Julianah. He strode into protective mode on autopilot. Eris ceased being the Goddess.

Tough timing. Just then. Eris types again.

Ping.

"You checked any of the hotel links I sent?".

He furiously types to her before she even finishes:

—What is this? You're marking your territory? I will come to you. Patience. No need to kill Julianah. I know you hate her. Haven't you hurt her enough? Wait for me to come to you.

Johnnyville is and will remain her safe space.

On the other side of the mountains, Eris receives these words from a pastel green screen. Some tunnel forms, again. Pulse off the rails. Just earlier she had floated on his love, caressed by dozens of roses.

Now, he cast her down again.

Some echoes in her mind. She recognizes the words. She is triggered.

—What course is this anyway? Her long lost dad barks at her in a hazy memory, long buried. I don't trust these courses, it's dollars out of the window.

—You didn't say that when you financed Aronia's uni fees in Canada and her failed business as a result. That was 100 times more cash than I asked for now.

—Yeah, but she's my wife.

—And I'm your child.

She shakes her head at the memory. It's happening again and she knows it.

"I offered happiness, you rejected. Now all I can offer is misery. You're a mountain of stale repression."

Daniel reads the message, thinks. What has he done?

"Look, I don't' want to be harsh. I am sorry. I will come to you. The right place for us is Dahut. I'll come collect you from Belmont. There, we'll have time and stuff. No need to rush and hide in a hotel like criminals. I mean…I am pretty sure you don't want the risk of running into her. That would be most unpleasant."

She throws a pillow at the wall, downs a whole glass of something or other.

"I hope you enjoy your stellar partner. How's your shoulder wound by the way?

Good night."

He is hurt. He's used to this hurt, but now she's really twisting the knife. In Julianah's knife wound.

"Why don't you go to your stellar oaf?!".

But his silent shriek lost in the digital ether. Eris switched off the chat. She has disappeared again. And he has to walk all the way back home.

To a bed with her. The Lady of the Knife. His very heart winces. His fingers inspect the wound, yet unhealed.

He walks home, forlorn. Combination of resentment and guilt towards Eris. He hates her a bit every time she highlights his ill logic. He understands her too. He longs for her too.

Up in the sky, stars blink and gossip. They look down with superiority on the never-ending human tragedy, the farce of the human comedy. Even the trees rustle with contempt.

Something's gotta give. Something will happen. He knows. Julianah knows.

Eris? She felt the Grandfather Clock chasing them through corridors. "Time". Or its pendulum hovering above the lovers, threateningly. Like a blade.

Tic. Toc.

"Is this check mate?" Eris asks Abe on the phone.

—I tried to ask Daniel about his historical family issues and what's going on there and why the weird rejection when he claims to love me.

She speaks in one breath, playing with her hair.

—And his answer?

—Well he doesn't want to talk about it.

—Why? Did you walk in with your boots again all over his delicate psychology and what I assume is ... mommy issues?

—Yeah, it's not mommy issues. More like me.

—Oh? Daddy issues?!

—Something like that. He sort of sees me at some level as the dangerous dirty mistress he has to defend his poor angelic mom from.

—Oooh. I see. Pause. Abe goes: So Julianah is the mom then.

—Yes. Poor Daniel is the white knight forever defending the defenceless damsel.

—You're very astute, Eris.

—Well I had time to think about it, it's kind of my job.

—Ah, Eris the psychotherapist...

—Well, my job is to think of human behaviour. Think about it. He's been a careerist, a focused scientist since the age of 19. He shoved away any self reflection. He's very repressed. He won't confront these things and by working hard from a young age he avoided serious self reflection we all have to do as part of maturing. And now, when love and the four people situationship (sort of polyamory, but not quite) demands even more thinking, he hides his head in the sand even more.

—Maybe he doesn't.

—What do you mean?

—Well maybe he just genuinely loves her more than you.

—Ah. So I'm really just the mistress.

—Well, think about it, Eris. You wanna see him as the poor innocent victim child in this, Teutonic whatever knight nobly defending victims etc. What if he's ...his dad? You are the mistress. The other woman. Would definitely explain everything.

Eris goes quiet.

—I don't know, it's hard. Of course I often accuse him of that and he vehemently denies. Our love is really intense. I also made some mistakes.

—He wants you to think it's your fault. Were they really your mistakes? What, you didn't want to leave your husband after a week of frolic? No. He's using these things against you to neuter your expectations. To keep you in the box. Make you think it's your fault. But in fact he's not able to leave her.

—So you're saying he's really like a bigamist?

—Well I didn't but now I start to think so. Some people are. You're the passionate love, the excitement. The exploration. She's the compassionate love, the warm nest. The exploitation. He wants both. Oh. Eris puts the phone on loudspeaker. Suddenly the device weighs a ton. She's sitting down. She can hear a cricket from across the neighbourhood gardens. Damn cricket sounds like a fire alarm. Head spins.

—So... Bit like me then?

—Like you? Abe says, picking his teeth with a sewing needle. He leans over the bathroom mirror to admire his pores. Freshly shaven. Such a good job, the new shaver.

—Well, yes, like me, goddammit. Didn't I also sort of keep Stan close?

—Thought you served him divorce papers.

—I didn't. I said I would. But not yet.

—Oooh. Abe stops admiring. Actually listens.

—Come on, girl. You're as bad as poor old Daniel.

—Well, yes. And no. Don't you understand?! She shouts. Head in palms.

It's a fucking feedback loop, Abe. The binary choice is... it's a competition. When fucking Daniel fucks up and puts that... let's say, woman, above me, I lean more towards keeping Stan. Stan looks better the more Daniel errs. It's a fucking binary choice. I'm sorry. It is.

Lately Daniel's been a complete fuck up. Says and does romantic things. But look, Abe. He's not here. He's with her. And I get these excuses. I've heard them all before. But cold reality is ...he's not here. That absence speaks like thunder. So of course poor Stan looks better. Stan calls me everyday, asks how I am. Puts my well-being first. I can actually still now talk to Stan like normal people—none of this psychodrama, this tango of mutual guilt, this hall of mirrors: "yes, but you did this, yes, no, but you did that". And think how much I hurt poor Stan. Yet no guilt tennis, no gaslighting.

I love love. I love passion. And all my passion goes to him.

—Who?

—Daniel, of course, Abe! You not been listening?

—Dunno. Sometimes I wonder if your real passion isn't Stan.

—No, no! Exasperatedly she slams the wall. Stands up and paces back and forth.

—I love Daniel with a passion out of this world. When we're together, ...but she stops for an intake of breath. Then she continues.

When we hold hands, the world is still. There is peace in the Middle East. And bombs stop in the sky. When I hold him close, nothing else matters. And his physical proximity answers metaphysical questions. I can't let go of that, and what would happen if I did?

Our belated teenage romance irrupted in both with the power of a neutron star collision.

But I can't fucking trust him. I'm a rational person. I need someone I can trust. I trust Stan. I'm not attracted to Stan.

—You never been? Abe gets curious.

—No, I was. He wasn't always like this. He let himself go. He ignored me, chased bar girls... But when I was, it was never as magical as it is with Daniel. But long term I have to ask myself... Do I need magic, paid for in so much pain, and an absent lover? Or do I need someone I can trust?

Abe nods though he can't be seen by the friend at the other end of the line.

—I don't know what to tell you. But forcing yourself to be with someone because it sounds good on paper when your heart wants something else won't work either. Maybe you need to fight for this love to the end.

—What do you mean? Eris sees the light in Abe's words. What do you suggest? Her heart races.

—I think you should fight for it.

—But look what he's doing to me!! You said yourself he's a player. She cries.

—Yes, but can you get over? Maybe your heart knows something you don't. Maybe you'll save him and yourself from your shared daddy issues. Maybe you'll make him see the light. He's a bit smart, isn't he. Or maybe not. Either way, worth trying. Can't live like this.

Eris thinks, frowns hard.

—I can't fight for him any-more. Not after the last rejection.

—So can you let it go?

—No. She says without thinking.

—There you go. Then you know what you have to do. It's not for him, girlie-o. You don't do it for him. You do it for yourself. To live it till the end. So you at least know. You fail, game over, you know. But at least you're not living the rest of your life in purgatory. Texting him secretly on shopping trips to town. Begging for phone-calls when his handler lets him.

—I don't know how to thank you, Abe. You're pretty fucking good.

—I know. He beams. I know. But you're not too bad either. And one these days you'll find me a man too and everything will be alright.

—Jesus. I can perform miracles, Abe, but find YOU a guy?? Impossible. They chuckle, like the old buddies they are. In the last minutes of sunset she texts him again. The Daniel. The broken exhausted resorts of the heart start spinning again, fuelled by faint hope. Even the faintest drop of hope breathes life back into the oxidized cogs and wheels of the heart mechanism.

"*My dearest Eris,*

I love you. To me, you are the swan of Belmont. The Queen of Albion.

I am lucky to be alive at the same coordinates of our four-dimensional world as you, somebody like no other, somebody of infinite value.

The woman who captured my heart forever, you define life; you are the definition of everything, the measure of things; alongside you, everything is dull and antiquated. One second with you is worth hundreds of years of life elsewhere.

You were very correct when you said I will never get over you. I won't. I don't want to.

I am in awe at the power of your persona. You opened new worlds to me, I've grown so much through knowing you.

You've revealed so much about me, enhanced me, my ambitions, my horizons. You even made this boy into a man.

Feels like now is the time I should talk about my concerns too. I feel we're a perfect fit. Longer plans? We both know there is uncertainty.

Here, I am losing someone alongside whom I used to function well. With Julianah, my brain had high capacity to think about stuff.

Me and you, we don't have any experience in how well we can work together—an uncertainty that I think bothers both of us. How good are you for my brain?

Our trial in fall crashed and burned. We are both scared.

All I want to is to clear these doubts, so we can be together, finally, like we've dreamed.

What will happen to you when you're old? What will happen to our differences? Will you cast me away, when

you fall out of love? I want relationships that last for-
ever. What if you tire of me? Like a toy. The words you
said a year back are burnt into me. A fear I live with.

I just want to stop this pain, for everyone. Please give
me some time. I can't just throw a certain someone into
cold water. I love you. More than anything.

Sorry if the letter is not great, I am exhausted, things
are hard here. Why is life so painful?!

I'm out for some extended exhaustion—a long bike trip
to the mountains. Let's wipe the tears with sweat and
return to glory".

Eris holds the phone in her hands. Reading with
febrile speed; shoddily, in criss-cross: first the middle,
then the start, then at the end, the first paragraph.

Letters fly of the screen, they seem to intersect each
other in a daze. Letters run away and she has to chase
them with red eyes and bring them back.

As per habit with Daniel's communications, actions
and whole interaction—a huge confusion grips her. It
takes her minutes to comprehend what is said.

She's still not sure.

"Maybe he wants some assurances before he comes
to you?"—Abe says, Cinco agrees. On disparate calls.
Emergency conference called with all her advisors. This
is a big day.

Internet calls and everything digital have due to the
pandemic become the new reality.

Reality with trees and friendly faces, a distant memory.

The poor lighting of zoom calls like ghost visions into
others' houses and endless typing and talking. Everyone
has super-fingers. The Arnold Schwarzenegger of fingers, on hunchback, pasty computer bodies.

It's not even that bad. Eris and Abe became closer
friends. And so her other "advisors". More free time.
Why not enjoy the free lock down time? Time to study
emotions. Look inwards.

—You don't think it's insulting??

—If you want to see it like that. He's got fears. It's weak but... He needs some reassurance. I think it's normal. You might as well give it to him. What else can you do?

I mean, it's worth it, for the best sex of your life.

—What?! It's not just sex, pal. We're deeply in love. It's love making.

—But you always said the sex is unbelievable.

Eris blushes even on the phone. Uncomfortable, she covers her mouth to say the words:

—Look... it wouldn't be sex if there was no love. Understand? I cannot have sex with someone if I don't love them.

—Ah, you damn pervert! So your kink is love, then? You're this type of pervert called demisexual?

Eris frowns, head exploding.

—Abe.. you serious?? This is the normal. This is the human default. You guys having sex in alleys and public toilets while drunk, that's the perversion. I mean, how can you even give your body to someone you don't respect? Or love? Or know at all?! Have you any idea how romantic and divine love making feels?

—Jesus, you damn weirdos. Take it away from me. I don't like! I never, not once, made love. Eugh.

—So you were on board with me and Daniel slapping and flogging each other, or the idea of poly—whatever you call it.. polyamory, bigamy, pervery?.. But you draw the line at making love.

—Sugartits.

Eris' eyes grow like saucers. Defensive snarl forms at the corners of her plump mouth.

—Sugartits. And Abe almost touches his sensual parts. Tell me how well this is working for you. You love him, you can't stand him, you want him only, but you can't be with him. He doesn't want you. He wants you but. Who's the sucker here? Who's hurt?

Do you think I give a fuck when I get my fix in a toilet? I don't even ask their names. Not that that actually happens much any-more. THANK YOU, Coronavirus.

By the way—I know about this place. Like, a really good place. No masks. No Covid pass, no vaccine, no social distancing, no nothing. Let's go. We're all going. Music all night long.

—Who's we?

—The whole gang: Cinco, me, ... Stan.

—Oh. Stan. Oh. Anyway. Abe. Look. You people are weird. The most natural thing in the world is to tie sexual desire to love. To separate them leads to a sort of loss of the soul. Good sex? I don't get it. Good love making? Yes. When you worship the other. When simply breathing next to their head, grazing the skin of their cheek is the most intense experience of your life.

—Eugh! Get away with this stuff. I don't like intimacy, I don't want cuddles, I can't stand people after sex. And now I am going to make some lockdown cocktails with my neighbor. You know, just to cleanse the taste of this conversation.

I much prefer porn to any of this.

Eris stops and thinks.

—I actually think porn damages something deep and intimate in the soul; like chasing sugar and burgers and cheap thrills to reward yourself, in absence of merit, no proportion to effort applied. Food isn't meant to be had for leisure fifty times a day. Constantly filling the emotional void in your life with empty calories.

Same with porn and casual sex, Abe. You are a bi-ological machine that's evolved chemical rewards to propel you forward to do things. To get better. Sexual pleasure is meant to motivate people making and then raising kids. People in this capitalist age just separate the reward button on its own, and press it like monkeys to buzz themselves to death; to obesity, to depravity, etc. Shopping for dopamine, not because you need stuff. Isolating intimacy from the sex is like the Christian loss of the soul. It doesn't just affect women. It affects men too, as much as you guys claim you can shoot sperm left and right with no psych consequences. Well it ain't like that: you pay a price. Deep intimacy and love, that feels divine, the best approximation we humans have to the divine. Deep, meaningful, healthy. Sacred.

I've had this with that idiot. It was too good. There's no going back. You perverts can go somewhere and fuck each other to death like numpties. I'll keep my beautiful pure soul romance.

—And tell me, Eris. In this pure body soul romance Christian utopia: do you provide oral? Yes or no.

—Fuck off.

Eris walks along the park alleys, stopping every three minutes to reply to texts.

She hasn't replied to Daniel yet. He checks the chat often.

She feels fury. Fury and outrage.

But the weird thing is she feels even more adoration somehow. A cognitive dissonance that hurts, that is deeply intrinsic to loving or even knowing the Daniel.

She does what she does best: type to him, from a bench. Cold fingers typing furiously, dark silhouettes spying from the shadows. Big cloud of paranoia and doom over all of them.

"*You feel distressed, unhappy, captive. You make your own life and take your stubborn decisions and listen to no one.*

But you're very amenable to a certain person's coercion and the gestures you do under that influence lead your life into ruin.

Happens when you lack your own moral system and will; when you act more out of pity for the weak than the pursuit of positive but hard constructive things. A path to misery and destruction.

You invest your energies in saving the sinking dependents; the professionally weak. Then you wonder why your life a mess.

You get what you invest in.

You vaguely want me, the so-called Goddess. But you are so often available to the emotional manipulations of the aimless, that what you actually build is commiseration. An island of aimlessness, propping each other with delusions, fighting hard to just stay alive, just pay the bills, just keep depression at bay. Shove problems under the rug, carving one more day of illusory entertainment off life: one more slice of cake, one more superhero movie, one more couple's crochet class. Meanwhile, the monsters under the rug ripening, ready to devour. The abstract monsters the menial eyes of Disney housewives can't see.

You act like rats in a lab experiment pursuing short term gain: faux comfort, absence of confrontation, fear of inducing heartbreak, of leaving someone who's grown too dependent, domestic peace, inertia. These small, glory-less things ruled your life decisions these past years of your life and our year of relationship more than concepts of long term benefits and the courage of pursuing something great: our spectacular love.

All settling, no aspiration. Sleep of the soul. Decay.

This is not just you by the way. It is a scourge of our times. The meek inherited the world. The meek, weak, mediocre, are put on a pedestal. People of value have to apologize for being talented. She is rewarded by having the Prince.

Her meager artistic efforts, though scorned by professionals, receive your cheers, because look, the poor girl, she's trying, let's give everyone a participation trophy.

But I am "arrogant".

Typical of the age of the Worship of Mediocrity.

She is beautiful on the inside, nice and kind, because she has achieved nothing and all she has to give is passive support and bovine obedience without question; raising no intellectual questions, not challenging you with ideas. Welcoming you home from tiring work with wifely offerings, muted.

You are a slave at work and at home you have your own slave. What a hierarchy. That's history for you.

And despite your progressive leanings, despite your young age, your education, you arranged your life in this patriarchal way, and with your subconscious impulsive decisions, have put your whole energy into preserving this status quo—because you're terrified of the alternative. You have fear of heights.

You aspire to me, but that requires courage and big gestures; easier to fall asleep on the conveyor belt in your own abattoir. Despite your scintillating career, this life reeks of inertia. The delusional comfort of losers. You don't apply your own scientific mind to your own personal life.

You aspire to me with all your being—it's why you can't sleep at night, and wake up twenty times to check my digital communications. You could be with me in Albion, curled together on the sofa, asking me directly what I am doing. Doing it together.

But you know you can't handle me. I challenge you. I put up a mirror you don't like. I unmask you. I dismantle the "savior" mythologies you crafted of yourself. Knight in shiny armor. And you resent me for casting light on them. You try to forget me every morning, and by evening you discover your hand in your pants dreaming of me, compulsively, possessed by me, entirely. Hand on your soul. Consumed by that which you do not grasp, and are too weak to stand up and reach.

Yet with your whole being, you resist. You prefer this torture to living.

At first, you trusted me, blindly, you let me lead the dance. Now you claim I'm a tyrant if I suggest to meet. You're not meant to lead, but you won't be led. Conundrum.

You prefer this life, this purgatory. You try to cleverly joggle the tortured emotions of two women. You think by being there for her in this half hearted way it's still better than letting her live her own life. Or maybe you know she'll completely sink without you. Too weak to truly let go.

Do you ever ask yourself what you want?

And think by sending me virtual hugs and vague promises, you keep me. You dream of a vague abstract future with me. Just not at the cost of cutting this invalid off entirely. You think I will understand. That I will wait. Let the Goddess wait.

I don't need your virtual hugs. Hug emojis? Are you a teen?! I don't even need them in person. Hugs can't help when your mind and heart are set against me. I don't need body heat. I need understanding. Which is absent.

Just so you know, the "Goddess" also has a heart. She's not the only one suffering. I am collecting the pieces of my soul, shattered on the floor of a blood bath.

I stand by all this. I know your limitations. You flew high with me, for five minutes; but your wings broke from the superhuman effort of keeping that altitude.

I know all this. I resent the way you reject my analysis because to you keeping fake mythologies of self is more precious than the cold fresh air of truth. Life affirming, renewing, truth, that can help grow, and conquer heights.

But.

But. But. But. This is my mind speaking. My mind, a constant exertion that spins into a vacuum like a broken mechanism no longer fit for purpose. And it's no longer fit because there is something here I don't understand. A variable I haven't fed into the equation. Or fighting against something stronger. Not bigger. Stronger. My heart.

But guess what? Too late for me now.

Unfortunately love is stronger. Don't know why, can't explain.

I am done following my head. I only have my mind. I've the burning ruins of conclusions and calculations that lead to me to disaster; and the strangely untouched column of light emerging from them that is my love. Stronger than ever.

I was proven wrong. My mind failed. So all I have is my heart—my love. It is all true. But through your repeated cowardly rejections, I swapped back and decided to agree with my mind once more. Often decided to fight and hate my own heart for being wrong. Block or ignore you for weeks at a time. And it's hard. It is my own heart, after all, and yours.

So despite all the above, I have to let go. For now. I won't fight my heart any-more. Be what may. Come to Belmont to pick me up. Meet me in Dahut. Choose the date. What will be will be. But be warned. This will be your last chance."

—A year of this, can you believe?

—I know!! Like yesterday we were still free.

—What you talking about?! Says Abe, grabbing the necks of his pals. We still are!!

The clothes wrap tightly on the hot bodies. Girls in their twenties dance with sparks in their eyes. Drunk.

Boys keep their lust under check for later. No one wears masks. Some strange character in the corner with a FFP2 mask on like a grandpa. Stan, actually.

The music makes it hard to hear but no one is there for the conversation.

—So happy to see people again!! Shouts a young girl in Eris' ear as she passes by with drinks in both her hands.

Yes, yes. Eris nods. She is wearing a vintage overall, with heels. Tied at the waist, unbuttoned. A certain pendant hanging from her neck on a Venetian gold chain. She touches it from time to time. It's like it's from him, from what seems like a previous life. Her hair down. Posture tall and neck sinewy, heavy under so many thoughts.

Also bit of happiness.

From literally minute to minute, she feels her phone in her pocket. Checks it out.

Puts it back in, annoyed.

—Stan! Are you okay?

Stan isn't. He doesn't want to talk. His checked shirt nearly undone. Not to be sexy, but because he doesn't care. But he approaches, gaunt. Dances a bit, hollow eyes. Eris is at once annoyed and tear eyed.

—Oh, okay let's give you a hug.

The hug feels like a gorilla clasp. He nearly faints into her, she suffers it quietly, waiting for him to release her.

—You look so much better!! You well? You haven't come to collect your last box.

—I don't care. Are you still with him? He says, sweet eyes but defensive voice. Stan is the master of carefully calibrated emotions and nuances, direct statements too. He is also bit relentless. Resolved to never let go. Wait patiently. She has to see the light.

She's saved by Abe, coming in, dancing with them. She dances.

Flicks her hair around. All eyes on her. She's not out to seduce. Her mind obsessed with him. Every thought. She takes a selfie, sends it to him.

A love gravitas sobers her facial features, but they still look young; the architecture of her face still angular, solar. Not even the ritual rejections of Daniel in favor of the little woman managed to destroy her confidence.

The rest of the night is a hysterical back and forth between violent dancing to indie songs and arguing or chatting to the Daniel. The boy that wasn't here.

He's happy for her. He's also jealous.

"Wine really loves me!" she flirts. "Awesome" —his retort comes: "wine also isn't jealous when you drink beer. Perfect."

"Why jealous, darling?! Shouldn't I be?"

But he disappears. Maybe he's cooking dinner. So homely, the scientist. So serious. She thinks. She's drunk. "Call me". No response. So she dances with some twenty year old who thinks it's his lucky night. Boys always do that—they mistake her general aura for seduction of them. But being healthy and full of life isn't a siren call to every man and boy that happens to cross her path. Boys don't really understand biology, do they? She'd explain it to them, but she's busy thinking of one specific boy.

Hour later, Daniel texts back. "Sorry, was busy". "Don't worry"—she texts. "A bottle of Pinot Noir called me instead and it really loves me!". "But I love you!"—he insists.

Truth is, the boy found time to quickly check his messages, on a break from the Marvel movie he's sat with Julianah to watch, on the sofa in Johnnyville—when Julianah dashed to pee. Soon as she's back in the room, suspiciously, his phone back in his pocket. On silent. He reaches his arms to cuddle her. She leans in for a bit of a kiss. He turns his cheeks away, pressing "play" on the video. His cheeks are for Eris only, he thinks, clenching them.

By the sofa, his luggage is packed. He's aware of it as he returns to the broken harmony of the sort of former couple. He is looking at the screen, but thinking of "her". The eternal Her. Her last letter. The future. Maybe he learns from his mistakes, she from hers. Maybe.

Julianah is looking at the screen, thinking of her own plans. The pulse of both racing, anticipation, excitement. But different internal worlds altogether. Resolutions profiling on the horizon for both. No common narrative any-more though. They may not be divorced in facts, but they are totally divorced in narratives.

Dancing under the improvised disco lights, Eris looks alive and happy. Her arms snake around with grace, energy shooting off her hips. You wouldn't even tell she's dead on the inside.

He is riding a mustang; fierce in controlling the animal. Riding through the desert, shirt undone, cowboy hat on, kept with his left arm while the right on the horse.

He's squinting, hard, to see through the blaze. Something catches his finely tuned senses... somewhere there is danger. Through a torrid landscape he dreams obstacles and races to an objective he doesn't yet know; then. Stops. In the horizon, reflecting like *fata morgana*... perhaps an illusion. An illusion in a dream. But a vivid dream at the gates of dawn.

He sees her.

For some reason, she's wearing a long cotton skirt, a ripped cotton check shirt. The ripped cotton flies in the wind like a curtain, dancing in the air around her. Lifting her up. He just sees a cloud of red fabric twirling, flipping, covering her, trying to take her away. Her screams, muted. Her figure, slimmer than ever. Gaunt. Cheekbones cutting through space.

His heart thumps. Eris! Has to save her. He gallops. But unable to reach, as though the faster the horse gallops, the farthest she disappears into the horizon, melting with it. Who is she running from? A large, dark, dragon, with a kippah atop his messy hair. Holding his tortoise shell comb like a weapon. Letting out fumes and a gnarl. So fierce the sky darkens when he stands up. He wants to kill his love. Daniel dashes to save her, and it is the inescapable feeling he can't, he isn't anywhere near her, that consumes him. Not just the desert heat, but this heroic impotence, this futility... his dream feels like a nightmare. Sweat, sweat rain, water, heavy eyes like he's about to faint with heat stroke. One more time her faint scream. Where is she?

Then he wakes up. Next to him, a gently snoring, plump faced Julianah. Occupying the whole bed. He lies perched on one edge, almost defying gravity. He's thirsty. What time? He grabs his phone, where he knows she is, where he can check for signs of life from her.

And alas!—she also has been awake all night, he can tell. In the kitchen, he pushes the cold glass of water into his neck, his forehead. To chill. Chilling is needed.

⬥————⋘⋙————⬥

Rolling in her satin sheets, under the Venetian chandelier, she's clutching the pillow, grinding her teeth. Having a nightmare.

It starts like a garden party in a castle. She's there, like in one of her socials, before the apocalypse. Holding a glass of this or other fancy booze—Bellini, her favorite cocktail; laughing, making poignant points to various erudite interlocutors while punctuating with a florid arch of her brow. Then jumping to the next person, next flower to pollinate, next victim to insert a virus of psychosexual seduction into the brain of; talking of this and that current affairs with confidence with a bit of Seinfeld about her, and a bit of Marilyn Monroe. Many good points were probably made, which only she could make, but—alas!—they'd be a tad lost on her audience, who was always too dazzled by the glamorous glow of the way her precise doll face drew shapes in the air as she talked—to hear what she actually talked about. And in her dream, she knew this clearly from the befuddled eyes of people she glazed over in a frantic but self-controlled search of her love.

Often checking nervously to locate a friendly hypnotic presence, a sweet torture—the one presence that mollifies her dominant vocal tones, the one man who can elicit sweetness. The boyfriend she came here with. The Daniel.

A dominant femme fatale to all people everywhere, a sweet little girl to him—a puddle of shy innocence. Him and only him had an involuntary skill to dissolve layers upon layers of adulthood and experience to reveal the needy girl who liked attention and demanded it loudly, stamping feet and throwing paper planes to punish the intended, otherwise busy audience.

In the castle party, silhouettes mingle at sunset; a sweet murmur and roses, cascading over gilded arches, and over white cloth tables. And a blue sea sparkling on the horizon, ready to absorb the world as soon as the little people stop their little party.

She winces. He's there. She located him in the corner of her eye while chatting impatiently with an elder lady whose elbow she gently taps to excuse self.

He is charming people too, in the halls of the castle, sipping cocktails defensively while disagreeing with various parties. Looking nervously left and right, trying to act interested, looking for her.

And then they randomly clash together, back to back, the clink of the glass against their teeth, liquid spraying over their chests. Bewitched, they turn to each other; their eyes see each other for the hundredth time like the first time; mist melting the contour of almond shaped eyes; pupils like saucer plates. Electricity drives their fingers together, which touch with a deep mutual sigh, as they drop head back heavy under the weight of emotion; inhaling each other, drawn together in a magic haze floating in the sunset light.

—You are wearing the shirt you gifted me! Daniel giggles.

—well you didn't like it, dear, you said "I'M TOO MUCH MAN FOR SALMON PINK"; you don't wear pink. And she talks while tracing a line on his neck, inhaling his hair, defying gravity in golden curls framing his head like a Botticelli painting. His white skin responds to her breath, incandescent with love.

—But it's a men's shirt. He protests playfully, just to say something, anything. He often does. "His neurons affected by her"—his excuse; "what do you expect when you torpedo my neurons with your hotness?".

She tears away from their surreal embrace to look down at her pink masculine shirt, worn loosely over a very thin silk summer dress. The shirt fluttering long in the wind barely covers the areas that the silk dress uncovers around her lithe body, in random cut-out triangles here and there. Her body comes alive next to him, like she's a dancer, a fever possesses her muscles, arched and ready to take off with him somewhere. Anywhere. Out of here.

She smirks and whispers into his ear, even closer, so close he receives her voice straight into his brain:

—Well... I decided to be the man I wanted you to be. He sprinkles in laughter, drawing her closer, into him, they curl their necks together, like swans.

But then. He walks off, holding her hand. Pushing the crowd aside. The muted evening scene unravels for them, like a parted Red Sea. Then among all these guests, his hand gets lost. Him too. She looks at her hand, which feels incomplete without his. The crowd has swallowed him, and she's standing alone, looking left, right, but the sun blinds her, a huge, huge, massive sun, drowning violently in the sea with the explicit intent to take the world with him.

Her dad. Her dad is there, in the spot on the dance-floor where she lost Daniel. It's still hot, the party has moved to the mountains. Her dad turns his back to her. He says to his party, don't know who she is, let's move on. Left her there like a beggar with a stretched hand. She looks at her hand, shudders. Blood forms in the crevasses of the hand. Then looks once more at her dad—he turns around to look, as if he forgot something. This time it's him. Daniel. It's his face. His party of female friends laughs at him for wasting time, at her. She sees their contemptuous grins lined up like a parade of horror. He doesn't want to be laughed at, so he grabs the arms of his companions, and goes.

She's talking to someone. About the whole thing. The talking feels meaningful, but it's just a dream. It is gibberish. She walks back home, but what is home—the home of her youth? A composite of all the homes she ever had? It's a home, anyway. And it feels like she has friends marching home with her, supporting her weight, as she grows feeble, and faltering. Sort of fainting into these supporting arms.

She calls him once more from a pay phone, like a single phone booth atop a sunset hill. Almost a British old fashioned booth, like they used to have. Inside, it's scorching, and she suspects fever. She calls. It rings, like a fire alarm. Rings incessantly enough to wake up the whole town but not enough to get him. He doesn't pick up. Nothing new, then.

So she wakes up. Eyes glaring up. Something a bit wrong, she feels. So she grabs her phone to check what he's doing.

Instead of signs from him, it's a message from Stan. That's a pattern that keeps happening. She hopes for Daniel, she gets Stan.

"Chag Pesach. Want me to bring you anything? Could dash to you, I am nearby. No trouble. Matzo? You like them."

"What the fuck? I actually really don't like them"—she mutters to self.

Eris ignores. Rolls back into sleep, phone under the covers. Really dreaming, hoping for messages from him. The Daniel. The princely ghost tormenting her soul.

"Have to send a correction to something I said in my last letter—I don't think beauty doesn't exist anymore (paragraph 12): just spend a whole evening checking out Kitty Spencer's Instagram. Bella Hadid too. No, there is still beauty.

Just thought I would send this for precision's sake. You know I don't like to leave a record of falsities."

Then she inserted an upside down smile emoji.

She went by her day.

No reply.

He just wasn't as concerned with beauty as her. Beauty. Such a strange concept. Not like kindness, or loyalty. Or cooking a good barbecue.

—Julianah! Where is my charger? Need to go out for a bit. Stay put. Working for an hour then coming home.

———⚬⚬⚬———

Eris locks the door. Even locking the door reminds her of that other door; she finds composure and steps out, one step at a time.

Empty streets. Pretty park further down. It's where prisoners live their allotted open air time. Socially distanced, masked and muzzled.

Martin there, on a bench, waiting.

As she parades down the alleys, all sorts of lockdown spectacles.

She notes two twins in a baby carrier eating ice cream that has all melted down their chests in rainbow colors. Baby-faces looking up at her, bit dumbfounded by life. The mother, seeing her spawn transfixed with Eris, worries they'll catch Coronavirus from her; so speeds up, face down and away. There is a little furry white dog chasing its tail, looking like a globe with beady eyes. "What's that cushion doing, running down the road "—Eris jokes to self as per habit, pacing self to arrive to meeting point in time.

—So. Martin. What say you? Isn't lockdown awesome? ...Less fucking people around?! .. finally, some privacy? And she chuckles in her typical fashion that makes her pearls sparkle, curls bounce.

—Yeah, kind of. Finally have time but no lust to use it? Actually got ill, lost people, brain cells, the works...

Eris hugs him with a bit of a buffer zone.

—Sorry, Martin.

Well, if I am honest I am a bit shit too.

—Yeah, Eris, tell me. What is this clusterfuck? You turned Mormon on me, they say.

—Who says?

—a little bird—his words come out with a sniffle. Come on, tell me.

—I am not Mormon, Martin. I am ... in a complex... sort of amorous situation...

Like a faux polyamory situation. Poly more on his side than mine. Really I want it to be monogamous but the.. complicated object of my affections seems a bit reluctant to... erm... don't know. Don't know.

Short, stubby, cute, full of heart, Martin frowns hard, to understand. To support his friend and client.

He is referring throughout this effort not so much to his own life experience, which is limited, but literature he read, which is enormous. And many friends he advised on similar park benches, elsewhere.

He pats his friend on the back.

—I know. A failed love is a death. Something permanently dies in you. You can find new things to care about, but that hole stays there.

A heavy prophetic silence breeds great promise on his side. He also has stories to tell.

Eris kicks back her head, surprised. No. She won't let the discussion float to his stories. She's not told hers.

—No, what?! I don't think it's over. Don't want it to be. I am still going!

—Oh. Sorry. Was my understanding ...

—Yes, you're correct. Daniel isn't exactly here. It's hard. Harder to explain. She looks outside for help, playing with her wrist watch.

Oh, God. Feel like I've been through a cycle in a really aggressive cosmic washing machine.

Look. He's not here. But we talk. It's hot. We want to meet in Dahut. Resolve once and for all. There are snags, you know, as you've heard.

—Big snags if I heard well... Martin adds semi-shyly, ascribing a circle in the warm air with short fat fingers.

Eris is set on not giving too much technical detail. It's more about the feelings.

—I feel strange. Like a Don Quixote born in the wrong place wrong time battling windmills with missing limbs and a cage around my neck.

Martin looks a bit lost.

—Don Qui...?

—Well you know!! Like I'm battling windmills on my jagged horse believing in fucking medieval romance that probably isn't there.

—Really? Not at all?

—It sort of is there... when together. When apart, it's conflict and pain.

There is a reality in his arms and another in his deeds.

I tried to let go because he's bad for me; but then I remember the magic ... it won't let me live. It won't!

Bulbous eyes and exasperated hands underline that statement, exploding forward, in an attempt to leave the body that drags her in the direction of Daniel like an evil gravity force.

—The mind forgets. The heart doesn't forget. Right? Her friend asks with weighted words of an Oracle, patting her on the knee. Bit of a wordsmith, this Martin; and he knows it.

Pause. He shakes head, pursing lips. Am I right?!

—Erm.. what do you mean.

—Think your mind says one thing, your heart another. He did you wrong, you forget that; but can't get over the good bits. The passion.

A crow flies out of the bush straight into their faces, confused. Young and aimless.

Eris hides behind her bag.

—Well, I can't get these things past you, and she giggles. You read the situation too well.

Although to be fair I did frankly sort of just said it to you myself. Didn't I?!

—yeah, yeah, just not exactly the same. We're trying to get to the bottom of this here bit by bit.

She continues speaking, from her mental tunnel. She's not as as in control as a year back. Her mouth an outwards projector of the film of love that spins her thoughts in an internal merry go round; daily, to exhaustion. Hoping, trying, to make her friend see the same film, understand. Escape the loneliness of her thoughts a few minutes. Sharing is like opening windows in the stale bedroom of a moribund.

—Can't fight so many feelings. Got a duty to pursue my heart, because even if I stifled these emotions, because the mind said so—I won't sleep at night. Just common sense. Who knows, maybe the heart (the subconscious, the hormones, whatever)—knows something I don't.

—Ah, yes; **or** the subconscious just wants you to repeat bad scenarios your parents put you through in your youth.

Slight dent in the perfect glamorous composure of Eris.

Slight bags under her eyes. The collagen, the yoga, the treatments don't hold together this skin anymore; she's finally showing her years. Sleepless nights and daily crying weakened the structure of her face. Thoughts carved new relief in the musculature of her pretty face.

—Martin, so ...I worry about that. You sound like Abe! He says this to me.

My phone is pickled in tears of frustration! I cry in that damn chat with "him" every single day.

Our bodies united, our minds in conflict...

It was stolen divine moments even as my heart was being made into mince meat. By this someone. That someone doesn't matter. I lived this love alone. And my friends who had to listen to so much soap.

I guess if it needs to happen, it happens. I wouldn't have seen this coming, thought I was too old for this. But life comes at you, manifests your fears in these boulders that dominate your mind for years. Manifests your childhood demons, your unsolved issues. Whatever your parents did you wrong. You're lucky if you can dust yourself off at the end and move on. Lucky if you understood what happened to you. Most people don't. Have to really be aware and pay attention. Analyse everything, critically. Don't forgive yourself, don't entertain delusions. Don't allow self flattering illusions. Don't let your understanding of what happened to you drown in a sickly sweet high corn syrup.

She wipes her nose, inhaling the pride of what she's just said. If only her pal and agent could also appreciate the artistry, the sentiment...

—Yeah, don't give me this inspirational Instagram wisdom. Look at you. You cry. You fear. You snivel. You're human, Erissy! Who do you think you are??

—The thing is not that you don't feel these things, Martin dear. Fear and sadness and all the less pleasant impressions of reality on the human mind. We all do, of course. The idea is what you do with them. How you react to them. Do you see me hide under a rock and cry life's unfair? Build a fort of delusions telling myself it's everyone's fault and winners must have slept with the jury and that grapes are sour? No. I fight. I take my fear, and invest the adrenaline into my fight. I take fear and invest in growing like a businessman. Fear is an asset. Not an excuse to crawl and wait to die. I don't want to die. I won't accept anything that seeks to make me die. I won't let this crush me. Won't let anything crush me. I'll fight it. OK???

Such wise words, Martin whispers in response. See? You're fine. You don't need my advice. You know what is what.

Half bored, half thinking of himself—is he analysing himself? Does he entertain delusions? Is there a life after death? Shall we pursue eternal youth? Do they still sell cheeseburgers in that shack down the left gate of the park?

Pause.

—Well, see darling? He starts to get ready to go. You know what to do already. Now what exactly does this mean in terms of actions, or...?

CHAPTER XV

His zip is stuck; he is stood there with his luggage, ready to go. Suitcase at the ready. Damn zip won't budge threatening to rip his whole skin with it.

Nervous, he looks over his shoulder.

He just about escaped her attention. He has to say goodbyes. Will be gone with the evening train.

Just to take out the trash and a few more chores, then he's free.

He's elated and excited. Like that first time he hopped on a train to her for the first time. When he knocked on the door of the Albion cottage not knowing what would be there. What could there be? But life, excitement, romance. He had dreamed. Full smile lit his visage. It paid off. He got her. He is THAT good.

Maybe she isn't here with him now... He shuffles uncomfortably, still struggling with the zip—but he has her obsessed. She loves him. That tickles him. Makes him feel important. And somehow, the fact she's suffering and crying for him, makes him feel even more so. Like, if they just had happy times together, it somehow wouldn't feel as much of a victory? Somehow, the fact it's hard, makes him feel a hero; a battle hard won. If she's with him DESPITE all this, then it's love. Everyone can be together in health. When times are fun.

Chin up. Hair off his face with an intrepid head shake. Up and forward, is the future. This is it. Life is happening now. He's going for it. A hero's journey.

He feels a pleasant circularity, satisfying sense of chickens coming home to roost. He has her at his feet. She repents. Took all the guilt on her own yoga defined shoulders; ready to give him a hero's welcome, probably drop to his feet.

His chest puffs up; like his pupils.

March of triumph in his ears, and he even gets a little erect in the nether regions. This type of architecture of events feels right.

Then something happens. Something entirely predictable and yet so unexpected. Something that destroys the beautiful castle of cards inside his head.

Daniel turns his head, unsure. Has he really heard Julianah cry? Was it really the unmissable sound of the weeping woman of his hopes and compromises.

Her fingers in his side. Her breath on his neck, as she stands on her toes to reach.

—Let's say goodbye properly. She whispers, suddenly seductive.

His breath freezes.

—I know I can't convince you to stay. Go and find your happiness with her. But just give me two days!! Switch your phone off, we do nice things, like the old days. You owe me that much, after all we've had. That would be the chivalrous thing to do, for a man like you. A good bye gift. Then I'll leave you alone.

He takes moments to think, sweat rolling greasily down his neck, eyeballs rolling heavily around the room, calculating possibilities. It can't hurt, he tells himself. He is after all deeply kind.

—It can't hurt, she whispers. Licking his neck.

He feels uneasy. But... That old thing. That old sense of duty, of divine over arching pity. A strange sense of obedience to her emotional tactics. Deep down he's made to follow, and she knows where the button lies.

He turns around. Stares behind her ear, tensely. She continues seducing. Hand in his pants, chest pushing into him, unbuttoning his shirt and licking his chest.

—Okay. He looks down. Hesitant. Okay. He utters loudly, again.

Ping is heard and ignored from his pocket. He reads later in a private moment, quickly.

"I don't know why, but the room is spinning. Think it's love?"

Yet another playful Eris text. Like usual, he doesn't understand her humor. He switches the phone off entirely. "It's disrespectful to leave it on, babes, it's like you are not even present with me; the phone is her; I am me, and I'm here"—smiles Liddel sweetly, tilting her head submissively.

He walks back into the chintz sitting room, like beckoned by an invisible leash.

Nodding to himself, "this is the right thing to do. Eris will have me forever; let's give this poor girl something. She deserves it, after a decade of loyal service".

Inside, Julianah has prepared. The room is lit with candles.

She removes her jumper. She stands there nude, in just her Hello Kitty underpants.

She looks even plumper than last time he's seen her naked; in fact so much so, that the belly hangs over the nether regions, and the weight of the breasts pulls on her back furthermore. There is no neck, it has disappeared into the flab, and as she stands there bright eyed and bushy tailed—a monument to the perils of gravity—he feels nothing. Vague queasy feeling swiftly recycled into a duty of care for the weak. Like weakness is a virtue, because it soothes the savior complex of the half living.

———⬦⬦⬦———

Cinco stands on the side-walk in a hazmat suit. His staff too. Everyone is excited, as excited as they can be in the midst of so much death and suffering. Life had truly become a horror movie. Broadcast in apocalypse tones on every Twitter and Facebook channel and every private conversation. A digital chorus of horror.

Deep eye circles, lack of sleep, too much screen time, in and out of work. Everything is now gazing into a screen. All the procedures of constantly sanitizing, putting layers and layers of disposable plastic between themselves and the world; makes everything feel unreal, muffled. Muzzled. Humans through these rituals more and more removed from the reality of the senses that tells them they have each other. Like they don't even have each other. Just the protective gear.

But. The glimmer of hope is about to arrive. In a van. The first batch of vaccines. For them, and for some of the patients. Bit of sunshine through the clouds again.

—I don't know why they're so late, again. We've been waiting for a fucking year. It feels like a year.

—Don't worry, they I'll turn up soon. Says one of the older docs. A surgeon. No one has any interest in not being here before the curfew. Through the masks and everything, sounds travel muffled. It's hard to hear other human beings, so people learn to give up; unless truly necessary, in which case they need to shout—so because they can't shoot all the time, they only speak and listen selectively. Everyone with their own internal priority scale. Here, saving lives, being all medical, is it. Disgust, physical disgust. A sense of tiredness and constantly being on the verge of retching. This group gathered here on the pavement are technically survivors, but none of them feels as such. Medical school is tough training, but not tough enough for this. See, in normal tough times, you have your jollies, your little rewards at the end of the day. Bit of social time, a good meal, bit of alcoholic frenzy rubbing yourself against someone in a bar after work. Not now. All you have is your laptop and your cat at home—if lucky. And portioned daily walks and supermarket trips. That everyone gets ready for like it was the prom.

But no more. All this will soon end, they say.

—It's over, isn't it, brother. Says a young black doctor with youth in his eyes. Now we have the vaccine, we can pop champagne and book those summer holidays.

—You do you, Dean. But I am not sure it's all over yet as such. The vaccine helps. It's no miracle cure. And it will be a long way to vaccinate all, and look at all the numbers who'll say no.

—Look at them how? Where?

—Well I mean, feel the pulse online. A lot of folk just don't wannabe lab rats, you know?

Here is where nurse Hatch feels it's her moment to shine, from behind her face visor:

—All those damn conspiracy theories. The dirty conspiracy theorists with blood on their hands, they tell people not to get the vaccine. They oughta be shot if you ask me.

Bit of quiet follows. Dean coughs into his suit.

—There's a lot online. Good, bad... Just got to take it with a pinch of salt. Judge for yourself.

—You oughta trust the science, that's what you gotta do!! The nurse underlines, louder than before.

—Well, technically, Sarah.. says Cinco while winding his quartz wrist watch. Technically... And he shakes his head to refocus his derailed train of thought.

Yeah. "Trust the science" the dictum doesn't make much sense. If you think about it, the very nature of science is the opposite of blind following. Science also isn't one unitary block. It's just a system of trial and error. Science isn't religion. You don't just obey. That's precisely what humanity did with the advent of the scientific paradigm: shifted from one obedience based paradigm of "believe and do not question", to a paradigm of "question everything, test everything". Science means we no longer repeat inherited wisdom and replay it ritualistically hoping good rewards fall from the sky for being a good puppy. Science means we take matters into our own hands and test the universe, brick by brick, to find out what it's made of. Not believe old scripture about it. Science means healthy scepticism; asking questions, informing yourself. People who say "trust the science" are importing religious thinking and applying it to its opposite. It's a bit like shooting yourself in the foot if you like. Shows people are overall very submissive and even when science tries to liberate them, show solutions and forward thinking, they still act like servants of God, sitting there waiting to be told what to do, what not to do, to be patted on the head for doing good, and punished for thinking astray. Except God is now "health bodies". Or some TV scholar. Who's also on the state payroll.

Dean chortles. "You sound a bit harsh on people, Doc. Most white collar professionals think with their mind, that's what they're paid for".

Cinco winds his watch some more.

—I'd say they are paid to not think outside their little field of expertise, if you ask me.

Dean goes on with an agreeable smize.

—Not that I disagree, to be honest. But the science on this is solid. On the vaccine.

—Maybe. Says Cinco, tensely. But the idea you just obey the current science and that's it, is wrong. Gotta use that critical thinking.

The nurses shift uncomfortably. The van approaches. The delivery of the first batch of the vaccine is here. Officially. General deep sigh of relief. From the heroes of the forefront of this particular war. They've had enough. What wouldn't they do to return to just a bit of life, and bit less death.

—It's them dying alone that gets me, you know. Says Dean. How they're left there, choke to death, not able to see their family. Awful, you know. Might have shell shock by now, I think.

Sarah jumps with "think you'll find the word for that is PTSD these days; more politically correct". Wave of Thatcherite authority washes over her blond wrinkled face.

Cinco laughs.

—Ha, what are you doing Dean, my man. Speaking in antiquated language to trigger the conceptual police.

—The what now? Police what? Says the nurse, bit of cookie falling off her mouth as she speaks.

When Eris opens the door, myriads of petals invade on a breeze. Spring is here. She never enjoyed the blossom with him, she thinks. So much she's not enjoyed with him. Breathing in the morning air on her balcony, lips kissed by pink blossom. "Sakura", like that tea house she likes down the road.

Room suddenly spinning. "Wow, this spring air is strong stuff!"—she jokes to self, as per habit. She's got this habit of being cordial to herself. Why not? She's always been her best friend, through all that life threw at her.

Puts the dizzy spell down to love. Yet another physiological symptom of such obsessive love. How many have there been? Dozens! Life's become a fucking parade of them.

She wants another sharp intake of this flowery oxygen. Tight chest, slightly new sensation. She has to clutch the balcony balustrade lest she falls, looking down from the second floor trying to shake off the vertigo.

She wraps her robe and walks back in, determined to go Albion. Luggage in the car already. Smaller suitcase lying open ready to be filled. Full of dresses and dainty things. Frippery. She likes it, props in her theater of love.

Enthusiasm drives her mind but her body says no; by the time she descends the stairs to make coffee, her energy wasted. She once more dismisses the thought of anything serious and just soldiers on, powered by love.

It is at this stage that she texts him playfully "I don't know why, but the room is spinning. Think it's love?". "Earth spinning round our love"—she thinks, but doesn't send.

She stands there coffee pot in hand waiting to see his reaction. Is message read? Yes, it is. Does he reply? She wants him to reply. Ask if she's okay. She plays the dialogue in her mind. He says "I worry about you"; she says, "don't worry, I am made of steel"; "of course you are, darling, but take care of yourself"; to which she would reply—"but don't worry, darling; whatever it is, seeing you will be the cure". She paints all this in her head, in the space of feverish seconds.

Coffee brews. Breakfast ready. Continental, like the good old days. The good old Daniel days.

Coffee drunk. Kitchen table sitting like a battle field of casualties; appetite low and she struggles to swallow. But his reply? Nowhere yet. In fact he isn't online. Not for the past hour or two.

Which is new. Even when he's not saying anything, he's online. Checking. Re-reading. Using the chat box as a proxy for love. Sometimes just staring at it.

She isn't happy with this inexplicable distance but she has things to do. Preparations to go somewhere, anywhere, are an industrial project. She wants everything well packed. This time, it feels much more important. So much more to do.

"Let's make another coffee; feel bit weak"; she peps herself up. But standing up feels hard.

So instead of boiling the water, she slowly drags herself to the sitting room. Where she has the presence of mind to play some of her favourite love music, the music that invokes the love, vividly, like it was played before her eyes, in the internal cinema of her mind.

It's this cinema of love that has been her world far more than anything else that's been going on since the pandemic. And not exactly like much has been happening in the pandemic either; but it doesn't matter

anyway, because her internal world—with or without
the boy that's spurred it—has been an utter delight. Pain
and pleasure roller coaster and an orthodox icon of
saintliness, an angelic halo, floating high on the horizon
of a promised metaphysical love. Still riding that initial
impression, despite the fact that events since beg to
differ.

"I'll rest a bit. These past months been hard. I need a
micro nap".

Her lithe body sprawled on the sofa, robe sweeping
the floor, peach sunshine caressing pale cheek.

Everybody loves her; with small exceptions. Everybody, including the loving sun. But the boy's not there,
hence her withering.

The only sun this flower needs is Daniel's love. And
she lives in perpetual night.

Painting love scenes with her mind on the high ceiling
that is now high and tall, like the Sistine Chapel of this
new, apocalyptic scripture of love. It looks mythical, and
you could gaze into heavens. A very specific and erotic
heaven that really happened for her on the eve of the
pandemic.

She looks in the direction of the angelic silhouette of
a certain blond young man. He was dancing with her.
She was dancing too. Like ballet dancers in flesh colored
leotards, their bodies like nude but de-sexualised by the
fabric. Statues, dancing. She twirled around him, flex-
ing all the way back, nearly dropping—when he caught
her and grabbed her up and carried her on stretched
arms—almost like he did in reality in Albion.

He stood tall while she tried to animate passion into
him, dancing fiercely... until a massive red fabric is
drawn from her side, undulating with her body's wring-
ing moves, floating high in shapes reminiscent of clouds
in the sky; she jumped, she dropped to the floor. She
leapt against the boy, thumped back, launching the red
silk like a flock of birds; she nearly floated. He danced
less and less, inert and withdrawn in himself.

The electronic riffs of the album invade the room, like a wall of sound washing ashore her yearning. As she sinks into a state of dangerous sleep, her mind's eye projecting images inside.

On a blank void it's him and her still dancing together. Their torsos intertwined like loving swans' necks on a lake.

In her dream, fluttering yards of gauzy fabric around the absent figure of Daniel. And she dances with all the power of her thoughts. Every little emotion and all the big ones.

In the cold void their silhouettes generate so much heat.

Stan. Stan usually texts, checks in on her; sends funny texts, memes. Anything to make her laugh or keep that little fire going. She usually replies. She is not set against him. He's used to getting a reply, she's always online. In fact when he sees her online he knows it's "him" she's there for—his rival; but she always texts back, kindly. Even when her heart's not in it.

His texts pour, unanswered. He knows her for long. He worries. How can she not answer for hours? Whole internet hours? That's not Eris. Never. Eris IS internet.

And it's Passover, Thursday, April 11, 2021.

Justice's "Woman Worldwide". Such a romantic album—a high powered continuous mix, summer romance in digital tides that emulate the heart rate of being powerfully in love. It was an album she often played. It often made her think of love.

The red fabric swirled round and round on a magic sky of love; perpetual entanglement, in a dance of souls.

But then he fades away. And it's just her. She dances, to the tune of "Love S.O.S".

The sirens of the song calling for help. She is slipping into a coma. She can't properly breathe.

The song calls for a love ambulance—the song plays it on repeat in the room, and in her mind; her mind's active playing the love. The love that never got to be.

She is sick. She doesn't know it, but she can't know anything at this stage. There is nothing to know. For her, the only thing needed to know is the dire need of a beating heart, the urgency of blood filled lungs.

The red scarf of her daydream twirls out of her lungs, onto the air of the living room. Her hand slips down by the side of the sofa. Fingers graze the floor where blood drops form.

Her body starts to die, but her mind can only dream of him. A longing so hard, so extreme. So betrayed. Still rising up like a column of light.

He is the dancer in the sky, his eyes have burned her soul.

She looks over her shoulder: through the red veil, to the Albion door scene, where he once stood. He stood there once and life's never been the same. A fire that will never cease burning. A fire that will keep burning even if it extinguishes her breath.

Quarters of her mind have switched off one by one, starved of oxygen. But in her subconscious the film keeps playing: a ghost at the door. His naked lithe body, curls round his face, eyes of abandon, a moment when existence opened its doors to a portal of hyper-reality. It enhanced their senses so they'd feel the high definition air; sparks, minds merging into one. Minds melting into the air between them. No, earth has never been the same since.

Souls connected, generating a sacred electricity that filled the atmosphere. The energy of which still hangs in the universe. A whole galaxy of baby planets born. They are still in love and locking eyes in that hyper-blast of pure energy.

The blood drips. It forms a puddle around the phone lying unanswered on the floor. The ringing cannot be heard and wouldn't be heard over the loud music. "Love S.O.S." plays over and over in her mind, or what's left of it.

Stan bursts through the door. Emaciated but animated by love. He congratulates himself for keeping the keys despite her daily protestations, and acts quickly to save her—all in a fraction of a second.

Cool and collected but raging heart of despair. She has the highly infectious Covid, but he doesn't care. Ambulance arrives soon to take her.

The sirens call like in her dream. In her comatose dream of him and the song.

***

Julianah steps up. She grabs her breasts off her waist in tiny fists. She brings them up to her lips and licks. She looks at him, between fake lashes.

His heart stops but a sense of autopilot-duty keeps him going.

—Look, Julianah, I stay, but let's do something fun.

—This is fun. Remember?

—Remember what? We never used to do things like this. You denied them to me, remember? You had your men who were more studs than me.

—Yes, we used to! You just don't remember. It used to be so good. We were the best couple alive.

—We were?

—We were.

Sad statement from a lustful face. Something clocks wrong. Like mechanisms dysfunctional across the galaxy and planets losing gravity. His own sense of gravity pulling elsewhere but he can't listen to that siren call; not just yet, not until all is taken care of on the home front. All the accounts settled; all the loose ends tied. He's neat and tidy, after all. Noble and duty bound.

A nagging feeling encompasses the space between his temples—"Eris". Like a whisper in his ear. Like the silk of her lips, the way it used to magically touch his neck, in the sunset overlooking the river. A feeling of beauty and sensuality yet unknown, un-hoped for, he remembers swiftly but—then! back in the room. To the matters at hand.

He advances slowly to Julianah and hands her the hoodie. Frowning, "please".

—Let's just go out to the river, enjoy a picnic. Take your dolls if you like. Please.

"Earth is spinning."

What did Eris mean, it's spinning? Her silly jokes. She is always so over the top romantic. Well, of course, she is, he deserves it. Her words cut, and hurt. Let her wait a bit. She is wonderful but she has hurt him. She is the Goddess that needs knocking down a peg.

Always "me me me". So self centered, he thinks. Eris, the self centered narcissist: so many selfies, so many designer dresses. Look, Julianah here is the physical embodiment of selflessness. Her physical degradation a monument to kindness, he almost thinks. "She cared for me so much, she neglected herself".

With a pink picnic basket the two wounded souls walk together. Propping each other physically, minds worlds apart.

Julianah's plimsolls make a flapping sound with each step. She stops here and there to rub certain areas, for her thighs chafing.

—Do you love me more than her? She says, reaching out to push his hair behind his ear. She looks positively radiant. Her love emanates from her ample bosom like vapors off a steaming pot of stew.

She stands up on her toes to reach him, eyes longing with desire, and betrayed love. Seeing not the reality before her, but the past. And her dreams. The little paintings on her wall, of floating princes and princesses from their shared youth. They used to watch manga together. They used to bond over that. She used to show him the world. He used to absorb it all with a grin.

—Do you remember, darling?

—Yes, yes, I remember. His heart chopped to pieces. Inside, a subcellular squeak.

He finds a place to lie down. It's unusually warm and sunny. Ethereal light. A metallic mist. April ejaculates this pink blossom over them in a magic rain. And scents envelop the landscape. The river gently murmurs.

She bends over to pick dandelions. Puts one behind her ear. One between the breasts. She smiles, with tears. Tear blind.

—Will you phone me? Will you phone me every day?

—Every other day, yes.

—Will you come back?

Will you come back to me?

Will you take care of me? I am the soulmate, she is the lover, yes? You will remember us?

You know I am the one, the natural real woman, you will come back to, you will one day open your eyes and see she was nothing. NOTHING. A siren of vice that seduced you from me. I am amazing.

Daniel, irritated, stands up and walks two steps. Looks away from her, into the distance.

—Julianah... I didn't stay to hear this.

—OK-OK-OK, she says in one breath. Desperate to please. Knocked back into pleaser mode.

She crawls to his feet and hugs them:

—I love you more than I love myself. She doesn't love you like I do. She cannot. No one does. I will do everything you want, everything. I will get a job. I will do everything she does.

I love you.

His lip curls downwards but makes sure she doesn't see his strain.

"She loves me more, if only you knew"—he finds no courage to say this on the outside, so he says it to himself in a loop.

The rest of the evening, the loop plays.

They drink wine. She knocks him over in the grass. Removes his top. He lets her, feeling generous.

She starts nibbling his ear, his neck.

He mentally compares this to the passion felt in Albion, where he's active, like a man. Not bad, he thinks, this is relaxing... could enjoy this too, from time to time. Different, and he shrugs to self. Like, this, here, it's about him—less about Eris' beauty. "Not. Bad".

Julianah's salivary track descends into his collarbone. She goes back up, round and round. Bites into his neck a bit too much. With a purpose. The salivary path rewinds, swirls. Checks his gaze—he's relaxed, accepting; she's emboldened. She bites again, this time with courage. A mark forms. Drop of blood. Scintillating in the thick sunset light.

She wants it to be there. She marks him as hers. Glee on her supersize cheeks.

A message, she thinks, for the woman at the other end of his journey.

He finally realizes what's going on and pushes her away. Julianah!!! Stop.

—Why??! She growls. A growl that ricochets off the trees and rocks and reverberates deafeningly. A growl like a pig slaughtered for Christmas.

———⊰❧⊱———

—She's got the virus? Cisco bellows over the many nurses and the ambulance driver ushering Eris on a stretcher. She's not the only one brought in unconscious. There are dozens of them. Thousands, over the week. A veritable spring harvest of dead bodies, breath hanging by a thread.

—Yes, I think so! Shouts Stan. He's frightened to death but he mastered the skill of siphoning fear into focus strong on survival and protection. The kind of guy you want on your side when you're in danger. He is determined to push for her to get the best treatment. Doesn't hurt he's mates with the hospital director.

—Yeah, yeah, man, I know. I mean, look what's here. You have to go into quarantine though. You weren't even meant to be here!

Stan steps back. "No".

—Yes, man, sorry. Look, it's the damn rules.

He's shouting.

—We all follow them, sorry, mate.

Stan tries to speak over the loud noises in the hospital emergency entrance, a doorway full of heaving choking corpses. His mask slips down, and his panicked body resists the nurses taking him aside, he can't, he won't leave Eris but she's slipping away. And either way she isn't here in a true way. A cascade of strong emotions possess him—eyes on the prize; he can't let go. Momentarily, yes, but he shall re-group. The woman is the goal. The utmost focus and priority. Her life, above all.

They're taking him into a room.

Cinco is the leader the hospital needs. He is struck by grief for his friends. But he is so used to this.

—It's a war scene here, mate.

Nurse approaches. The desperate people at the gates that come out at night, haunting streets, masked and impotent. They are here again, she says. She is a bit scared. They look like angry homeless people or escapees from a mad house.

—Can't you give them something? Throw them something they want?

What does it say on the TV? Nothing?

—No, like they don't exist. Don't think the federal government wants to acknowledge they exist.

Cinco wipes his forehead sweat with his cuff.

—Please throw them some masks and stuff. Close the back doors.

—We can't boss. We need access.

—Secure it with more locks and put a guard. Only let in those who ring and speak into the videophone.

Secure everything you hear me?

—OK, OK, chief.

The man walks off muttering.

Sirens, choking, heaving, sputtering and wailing: a spectacle from hell. These people—the staff, it's gaunt eyes that haven't slept in ages, barely standing up. Fighting a war, but a strange type of war of saving lives. From these ambulances that deliver a constant stream of dying people.

—Put ... Eris... Clemens... She was just taken in... Put her in a single room. Ventilator if needed, the works. Only if needed. The new medication, high dose. I'll log there, take a look at her myself soon.

Receptionist stares at the screen taking down these commands on autopilot.

—The patient in room 3 died last night, you know that, correct? She says emotionless.

—Yes, I know. The mayor's wife?

—Yes. And her daughter in another room...

—Really?? He stops and looks over his glasses. I thought ...

—We gave her the vaccine. Yes. Now the typist stops and looks at him with gravitas.

In fact the mayor's wife too. In fact she got very ill right after the vaccine.

Cinco taps his feet thinking, frowning. For a split second silencing the chaos of death and suffering that bellows in his hospital day and night.

—On the other hand, the lady continues. On the other hand... yes, I'll be there! She shouts to a nurse who wants something from her. Everyone wants a piece of me!! Slow blink to contain an irruption of controlled anger. She's got this.

The other vaccine recipients did well—she continues. My brother got the vaccine day before yesterday—she leans in and looks the doctor in the eye—then he got the lurgy... She gestures with her head.. And he's fine. Totally fine. Symptomless.

Cinco looks at her carefully.

—This your overweight brother?

—Yes.

Ian. He'd have nearly been killed if not vaccinated.

—I know. Like so many. So many we've seen, isn't it?

Cinco agrees with his colleague's point via his nodding eyebrow while the other eye already onto the next task; and walks off, focused.

In the single room they assigned her, Eris lies motionless with a respirator invading her throat. The movie is spent, now it's all a fight for survival inside her body. Cells compete with cells to live, to outlive the sickly ones.

Nurse walks in.

—This your famous lady friend?

—Yes, the writer. She's a good family friend.

Cinco is sad.

—Sorry, doc. Nurse's hand on his back: She's quite beautiful.

She withdraws her hand and looks at it, awkward; rubbing it against her pockets, secretly.

—Quite so, he approves, looking down. Not like it matters now.

—Who knows? Maybe it helps her. Health, youth, fitness .. it's here that they pay off. Good immunity also accounts for something, fuck's sake.

He shrugs: She's lost lots of blood. Needs transfusions. In fact.. Did you put that man in isolation like I said?

—The rabbi? The tall loud fella? He's in room 67 under observation.

—Yes. It's her husband. I'll go talk to him.

———❧———

Evening sets in over Johnnyville in quiet lockdown tones, with murmurs and kids' screams heard infrequently. Car engines sometimes crossing far off roads, elsewhere. Not here. Nobody is doing anything here.

Daniel's given up on the idea of trains. Trains sparse and unreliable anyway.

He's slowly setting towards the car. Late night. Very late. Almost morning. Hopes to escape again.

All packed up and ready to go. Looks left, right, walks to the car. Sits inside.

Starts the engine.

Deep sigh of relief. NOW he can start the rest of his life.

When... in the dark, a slimy object in his nape. Startled, he freezes. Bit sharp, the tip of whatever is touching him.

—Don't move. If you move, it'll stab you in the neck.

The incredible words roll off in the Southern drawl of his now ex fiancée's lips from the back of the car, though sounding like they're ASMR-ing through the sound system, the voice of a jealous pagan God, or an Alexa gone haywire.

—No... what in God's name you think you are doing, Julianah? He vocalizes each word tensely like pouring calm into the vowels will calm her down.

—Look. Don't you worry. We do it my way, everything will be alright. I just want you to drive me to your meeting point. I wanna see your lady. I want to do the hand over. I'll let you go. I'll drive back.

—Erm.. you don't have a license, sugar pops.

—I am OK. I am A-okay, "sugartits".

Somehow the gloves are off. In the rear-view mirror, he sees her eyes gleam in the dark of the backseat. Body frozen. Feels like he's just now hearing her for the first time. As she is. Like he's never known her. Slashing his arm with a broken whiskey bottle still child's play. This.. now, this, was hardcore. He's finally, ten years in, getting to know her.

She is sitting there focused, all her life's woes poured into this. She dressed up for the occasion: school girl skirt revealing ripped tights, her signature pigtails forming a wispy mess around her physiognomy. A crop top finishing above the navel, and many layers of jewels, cascading, making a threatening clinking sound with every swerving of the car. It is that clinking of cheap metal that lets Daniel know what she's up to, as he tunes his ears.

She spent an hour layering the beads, and the chains, and the rings, and the heavy makeup. Like a warrior getting ready for battle; mixing tears into the caked Kohl of her lids. Fake lashes askew, nose ring glistening with body fluids.

Suddenly things have become a hardcore life and death play. He thought he was the hero of an epic romance. Turns out it was horror all along.

Pity? Pity for her?

After all he'd one for her? Hardly. He's incredulous. All pity has escaped him; he will do as she says, but hopes to get away. Sort of calm. Mr. Sortoff is sort of calm in front of the storm. But tears and despair forming too. Somewhere, yet brushed off; soon to bubble up and irrupt like a volcano.

He always thought he's strong; well, he's about to find out how strong.

Engine starts. In the silent night the brakes cut a shriek that triggers a hysterical dog concerto all round.

"She's barking mad, she is!". These words sound in his own head, echoing in a dreadful internal silence.

He drives, eyes flicking between the dark road and her eyes on the back bench, glimpses of which pop like bullets in the mirror. The metal in his neck. The unicorn knife. Her favorite of many toys. A cute pastel colored item—"the innocence of childhood". Now it could scoop his spine off. Almost like being a 30-year old toddler isn't even that cute anymore.

One wrong move, one hop on the road, he's dead.

The hero starts to unravel internally, bit by bit, blow by blow. The road unravels before them. The map to Belmont on his Sat Nav. He knows it by heart anyway. It's his love map. No chit chat to Julianah now. Just the engine and the stars. And his love for Eris. Etching a plan. Love and hate both driving this car, weakness having created this maze.

———⟨≫⟩———

—You're not going to fucking believe this.

The radiance on Cinco's face assures Stan this is good news. Pacing up and down in his little hospital cell has wasted him for the night. So had donating nearly a liter of blood to his wife; luckily compatible in blood like in all important things.

—You are not going to believe it, my man. Never in a thousand fucking years did I expect anything remotely like this shit. I swear.

What? His eyes say. His voice, usually booming, is spent. "Tell me", he whispers in baritone. What?? What?

Cinco takes a deep breath.

—This. THIS. If true, if what I saw correct.. is REVO-LUTIONARY.

Look, I am a man of science. I only have correlation, no proven cause and effect. I cannot say for sure.

—Come on, MAN, TELL ME HOW SHE IS!!! Is she better?? Is she?? He almost shakes his pal's shirt.

Cinco snaps out of his little bubble of scientific ebullience; surprised, almost, to see Stan there.

—Pal. You don't understand. Yes, she is better. Stable. But what's more, she is ... how can I say this?! Radiant. In the 12 hours since administration, she's... well.. She made a magnificent recovery. It's like she's 20!

Stan snorts in disbelief and impatience. Yes, yes, good news, but can I see her?

—You can see her on a tablet. She's starting to wake up. Grabbed a nurse's finger. Not awake yet.

—Wait, how is she like 20? What exactly..?

—Organs, blood tests. All tip top. Her body's made an unprecedented 180 degree turn. I am not sure you know how bad she was. I didn't want to scare you. She's off the respirator now. Only thing I can think of is the interaction, maybe, between your blood, and some of the new, large dose Covid medication.. you know? But never is recovery so dramatic and fast.

Cinco looks at Stan wide eyed. Medical elation he's not hoped for since this apocalypse started.

Stan thinks, chewing in a vacuum. Something in his teeth. So can I see her?

—VIA TABLET!!

—FUCK OFF, man. In person!!! You just said I saved her life, what, I can't even see her??

Cinco rolls his eyes. I don't have time for this. You know the rules. She is still contagious, it is very dangerous. You are in quarantine. Here's the tablet. You can perhaps try to wake her up, voice of a loved one good for this type of thing.

He puts up the app, rings. Connects. Nurse answers, masks over mask and visors and all. She smiles and aims the camera at Eris.

Peaceful, radiant, asleep—gently moving her lips. Like she's dreaming. Indeed, looking younger. The two men look at each other. In disbelief.

—Eris!! My sweet, sweet, darling bunny. Can you hear me??

She murmurs, moving head sideways. Skin translucent and luminous, like she's not even been half dead.

They notice, the two friends. And nod at each other, ...

—You think... erm... it's my blood that did this?! My blood heals death? He lets out a laugh of relief.

Cinco lifts hands up in despair. Maybe?!.... I don't know? What can I say? We've done this and some combination of breakthrough meds. You did say .. was she fasting?

—She does every month. NAD?

—NAD!

They stare.

—My blood?! Stan wonders.

— Haven't seen any other patient with quite this particular reaction to infection, you know? The whole thing rather bizarre. We'll have some detective work to do in the morning. The coming days.

Congratulations, man, she's out of the red. And you've got yourself a fresh and young looking .. erm.. ex wife? He laughs, awkwardly. And leaves to save more lives.

—Eris, sweetie. My sweetest baby. Can you hear me? The sweetness in his voice could melt steel. In fact the nurse by the bed is very emotional.

Eris smiles. She responded to the love, his love wakes her up.

Stan is elated. No one has ever smiled like him right now. It's like every pore of his skin a smiling emoticon if you zoom in the cellular level.

Eris, in her bed, immobilized, moves her lips. Her neck, a bit. Opens delicately... the universe stops.

—Daniel.... I knew you'd come. Daniel...

———— ❈ ————

She wakes up. The second night of her hospitalization. No more respirator, but a little drip. She feels weird. Doesn't recognize the place. "What the fuck is this".

Doesn't care where she is.

"Daniel"... No phone. No one in the room. No way to communicate.

She sits up. Unusually strong for what she's been through, not that she knows. Her strength multiplied. She is mentally focused though convalescent. Strange energy runs through her. One thought only: "Go to him". "Albion, Albion".

She listens. No human sounds. Just beeping from various equipment.

Wants to read her stats on the monitors but can't work out what is what. Just has a surreal sense of confidence that she's OK, she can read her own body signals, through her unusually sharp senses: she is strong.

She disconnects the drip awkwardly. Looks at her hospital gown. Bit large, long, gray. Shrugs. Looks around. A single cone of light from a street lamp illuminates the cabinet where her keys must be. She rummages through. Keys found. No sign of phone. That phone is everything.

"I am in room 67 in quarantine, end of corridor. I love you. Stan. Cinco saved you. Abe here too". She reads and throws the note before she gets to jump in some Crocs laid for her by the bed.

She opens the door. No one. Dull voices, snoring, some wailing in the distance. Sounds of death, sounds of survival. Murmur of nurses used to both.

She tip toes. Gently. Gentler. Like a ballerina. Or a cat.

Out on the pavement, in the cool air—she looks around. The hospital hill. The flickering lights of Belmont down below. How to get home, to her home, the car?

Streets after streets of running and hiding—it feels exciting and worth doing, because she has a goal.

She looks back over her shoulder.

Silhouettes rustle behind the trees and she knows exactly what they are. Plus it's a curfew. Everything has to be exacted with prudence. Such hostility in the air, from so many directions. Abstract and not.

Running is, she decides, the best idea. So she runs, sometimes barefoot. Hides from time to time. To watch and listen. She can see and hear them. The damn monsters. Creaking of their mobility scooters. One comes out, looks at her. Mask, and atop, a pair of empty eyes. It's like he wants to get her fucking brains.

They're everywhere, their hard breath giving them out. Their primal spite shining out of them like daggers. No reason to chase but feral envy she's healthy and their brains eaten out by the virus. A feral envy turn to gory desire. And she with her sharp senses, even sharper now,

can sense it. One look back, sharp breath. Out of step.
Dashing out of the bushes, downhill on the very steep
slope of the hospital dwellings. To the car, her passport
to love and freedom, down below on the quaint streets
in the valley. Her steps kick pebbles into the abyss,
giving her away.

A hiss. A banging sound. A presence she can't quite
pinpoint.

A crossing. No waiting for the red light now. She dashes, quickly. Out of nowhere, cop appears.

—What are you doing here, young lady? Shocked with
her appearance.

—Nothing, just chasing to my car.

—Watch out young lady. Nasty people, nasty hooli-
gans about. You know it's a curfew, he admonishes gently. Please wear your mask.

—I don't have one. He hands her a blue FFP2.

"Hmm"... he's not sure why she's there dressed like
that.. but as usual, even in hospital rags, Eris gives off
a respectable charm, a halo of feminine authority. The
air that all is well, on a serene curve upwards, calculated
with precision by her very eyebrow, that moves in strict
rhythm with the events she dominates. The precision of
her limbs in motion, an outer manifestation of the clarity
in her thoughts.

—Here, take care. Watch out for them nasty people.

—I will, thanks.

A winning Eris smile; dazzled by beauty, the officer
gestures to his cap and shoots off. She thinks of asking
for details. Steps back to call the man. But he's gone. The
temporary bubble of safety gone like smoke.

But she's close to home now. Closer to her little home,
the car. Looks left. Right. Moon shines in her pearlescent cheek. Hospital gown fluttering in the wind. She
flies with the grace of a cat. Strange streams of energy fuelling her: the reviving meds, the blood transfu-
sion—Stan's; her explosive internal youth that's powered her through decades of fight and success. The

LOVE. The LOVE. The love that feels ethereal. Projects images of the final goal—Daniel's sweet face on her pillow in Albion. To caress, to kiss. To absorb his abandoning gaze into her. A child that needs her.

She's nearly nude in front of her house, on Belmont Avenue. Her car glitters in the dark—two beeps like it's recognizing her, a loyal sentient servant; she jumps in.

Inside, she's safe.

Another sharp breath. Starts the engine. The engine is quiet but something triggers the creatures. The Covid zombies. All at once coming out. A concert of mobility scooters, heaving coughing chests and for some strange reason banging pots and knives against each other; pans with butcher knives with other kitchen paraphernalia from hell. They suddenly advance towards the woman inside the steel cage. She starts the flood lights, which startles them but horrifies her. They look atrocious. Curfew makes sure no one on the streets.

"What the fuck are they so ugly for?"

—Why are you so angry? Aren't you supposed to go home and die in isolation on doctor's orders?!

Her voice surprises herself.

Thought shoots through her, memories of chats she usually ignores because they're not about Daniel. Covid ate their brains. "The virus made Swiss cheese of their brains." She sees Cinco before her, his permanent worry frown.

This is what they're reduced to. She doesn't exactly feel pity.

She couldn't. She needs to get out.

A sense of tragic rage that fellow humans have become this and turned into your enemy; you could have felt bad for them, offered a hand; instead you have to roll your car over them and hear their ribs crack. Harder. Faster. Like a demented music of cracked ribs; ah, the sweet sound of survival.

Fierce internally but outside frail; in her steel cage she feels anxious when the deformed faces push against the shield; trying to burst through; her car too slow, stops and fails. And the zombies circle her, again. A paroxysm of despair but which awakens even more resilience and determination in her. Lined up dreadful faces knocking on the glass, knives in hand, masked deformities.

Eye contact with them hurts; her skin crawls, terror pangs.

Then she hits the pedal and shoots down the road. To Albion.

In Dahut Graciella stands in the window, hoping for night time spectacle. Some things he saw, some things he felt.

Tonight feels particularly scary to him. His senses have picked something vague and remote.

He wants to warn people but he's long given up, bit of Cassandrafreude; no one believes his warnings, because he delivers them while distressed; which people seem to take for evidence he's wrong, or hysterical, or Goddamn knows what. And when facts prove his fears correct, post priori—no one is quick to apologize for laughing it off. Story of his life. Story of life in general. He has yet to die a few lives before anyone will acknowledge all the time his warnings came true.

No one ever said sorry.

He turns weak at the knees.

The weight of this world too much. For anyone, let alone Graciella's arthritic knees.

He remembers his mom. Sitting down, petting the plants. Waiting.

Rustles and far off sounds he can't comprehend. "I am not even going on that online machine no more, who's to say any real people there. They don't understand. Everyone crazy".

With his tired eyes he slips into a deep sleep. Eyes on the road. Internally as externally forever closed.

A fox crosses the lane, easing into the bushes on the Albion property. Disturbing some ghosts.

Crickets. A far off loud boom. Enormous, like the sky fell. Triggers car alarms and dogs. Night.

At that exact second, Napoleon escapes his little cage in Belmont, after chewing incessantly in a state of suspension at the net that covered it. He runs and runs, out of the window, into a new and exciting freedom.

An hour and half is a long time to drive with a knife in your nape.

But Daniel has that self control he likes in Western movie stars of yesteryear, come to fore in his life, like a hero. Of the ages. Hero of surviving the kawaii unicorn bedazzled knife of your former future wife, not quite yet future former.

He sits there drowned in his own cold sweat. Eyes on the road. And boy is it a dark road. A dark dangerous high road through mountains.

—I will take one look at your bitch and hand you over to her. I will do it myself. I wanna make sure she takes care of you like I did. I made you pancakes. You can eat them together. You can sit there and enjoy what you've done to me. How you have both plotted to knife me in the heart, I will show you. How you both set out to destroy me, innocent little me, I never hurt nobody.

I helped you through everything we did. Every victory of yours, is mine. Every little trophy, mine. I was there. Was there. Took care of you. Brought you little cute bento boxes to work. Walked you back from work on tired nights.

Daniel feels her, but feels the knife. Paralyzed. Road is dark and he can't work out any plan. He starts to gently sob, unheard.

—I did it all, for you. All for you. I am "the Liddel", remember? "Little you"—I am you, you are me.

And look at this. You leave me? And for who??

If you left me for a normal woman. A good woman. I would have understood.

You leave for me a two penny broad with no tits. A nobody, a hag who's older than me. A corrupted woman. Everyone knows she's fucked her way to the top. Not honest like me.

You'll see. You'll see what you both done to me. You'll take one look at her, one ...

—You mean unlike you, who cuckolded your way to the bottom? Daniel's bile irrupts finally, slowly, through gritted teeth. His glance in the mirror not met by her.

A decade of repression finally, for the first time, letting out. His jaw about to pop, so tense.

But the girl doesn't have ears for this level of truth.

—Look at me. See us side by side.

And then you will voluntarily—I tell you—say, oh boy, I have been stupid.

Just see us side by side.

Just you watch.

And you will say, sorry babe, and come home with me.

And we go back home like the old days and eat cheeseburgers and fries and pie and I will tell you stories and you will laugh and we will have a baby and...

Daniel irrupts in loud crying. Loud, choking, sobs, with centrifugal tears.

The viaduct not far ahead.

—And...

—And...

Swerving that thing like a Formula 1 racer, for survival. But no easy way out. Corpses and bones and trash everywhere and yet a lot more out of the bushes. How were they so many?

Why, on this dark old night?

What happened to humanity?

Racing at her. In front of her, road blocked. High on the dam, another dam; a human shield, just not so human after all.

One hideous creature slams against the wind-shield—bulbous eyes, animal growl coming out of the bloodied mask. Steam forms and she hears the drowning lungs, the rotting flesh. Those damn empty hungry eyes. Growl again, gesturing to his mouth.

—Really, pal? And you're saying that with all the weight of your fat-mobile?!

She slams that acceleration. Slalom through Covid zombies—zomvids.

Bit mad, she thinks. No turning back. Teetering between an abyss behind, an abyss ahead.

She has nano seconds to think. She knows that place like the palm of her hand but not the inside of the dam. The guts of the dam are a dark cold thing. Those Instagram kids? TikTok stars? People who delved in to look at the guts of the maze and died.

And she delves too. But not to die.

But the idea forms and grips her in those brief items of time that her destiny is decided. And not even just hers.

So she looks everywhere, calculates everything. The hospital is high up on a hill. She knows where everything is.

Her love is ahead. He is safe.

She drives the car aggressively round and round through the area round the main entry of the dam. Not even staff cars parked there. Almost nothing, like a post apocalyptic landscape.

What a year of this has done.

What a bunch of Covid cretins are doing. She thinks. She has to think fast.

Behind her, around, the martyrs of Covid madness advance in their horrendous garb; eyeballs hanging on the outside, guts in hand. Could be, she is not sure. Looks that way.

They all somehow wear masks. And the knives and mallets and pans and the deafening clink and clank—approaching like a circle of death.

She parks, rolls out of the car, tumbles down a few times. Speed. Speed of the essence here. It's her one weapon. If she only outruns them—which isn't hard, their lungs being fucked, their scooters slow, their frame heavy and joints fucked. If she is agile and fast enough she can run through that door. Once inside she has to keep running.

No choice but to run as fast as she can—which is suddenly very fast, like she's about 16 and on speed.

So little time.

She has to run round through the dark, sub zero, guts of the dam and emerge back out and into her car—if anything left of it, but they're not attracted to the car. They want flesh. They want youth. They want her. It's the fresh healthy human they hate, they're after.

She had never been a runner but they were suffering with an illness that ate through their lungs.

She runs. She runs as hard as she can through cold wet galleries, of a dead industrial past; some engineering giant made of cement with bones of steel; Celsius dropping to minus 5; minus ten, the further she goes; then lower and deeper. No sign of control panels yet. She needs the controls that calibrate the 30 blocks. No maps on the side. This is hard, she thinks, but most of all—she runs. She has to run for her life. She can see her breath, she can hear it. She feels superhumanly strong, but fear still powers her more than anything. In these nano seconds the idea forms that she's not even just running for her life.

For love yes.

And what a love that is.

She runs with his image like an icon in the night sky, guarding over her.

But she feels she's sort of running for everyone to save them all from the herd; the dismembered herd with the Covid breath and bloodied masks full of pus running, rummaging through the corridors as fast as they can—which luckily isn't very fast.

She has to keep tip top speed to stop the freeze.

Minus twenty. Her hospital gown more like ropes round her neck now. No stopping. She finds them. The control panels. She is in front of one, frozen, her fingers cannot reach, cannot bend. She finally hits with elbows, looking desperately left and right, hearing muffled nightmare sounds coming through the hundreds of meters of dark galleries; the single bulb at her side drops dead. She's in the dark now. Her phone? No where. No phone, no light, how the fuck to get out of here?

Panic and hope hit simultaneously, both stronger than any emotion she's ever felt. She thinks she's powered by love, a supreme love; she's defeating ill temperature with the mere power of love but there is more.

She keeps running, this time crawling by the wall, clutching it like an old pal.

His image shines over her head, a pallor of life and death at once invigorates her; the images haunting her brain in quick succession there to motivate survival. And it hangs by a thread.

"*Would be quite stupid if I froze to death here and those monsters weren't even out to kill anybody.*" She laughs sardonically to herself. "*Maybe they just wanted a snack*".

Some pathetic figures catch up with her, by virtue of mere accident in the labyrinthine galleries. They surround her, confused. One reaches his arms and blood-shot eyes, the other nearly touches her hips.

She giggles almost. She panics too, but fights it, and in a fast twirl, escapes through their limbs, runs away.

—Die, you damn undead Swiss cheese brain Covid-iots!!!!

She'd like to stay and see the look in their eyes, but no time; so she runs, crawls, picks up, runs again, crawls and crawls and keeps eyes on the prize.

Something snapped, a fright of death. Level lower and lower into survival mode, adrenaline and instincts laid bare; an empty skeleton of reality reveals itself and she likes it, afraid and hallowed but excited. Excited to be down here in this level of pure bare bones reality of what life is. This race for life. It's what life is most of the time, but in too slow motion, so you cannot see the threat; the threat is abstract and obfuscated; but this? Condensed experience, you see, you smell the threat in high speed like you're meant to. Feel it in your lungs. Refreshing for once. Refreshingly HONEST.

She starts being delirious as she crawls the wall; she doesn't even realize her legs, her limbs frozen, and pur-ple. She can't even remember when she descended in the guts of dam, but she knows the aim.

A second panel: more random commands, with her forehead smashing, picture waning in her mind.

A high of life and death keeps her conscience going.

"Where am I?"

"What am I doing?"

Running. Running.

Ignoring limbs, sounds, haranguing from the pot and pans and knife brigade.

Ignoring all, on pure energy.

Her face looks beautiful when it glitters under the one functional bulb; she doesn't know but she's back up, a level under the surface.

In the guts of the dam the 30 blocks start to shift. Her random commands trigger its demise.

The clockwork precision that's required to subtly move them in unison, a marvel of engineering—has been kicked in the head; by hers. Setting chaos between the giant blocks with roots deep in the mountain.

It only takes so little to destroy. She thinks. All that immense work of ten years of putting rock over rock and blocks of cement deep under the surface and perfectly calibrate them to withhold a mountain of water. And now she destroyed it all.

With elation of both destruction and creation—she can't know which is which, she crawls out into the moon light on bruised and frozen hands and knees.

The idiots, the Covid idiots, the zomvids, whatever, lost in the galleries. Frozen or dead from running. They're trapped. Some still emerge from the bushes.

Endless supply of them monsters it seems. She has time to throw a sardonic laugh.

"You fucking bastards". A SARDONIC LAUGH. She's won, she knows it.

But her body is ailing. She barely can move, she's run a mile through a freezing secret winter capsule in a dam.

She looks in her bra; the car key. Stumbling, grappling at the path, in a dim street light—she turns on the car. Beep, beep—it's recognized its owner. Every little step has to be calculated so the bastards don't jump in, don't cut her off. They're armed, she isn't.

She crawls, jumps, jumps up to her feet like the dancer she was in her comatose dream.

Strange high and sense of power through her veins. Inside. She's inside.

She has seconds.

She's laughing at them, a hysterical controlled laugh against adversity, a calibrated set of vocalizations to let out the triumphant release of emotions; she's thrived. Cascading against the mountains, reason over chaos.

She overpowered, overcome. It feels damn good. But no time to waste, she's aware. Powerfully awake. Looking everywhere, taking in every detail. Senses hyper awake. She's starting the engine.

Just then. Oh, no. The song starts with the engine... It is beatific. The sense of rebirth and cosmic energy coming off... washes off her bad energies, her tension, her fear and the colossal amount of unhappiness endured.

It's "Sunrise", the song by Pulp. Her and his favorite English band. She hasn't listened to it since the boy languished nude in bed with her in *illo tempore*. Its coming on now feels prophetic. She rides that song into the night. Hour before dawn.

It is the beginning of the end. And the end of the beginning. Both these statements are true.

It is the apocalypse behind her. The new start ahead.

She spares a few moments to think of the protected Stan, Abe and Cinco atop of the hill in the hospital.

The rest... the rest is gone. Everything. Drowned the whole world behind her and she doesn't even care. With the sunrise soundscape fuelling manic grandeur.

Clutching onto the steering wheel like a lifeboat she gazes into the rear-view mirror: no sign of anyone chasing her. It worked.

Like a plane that's done the hard bit taking off and is now just gliding through air, she's just focused on the road ahead through the woods.

The scary bit is always the narrow viaduct.

Viaduct suspended through virgin forests, infernal dark and doom. She drives to a new world, to victory.

She's afraid to look back, but how can you not? Who's ever seen anything like that. More than a force of nature. A force of man. It makes her tremble like she's never trembled before but at least the crazies are gone.

—I'd love to eat popcorn and watch you drown, losers!!!—but lucky for you, I've got somewhere to go. Byee!!

Something in her says she just has to keep going, like it's always done. So she hits the pedal and drives onto the damn viaduct.

Sometimes, apocalypse after apocalypse keeps happening and it's not even slowing down. Feels almost too much for the brain to cope but there's that resilient core in her that clocks forward: keep moving, keep running, like she's run through the galleries, through life.

Her breath still short. It feels like it's always going to be. In the thirty seconds or so she ponders all this semi consciously, the lake, the valley as she knows it starts to loudly disappear. A crack like earth's plates shattering. Tsunami going to drink Belmont. Maybe it's better that way. Maybe you need to kill an apocalypse with another. Hard times, hard measures etc. It's ... Transfixing her. Just her alone, and the city about to drown under this giant monster of water behind her. With all she knows and holds dear in it. Well, not all. Because, something, ahead. Something precious. Beyond the mountains. After the world is drowned, her love remains, sweetly, in a cottage. Perhaps waiting for her. She pushes on. As the engine starts, the pebbles on the bridge, suspended over the ongoing water apocalypse, start to fall. The distance between her and the waterline growing, but she only has split seconds to notice in her side eye as she pushes forward to get away from it all. Tense, frightened. Teetering between death and glory.

She sees barely anything, the road ahead a dark grey blot and the shiny moon unsettling dark trees and birds.

She glides.

From the other side a set of lights approaches fast. Too fast. She stays on, doesn't know what to do. To swerve is to jump into the abyss, an abyss that is becoming stone more than water. With the world exploding behind and this car ahead what is she to do??

No time to think.

The other car approaches fast, unthinkingly.

Daniel. Daniel driving the car with a knife in his back, grazing his neck, body frozen in a superhuman effort of self control. He sees the light, he doesn't know the car; but he has to make a swift decision.

A decision to swerve in the abyss to his left, in what he thinks is the reservoir; may be water still but going fast; nothing makes sense tonight. All is the end of known times; the car jumps off the high path like an arc of death, two silhouettes irrupting from it into the chaos below.

Eris stops. Something stops her as the song ends in an electronic growl.

Some very grabbing gut feeling crawls up and grips her, perturbs her euphoria. Screeching tires. Opens the window to gaze back into the abyss she didn't want to hang around to see.

She doesn't see much, but a world sinking and a car floating between rapidly lowering levels of water, and rocks.

Two bodies floating. Like ants. Dim dots shining in the moonlight.

Two sad ants floating aimlessly... together.

She has a very bad feeling. Very. Frowns, tries to chase the bad feeling.

Why bother? "Why am I bothered??? Let's go".

She goes, but the rest of the drive to Dahut is tense and confused, bitter eyes. Haunting the road for AN-SWERS.

Floating Daniel the knight.

Down there, floating unconscious. The knight. He really got the girl. He fought the obstacles and flew straight into the lake. A waning lake. The moon shines and glitters over the water doom as his and her body float, groan, submerge. He rescued his princess in the end. Just not the one he wanted and not in the way he dreamed. The trouble with these Teutonic knights is they're big on imagined duty and self sacrifice but not so much on survivalism. And this pandemic? Well, it was the time and place to be just that: survivor. You survive that, you survive anything.

The poor town of Belmont stood no chance. As soon as by virtue of the now rejuvenated hands of Eris, the 30 blocks collapsed in a galactic doom... all the content of people's lives and suffering and even joy was drowned in seconds, minutes. So much less than it took people to turn around and see what their ear was trying to say.

On a quiet back street a man stood quiet for seconds, terrorized. What is this? Suspected an atomic bomb. By the time he took his phone out to text friends and family, his narrow eyes could make out a monstrous mass of ...water. River of water in the sky. Like warrior queens galloping on giant water horses straight at him. The man, in his fifties, masked and red haired, felt his heart stop like a scared mouse. And pondered for seconds. What do. Thrown into a new and as yet unknown primal level of obviously superior computational powers, like awake from the torpor of 21st century life... he ran. The primal force, bigger than him, shared with all creatures, a force that is there on standby, muted by comforts, until something like this happens. Disaster. But alas! As ginger man running down the road, the sky shapes catch onto him and ...drown him. From his hands, the phone escapes, finally free.

Floating in the new sea-world just created, a news notification comes on the screen: "It's over! The crisis is over. Experts say we have to learn to live with Coronavirus, as part of life. Coronavirus is now part of us". And quickly, then, the phone itself drowns.

And all of Belmont. Muffled screams of despair, a faerie of floating pieces of life like displays in a museum. Kids, cars, a pink vase, someone's uncollected laundry on a line. The city is dead yet alive.

Dreamy pergola drenched in roses and lilacs. A pond. Ionic columns towering over a vast green oasis of the garden of Eden.

Nearby, a quiet sea. Eris. Very youthful and beautiful, a veritable princess; but her hair fully white. She turns to her also white haired friend:

—Isn't it funny? The more advanced we are, the more our definition of paradise is bits that remind us from where we came. Bits of unspoiled nature. What luxury. What was once everywhere and free—now a treat for the super lucky. To remember something we lost. And the higher we climb the more we yearn for what we've lost. The simple things.

Her friend, tall, grabs her elbow. They descend the stairs to the ball. The eerie sounds of Scratch Massive's "Take Me There" can be heard, a soundscape that takes you with it, above the waves, the trees, the clouds. Eris has prepared long for this. Most everyone is there. A crowd of old souls, young faces. She's elated, but like she's learned in her adult life... nothing is easy. Good feelings can be doubled by dark feelings, layer below; it's all layers, wavelengths of the soul that sing different tunes. Lucky if they sometimes sing in tune, or work together to a plateau of anything. Never stable.

Never complete. And what if it was? Then there would be stagnation. She tells self, to propel forward. Always propel up and forward.

Her gown, heavy peach satin, scintillates in the honey glaze of the setting sun; giant bow sweeps the floor; her back uncovered. Hair a monumental updo like a Greek Goddess. A splendor of jewels, as usual. Pearls shooting light reflections from the corners of her princess facial contour; colored rocks on her fingers mark every movement of her hands with more light, always light.

She feels her necklace with her fingers. The rubies have faded, their edges not so sharp. But the smiley face there. She flips the medallion between her fingers a few times, like twisting a memory mechanism. Sharp pang in her stomach. Face drops. Hides a bitter thought. Tense curl of her lip to suppress a gust of tears, frown like lightning on a beautiful face. Torrid moonlit scenes haunt her for a bit, until she shakes her head off them. Deep breath, chin up. Takes her friend's hand. In the crowd, a kippah on a tall curly head: Stan. Abe's witchy laugh. Party's about to start.

Step by step downstairs, until they're all submerged in music.

"Hyperaeon, you that from chasm
Uprise entire realms,
Ask not for wondrous signals
That lack clear name or form.

A human wish you be?
Their likeness want to lend?
But should they perish all,
Others would take their place.

They merely build upon the wind
Ideals vain and faint;
When waves wash into a tomb,
New waves catch up abaft.

They, depend on lucky stars
Harassed they are by fate;
We—know no time, no space,
Death, we know not.

Off yesterday's eternal womb
Today lives what tomorrow dies;
Should a Sun extinguish in the sky
New Suns soon come alight;

Like in perennial sunrise,
Mortality still chasing it in kind,
For all is born to die
And dies to come alive.

But you, Hyperaeon, remain

Wherever your light be cast.
Ask for wisdom, not death,
You must.

Who even this mortal be?
For whom you wish to die?
Go, make for that wandering earth,
See what you shall find."

("Hyperaeon", M. Eminescu)

(To be continued)

Support the rise of new literary fiction by leaving an
Amazon review.

Next in the series:
HYPERAEON VOLUME II
A Tale of Awakening.

+

Find me on:
hyperaeon.co
X : ErisHyperaeon

Printed in Great Britain
by Amazon